$19.95

ALEXANDER I

Russia's Mysterious Tsar

M. K. Dziewanowski

This is the story of Russia's mysterious Tsar Alexander I. The enigmatic grandson of Catherine the Great was an "enlightened monarch," hamstrung by the history and traditions of an unwieldy empire. His complicity in his father's death, and elusive marriage, romance with his sister, and the ultimate mystery of his final years, speak of a tormented soul.

Did Alexander die in 1825? Why was his grave empty when the Bolsheviks opened it? Did he live out a long old age as a monk in Siberia?

Based on extensive research and a visit to the Leningrad State Archives, this is the first account to develop the underlying psychological themes of Alexander's life. The reader is drawn to the minds of the characters, and th world around the court of St. Petersburg, and on the wider stages o Napoleon's Europe.

ALEXANDER I
Russia's Mysterious Tsar

ALEXANDER I
Russia's Mysterious Tsar

M. K. Dziewanowski

HIPPOCRENE BOOKS
New York

For information, address:
Hippocrene Books, Inc.
171 Madison Avenue
New York, NY 10016

ISBN 0-87052-898-X

Library of Congress Cataloging-in-Publication Data

Dziewanowski, M. K.
Alexander I: Russia's mysterious tsar / M.K. Dziewanowski.
.p cm.
ISBN 0- 87052-898-X :
1 Alexander I, Emperor of Russia, 1777-1825—Fiction.
2. Soviet Union—History—Alexander I, 1801-1825— Fiction.
I. Title. II. Title: Alexander, the First.
PS3554.Z5A44 1990
813' .54—dc20

90-46687
CIP

Printed in the United States of America.

Contents

	Preface	7
Chapter 1	Between Moscow and St. Petersburg	9
Chapter 2	Tied to His Grandmother's Apron Strings	21
Chapter 3	Between Two Worlds	39
Chapter 4	Necropolis, Lesbos and Cythera	63
Chapter 5	Am I My Father's Keeper?	87
Chapter 6	Reforming Russia	119
Chapter 7	From Domestic Reform to Foreign Adventures	139
Chapter 8	Austerlitz	165
Chapter 9	Tilsit	185
Chapter 10	"Napoleon's Prefect in Russia?"	201
Chapter 11	War Without Peace	237
Chapter 12	The Triumph	265
Chapter 13	The Victors Amuse Themselves	273
Chapter 14	The Baltic Baroness	295

entered in Latvia

Chapter 15	In Search of Salvation	307
Chapter 16	Why Taganrog?	333
Chapter 17	In the Siberian Wilderness	349
Chapter 18	Epilogue	381
Index		385

Preface

Writing in his diary about the revolution of 1905, Count Leo Tolstoy was deeply depressed. His personal troubles, the bitter feud with his wife, strongly colored his pessimistic outlook on the Russian society; he found it in desperate condition from want of ideals of simple life and lofty spirituality. Everybody, he thought, was obsessed with "Science" and consequently "there could be no room for religious and moral understanding."

To get away from his gloomy reflections, Tolstoy thumbed thorugh a recent book about Tsar Alexander I, a huge four-volume study by N. K. Schilder. Alexander obviously fascinated Tolstoy. The enigmatic Tsar exemplified to Tolstoy many elements of Greek tragedy. He was torn between unsolvable political problems and his private agonies: his complicity in his father's assassination, his romance with his sister, his numerous love affairs. While on the throne he had tried to reform Russia—struggling with the overwhelming problems of his unhappy giant of a land: its vastness and power, its backwardness, its historic mission, the ambivalent Euroasiatic identity, its relationship to the rest of the world. At the same time Alexander was wrestling with his own frailties. What impressed Tolstoy most of all was Alexander's conversion to mystical Christianity, so similar to Tolstoy's; he was also fascinated by the Tsar's enigmatic death at Taganrog.

Could it be true that Alexander only pretended to die in 1825? That he became a holy man, living for over thirty years under the name of Fyodor Kuzmich as a saintly hermit in Siberia? This second life of contrition of the frivolous and lascivious Emperor, turning to penance, good deeds and spiritual meditation fascinated Tolstoy. What a story! After some research of the controversial problem that split Russian historians into two camps, Lev Tolstoy began to write the story of Fyodor Kuzmich, a Casanova transformed into Saint Francis of Assisi. He thought it was the greatest of subjects for the historian-novelist. But Tolstoy never finished the book and left only a brief skeleton of his project.

Tsar Alexander's story has been told many times before, but never with enough attention to its manifold ramifications. The present narrative is an attempt to deal with some of them. Although a great deal of research, including a trip to the Leningrad State Archives, went into writing this volume, it is not a scholarly book. It is a novelistic rendition of the drama of the tragic mysterious Tsar. The author believes the fictional form is a better medium for conveying to the general public the strange story, and permits him to dispel the contradictions and gaps by imaginative reconstruction.

All dates are given according to the Gregorian calendar, common to the Western world, rather than the Julian calendar, which was utilized by the Russians until the Bolshevik revolution. As far as possible, I have used the commonly accepted system of transliteration of Russian except when English usage commands an alternative spelling more naturally acceptable to the general reader. For arbitrary variations of this kind I ask the indulgence of linguistic purists.

In my work I was helped by some of my friends. Professor Roland Stromberg and Alex Jordan read the first two chapters and made valuable corrections and suggestions. The entire manuscript was read by Mrs. Rosemary Schaefer and my former student, Charles Schaefer, who have both greatly contributed to its final shape. I am most grateful to all of them, not only for their proofreading, but also their advice and encouragement.

—M. K. D.

CHAPTER 1

Between Moscow and St. Petersburg

*B*y the middle of the eighteenth century, Russia resembled the two-headed Byzantine eagle of her coat of arms: one looking east, the other west, one forward, the other backward. The Empire's view was bifocal, split between the two capitals, ancient Moscow, and the new capital, St. Petersburg. These two centers vied with each other for primacy. They were the clashing symbols of tradition and modernity, the Slavic and the Western, native and foreign, continental and maritime trends.

The dichotomy began with Tsar Peter the Great. In May 1703, during the Great Northern War conducted by Peter against Charles XII of Sweden and his allies, Russian troops scored their first major victories by capturing the Baltic provinces of Ingria and Livonia. When Peter and his suite came down through the Ingrian forest, which covered the mouth of the River Neva, they found at the seacoast little except soggy wilderness and a few hamlets scattered around the swamps. In its last few miles before emptying into the Baltic, the westward-flowing Neva divided into four branches and formed several marshy islands, overgrown with thickets. On May 16, excited at reaching the sea, the giant Tsar shouted, "Finally! Hurrah! Follow me!" Then he waded knee deep into the water, humming the song which he had heard his soldiers so often singing around camp fires: "O my Baltic, Baltic sea, O how long I've dreamed of thee. . . ."

He took a musket from one of his soldiers, and with its bayonet cut two huge strips of sod from the shoreline, saying, "There shall be a fortress and a capital city here. I will name it after my patron saint." This was a momentous decision. By ignoring the ancient capital he challenged old Russia, with its primitive customs, its tradition-bound way of life. At the time of its founding, the capital of a new Russia actually consisted of only a few mud houses inhabited by a handful of Finnish fishermen. When Peter's close friend and co-worker Alexander Danilovich Menshikov remarked that this was still a front line in the war and that Ingria might be lost, Peter replied, "Are you a true Russian, Alexander Danilovich, or not? A true Russian never abandons any piece of land which he has conquered. He is like a bulldog who does not let go of what he sinks his teeth into!"

Then he commanded that work on the fortress start at once. Obeying the Tsar's order, thousands upon thousands of serfs, requisitioned from all over Russia, began building a fort. In a few years the powerful bastion, named after Saints Peter and Paul, stood boldly covering the western approach to a city under construction. As flood waters often inundated the shores upon which the city was being built, the initial task was to raise the level of the ground above the water's reach. Lacking for the most part not only wheelbarrows but even shovels, the workers had to scrape dirt with their bare hands, pack it into bags and carry it on their backs to low areas of the precarious shoreline. At least 100,000 of the men conscripted to build the city perished in the malaria-infected bog surrounding the mouth of the Neva.

It was Peter's extraordinary whim to establish his new capital in the middle of a war, at the exposed, inhospitable northwestern border of the Empire, amid a wasteland that bore almost nothing except pines and hemlocks. Consequently, all supplies had to be brought in from far away to keep the capital alive. There, not far from the Arctic Circle, snow often fell at the beginning of October and by the end of November a thick blanket of it covered the ground. The short winter days began with dawn around nine in the morning and ended about three in the afternoon. The long "white nights" of summer upset the natural rhythm of human life. At the height of the season, the heat and humidity of St. Petersburg was almost unbearable; the air did not cool down even during the brief hours of the night when the sun mercifully disappeared below the horizon. This made life in the new city extremely difficult. But the caprice of the autocrat had to be accepted.

By 1712, three years after the decisive Russian victory over the Swedes at Poltava, Peter ordered most government offices transferred from Moscow to St. Petersburg, though the latter was still in its first stages of frenzied construction. He then issued a decree proclaiming the city capital of his Empire. But this all-powerful tyrant could not change the centuries-old instincts and habits of the Muscovites, who continued to cling to the majestic old capital, with its ancient citadel, the Kremlin, where every Tsar had been both crowned and buried, and where the Metropolitan of Moscow, head of the Orthodox Church, had his traditional seat. If by the close of the eighteenth century, St. Petersburg had become the administrative head of the Empire, Moscow remained its heart, perhaps its cultural focus (though powerful currents of the European Enlightenment poured also into Petersburg), the spiritual center of Holy Russia, as well as her busiest commercial hub.

They were two very different cities, one conceived in the head of a single person, the other having grown spontaneously without prearranged plan or pattern. By the eighteenth century Moscow had many of the features of an overgrown village, erratically sprawled around its architectural center, the Red Square in front of the Kremlin with its imposing cluster of palaces and churches. St. Petersburg, on the other hand, from its very beginning was a planned city, with a rigid geometric pattern. The Western architects hired by Peter and his successors lined its streets with Western-style buildings, emulating the finest in Europe. Wide avenues crisscrossed in a rectilinear grid. The favorite child of Peter I and Catherine I, the Empress Elizabeth, hired Italian architect Bartolomeo Rastrelli to build two magnificent imperial residences, the Winter Palace, in St. Petersburg, and the Catherine Palace at Tsarskoe Selo, or Tsar's Village, just a few miles south of the city. A symbol of the Westward and maritime orientation of the new capital, the Admiralty Building, with its high spire, faced the Baltic Sea. St. Petersburg grew like mushrooms after rain, and celebrated every May 16, the day the Great Tyrant conceived his daring dream.

A product of nearly seven centuries of spontaneous growth (nobody knew when it was actually founded), Moscow resembled a huge marketplace interspersed here and there with ancient churches and old-fashioned country mansions. The rigidly planned cluster of Western-style palaces and office buildings in St. Petersburg were surrounded by the many barracks needed to house numerous soldiers and sailors. The streets of Moscow were filled with people running about on their own affairs—busy merchants, shouting street peddlers, gesticulating peasants selling their produce in the open markets. But in St. Petersburg everything seemed regulated and constrained. The bureaucracy with its pomposity and protocol dominated the scene. Courtiers, officers, officials, all in the prescribed uniforms of their various ranks and functions, moved silently and haughtily through the streets carrying orders to or from their superiors. Occasionally a messenger would be seen galloping on horseback to some provincial governor, or a closed horse-drawn carriage carrying unfortunate victims to exile in Siberia or to another distant part of the huge sprawling Euroasian Empire. Every day, rain or shine, military detachments marched to their drilling grounds and returned to their barracks. As spiteful Muscovites were wont to say, "In Peter (as the capital was colloquially called), one does not die or even breathe except with official permission or by order."

While Moscow grew slowly, St. Petersburg exploded. In the last half of the eighteenth century, Petersburg's population doubled, from about 100,000 to 200,000. There were thousands of foreigners there, more Germans than any others, but many Frenchmen, and even several hundred Englishmen. A flourishing trade brought in British manufactured goods in exchange for Russian hemp, iron, tallow and lumber. On Nevsky Prospect a resident could buy excellent English beer or pottery made by Josiah Wedgwood.

The contrast between the two cities extended to building materials used: brick and stone in Petersburg, while wood was used in Moscow for almost all the buildings except the Kremlin and a few churches. Even aristocratic palaces there were built of timber logs. The main streets of the city on the Neva were paved and lit with lanterns, whereas Moscow's thoroughfares were rough wooden planks and secondary roads of dirt and clay became impassable during the autumn and spring rains.

Inhabitants of the new capital laughed at the backward and old-fashioned Muscovites, while the latter scorned the cosmopolitan crowd of St. Petersburg as pretentious, foreign, and perverted in their pursuit of pleasures and government careers while cutting each other's throats.

In the later years of the eighteenth century many people complained: "I tell you, it was a great blunder, even a crime, for Peter to have made this place, and at such a frightful cost! It's an unnatural place. Moscow is the real heart of Russia. Here in St. Petersburg everything is cold, heartless. . . . People even speak French or German rather than Russian. And what do these French and German snobs tell us? That Russia is miserable and savage, that it must be made over in the image of foreigners. That is disgusting!"

The response was: "What are we to do? Not a single truly Russian work of literature exists, not even a novel which realistically depicts Russian manners and customs. How can we have a cultured society without reading the great French, English, German writers? To return to the culture of Moscow is to revert to a miserable savagery. We have got to keep in touch with the thought of the West."

* * *

St. Petersburg was a narrow window which Peter the Great had forcibly opened to Europe. Through this window streamed Western scientists, artists, and not least military experts, as Peter tried to make his country a great European power, equipped with efficient armed forces, and especially a newly built navy. All of Peter's reforms notwithstanding, the overwhelming majority of people in Russia remained what they had been for centuries—an amorphous mass of poor peasants, brutalized by backbreaking daily labor as well as by vodka, and, in the eyes of the Westernized upper classes, fanatical and superstitious. For most of them Greek Orthodox Christianity was more a way of life than a body of dogmas. Some landed gentry regarded the serfs as happy and well off. Toward the end of the century sentimental native operas depicted the peasant as filled with simple bucolic joy and virtue. Such idealization was countered by the picture presented in 1790 by Alexander Radishchev—first of the "repentant nobles"—a picture of misery and savage mistreatment for which the author of *Journey from St. Petersburg to Moscow* was banished to Siberia.

The peasant-serfs regarded their rulers not only as masters of life and death but as almost god-like creatures. Their proverbs reflected this view: "The sun shines in heaven and the Tsar on earth." Another saying expressed the peasants' organic ties with the land they tilled: "The Tsar is the father, the earth the mother." But, alas, most of the earth that nourished them did not legally belong to them, but to the masters who allowed their serfs to live and work on small portions of land only in exchange for heavy labor on the masters' estates. But in a deeper sense, the lords belonged to the Tsar, because of the obligatory service they owed to the State.

The squire's power over his serfs was near absolute. By 1765, it included the right to send a serf to forced labor in Siberia without reference to any tribunal. Customarily the peasant and his family worked half-time for their masters and half for themselves. But in addition to their regular work, most landlords frequently imposed additional labor at certain times, for instance at haymaking or harvesting. Such a situation corresponded roughly to that situation in Western Europe during the early Middle Ages. But whereas serfdom had all but ended in Western Europe by the eighteenth century, it expanded in Russia and became more severe. The peasantry, while sulky and not infrequently rebellious, bore the burdens, retaining an almost mystical attachment to the land. "We are yours, but the land is ours," a folk saying ran. "We need land, land, more land," was the constant lament of the great majority of peasants, in the largest country in the world.

The wealth of a Russian squire was measured by the number of serfs he owned because they were his main labor force. Without them the land was worthless. The nobility shared the monopoly of land and serf ownership with the Crown and the Orthodox Church. By the end of the eighteenth century the traditional practice of dividing possessions among all male heirs had reduced most of the squires to dire straits. In 1772, some one-third of them owned fewer than ten serfs each, while only one in four owned more than twenty serfs. Thus for most of the poor landowners, life was also a struggle for survival. Service in the armed forces or government administration offered the only way of bettering their lot. A small group of powerful noblemen, families like the Golitsyns, the Shuvalovs, the Strogonovs, did indeed own thousands of "souls" and lived in luxury, occupying most of the lucrative positions of state as well. The gap between the bonded peasant grinding out his life in the fields and a small stratum of the Europeanized nobles isolated in their manors or in the palaces of Petersburg or Moscow was practically unbridgeable. This alienation preyed on the consciences of some penitent, guilt-ridden aristocrats whose minds began to turn toward reform or even revolution.

In the eighteenth century a revolution was most unlikely, but its distant rumblings could be already heard. They were reflected in a series of peasant mutinies, the most dangerous of which was to take place half a century after Tsar Peter the Great named his capital city on the Baltic.

* * *

Peter's death opened a period of political instability lasting for thirty-seven years. Peter, who cruelly tortured and finally killed his own son Alexis, because he opposed his Westernizing reforms, abolished the traditional rule of primogeniture and replaced it with the right of each sovereign to choose his or her successor. In actual practice, the guards regiment and other elite military units stationed in and around St. Petersburg decided who would be elevated to the throne. They made the Russian crown neither hereditary nor adoptive, but rather occupational. From Peter's death in 1725 to the accession of Alexander I in 1801, every sovereign ruled with the consent and support of the guards. They were the actual kingmakers and promoted those who seemed amenable to sustaining their class interests. Of Peter's immediate successors, three were women, one a boy of twelve, another a year-old baby, another an idiot. The two oldest guards units, the Preobrazhensky and Semenovsky regiments, both stationed in St. Petersburg, played a special role in the process of establishing and maintaining sovereigns on the throne. They were similar to the Pretorian guards of late imperial Rome in this respect.

The Empress Elizabeth, daughter of Peter the Great, soon after mounting the throne in 1741 tried to reassert herself and prepare her succession in advance. She summoned to Russia her nephew Peter, son of her sister Anne, the Duchess of Holstein, to be trained as Russia's future Tsar. This was a strange choice. Peter was a German princeling of feeble intellect and deceitful character, narrow-minded and childish. He was an obsessive admirer of all things Prussian, especially Frederick the Great's military organization and practices—the drills, the uniforms, the way of life. Elizabeth knew of these limitations, yet she persisted in her dynastic scheme, arguing that "The blood of the Romanovs flows in his veins. That is the most important thing. . . . In due time he will learn how to be a ruler of Russia. The clever Germans have a saying that 'wisdom comes with the office, *Verstand kommt mit Amt*. . . ." And indeed, the half-witted, capricious Peter was established at the St. Petersburg court as Grand Duke and heir apparent, or Tsarevich.

Elizabeth was an overprotective aunt and a petty despot. In 1744, she brought Peter a German bride, Princesss Sophia of Anhalt-Zerbst, daughter of one of the field marshals of Frederick the Great. She was born in the Baltic city of Stettin in 1729. Elizabeth didn't know her personally, but when she saw her portrait she decided that Sophia, a healthy looking girl with rosy cheeks and an angelic smile, would be a most suitable bride for her nephew. Sophia was brought to St. Petersburg at the age of fourteen with her coffer full of Western books, but only three dresses and two nightgowns, bought out of the traveling allowance sent by the Empress. "I remember," a courtier noted in his diary, "when she showed up with her mother, she was introduced to a gawky German youngster, about to be married to her. She was in for a shock when she saw him." But the clever and adaptable girl pretended not to mind it. She accepted the inevitable and immediately began to learn the Russian language, which she soon mastered to a high degree of perfection. She also studied diligently the Russian Orthodox religion, renouncing her native Lutheranism, and was received into Orthodoxy and assumed the name of Catherine. After her marriage to Peter, she was given the title of Grand Duchess.

Catherine had a quick and cunning mind. She quickly grasped that her husband was immature and apathetic, a dullard who took no interest in her whatsoever, and except for military matters was uninterested in public affairs. On the honeymoon he played with toy soldiers, neglecting his bride altogether. He surrounded himself with people of his kind. This included his empty-headed mistress with whom he lived quite openly. "Peter's favorites were fools or traitors," said Catherine to one of her ladies-in-waiting whom she trusted. "He indulges himself in the most dissolute debauchery and drunkenness. His mistress is ugly, stupid, and offensive." Most courtiers, except those which were as depraved as Peter's, were eventually alienated from him.

Catherine soon concluded that her husband was a hopeless psychopath. The ambitious and energetic girl read Voltaire, Mme. de Sevigné, and many other French writers fashionable in the Age of the Enlightenment. She admired their Gallic esprit, their sparkling style, their fund of new ideas among which the notion of "enlightened despotism" was so prominent. Outwardly she ignored her husband's eccentricities and took Montesquieu to bed with her. In her memoirs she recorded a burning amibiton to become "an autocratic empress of all the Russians." This Germanic girl with a French education also began to cultivate the Russians who could help her achieve this ambition, namely, the officers of the two key guards regiments.

Among the more daring and better looking of these were Colonel Sergei Saltykov and the brothers Orlov, Alexis Michael and Gregory. In 1754, Catherine gave birth to a son, Paul, whom Peter recognized as his own but whose father was probably Saltykov. He was shipped off to Sweden after that and his place was taken by the brothers Orlov who alternatively shared her favors.

Upon succeeding Elizabeth in 1762, as Peter III, Catherine's husband proceeded to reveal his incompetence. His actions were a constant affront to patriotic Russians. He ended Russia's hitherto successful participation in the Seven Years War against Prussia ruled by the tough and resourceful Frederick II. During this war, which Russia had conducted since 1756 as an ally of the French and Austrians, her troops had captured most of East Prussia and even Berlin. When Peter came to the throne, Frederick II was at the end of his resources and about to capitulate. Overnight his situation changed when the new Tsar ordered the Russian commanders in Germany to abandon their conquests and switch sides. The Russian troops evacuated all of the territory they had conquered. Thus Frederick's Prussia was miraculously saved from total defeat.

In his obsessive adulation of Frederick, Peter went to far as to publicly kneel before the bust of the Prussian ruler, crown it with a wreath and kiss it! At the same time Peter surrounded himself with Germans from his native Holstein, ordered the Orthodox priests to dress like Lutheran pastors, and talked loudly during religious ceremonies at the court. He once stuck out his tongue at the bishop officiating at a High Mass. No wonder the Chancellor of the Empire, Nikita Panin, called him a fool and traitor.

While violating Russia's national interests, Peter also provoked his wife, publicly insulting Catherine and threatening her with divorce and confinement in a nunnery, to her a fate worse than death! These threats spurred her to action. Realizing that she had support from many of the younger officers, she formed a conspiracy to seize power. In June 1762, when Peter's secret agents arrested one of the conspirators bringing the danger that torture might compel him to reveal the names of his comrades, the other plotters hastened to act. Catherine's principal lover at the time, Alexis Orlov, spread the rumor that Catherine was being physically threatened by her half-mad husband, Peter. Supported by his two brothers and other fellow-conspirators, Alexis Orlov brought two guards regiments and other units to St. Petersburg. At the head of some 14,000 troops, Catherine marched to the capital dressed in the green and red uniform of the Semenovsky regiment. Speaking from the scaffolding of the still unfinished Winter Palace, Catherine with her eight-year old son Paul at her side addressed the troops in Russian. She urged them to defend her against her tyrranical and insane husband, "I am a poor woman. . . . My husband is a fool who doesn't even bother to learn our language. He has not only dishonored our sacred national banners, but vilified our holy Orthodox religion. Now he wants to murder me. . . . Together with my little son I throw myself under your protection. Help me! Help my poor son!"

At the same time Catherine's agents distributed a printed manifesto which proclaimed the dethronement of the incompetent and treacherous Peter III. Cheering soldiers, under orders from their officers, surrounded Catherine as officers, priests, and nobles approached to swear allegiance to the new Empress. Meanwhile the indolent and confused Peter waited passively at the suburban palace at Oranienbaum. He was soon arrested, without much resistance, by Catherine's supporters. Ordered to abdicate, he made a humiliating submission, asking only to retain his fiddle, his black servant, his dog and his favorite mistress. The meek surrender did not save him; the Orlov brothers strangled him amidst a drunken brawl. The world was told that Peter had died of colic.

CHAPTER 2

Tied to His Grandmother's Apron Strings

The logical candidate for the throne vacated by Peter's death was the heir apparent, the eight-year-old Grand Duke Paul, whom Peter had officially acknowledged as his son. According to the law of succession Peter the Great had enacted, the Emperor was entitled to appoint his heir. Peter III had applied the law only negatively. On his accession he had not proclaimed Paul as his heir. The oath of allegiance to the new Tsar taken at that time mentioned only "such heir as he shall appoint," without naming Paul. Catherine took advantage of this ambiguous legal situation to proclaim herself Empress "by the grace of God and the choice of the Russian people." She declared her stand for the defense of Orthodoxy, the honor of Russian arms and for public order. With a remarkable vigor of body and mind, she immediately immersed herself in affairs of state. She was as resourceful and often unprincipled as she was highly intelligent and literate. She proved a tireless worker, a brilliant diplomat and a skillful administrator.

Meanwhile the stream of lovers continued. Alexis Orlov was succeeded by his brother Gregory, the handsome artillery capitan who had helped her to the throne and then he gave way to the mad Grigory Potemkin. "A crooked, squinting, huge, swarthy, sweaty, filthy giant," as Lev Tolstoy described him, "but. . . . what a man. A true Russian, larger than life. And he had great knowledge, it was said of him. Also, what a crook. He lined his pockets well. Yet he added much to the Court. There was never anybody like him." He often acted as a monarch and received envoys while in bed, clad only in a dirty, tattered robe, and wandered the palace in his dressing gown or a cloak with a pink kerchief around his head. Yet Catherine soon moved from Potemkin to a succession of younger men. Her appetite for young male flesh was titanic. During the thirty-four years of her rule she had some forty bed companions. There was Zorich, a vagabond Serb, young Rimsky-Korsakov, who lost favor because of cavorting with a lady-in-waiting, then Lanskoy, only twenty-two, when Catherine was at least forty. When Catherine was over sixty she had a lover in his early twenties, Platon Zubov, an empty-minded playboy.

Catherine combined coarse sensuality with pedantic calculations of the smallest practical details. Around the age of sixty, she came to the conclusion that her time was too precious and that she deserved only the *crème-de-la crème* of Russian masculinity. When erotic athletes like the Orlovs or Potemkin had passed their prime, the aging Empress found that younger men had to be properly schooled to perform prescribed duties. Consequently, before being allowed the honor of slipping into her bed, a candidate-lover had to pass a strict preliminary examination that usually took place in rooms adorned with pornographic pictures, most of them cheap French and Italian engravings meticulously arranged on the walls of what she called "my little gymnasium." The task of testing and training the selected candidates was assigned to an experienced woman, Madame Protassov, who bore the official title of *l'eprouveuse* or "testing woman." Then the top graduate would be assigned to the Empress as adjutant, secretary, or some other nominal office, and had to serve as her bed partner at her pleasure.

Catherine, who as Grand Duchess had led a rather simple life, changed her ways soon after her accession to the throne. Residing mostly in the Winter Palace and Tsarskoe Selo, she came to believe that display of luxury and splendor was an integral part of the effective exercise of power. Her court surpassed that of previous rulers in ostentation. An immense retinue of courtiers always preceded and followed her. Her bodyguard, composed, of course, of tall, handsome young men, wore sumptuous attire, the officers sporting solid silver breastplates, gilded swords, and dresses richly ornamented with precious gems.

Service in this elite guard regiment, originally a serious duty, degenerated by degrees into a sort of sinecure. While ordinary units of the armed forces performed front line service, the guards regiments under Catherine were reserved mostly for ceremonial duties. The road to officer rank in the guards led chiefly through the Corps des Pages, an exclusive academy preparing youngsters for either military or civilian careers of high rank. Parades, dinners, and balls made up the social life of the guards regiments, while military drill was essentially in the hands of noncommissioned officers. More important than strictly military training was good performance on the parade grounds. It was this body of personal guards that constituted the nursery providing the Empress with a supply of lovers.

Her erotic achievements were paralleled by feverish propagandistic and intellectual activities. She was a correspondent and friend of the great French *philosophes,* one of whom was Voltaire. Diderot, editor-in-chief of the great French *Encyclopedia,* visited her at St. Petersburg. Both men received generous subsidies in exchange for which they sycophantically praised the "Semiramis of the North," comparing her to the Holy Virgin and extolling her French writing style above their own. Though Catherine was tone deaf, she encouraged Court musical careers. She subsidized the translation of carefully selected foreign books that served her purposes. While she spoke mostly German or French she encouraged the development of the Russian languge, for which no grammars or dictionaries existed at that time. Low Russian, the speech of the people, was considered too coarse for polite usage. She was a promoter and pioneer in the field of education, including women's education. She founded the first institution of secondary education, the Smolny Institute, for girls of noble families.

The exciting fruits of that intellectual renaissance known as the Enlightenment flowed into Russia, even though Catherine was cool toward ideas which she considered dangerous for Russia: Voltairean attacks on the established church or Rousseau's creation of a cult of the common man. She often said: "I am interested in uncommon men."

Realizing that she had ridden to the throne on the shoulders of guards officers who were members of the nobility, Catherine protected the rights of the landowning class. A Charter of the Nobility recognized the landowning segment of society as a separate, privileged estate, reassuring it of freedom from compulsory service and direct taxation, as well as from corporal punishment. The squires could dispose of their lands and their serfs as they wished. This included the right of buying, selling, pawning, and flogging them, and even banishing them to Siberia without the right of appeal.

As a result, what was paradise for the squires was hell for the peasants. Catherine thought that "under a good master, the Russian peasant was as well off as any in the world." But during her reign, Cossack warriors and Ukrainian free settlers were forced into serfdom and attached to the land. Local folksongs and ballads reviled Catherine as the wicked woman who crushed the Cossack autonomy and fastened the Ukrainian peasant to the soil: "Katerina, devil's mother, what have you done? To the wide steppes and the happy land you have brought ruin and serfdom," ran a Ukranian song.

Catherine's policy of extending serfdom was the cause of the series of savage peasant uprisings that marked her reign. A colorful, charismatic Don Cossack, Yemelian Pugachev, led the largest and best known of these, one that caught the imagination later of the great Russian writer Pushkin and inspired him to write *The Captain's Daughter.* Proclaiming himself to be Peter III, miraculously saved from the hands of Catherine's henchmen by Archangel Michael, Pugachev raised the standard of rebellion first in 1773 in the Urals; from there it spread over a vast area of southern and central Russia. It was one of the greatest rebellions of all time. Pugachev's followers succeeded in capturing Kazan, Penza, Soratov and many other cities, before he was betrayed by rivals, captured and taken to Moscow to be tortured and executed in 1775. Massive and barbarous reprisals ensued, as serfdom in all its severity was reimposed. Catherine herself followed the practice of bestowing thousands of "souls" as gifts on current favorites and on nobles who performed meritorious state service.

★ ★ ★

Meanwhile, Catherine's son, the Grand Duke Paul, led a secluded life as a veritable orphan and did not, at first, realize what his legal position was. Born in 1754, he was only eight years old at his father's death. From the beginning his mother treated her ugly and awkward child with cold indifference and even scorn. By the nature of the situation there were barriers of suspicion between them. Were not enemies of the throne potential rebels among the restless nobility, capable of using him as a weapon? Yet, the fact that his mother was a usurper only gradually entered Paul's mind. When he appeared in public at the age of nine at a military parade he had been much surprised to hear several officers shout, "Long live the rightful Emperor, Paul Petrovich!" He was in Hamlet's position: "Your mother and her lover murdered your father," people might have whispered to him. "Avenge him!"

Paul was most unheroic in appearance. He had an extremely small, almost flat nose, a large mouth, prominent lips, a protruding jaw, and long yellow teeth. This together with premature baldness and a pallid complexion earned him the nickname of "Death's Head." His short round figure further added to his grotesque, even repulsive appearance. Always dressed in extravagant costume, he was more a caricature than a court figure. Catherine, so fond of shapely masculine form, hated him as a reminder of one of her brief, accidental and least satisfying romances. As the boy grew, relations between mother and son became extremely tense despite mutual attempts to preserve outward appearances.

The first marriage of Paul to a Hessian princess, ordered by his mother, ended in the death of the young Grand Duchess in childbirth. Her demise was followed by a scandal when the opening of her private papers revealed an affair with Prince Alexei Razumovsky, whose child the ill-fated infant surely was! Razumovsky was bundled off to Naples in a hurry. There were even rumors that the Grand Duchess had been murdered, or allowed to die. After that, Paul found a happier marriage, also arranged by Catherine, to a Württemberg princess, Sophia Dorothea. Rebaptized and renamed in Russia, as was the custom, Maria Fyodorovna bore the Grand Duke eleven children. The oldest son was born December 24, 1777, and christened Alexander, in honor of Alexander Nevsky, the Muscovite national hero who had defeated the Swedes and the Teutonic Knights in the twelfth century. Insisting on that name, Catherine also had in mind Alexander the Great, legendary world conqueror of ancient times.

The handsome blond, blue-eyed infant, who inherited the good looks of his mother, immediately captured Catherine's affection. Born two years later, the second son, named Constantine, was far less attractive than Alexander. Red-haired, with an ape-like Mongoloid face and a ridiculously small nose and abnormally long hands, he more resembled his ugly father than his good-looking mother. Catherine paid considerable attention to this ugly boy, but from the beginning she preferred the good looking Alexander.

After 1783, in the last decade of the Empress's life, Paul lived an isolated existence at Gatchina, a large estate given to him by Catherine, a place some forty kilometers from St. Petersburg. There, she thought, he would be less dangerous, as well as less uncomfortably present to her sight. He lingered there in a world of military play-acting. Paul hired architects, engineers, ballistic experts and others to fortify the residence and build enormous barracks, where he trained his own little force of small detachments (some 2,400 men) known as "His Imperial Highness' Battalions." He dressed them in Prussian uniforms and drilled them daily to exhaustion, as his private army, separate from the rest of the Imperial forces. He governed Gatchina as his own tiny kingdom, while he nursed his bitter hatred of his scornful mother, her artificial licentious court, her pseudo-intellectual ways—all she stood for. Prussian manners and methods were his ideals and Frederick the Great of Prussia, his idol.

What of the children? Catherine cunningly took advantage of the absence of the Grand Ducal couple (who in 1781 were sent on a tour of Europe to get them out of the way) in order to transfer the boys to the Winter Palace and then to Tsarskoe Selo. They were to be educated under the watchful eye of their grandmother and the tutors she chose for them. Alexander was to be prepared for the throne of Russia. Constantine, one day perhaps, would live up to his name by ruling from Constantinople over a reestablished Byzantine Empire, wrested from the Turks. Catherine ordered that the parents were to see their sons only with her permission, which often would not be granted for months. When Paul and Maria protested, Catherine simply said, "I ought to raise the boys. Am I not mistress of the art of governing people? Haven't I proved this by what I have accomplished?" When the Grand Duchess Maria Fyodorovna wept and insisted on reclaiming her own children, Catherine stamped her foot and cried, "The children belong not to you but to Russia. They are state property. It is my duty to raise them as they should be raised to fulfill their sublime destinies." When Maria Fyodorovna gave birth subsequently to other children—she had four daughters—Catherine told her, "Now you have four children to assuage your grief. Isn't that enough for you?"

As a result of his mother's tyranny, Paul's anger and frustration grew stronger and deeper. He developed a persecution complex. One night Paul woke up sobbing and told his wife of his nightmare: he had relived the day of his father's death when as a boy he was driven to the palace in his nightshirt to receive the acclamation of the crowd at the side of his mother. But in his terrible dream the carriage never reached the Winter Palace. Instead it took him to the

Senate Square where he was led up the steps to a scaffold. "And they all shouted that I must die!" he wept. Such nightmares haunted Paul more and more frequently as his despair and frustration, nourished by fear and suspicion, deepened with age, and he gradually became paranoid.

★ ★ ★

Meanwhile Catherine proceeded to pay passionate attention to the education of the two boys. She, of course, adored Alexander, calling him "my little monkey," "my darling angel," "my delightful urchin," or "my future Alexander the Great." To prepare her grandsons for their roles, she ordered instructors and tutors to apply Rousseauean or "natural" methods in which she took great pride: plain food, loose clothing, plenty of fresh air and exercise. This simple, healthy life included cold water baths every morning and sleeping on flat iron beds with straw-filled leather mattresses. The room temperature was to be kept at 14–15 degrees Centigrade (about 58 degrees Fahrenheit). To keep the air fresh, no more than two candles were to be lit at a time in their respective rooms. Alexander had a Russian wet nurse as well as a French governess. Constantine also had a Russian nurse, but his nanny was Greek, to prepare him for his future destiny as ruler in Constantinople.

Despite her many duties and pastimes, Catherine always found time to spend with her grandchildren, teaching them to read and write, playing games with them using toys she frequently designed herself. She wrote instructive tales, nursery rhymes, and digests of old Russian legends for them. Her views on education stressed shaping of character as much as formal instruction. She encouraged both children to till their own gardens and grow their own vegetables. They were urged to be dignified yet practical, self-confident and self-sufficient.

As a boy Alexander loved outdoor life. During the summer months he walked, enjoying the masses of greenery, or climbed into a small rowboat and cruised the canals that crisscrossed the vast park at Tsarskoe Selo. He liked to pick mushrooms and berries. In winter, which in St. Petersburg might last up to five months, he built big mounds of snow, then sprinkled them with water to freeze and form ice mountains and splendid runs for sleds and toboggans. In 1781, Catherine selected as tutor for Alexander and Constantine a young Swiss disciple of Voltaire, Rousseau and Montesquieu, Frederic Cesar Laharpe, then twenty-five years old. Saturated in the thought of the French Enlightenment, so near to his native Vaud, Laharpe had developed a fierce independence, a love of republican virtue, and a hatred of tyranny, which had brought the young lawyer into conflict with feudal authority in his native land before he was contacted via Catherine's friend, the German Enlightenment writer Grimm, to make the journey to St. Petersburg. Laharpe was a good devoted teacher, and Alexander loved him.

At the same time, the Empress had appointed old General Saltykov, the father of her first lover, to supervise the boys' military education. He taught them horse riding, drill and general discipline necessary for their duties as princes and military men, while languages, history, mathematics and natural sciences were Laharpe's task.

Catherine liked history most of all. In the course of studies she outlined for Laharpe to teach "the orgins, the decline, and the fall of empires and civilizations," as well as biographies of great state rulers, principles of legislation, foreign policy and commerce. But he was to stress conduct and character as much as learning, courtesy, self-possession, and "principles of humanity." The young Swiss lawyer was up to it. "A solid head," Catherine called him. She liked him, and he succumbed to her flattery.

Laharpe exerted a deep, lasting, lifetime influence on Alexander, with whom he got on well from the start. The coarse, volatile and vicious Constantine, on the other hand, despised Laharpe and once even bit him when Laharpe scolded him for not studying enough. The serious, earnest Swiss functioned as the first of the father figures in whom Alexander found a substitute for the unstable and usually absent Paul.

Laharpe tried to pass on his Enlightenment outlook, including religious scepticism, to his pupils. When Alexander asked him who Jesus Christ was, the mentor answered, "A fanatical Jew from whom the Christian sect took its name." Until his last years Alexander would adhere to a kind of deism in which religion was a rational humanistic morality, with all the sects and creeds being essentially similar. The veneer of the various theologies was considered irrelevant, usually complex rationalizations of the particular interests of the corresponding priestly group.

On this point Catherine and Laharpe were in perfect though tacit agreement. Her own deism, or perhaps agnosticism, was concealed under her careful, regular, demonstrative observance of the rites and customs of the Russian Orthodox Church. These were numerous and lengthy. Some ceremonies, for instance the Easter Sunday service, lasted two or three hours. Everyone had to stand during these liturgies, which were followed by interminable sermons, lasting much longer than Protestant or Roman Catholic ones. Catherine submitted patiently to these ordeals. Her loose moral life did not prevent her from frequently receiving Holy Communion and performing the outward signs of the Orthodox faith in a manner worthy of a most pious nun. Meanwhile, she was confiscating large tracts of Church lands which she distributed to her lovers. When the Metropolitan of Rustov opposed her secularization policies and rebuked her for lacking real spiritual values, she became mad with fury. She ordered "this big mouth stopped" and had him defrocked and confined to a distant monastery in the far north. Most of the hierarchy meekly submitted to the Empress' whims and excesses, and tolerated her secularist outlook so long as she paid her respects to the outward formalities of the Orthodox Church.

Alexander, at first shocked by Catherine's evident hypocrisy, learned from Laharpe the Enlightenment doctrine that religion is only a useful political tool. "Religion is one of the main instruments of statecraft," Laharpe told his pupil. "It has to be used skillfully and cautiously. . . . Remember that on ascending the throne you will also be head of the Russian Orthodox Church. Whatever your private feelings and convictions are, you must conform. You must behave as if you were a faithful son of your Church, thus setting a good example to your subjects."

The Empress' choice of a religious instructor for her grandsons was also peculiar. For the task she selected the unconventional Orthodox Church Father A. A. Samborsky, who had lived in London for a long time, married an English woman and taken a liking to the Anglican ritual. Although a Court chaplain he was in fact more interested in economics than religion, and was a pioneer in bringing to Russia some understanding of the new science that the French physiocrats and the Scotsman Adam Smith were creating. Samborsky's house was the meeting place for all those interested in English ideas, and for all visitors from the British Isles. He shaved his beard and Catherine even allowed him to wear secular dress. The Orthodox hierarchy suspected the purity of his faith and some bishops refused to conduct services with him, considering him a libertine and a heretic.

On the whole, Alexander's education was reasonably extensive. In addition to languages (Latin and Greek as well as French, German and English) and history; it also included mathematics, drawing, fencing, and music as well as scientific subjects, very agreeable to Laharpe as a man of the Enlightenment. Like many people of the Court, Alexander knew French, English and German better than Russian, which was not yet considered a suitable language of civilized discourse. It might be objected that his education was limited by the fact that he rarely traveled outside the St. Petersburg area, and imagined that the rest of the country resembled the artificially idyllic world that surrounded him. Peasants he saw only from a distance in a few model villages that Catherine and Potemkin created for the sake of exhibiting them to foreign visitors. Dressed in colorful regional costumes, the carefully selected peasants had to sing, dance and display ethnic customs. Only a few of the more daring servants whispered to Alexander about the sorry lot of the serfs. When he repeated the stories to Laharpe, his tutor explained, "You must not forget that Alexander of Macedonia also had slaves. He perpetrated many horrors and sacrificed liberty in his empire. He laid waste to Asia just to imitate the heroes of Homer and please his minions. But you must never take him as a model. The happiness of your subjects should be your goal."

Alexander was surprised and responded, "But my grandmother wants me to be another conquering hero, like Peter the Great. Didn't she build a monument to him at the Senate Square?"

"Yes, my boy," the Swiss answered, "Peter the Great did not only say that he was devoted exclusively to the good of his people but he also worked hard to civilize them. Maybe some of his cruel measures were necessary for the barbarous Russians of his day. But almost a century has elapsed since that time. With the changed conditions one should alter the methods of governing people. Your Imperial Grandmother's wise reforms also have gone far toward civilizing your country. By the time you are fortunate enough to ascend the throne, the Russian people should be ripe for further improvements of their manners, morals, and the milder, more compassionate way of ruling them. . . ."

"What a wise man you are, Monsieur Laharpe! I wish you would stay at my side for a long long time. I will always need your advice."

"I am here as long as it pleases Her Imperial Majesty for me to remain, and wants me to communicate the principles that, in my opinion, ought to permeate every enlightened prince. Human beings should not be bound hand and foot to the caprices of another single human being. . . ."

"But what about our serfs, Monsieur Laharpe?"

"I hope that your Imperial Grandmother will in due time alleviate their lot. The Pugachev rebellion has been a warning. And it will be your task to do away with this institution altogether. Indeed, I am about to submit a memorandum to her on this subject and on that of a constitution for Russia."

So he did, in June 1784. When the content of the memorandum leaked out to courtiers, they were sure the Empress would send Laharpe packing his bags and order him to return to his Switzerland. But nothing of the sort happened and he was allowed to continue inculcating Alexander with republican ideas. Alexander hung on every word of his mentor. He listened to Laharpe's "principles of the dignity of the human person, of respect for every man, whatever his status in society," yet, occasionally, he voiced his doubts:

"But what about our ancient autocracy?"

"An enlightened prince," Laharpe insisted, "should be a benevolent father to his subjects, the first servant of his country, and not their oppressor. . . . Ideally there should be no princes. Each country, under the rule of just and impartial laws, should elect its most worthy citizens to fill the offices of government. I trust you remember what Plato said on the philosophers ruling their countries."

★ ★ ★

The bright and precocious youngster matured rapidly. Catherine found Beaumarchais's "Marriage of Figaro" shocking and was oddly enough quite prudish in some matters. She forbade Alexander any contact with women, except for his dancing lessons, for which only the most aristocratic girls were selected, and taken away immediately after the prescribed hour. His tutors never discussed sex with him, except in the most abstract manner. But adolescent nature asserted itself. At the age of fourteen Alexander began chasing the servant girls who cleaned his rooms. One day he admitted to Laharpe, "I often have strange dreams at night. After last night's performance of "Figaro" I dreamt that one of the Italian actresses I saw on the stage came to my bed and embraced me very tenderly. When I awoke my bed sheet had wet spots. . . ."

This was duly reported to the Empress who had insisted upon being informed of every detail of her "little angel's development," including accounts of his bowel movements. When the nocturnal incident was reported to her, she decided it was time to start looking for a suitable wife for him. Meanwhile, Monsieur Laharpe was ordered to guard his innocence strictly and watch closely his contact with the servant girls. "His initiation into love should come only within marriage. . . . Until marriage, virginity is a necessity," Catherine insisted. Marrying her grandsons became a high priority of the Empress' schedule.

Russian ambassadors at the principal European courts immediately received instructions to submit lists of prospective marriage partners to the Ministry of Foreign Affairs. "German princesses are the best prospects. They are faithful, fertile and obedient. Pay special attention to the smaller German courts," the ambassadors were instructed. Information from the court of Karlsruhe in Baden mentioned two princesses, Louise, 13, and Frederica, 11. Both were pretty, well-educated, and their parents only too happy to have their daughters considered by the Empress of All the Russias as potential brides. Their age did not discourage the determined Catherine. "After all, when I came to Russia for the first time, I wasn't much older than Louise. I have to provide for their journey to St. Petersburg and their stay here. In the meantime, the girls will become accustomed to our ways and customs, while Alexander and Constantine are becoming more mature. . . ."

So indeed, the two frightened child-princesses arrived in St. Petersburg in October 1792. Soon after her arrival in January 1793, Louise began to study Russian and the catechism of the Orthodox religion. With her new baptism she traded her Protestant name Louise for the more Russian sounding name Elizabeth Alexeyevna. Catherine was captivated by Louise and exclaimed, "The more one sees her, the more pleasing she is. What delicate features! The profile of a Greek cameo. What lovely hair! What almond-shaped eyes! No one who comes near her is able to resist her charm. She is an ideal bride for Alexander." Even the Grand Duchess Maria Fyodorovna, Alexander's mother, usually critical of Catherine's judgment, agreed this time. "There is a strange charm about her person! Louise has a perfectly oval-shaped face and a voice vibrant with feeling, and such remarkable delicacy of manners that my Alex is bound to be enchanted by her. Who wouldn't be enraptured by her ash-blond curly hair, her milk-white complexion, her rose-bud cheeks? And her blue eyes framed in black eyelashes. . . . One would have to be made of stone not to love her! She is a true gem."

But Alexander disappointed both his mother and grandmother by remaining indifferent to Louise's charms. Their first meeting, which took place under the scrutinizing eyes of a few hundred courtiers, was a failure. Louise, alone for the first time with a strange young man, was paralyzed with embarrassment and fear. Alexander, on the other hand, feeling trapped, displayed a studied indifference. After several meetings, the youngsters did develop to the stage of a moderately vivacious but rather banal exchange of a few words. They chattered mostly about the early snow, the long exhausting trip from Karlsruhe to St. Petersburg, and the enormity of the Winter Palace. Later they exchanged letters that led to a few meetings in the privacy of Louise's apartment.

After a few weeks the Grand Duchess Maria Fyodorovna informed Catherine that Alexander admitted to considering Louise "more and more amiable from day to day." Once he even tried to kiss his prospective bride gently. She reciprocated shyly. Louise reported this in a letter to her mother at Karlsruhe: "You can't imagine how strange it seemed to me to kiss a man who was neither my father nor my uncle. What seemed even more odd to me was that it didn't feel like when Papa used to kiss me, always scratching me with his beard."

Since all letters of Louise were intercepted by the Court officials, the Empress was encouraged. This prompted Catherine to tell her secretary that "Alexander shows every sign of loving Louise, but he is too shy and does not yet dare show it openly. She is mature enough to marry him even at thirteen. We have to arrange their betrothal while she is still a virgin. At our court, as you know, that may not last too long. These guard officers are raving wolves, savage tigers, capable of all sorts of devilish tricks to seduce an innocent young thing like Louise, as long as her position at the Court is not well defined. Even I would be helpless to prevent it. . . . We must arrange for their instant wedding."

Louise was fifteen and Alexander had reached his sixteenth birthday when they were married. Paul, who had not been consulted about his son's marriage, first refused to attend the ceremony. Catherine had to force him to do so by resorting to a threat: "Either you attend the wedding or I deprive you of your allowance, your soldiers and your Gatchina estate." Paul complied sullenly. His bitterness and frustration deepened still more.

The wedding took place on October 4, 1793, at the Winter Palace. Alexander wore a long Russian caftan of silver brocade with diamond buttons and the light blue ribbon of the Order of St. Andrew. Elizabeth had on a magnificent gown made also of silver brocade strewn with pearls. Alexander's brother, Constantine, held the ceremonial crown over the heads of the young couple, a traditional Orthodox custom. The wedding deeply moved Catherine, who cried when Alexander kissed his bride, and whispered, "They look like two angels." The ceremony was followed by a series of banquets and balls, with accompanying displays of fireworks, theatrical performances such as "Cupid and Psyche," and festivities that went on for two weeks. Alexander and Elizabeth, now the Grand Duchess Elizabeth Alexeyevna, gave the impression of spontaneous gaiety.

The pomp and fanfare covered up instant marital troubles. Alexander's emotional immaturity accompanied a lack of experience as a lover. Reared in the golden cage of the Winter Palace under the gaze of his strict and overprotective grandmother, he had had very limited contact with women except for the hasty kissing and hugging of the servant girls. In his psychological makeup, shaped during his isolated childhood, there was a large element of infantile narcissism, an expectation of being loved rather than to love.

Elizabeth was still more childish and inexperienced than her adolescent husband. A good little girl, she had no accurate knowledge of the facts of life and was completely unawakened sexually. Alexander's clumsy attempts to satisfy her vague romantic longings for more than superficial kisses and caresses perplexed her. When they found themselves in the marital bed for the first time, they were both embarrassed. Alexander was paralyzed by shyness. Elizabeth was trembling and sobbing. Neither of them knew what to do. After some hugging, fondling and kissing, Alexander grew bored and sleepy. "The day was so long. . . . Maybe I drank too much champagne. . . ." He turned away from his bride and fell asleep. His snoring kept Elizabeth awake until the wee hours, until finally she too succumbed to weariness and boredom. It would be difficult to imagine a more pathetic aftermath of a brilliant wedding day.

After this inauspicious beginning, Alexander's more daring but still awkward attempts at lovemaking on the following night found Elizabeth still unresponsive. A week or so of this conjugal confusion led to the evolution of a sort of brother-sister relationship between the newlyweds and tender but incomplete caresses. Elizabeth was aroused but not completely satisfied. Only her innate delicacy prevented her from showing this to the outer world. Such was the beginning of a long and complex relationship.

CHAPTER 3

Between Two Worlds

For the newlyweds the Empress Catherine built a small, graceful, yellow and white palace at Tsarskoe Selo near her own summer residence. Located some thirteen miles south of St. Petersburg, Tsarskoe Selo was a conglomeration of buildings, the main one being the huge Catherine Palace that Peter the Great's youngest daughter Elizabeth had built in memory of her mother Catherine I, Peter's second wife. The various imperial residences stood amid massive expanses of greenery, in a large, scenic, English-style park designed by a gardener brought from London. The park with its vast artificial lake was adorned in typical eighteenth century manner, studded with picturesque pseudo-ruins of ancient temples, along with ornamental "medieval" bridges and replicas of a mosque and a Chinese village. Members of the high nobility and officers of the imperial household occupied the villas that surrounded the park. The Empress summered there. A special ramp was built to ease her descent from her chambers to the park, for in her advanced age she had grown so stout that climbing stairs was exhausting.

Tsarskoe Selo had its own high school, the Lycée, for children of the elite families. All this formed a world of its own, dominated by the imperial palace. Grand Duke Paul, as will be recalled, lived meanwhile in Gatchina, isolated from his hated mother by distance and the distinctive militaristic environment he created there. In Gatchina he felt sovereign, secure, and all-powerful.

As a young man, Alexander was uncomfortable visiting his father's domain too often because of his grandmother's jealous opposition to unsupervised contacts between them. But after his marriage and becoming established in his own palace free from close supervision, Alexander soon became an increasingly frequent visitor to Gatchina. Occasionally he would take Constantine, known as Kostya, with him. At first Alexander was a bit shocked by the ribaldry and vulgarity of Paul's rough, hard-drinking officers. Gradually, however, he came to enjoy the experience of a less formal environment and the thrill of commanding and drilling the Gatchina troopers. Eager to win back his son from the grandmother, Paul, aware of Alexander's fascination with the military, began to teach him and Constantine the techniques of command. What red-blooded young man would not find exciting the music of a military band and the colorful changing of the guard meticulously choreographed by his father? Or the mock charges of the brilliantly dressed hussars?

Gradually, under their father's guidance—with his sons, Paul suppressed his impatience with beginner's mistakes—the two boys learned the arts of soldiering and leadership. This was especially true of Constantine, harsh and brutal, a born martinet. Physically stronger than Alexander and a much better horseman, he was drawn to the Gatchina barracks. Kostya passionately enjoyed shouting orders to the guardsmen in his deep, sonorous voice. They responded to the commands of this ugly but robust martial figure. Constantine was an impressive sight on the parade grounds. The rough personality of this essentially physical being contrasted prominently with Alexander's hesitant, innate gentleness. The fact that Kostya, though far less intelligent than Alexander, was much quicker to adapt to the military profession somewhat undermined the bonds of brotherly affection.

The combined effect of Alexander's slender figure and his high-pitched voice made him something less than a natural military commander. Moreover, he was short-sighted, deaf in one ear and had a slight limp, all handicaps which generated a certain inferiority in his sensitive psyche. He grew jealous of Kostya's skills and of Paul's seeming greater affection for the son who resembled him physically and temperamentally and with whom he soon developed a closer psychological affinity.

Soon these increasingly frequent escapes to Gatchina gave to Alexander and Constantine an excuse to neglect their studies as parade-mania replaced scholarship. Paul insisted that his sons appear in proper attire for each military function, i.e., in the uniform of the unit they were to drill or lead on a particular day. Since Paul had five detachments at Gatchina, each with a different uniform, the boys had to change frequently. This was a chore but Alexander came to enjoy it. He found pleasure in contemplating himself in the mirror, admiring the extravagant costumes Paul developed from various Prussian patterns. These usually included high boots with fancy spurs, white elbow-length gloves, three-cornered hats, gold and silver sashes, powdered wigs with beribboned braids! With a sword at his belt and a cane in his hand, Alexander tried to imitate his father and carefully rehearsed over and over again in front of a mirror the gestures he would make and the commands he would shout during upcoming parades.

Thus, after a few months of this military training, it was obvious that Catherine had lost the battle for her grandsons' souls. She had tried to dominate the boys by intellectual indoctrination in complex, abstract ideas. This, however, failed to satisfy their male instincts. She did not know how to absorb the youthful energies of the brothers in activities more robust than the tedious, strictly regulated routine of the imperial court, where wigs, lace cuffs, and curtsies in the French manner were the rule. Paul, on the other hand, successfully exploited his sons' masculine pride and both brothers took increasing pleasure in fulfilling their military duties in the Gatchina world. This gave them a sense of importance and flattered their vanity without requiring much expenditure of thought on their parts. Adolescent rebellion took the form of turning against the authoritarian grandmother who had served as surrogate father (along with her instrument, Laharpe). Both brothers turned back toward their true but heretofore absent father.

Thus for the next three years or so Alexander lived a dual life, torn between his father's world at Gatchina and Catherine's domain of the Winter Palace and Tsarskoe Selo. This gave rise to all sorts of problems. Since Catherine did not tolerate Paul's uniforms at court, before appearing in her presence Alexander had to change into appropriate dress, a gold and silver braid-embellished court uniform which included long knee breeches, silk stockings and gold-buckled patent leather shoes. At Gatchina he behaved like a rough soldier; at the imperial court he had to be a polished courtier. Thus, Alexander became an actor playing two parts. But he enjoyed acting, one of his favorite hobbies being amateur theatrics. The psychological implications are evident: an insecure ego taking refuge in multiple roles, a narcissist admiring himself in the mirror.

Alexander proved to be a brilliant actor. When he played the leading role in a comedy called *The Liar,* Catherine herself congratulated and then kissed him on both cheeks, saying, "Sasha, you were really marvelous. I can't imagine anybody playing this role as well as you." In his amazing real life, far more dramatic than any fiction, he would later perform as an actor, too. Napoleon would call him "the Talma of the North," referring to the celebrity of the Parisian theaters.

* * *

Alexander soon found friends and role models among his fellow officers at Gatchina, something he needed but had not experienced before: the companionship of other young men. He was especially attracted to a second lieutenant of the cavalry, named Prince Alexander Golitsyn, an instructor in riding and fencing. Alex was the only son of a rich aristocratic landowner and the heir to a large fortune. His generous allowance permitted him to keep company with the spoiled set of young men. Swarthy and curly-haired, with an aquiline nose and a small dark mustache, he cut a smart figure both on the riding course at Gatchina and in the drawing rooms of St. Petersburg. His sharp wit and perceptive mind, along with his carefree disposition, captivated Alexander, who was rather repelled by the coarseness of many of the Gatchina officers.

One January day in 1794, seeing that the Grand Duke was depressed, Golitsyn said, "It seems to me that Your Highness could stand some cheering up. Maybe a visit to the Gypsies at the Red Tavern would help."

Alexander had never heard of the Red Tavern. When his friend explained this establishment and the sort of varied entertainment it offered, Alexander blushed and murmured, "My dear Alex, I am married. I wouldn't want to be unfaithful to my wife."

"If I may say so," Alex smilingly replied, "Your Highness seems not to be aware of a superior fidelity, heroic of which a Russian officer should be capable—fidelity to several women at the same time." Not entirely persuaded by this argument, but not wishing to appear less daring and masculine than the others, Alexander did not at first refuse the invitation. But after a few minutes of reflections he raised another objection. "My dear Alex, in my position, how can I go to the Gypsies without the entire Peter society knowing of it and gossiping about it?"

"Everything will be taken care of, Your Highness. You will wear a black wig, put on civilian clothing and be introduced as my half-brother, Peter, who has just returned from the Ukraine to spend the season at the capital. Moreover, I'll reserve the tavern just for our group, the Gatchina cavalry squadron, so that no miserable infantrymen or contemptible civilians will be allowed in that evening. Is this all right with you?"

"You are a genius, Alex! Let's go. How about next Saturday?"

★ ★ ★

And indeed the following Saturday night half a dozen kindred spirits set out in two troikas, the traditional Russian sleds drawn by three horses, for the Red Tavern. The drivers, wearing huge bearskin fur caps and thick fur-lined felt coats, sent the troikas along at a brisk clip for some four miles through the deserted snow-covered countryside toward St. Petersburg. The spirited horses were covered with a thick net to shield the riders from the slivers of ice thrown up by their hooves; they strained at their bits as they pulled the sleds over glittering icy roads, bright silver ribbons under the light of a full moon. They pulled up before a one-story, white-washed stucco building, its roof covered with thick snow supporting huge icicles from the eaves. The doors of the house were painted bright red, as were its eight window frames. This was the legendary Red Tavern, whose delights Golitsyn had so vividly described to Alexander.

As the visitors entered the hall, a young Gypsy helped them remove their heavy fur coats. Then the young officers were greeted by the proprietor, an old gray-haired man dressed in a short black oriental caftan richly embroidered with yellow and green silk threads and silver sequins. Bowing very low, he led his guests to a large rectangular hall lighted by a chandelier of wrought iron and a fireplace. Nothing adorned the rather shabby, plastered walls except two etchings in varnished wooden frames. One represented Peter the Great on horseback reviewing his troops before the battle of Poltava, the other Catherine the Great in her coronation robes.

Four young Gypsy waiters in similar gaudy caftans and baggy Turkish pantaloons seated the guests around a heavy oak table. In front of the open hearth and its roaring wood fire a huge feast was set. In the middle of the table a roast suckling pig and large chunks of broiled lamb were surrounded by lavish tidbits, caviar, cold meats and fish dishes as well as bottles of wine and vodka. As the guests helped themselves to food and drink, entertainers appeared from opposite sides of the dining hall. A semicircle of slim and swarthy young men in richly embroidered shirts and oriental pantaloons strummed their fingers over seven-stringed guitars and sang in harmony, as an equal number of Gypsy dancers swirled about in traditional costumes of voluminous skirts, silk blouses, yellow, blue and green kerchiefs around their heads, their necks adorned with glittering jewelry of gold and silver coins. As the guests ate and drank, the band played and the girls danced with tambourines in their hands, tapping rapid fanatic rhythm with their feet. Their teeth flashed. They sang sad, romantic, sensuous songs about Gypsy life and hopeless love in the boundless Russian steppes, or about trips to exotic lands, about lovesick hearts seeking consolation in desperate exploits or suicide. The golden coins around their necks jingled. The men of the chorus yelled. The women dancers sang with guttural, staccato shouts. The tempo became faster and faster. Finally, they reached out inviting arms toward the guests, proudly tossing back their heads.

The sound of these plaintive melodies, the whole strangely hypnotic, intoxicating scene deeply affected Alexander who sat watching, without eating much, but gulping glass after glass of the Caucasian wine which his companions poured. Then suddenly, from the rear of the semicircle of musicians, bounced a young, dark-skinned Gypsy dancer in white shirt, black pantaloons and red boots. He slapped his knees and made a solo pirouette. At a breakneck tempo he performed a frenzied solo until he seemed completely exhausted, ending the dance with a spectacular jump and collapsing onto the floor. The music and singing stopped. The show was over.

Waiters reappeared and served champagne to the guests in oversize glasses. Each guest took his glass, bowed low, stood up and drank the bumper in one draught, after which he held the glass upside down to show that not a drop remained, and then tossed the glass over his shoulder onto the floor. Wild drinking ensued. Not an experienced drinker, Alexander became quite dizzy. As the evening progressed the girls joined the officers, sitting on their laps, kissing them, and coaxing them to sing. The bewildered Alexander, brought up in such a sheltered, strictly supervised world, had never heard the songs, which everyone else knew by heart, or the orgiastic refrain:

> Without mighty Russian drinking,
> Without fiery Gypsy singing,

Any party would be sad.
Let's drink, let's sing
Let's get mad!

As his head began to spin, he noticed his companions grabbing their Gypsy girls and running off to rooms adjoining the big dining hall or to the attic upstairs. A novice at the Red Tavern, Alexander did not do so, and one of the Gypsy singers, a plump but still beautiful woman of about thirty, with swarthy skin and shining black eyes, observing his shyness, approached him and said, "Who are you? I've never seen you here before. Why are you so sad? You seem so lonely. . . . My name is Marusha. I am the leader of the chorus. I will cheer you up. . . ."

Then she gave him a long, passionate kiss on the lips, took him by the hand and led him to her room upstairs.

* * *

After that January night Alexander became a regular visitor to the Red Tavern. Marusha's fiery lovemaking contrasted with his tepid marital life, the docile and passive sexuality of the inexperienced Elizabeth. He had found an invigorating tonic that revolutionized his conception of things erotic, and became a turning point in his life. He wondered how he could have spent his adolescence unaware of this. Yet, he couldn't help wondering if Marusha's exquisite lovemaking was spontaneous, or simply the professional tricks of a cunning Gypsy eager to pry money from rich young men? After a few encounters, it didn't matter to Alexander. He lived in an emotional frenzy for several weeks. After a dozen visits to the Red Tavern, he was like an addict willing to pay any price for the craved narcotic.

Inevitably, Marusha began to question her lover about his identity. "You have never told me much about yourself. Who are you?"

"I told you. I am the younger half-brother of Alex Golitsyn."

"It is strange. You are unlike each other. You must be very rich. Nobody ever left me five hundred roubles for one night."

"Well, my father is a wealthy landowner and gives me a generous allowance. As a farmer's son I believe that money is like manure—it's no good unless it's spread around. But tell me about yourself and your people. Who are the Gypsies? Where do you come from? Is it true as my nurse used to tell me that you Gypsies are pagan devil worshipers who steal and kill Christian children?"

"What nonsense! We are also Christians! Perhaps not like you, the Orthodox people, but Christians nevertheless. After all Jesus Christ was a Gypsy since the Holy Virgin was a Gypsy woman. Since Jesus was one of us, we have many stories regarding Our Lord. For instance, my father and grandfather told me that it was a Gypsy smith, named Romi, who was commanded by the Roman centurion to forge nails for the crucifixion of Christ. Romi believed that this was a wrong, criminal act. He procrastinated as long as he could and finally refused to finish the job, claiming that whatever he did the nails remained crooked, and burning hot and therefore unfit for crucifixion. The centurion killed him for this. We think of him as the first Christian martyr. As you see I keep his icon over my bed with an oil lamp in front of it."

"Where do the Gypsies come from? How do they live?"

"I don't know exactly where we come from. My grandfather says we came to Europe from somewhere in Asia, many generations ago. Many of our men keep the tradition of St. Romi by working with metals. They make and repair pots and pans. They also make horseshoes. Some are smiths and tinkers, but some are musicians. As a matter of fact my older brother is a smith who works for one of the cavalry regiments at the capital."

"They say too that many of your people, especially the women, are clairvoyants and can tell fortunes."

"That's a fairy tale, Peter. Clairvoyance is God's great gift. Only a few people are endowed with it. Because they are so poor many of our people pretend to be able to tell fortunes in order to earn money. In a way we are like the Jews, a scattered, wandering, persecuted race, making our living in whatever way we can. Centuries of suffering have sharpened our intuition, our sixth sense. Honestly speaking, much fortune telling by ordinary Gypsy girls is simply bluffing and even cheating. They try to sense what their customers want to hear and cater to their wishes with predictions of love, money, travel, adventure. Isn't that natural?"

"But you, Marusha, can you tell my fortune?"

"Look, Peter, I could easily act like other Gypsy girls and make you pay for it. But you are so sweet, so gentle, so generous. I'm becoming more and more fond of you. Maybe I'm in love with you. . . . I'm not going to cheat you. I don't have any gift of fortune telling. I earn my living by singing, dancing, entertaining men. . . ."

"A pity. In my present state I would love to learn what life has in store for me."

"Maybe I can help you. My uncle Munro is an expert fortune teller and clairvoyant, a real wizard. Do you want to see him? He will read your future from your hand, from cards, from tea leaves, whatever you desire. He is also a learned astrologer."

"By all means. Where is he? Could I see him soon?"

Uncle Munro, as it turned out, lived apart from the tribe, in a suburb of St. Petersburg. He was married to a Moldavian Orthodox woman who was also something of a sorceress. Munro was a busy man, with a large clientele of important people; Grand Dukes, foreign diplomats, all kinds of dignitaries consulted him. But Marusha was able to arrange a visit within the week for Alexander, as a special favor.

* * *

They went together to a small house on the southern fringe of a St. Petersburg suburb, almost in the countryside. Uncle Munro's log cottage was blackened with age and had a thatched roof. When the visitors knocked at the painted doors, the old Gypsy, dressed in a long black oriental robe, let them in. Then he sat in a low chair in a large dimly lit main room. After a few words of introduction, Uncle Munro suggested starting with a reading of tea leaves. As Marusha withdrew into an adjoining room, an old, tall, thin woman dressed in a richly embroidered robe brought a teapot with hot water, a bag with tea leaves and two brass cups. When the tea-drinking ceremony was over, Uncle Munro emptied the leaves from Alexander's cup on a large white plate and gazed at them intensely. Then, mumbling strange incantations, he began to split the leaves apart with a long white goose feather. After a prolonged inspection of each leaf he gathered them together in his palm, added a handful of herbs and threw everything into the brazier standing in the middle of the room. Breathing the strong aroma that filled the room, the Gypsy seer began to whisper, "Women, women, too many women. . . . They help and hinder you in succession. . . . Family relations no good. Too much jealousy, suspicion, ambition, pride . . . and treachery. Your father is destined to die soon—a strange and terrible death! I abjure you to have nothing to do with this. . . . Then I see more blood around you. I see a huge sea of blood . . ., Confusion, intrigue, confusion! Your life splits in the middle. This I see quite clearly, but what it means I don't understand . . ., There is too much confusion around you. . . . I can't continue. I am old and tired. Maybe my wife, who is younger than I and sometimes has a clearer vision of things to come, can help us."

He sat back in his chair and rested for a moment, breathing heavily. Then he clapped his hands three times. The emaciated looking lady who had served the tea appeared. "I have tried to tell this young man's fortune," he said to her, "but I became too confused. There are too many strange and terrible happenings, things beyond my comprehension. Why don't you continue the session?"

Squatting down in the Eastern style before Alexander, the woman bowed low and began to stare at Alexander's forehead. Her green shining eyes set in a narrow, white face seemed strangely penetrating. After a moment of silence she drew a small bag of herbs from her girdle and began throwing them into the brazier. Again a powerful aroma filled the room, making Alexander a bit queasy. After a time the woman began to whisper, "You are not the person you pretend to be . . ., Why do you do it?"

When she received no answer, with an expression of acute pain and fear on her face she jerked about and began spitting out one short sentence after another. Her whisper gradually turned into a shout, "I see a man strangled. He is very close to you, almost next to you. You rise up very high, but foolishly challenge a strong man on a white horse. He crushes you, but then embraces you. You extricate yourself from his embrace. Treachery. War, war, great murderous war. Finally you defeat him, but you pay a terrible price. Then something happens. . . . something I can't explain. Long travels to faraway lands. . . . Long life as a hermit. Then another long solitary life. . . ."

"What about Russia? What is going to happen to our country?"

After a long silence, the woman reverted to a barely audible whisper. "I don't know. . . . I don't understand what I see. The horrible images that keep rising in my mind are far beyond my comprehension." She muttered something about a huge red flood overrunning Russia, about a great war with millions and millions of corpses. . . . "And then I see a yellow flood! Yellow, yellow flood, all over the country. . . ." She was seized by a fit of hysterical sobbing. Shaking, she fell over and fainted. Her face became chalk-like, her body motionless, seemingly lifeless. Uncle Munro clapped his hands twice and a Gypsy servant carried the rigid body away. The session was over. Alexander and Marusha left the room silently.

The invigorating encounters with Marusha and the Gypsies continued for several weeks. Then, suddenly, Alexander's euphoria was interrupted by the news that Golitsyn and one of his companions had contracted gonorrhea. Treatment consisted of painful urethral irrigations and instillations of sandalwood oil, accompanied by huge doses of strong bitter infusions. Alex recovered slowly. After his wild temperament drove him out one night in search of amorous adventure his physician ordered such a severe bleeding that poor Golitsyn, weakened and emaciated, could hardly get out of bed.

Grand Duke Paul was furious. The afflicted pair were his only riding and fencing instructors at a time when he had just received a band of raw recruits for his favorite cavalry squadron. To replace them, he would have to seek Catherine's counsel. In a fit of rage,

Paul declared the Red Tavern off limits for the officers of the garrison, including Alexander, a stunning blow, needless to say. Withdrawal from the addiction to Marusha's company and the haunting Gypsy music brought some painful consequences: loss of appetite, sleeplessness, mental depression. There were moments when he was close to committing suicide.

Shortly thereafter Alexander lost the companionship of his childhood friend and mentor, Laharpe. Aware of the fact that he was of no use, he left the palace with mixed feelings and married a sixteen-year-old girl from a Baltic Germany family residing in Petersburg. The wild Constantine had often tried Laharpe's patience. Moreover, the wicked ways of Catherine's court shocked the puritan Swiss more and more. Finally, the French Revolution brought him under renewed suspicion as a radical republican. Catherine herself, Francophile though she had been, was bitterly against the Revolution and anything connected with it. Laharpe had advised her not to join Prussia and Austria in an intervention against revolutionary France. Irritated at this, Catherine dismissed Laharpe in December 1794, nearly two years after the execution of King Louis XVI. Teacher and his student parted tearfully. Alexander gave lavish gifts to Laharpe, and the latter lingered in St. Petersburg until May, supported by the Grand Duke's private funds. "My dear friend! Do not forget me!" Laharpe never would.

⋆ ⋆ ⋆

Under the Empress Catherine the Russian Empire had expanded enormously. Inherent weaknesses of neighboring Poland and Turkey whetted Catherine's appetite for territorial gains. The Polish state had an elective kingship, so Catherine arranged to have her former lover, Stanisls Poniatowski, elected to the Polish throne in 1764. A revolt aided by the French brought in the Turks also, but the Russians defeated them soundly and grabbed not only the Danubian principalities, but also part of the Crimea from the tottering Ottomans (1769–70). These Russian gains alarmed not only Austria but also Prussia. To forestall an impending war, the cunning Prussian King, Frederick II, then proposed a partition of

Poland to Catherine and to Maria Theresa of Austria. The first of these banquets at which these monarchies made a meal of the hapless Poles occurred in 1772. Their cynical greed shocked much of Europe, but sharing the Polish spoils cemented an alliance between the three powers for almost a century.

Thus after the wars with Turkey, Russia had a firm hold on the northern shores of the Black Sea as well as a slice of Poland-Lithuania. Catherine looked forward to further conquests, especially Constantinople and the Black Sea straits. Was not her second grandson, the rugged Constantine, designated from birth to one day sit on the Byzantine throne in the city which bore his name? When in 1774 the Turks were forced to recognize the Russian right to act as protector of the Christian Orthodox peoples who lived under their rule in Greece, Rumania, the Balkans, and the Holy lands, Catherine found a magnificent excuse for intervention. She had been maintaining pressure on the Turks, however Russian schemes to dismember the Ottoman Empire were checked somewhat by an anxious England, joined by Prussia and Sweden. The long and momentous rivalry between Petersburg and Whitehall, centered on the straits connecting the Black Sea to the Mediterranean, had already begun.

The Second and Third Partitions of Poland (1793–1795), gained for Russia the lion's share of the once large Polish-Lithuanian commonwealth: Courland, Lithuania, Volynia, Podolia and Belorussia. Since the death of Peter the Great, the Russian Empire had increased its population from 18 to 30 million, mostly as a result of Catherine's conquests. Yet, not everything went smoothly. The second partition touched off a Polish uprising in 1794. Russian troops led by the hero of the Turkish wars, Field Marshal Alexander Suvorov, suppressed it.

Leaders of the uprising were imprisoned in the SS. Peter and Paul fortress at the mouth of the Neva. Among them were two officers, descendants of the powerful and wealthy Czartoryski clan. The brothers Adam and Constantine, whose father and grandfather had once been leaders of the pro-Russian Czartoryski faction, were too valuable to be kept in prison. Catherine ordered them brought to St. Petersburg to be closely watched but treated as political hostages in order to guarantee the influential Czartoryski clan's future political behavior. She had them assigned to the service of her grandsons; Adam was to serve as Alexander's adjutant, while the younger, Constantine, was assigned to the brother of the same name.

The Grand Duke Alexander took an instant liking to the tall, dark, elegant young man whose protruding jaw and vigorous movements betrayed a firm, active nature. Seven years older than his new master, Prince Adam was an accomplished gentleman, with refined manners and a wordly polish. He had studied law, history and political economy abroad, in Paris, London, and in Edinburgh, that Scottish source of so much Enlightenment thought. Well informed, he could speak intelligently on most questions of the day, and he possessed some of the qualities Alexander lacked: stability, self-discipline, depth.

The reverse was also true: Czartoryski was much impressed by his youthful Russian superior, whom he found handsome, charming, and more intelligent than he had expected. "Alexander's mind is lively, alert, and curious," he wrote to his father in Poland. "Despite numerous gaps in his education, resulting from Laharpe's haphazard methods of schooling and the Grand Duke's inherent laziness, his judgment is subtle and his intuition often astonishingly accurate. Although his knowledge is not great, he understands much."

Alexander did not hide his admiration for his adjutant's austere precision in expressing his thoughts, so much in contrast to the empty loquacity of most of the courtiers. "What a bright versatile adjutant I have acquired!" Alexander thought after their first encounter. While strict in matters of etiquette, the Pole was free of that Byzantine servility so prevalent at both courts, Catherine's and Paul's. "What a contrast," Alexander reflected. "He is a virtual prisoner, a hostage, yet he behaves like a free man and a grand seigneur." Alexander quickly dropped pretensions of superiority and assumed a simple cordiality toward his aide. He immediately began to call Czartoryski by his first name, an unusual practice at the highly ceremonial Russian court. Within a few days Alexander invited Adam to a private dinner at the Alexander Palace. From the first moment, Czartoryski was impressed with the Grand Duchess Elizabeth's delicate beauty and subdued charm. While often paying her eloquent compliments, he kept a proper distance from her. Thus began a long and intimate relationship between these three individuals whose lives were destined to be closely intertwined for the next generation.

★ ★ ★

A routine soon developed in which almost every day Alexander and Adam took long walks together around Tsarskoe Selo. In the new companionship, Alexander confided everything to his fascinating friend about the Gypsy days and other secrets of his private life. Fond of reminiscing about his childhood, Alexander often astonished his Polish companion by his frank recollections. "At the age of five my grandmother took me and assumed exclusive control of my upbringing. . . . When I was nine years old I began to grasp the nature of her relationship with me. For instance, I remember an encounter between her two lovers, Alexei Orlov and Potemkin. This took place in my grandmother's apartments before my very eyes. It was bizarre to see these two men confronting each other with hatred and jealousy."

Alexander dredged up memories and presented them for comment to Prince Adam. "Once our servants brought Kostya and me to see our grandmother. The huge room, with its carved and gilded ceiling, was crowded with courtiers. She was seated at her toilet table wearing a white powder wrap. Her hair was combed upward above the forehead and very skillfully arranged about her temples. Her maids were putting the finishing touches on the elaborate headdress. She smiled as she gazed at us and said with her strong German accent, 'Aren't they both handsome boys, my slender Sasha and my chubby Kostya!'. Yes, my grandmother petted and spoiled me more so than Kostya. But, sitting on her lap, I was aware of a repulsive body odor even though she used much French perfume. It irritated my nose. . . . I also disliked her hands. They were yellow, wrinkled, and damp. Her fingers curved towards the palm and were tipped with long nails. I thought the hands of a greedy witch. . . . Her eyes were misty, gray and weary and produced an impression of cunning and wickedness. . . . Although in private I referred to my grandmother as 'Granny,' in public I had to address her as 'Her Imperial Majesty'. . . . But these were the happy days . . . I still had illusions. . . ."

Alexander recounted to Adam that his initial affection for his grandmother had turned to bitter contempt. Czartoryski discovered this during one of their long walks. "Do you know that her present lover, Platon Zubov, a coarse, narrow-minded junior officer of the guards, is more than thirty years younger than she? Potemkin was also coarse and brutal but at least he had wit, personality and intelligence. He radiated authority and power. Zubov is a complete nonentity. Of all her lovers, he is the meanest and most insignificant. He is a zombie. He pays no attention to court etiquette and takes liberties with her that no sovereign should tolerate. . . . One morning I saw Zubov in his dressing gown coming out of the Empress' rooms. A little dog belonging to my grandmother was running after him, barking furiously. Even the two servants guarding her bedchamber couldn't help laughing. . . . I am humiliated to think that my grandmother behaves in this disgusting manner, like a whore. . . ."

Czartoryski did not know whether these words, which the eighteen-year-old Grand Duke spoke openly in a public place, were sincere, or were intended to draw him out and to test his feelings about Russia and about Alexander himself.

But with Czartoryski, Alexander also discussed more serious subjects, for instance, the matter of his planned, liberal humanitarian reform for Russia. The republican ideas which Laharpe had instilled in him dominated his political fantasies. Although young Czartoryski basically shared these views, he felt he had to moderate some of the younger man's more rash opinions. "Hereditary monarchy is an unjust and obsolete institution," the Grand Duke told his friend. "Supreme authority ought to be based not on the accident of birth but on the will of the people." Czartoryski, surprised, presented arguments against such an unorthodox view and warned him, "Look at what Poland has suffered from free elections of their monarchs! They have paralyzed creative forces in the Polish people. They have made Poland an easy prey for their better organized, rapacious neighbors. Look at the recent partitions!"

Alexander burst with moral indignation. "The partitions of Poland are one of the great crimes of our century! Why should Russia want more land? We already possess more than we can possibly manage. If I ever ascend the throne of Russia, I will immediately atone for my grandmother's treachery and outrageous violence by rebuilding a free Poland."

Prince Adam was puzzled. Was Alexander sincere? "You are the only person to whom I dare to speak frankly," Alexander reassured his companion. Yet the Grand Duke also confessed to Adam his strange fascination with military pomp and ceremony. "Kostya and I, when we were little, used to dress up in the dark green uniforms of the Semionovsky regiment. We especially liked the black plumed hats. While we rode in them through the streets, people in military uniforms saluted us while civilians removed their hats and bowed low, and the women curtsied. How delightful to be admired by large crowds! . . . As we passed the sentinels, the guard of honor from the Preobrazhensky regiment presented arms. I always loved to watch such smart soldiers standing at attention. I am very fond of military exercises, drills and spectacular parades. . . ." Thinking of Narcissus, Czartoryski might have murmured, "You like to see yourself reflected in the admiring gaze of others." But his haunting thought was, "Here is a radical republican and a professed liberal, yet also a vain militarist. . . ."

Alexander was a passionate admirer of nature. A flower, the verdant green of a tree, the view over an undulating plain, could send him into ecstasies. He loved the country, and dreamed of retiring to some simple rustic life, a Rousseauean dream perhaps containing memories of those pastoral plays so often performed at his grandmother's court. "I am sick and tired," he once told

Czartoryski, "of the artificiality and hypocrisy of the Court. Wouldn't it be lovely to retire, for instance, to an old castle on the Rhine, to read interesting books and cultivate an orchard or a vineyard or buy a cotton plantation in Virginia?"

In response to such outcries Prince Adam would smile and reply, "What about your country, your subjects? Would Russia benefit from the resignation of a potential ruler so well prepared for his task? You were born with a crown on your head. It would be an act of moral cowardice to renounce it. You are attached to your throne just as the serfs are attached to the land. It is your destiny."

★ ★ ★

Catherine watched with apprehension the mounting terror of the French Revolution. It ended forever her flirtation with the Western intellectuals, and any pretension to liberalism. The bust of Voltaire was moved from her study to the cellar. When the French ambassador to Russia took a leave, Catherine remarked that he would do better to remain in Russia and not expose himself "to the tempests." "Your penchant for the new philosophy and for liberty will probably lead you to support the popular cause. I shall be sorry. I shall remain an aristocrat. That is my *metier,*" she told him proudly. The riots and massacres, climaxing with the execution of the King and Queen in 1793, made her mad with fury. The guillotining of Marie Antoinette moved her more than that of Louis. She finally broke off all relations with France and decreed six weeks of court mourning after the execution. She closed the Masonic lodges in Russia in 1794, and forced French people living in Russia on pain of expulsion to take an oath of allegiance to the Russian state. A tight censorship now forbade the publication of books "likely to corrupt morals" or indeed dealing with the French Revolution at all, and it became illegal for Russian subjects to import French books, newspapers, even French wines and perfumes. The most famous victim of the censorship was Alexander Radishchev, exiled to Siberia for venturing to criticize serfdom in his *Journey from St. Petersburg to Moscow.*

Yet, though she wished them well, Catherine did not join the monarchs of Austria and Prussia in making war on the regicidial French regime. She was far too interested in digesting her acquisitions from Poland and Turkey for that. While this western war was going on, the wily Empress contemplated seizing more of Poland.

Alexander's view of the French Revolution was at first more favorable. Having been influenced by Laharpe, he was enraptured by it, as so many others. To be sure he had been only twelve years old when the Estates Generals were summoned, but he had followed the unfolding of the great revolutionary drama with keen interest. However, the execution of the royal couple, the victory of the violent and fanatical Jacobins, and the Reign of Terror sobered his enthusiasm. Yet, he regarded the execution of Louis XVI as a warning to monarchs to change their ways.

His plans of abdication were revived. Czartoryski continued to oppose Alexander's dreams as unrealistic and even harmful, saying "What about Russia? What about the interests of the Romanov dynasty?"

"What kind of Romanov dynasty? If a Princess Anhalt-Zerbst mates with a Colonel Saltykov, do they beget a Romanov?"

★ ★ ★

As time passed Paul's relationship with his mother Catherine became more and more acrimonious, so that eventually they could hardly bear each other's presence. For over thirty years mother and son had been pitted against each other in silent hostility. Speaking to his friends at Gatchina, in addition to calling her a murderess, a usurper, and a whore, Paul did not bother to conceal his disapproval of Catherine's policies in general. He called the partitions of Poland "highway robbery," harmful to Russia's national interests. "Why annihilate a Slavic buffer state?" he questioned.

As for Catherine, after a long period of indecision, she resolved to disinherit this grotesque and unstable son and relegate the throne directly to Alexander. She sensed that if Paul came to the throne he would reverse her whole political system, as well as many of her cultural innovations, and Russia would become "a Prussian dependency."

Before Laharpe's departure, she had summoned him and asked for his opinion. "Tell me frankly, what do you think of this madman? What would be the fate of Russia if he were one day to become ruler? This unspoken thought torments me. What a difference between him and my Alexander!" The Swiss teacher was aware that Catherine's decision to send him home owed much to his refusal to respond to her previous attempts to recruit him in her campaign to exclude Paul and to prepare Alexander for the impending succession. Laharpe knew how unfit Alexander was for the rough world of politics and how little he wanted to enter it. To Laharpe, Alexander had just recently written, "I am discouraged, reduced to despair by all I see around me. I would renounce it all for a rural retreat. . . . My wife shares this wish."

In any case, such an effort to bypass the legitimate heir was bound to present difficulties. Paul was the rightful heir in the eyes of many Russian people. And he had his well-trained praetorian guard at Gatchina. He was eager and anxious to rule. How was abdication to be arranged without Paul's consent? Paul might be eccentric, but was he certifiably insane? Who was to do the certifying?

Paul had been forewarned of Catherine's scheme to exclude him and it disturbed him deeply. Occasionally he turned on his own sons, Alexander and Constantine, accusing them of plotting with his mother. The threat of exclusion obsessed him. He would occasionally wake up in the middle of the night screaming "Treason, treason everywhere!" Fear of being killed in the manner of Peter III further upset Paul's already unbalanced temperament. Catherine tried to get Paul's wife to sign an abdication document, though what effect this might have was unclear. The Grand Duchess naturally refused.

Alexander at heart abhorred the idea of becoming Tsar and was evasive and noncommittal when his grandmother approached the subject. Catherine raised the question of the succession in 1794 in the Senate, an advisory council and supreme court made up of the top nobles. Its members generally agreed to exclude Paul from the throne, but some of them pointed out serious legal objections.

Catherine persisted, however. She sought a more satisfactory mandate from the Senate again in 1796. But the letter of abdication she had drawn up for Paul lay unsigned in her desk for several months.

Rumors circulated in the summer of 1796 that Catherine intended to proclaim her grandson heir on New Year's Day 1797 while she was still on the throne. She had decided in the autumn to draft a decree disinheriting Paul and appointing Alexander as her successor.

The autumn of 1796 was a tense and confused one. The absorption of huge amounts of Baltic and Polish-Lithuanian territory had complicated the problems of government, the most difficult of which was preventing Jews of Eastern Poland from penetrating into Russia. The doubling of the Jewish poll tax seemed to have little impact on their immigration and settlement in the two capital cities. All this bothered the aging Empress. Abroad, a young general named Napoleon Bonaparte was planning an onslaught into Italy and onto the dessicated landscape of the old order all over Europe, toppling ancient thrones, threatening to blow away all those painfully wrought schemes of Catherine from the Baltic to the Mediterranean.

On November 5, 1796, Catherine arose at her customary hour of 6 A.M. As usual she splashed her face with ice water, then drank five cups of strong Turkish coffee to bolster sagging energies. After receiving her young lover Platon Zubov and her secretaries, the sixty-seven-year-old fat woman retired to her dressing room and then to her newly installed lavatory. After several hours, when she failed to reappear, the valet and maid forced open the door and found her on the floor, slumped and unconscious. She had been felled by a massive stroke.

Alexander's walk in the snow-dusted gardens of Tsarskoe Selo was interrupted that morning by a messenger shouting, "Your Highness, please hasten to the palace! Her Majesty the Empress has had a stroke." Alexander arrived before his father, who had been summoned from Gatchina. They found the obese, shapeless body of the Empress, placed on a mattress on the floor. She was breathing heavily as the servants and ladies-in-waiting sobbed conspicuously and whispered about the incident. The surprised Alexander noticed that she lacked all her front teeth and that her nightgown was soiled and spotted. The mighty Empress lay helpless, object of pity or disgust and no longer fear.

Paul was very uneasy. Would she regain consciousness long enough to effect her cherished scheme of disinheriting him in favor of Alexander? Or perhaps might she linger on, semi-paralyzed, and decree a regency that would include both Paul and his two sons? While Alexander hesitated, Paul promptly grabbed the reins of power, issuing orders with the aplomb and the self-assurance of a well entrenched monarch. Meanwhile Catherine's lover, Platon Zubov, appeared. He could not hide his confusion. His pale features distorted and his hair disheveled, he searched Catherine's desk, seeking to find and burn papers that might compromise him.

As Catherine lay on the floor in agony, senior militarymen and courtiers weighed the advisability of declaring allegiance to the legal heir apparent. Should it be to Paul, or to Alexander? Most of them knew of Catherine's intentions. But as Paul took the initative to assert himself and Alexander remained passive, the courtiers, one by one, rushed in, knelt and paid homage to Paul. Alexander joined them. On his knees he kissed his father's hand and swore an oath of allegiance to him as the new Tsar. Alexander Bezborodko, a leading figure of Catherine's government also joined Paul and destroyed Catherine's last testament.

Meanwhile, all hope of Catherine's regaining consciousness vanished. Despite the efforts of her two German doctors she died about ten o'clock in the evening, some thirty-six hours after the stroke. A new epoch had commenced in Russia's history and in Alexander's life.

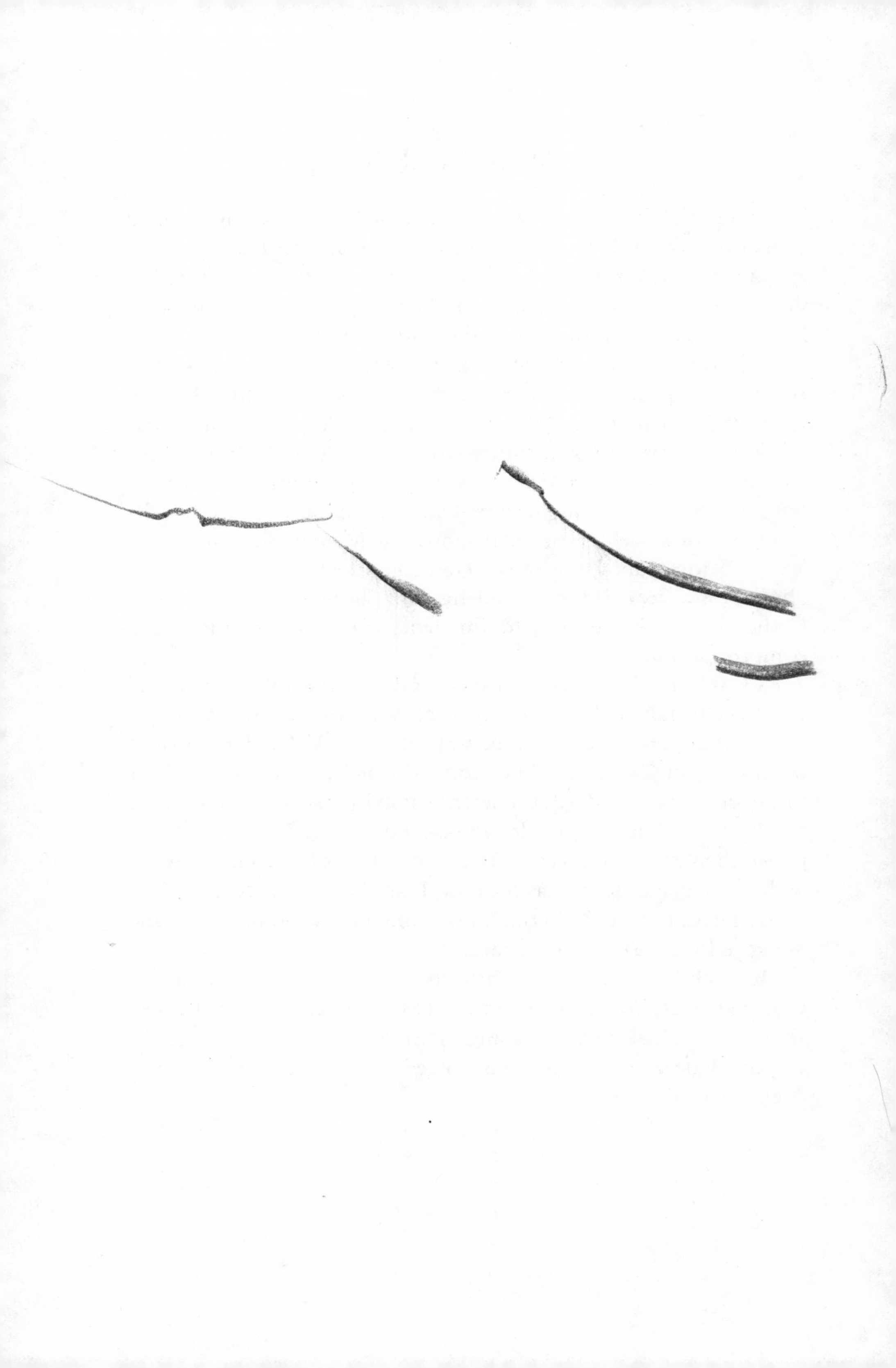

CHAPTER 4

Necropolis, Lesbos and Cythera

Never before were changes on the political scene so sudden and so sweeping as those following the accession to the throne of Tsar Paul I. Almost everything that his deceased mother had done was now carefully undone, or at least radically altered. One of the first steps of the new monarch was to grant his five Gatchina battalions the privilege of making a triumphant entry into St. Petersburg. The Gatchina detachments were placed in battle array at key points in the capital, displacing the regular guards attachments. This created much dissatisfaction among the aristocratic officers of the guards, who had always been showered with favors and treated with great consideration by the late Empress. Now they were brushed aside by "the ruffians and brigands of Gatchina."

Immediately, Paul ordered his officers to adopt the Prussian uniforms of Frederick the Great. The tight fitting uniforms were to be a model, first for the guards and then for the entire Russian army. Prussian headdress was also ordered. The curled and plaited arrangements required many hours of attention from the two barbers attached to each company, squadron or battery, and inflicted real torture on the unhappy wearers, whose hair was impregnated with a mixture of lard and powder. The concoction dried into a thick crust which often gave the men violent headaches. The uniform itself was no less uncomfortable. Paul insisted on it fitting so tightly that rapid movement was impossible. If a soldier fell, often he could not regain his feet without assistance.

Alexander and Constantine were in an advantageous position because they had already been outfitted with Gatchina uniforms and knew how their hair was to be dressed to please their father. On the other hand, the majority of the courtiers were most confused. Within a few days, they had to radically alter not only their dress, but also their hairdos and the rather relaxed behavior to which they had become accustomed over the previous years. Under Catherine, officers wore their hair long or short, straight or in curls, according to their own tastes. The new order was to wear stiff curls above the ears only, as well as the obligatory Prussian pigtail, the whole to be covered with pomade and powder. Under Catherine, the loose and comfortable uniform introduced by Peter the Great had been retained. During the last years of the Empress' rule, many dandies went so far as to wear their uniform smocks unbuttoned in order to display non-regulation richly embroidered vests. Such liberties angered Paul, who sneered, "You dandies. You sissies. Would you like to wear women's petticoats?"

While flooding the country with all sorts of radical changes, Paul systematically investigated his mother's private archives. With a small silver key, he opened a secret drawer in the desk in which she kept her personal papers. There, various packets of her most intimate correspondence were neatly tied with silk ribbons. During his search he came upon a sheet of crumpled gray paper tossed among her love letters. The writing was large, the letters crooked, obviously scribbled by an unskilled hand. As Paul began to read from the paper, his face became pale and his hand trembled. The letter had been sent to his mother and dated "Ropsha, at six o'clock in the evening of the sixth of July, 1762." In it, Gregory Orlov described to his brother's mistress how he disposed of Catherine's husband, Peter III.

"Merciful Monarch and Little Mother, how can I explain, how

can I describe what has happened? You will not believe your faithful slave. But as before God, I speak the truth. I am ready to go to my death, but I myself do not know how this calamity happened. We are lost if you do not show us mercy. Little Mother, he is no longer of this earth."

Here the words became blurred and barely legible as if the letter were stained with water, or perhaps, tears. Were they Orlov's or Catherine's? With great difficulty, Paul read the fateful message, using his spectacles, which he never displayed in public, because they, as he used to say, "make me look like a military doctor and not a Grand Duke and heir to the throne." Thus, he learned from the blurred sentences of Orlov's letter the details of the end of his father's life.

"But no one had thought of this, and how could we have dared to raise our hands against our monarch! But, Your Majesty, the calamity is accomplished. He quarreled with Alexis and Prince Theodore Bariatinsky at table. We had no time to separate them before he was no more. We cannot remember what we did because we were drunk, but we are all, to the last man, guilty and deserving of punishment. Have mercy on me, if only for my brother's sake. I have brought you my confession and there is nothing to investigate. Forgive, or command the end quickly."

Paul sat motionless in the armchair, breathing heavily, his eyes fixed on the letter that had fallen from his hand. Before him rose the image of the well-known Alexis Orlov, a Hercules of a man who, with his mighty hands, had strangled the man whom Paul considered to be his revered father and role model. Peter's death had been largely forgotten except by Paul, who thought of his father fondly because, unlike his mother, Peter had treated Paul with kindness, given him wonderfully painted wooden soldiers brought from Holstein, and played with him for hours. Before reading the letter, Paul had so much admired Orlov, a splendid soldier, a victor in so many battles, knowing nothing about his role in the death of Peter III. And there was the question of Paul's parentage. He had often heard tell of Saltykov as his mother's lover and his natural father, however, he did not wish to admit to this. It would make his craving for the crown a morbid illusion and the continuity of the dynasty a myth. Knowing that Catherine despised and worked to disinherit him, he refused to believe that he was also a bastard. "No, no," he murmured to himself, "Peter III was my father. He was. He must have been. I am his rightful heir. I must now become his avenger."

* * *

While Paul was experiencing a sort of masochistic pleasure in studying his mother's intimate papers, the body of the Empress was awaiting burial. No date for the ceremonies had yet been set, and no one could understand why the embalmed body of the Empress lay for a week in her bedchamber and was then moved into the throne room. The delay was coldly calculated, however. What Paul sought now was a joint, solemn funeral for both his parents.

A general perplexity increased when workmen began to build a splendid structure in the large gallery that was used for dancing on the occasion of court balls. Over a dais surrounded by columns, a rotunda was constructed. Black velvet curtains with silver fringes and tassels descended from the ceiling and draped to the form of a round tent, the traditional *castrum doloris* for two bodies.

In spite of Catherine's death, the routine of court life resumed. Servants did not hesitate to remark on the scandalous details and anecdotes of Catherine's private life. Courtiers, after coming to kiss the hand of the deceased monarch, hastened away from the coffin. Meanwhile, Paul ordered an urgent and thorough search for his father's body. "The grave must be found quickly. Investigate all those who took part in the burial. If torture is necessary, use it." The difficulties were formidable because Catherine had instructed the Orlov brothers to bury Peter's body secretly in an unmarked grave. While awaiting the result of the search, Paul continued to dig more deeply into his mother's private records. In the vicinity of her bedroom, he discovered two rooms filled with pornographic pictures—the training grounds of her prospective lovers. Each candidate had a separate dossier where Catherine kept Madame Protassov's written description of his peculiarities. The potential lovers were graded, like school boys, on a scale of one to five. Paul laughed sarcastically after reading that her last lover, Plato Zubov, age twenty-five, almost failed the test. He had been described as "moody, clumsy, and erratic, and inexperienced despite his twenty-five years and the remarkably good looks of a young angel." She added, "I would give him a grade of 3 or 3+ depending on his mood. I hesitate to recommend him without reservation. My suggestion is that your Imperial Majesty try him on Her own and then decide for Herself."

"This is wonderful!" thought Paul to himself, "I will have it copied and distributed among Zubov's fellow officers and ladies of the Court. This will punish him more effectively than a banishment to Siberia. It will make him the laughing stock of society."

Paul switched to the Empress' correspondence with foreign luminaries—Voltaire, Diderot, the brothers Grimm, and other luminaries of the European Enlightenment. Some of the letters were pompous and ridiculous; others were simply self serving. Most ended with requests for additional subsidies, more and more money. The most cynical and servile of all letters were those of Voltaire. He showered flattery on the Empress in a most cynical manner. He claimed to be enraptured by her wisdom, which he deemed greatly superior to all the philosophers of the world, and expressed his grief that he was unable to write in French as well as she. He went so far as to compare the Empress to the ancient queen Semitauris, and even the Virgin Mary. And although in almost every one of these letters he found occasion to ask some favor, Catherine, despite all her cleverness and worldy experience, genuinely enjoyed his shameless flattery. Voltaire was obviously convinced that flattery could never be overdone and leads everywhere.

"Oh, those Western intellectuals, they are a regular bunch of harlots. For a few rubles, they would kiss the devil's ass," Paul thought to himself.

* * *

Meanwhile, the search for the body of Peter III and preparation for the solemn joint funeral went on. Even though circumstances of his burial were shrouded in secrecy, with the assistance of some old peasants who had helped the gravediggers, the place was found. One of the peasants remembered the spot exactly, "It was just about half a mile north of the Ropsha village cemetery, under a birch tree." By the middle of November, the ground was solidly frozen and shovels did no good. Heavy axes had to be used to cut the marshy ground, now hard as ice. Paul, his face unearthly pale, stood near the gravediggers all the while, supervising their work.

Finally, the moldy lid of the coffin became visible. As the gravediggers lifted out of the earth a worm-eaten box of pine wood, Paul could not take his eyes from it. When the carpenter lifted its cover, he focused on the contents, as if hypnotized. There was nothing in the box but a clump of hair, a shattered skull, a broken pelvis and a few other bones, and half-decayed, high cavalry boots with spurs. There was neither a shroud nor the usual band of inscribed paper on the head of the deceased, not a cross or an icon. "They buried him like a pagan, like a dog," he whispered. Then he moved away from the box, drew his sword, and stood at attention saluting the remains of the man he thought to be his father. He crossed himself three times, and looked again at the decayed remains in the now fully opened box.

On Paul's order, and with great ceremony, the wooden box was placed in a silver coffin. Then it was covered with gold brocade and the Imperial coats of arms in the presence of the entire Imperial family, including Paul's infant son, Nicholas, still in the arms of his nurse. Alexander and Constantine, who together held a red cushion on which rested the imperial crown, were given a sign to approach the remains of their grandfather. Paul took the crown and placed it on Peter's broken skull. Then he shouted "Attention," and again with his sword saluted the remains. Two chamberlains, in mourning garments and black gloves, were ordered to transport the silver coffin on a magnificent hearse drawn by six black horses, and the whole retinue proceeded in several carriages toward the capital.

After a solemn requiem service in the Cathedral of SS. Peter and Paul, the coffin was closed. The new Tsar appointed an Imperial Commission to arrange a ceremonial "for the joint funeral of their

Imperial Majesties." This was followed by an announcement that national mourning for "the late Emperor and Empress" would last twelve months. All courtiers were to order for themselves black mourning clothes; officers and soldiers were to wear black armbands on their left sleeves. People were astonished by the request to mourn for a man who had been dead for thirty-four years and nearly forgotten.

Finally, the coffin was carried to the Winter Palace and placed on the dais of the *castrum doloris* next to Catherine's body. Tall wax candles burned nearby, casting eerie light on the coffins. A group of six guardsmen, changed every hour day and night, stood motionless at the corners of the dais. For days on end, crowds passed through the huge, dim hall in a tribute of homage to both monarchs. Mourners mounted the steps, kissed the Empress' hand and touched the closed coffin of Peter. In the half-light, the huge hall looked somber and majestic. Only the *castrum doloris* was bright with the light of the wax candles. During the week that the bodies were in state, the hall became a place of social gathering. People came night after night to socialize and converse with each other. Among those who came daily to pay their respects were the Orlov brothers; Paul insisted that they be present every afternoon at the peak of the visiting hours. They were furtively watched by the others assembled in the shadows of the great hall.

Paul had yet another surprise for his public. He decided that those who had taken part in his father's murder, including Alexis Orlov, should carry the regalia through the streets during the funeral procession. Afterwards, Peter lay in state next to Catherine in the Cathedral of SS. Peter and Paul, and when the priests incensed the bodies, they were put to rest in a single crypt, over which two marble statues were to be erected.

★ ★ ★

Following the funeral came a series of profound changes. At forty-two, after three decades of waiting for the throne, Paul wanted to reform everything, to reverse his mother's policies and practices. He abolished Peter the Great's Act of Succession whereby the Tsar could name his own successor, and decreed that sovereignty should pass through the eldest living son. Thus, Alexander officially became heir to the throne. Most of the dignitaries who had been influential under Catherine were dismissed by Paul. The only one of her ministers whom the new Tsar retained was Count Alexander Bezborodko, who was promoted from Vice-Chancellor to Chancellor and made Prince. This was due to the fact that during the last days of Catherine's rule, Bezborodko had dared to criticize Plato Zubov and to oppose the plan for making Grand Duke Alexander legal successor to his grandmother.

Paul so hated Potemkin that he turned his lavish Tauride Palace, a gift from Catherine, into a garrison and stable for a regiment of Horse Guards. The mausoleum that Catherine had built for Potemkin in the Crimea was destroyed and his remains were exposed to the elements. Plato Zubov, after being ridiculed by the publication of his "report card" from Madame Protossov, was banished to his estate, never to leave it to the end of his days.

Paul was alternately a petty tyrant and an enlightened farsighted reformer. Initially he had wished for peace and scorned his mother's wars. He had cancelled an army call-up decreed by Catherine two months before her death. Paul also sought to eliminate the arbitrary rule of commanding officers over their rank and file and to end the practice of service in the Guards being a mere sinecure. He tried to modernize the Russian army. On his fourth day in power, he set up a new organization of field artillery, and later developed his concept for the uses of the three main army branches. Here he did not slavishly imitate his idol, Frederick the Great. Whereas Frederick had used the artillery to initiate a battle, the infantry to attack, and the cavalry to complete the operation, Paul greatly broadened the artillery's sphere of action to include preparatory bombardment, support of the attacking infantry and shielding of its retreat. In all three stages of battle, the artillery was to act independently, and in the event of defeat, it was to offer protection to the withdrawing forces. His reforms of the artillery had good effects, not only in his reign, but in the next as well.

Paul had a keen sense of his Divine Right; he sometimes even accepted his meals wearing his crown. He tolerated no opposition. When existing law was cited as an obstacle to his reforms, he would thunder, slapping his chest, "Here is your law." To the Swedish envoy Stedingk, he said "Know that no one in Russia is important except the person who is speaking with me." He treated his courtiers like new recruits. When one of them met the Tsar, he was required to bow deeply and then, with one knee on the ground, to kiss the Tsar's hand while the Tsar kissed him on the cheek; the courtier had to withdraw without turning his back to his sovereign. This frequently caused confusion as one often trod on the toes of another who was coming forward to render the same homage.

Frequently Paul drove through the capital in a sled or an open carriage, accompanied by one of his aides-de-camp. When another carriage was encountered, it was required to stop. The coachman and footman had to remove their caps, and those in the carriage had to alight and make a profound bow to the Emperor, who noted whether the bow was sufficiently low. Sometimes women and their children were forced to descend into snow and cold, or into mud during a thaw, to perform this ritual. All who approached the court were in constant uncertainty and fear of being addressed by the Court-Marshal at any moment in the presence of the whole Court with some insulting message from the Tsar, and then sent into exile.

Balls and court festivals were arenas where each man risked his position and liberty. Paul constantly fancied that sufficient respect was not shown to his person. Often, after giving a harsh verdict regarding a man who had displeased him, the punishment did not, after reflection, seem to him adequately severe, and he increased it. All who belonged to the Court or came before the Emperor were thus in a state of constant fear. No one felt secure that he could maintain his standing until the end of the day and, upon retiring, it was quite uncertain whether or not, during the night or in the early morning, some authority would come with a verdict to take one off at once to Siberia.

Initially Alexander fared well under the new regime. By the age of twenty, he was Military Governor of St. Petersburg, head of the Siemionovsky regiments of the Guards, commander of the military division of the capital, Inspector of Cavalry, and president of the commission for the food supply, housing and police in St. Petersburg. From 1798, he also headed the War Department, and from 1799, held a seat in the Senate and in the Council of the Empire. However in the year 1800, all this began to change and Paul became increasingly suspicious. In spite of bestowing many honors on Alexander, Paul began to treat his son with surprising harshness. He thought Alexander was not sufficiently devoted to his duties. One by one, he dismissed from Court all of Alexander's friends: Peter Tolstoy, Victor Kochubey, Alexander Golitsyn and Paul Strogonov. He was both suspicious and jealous of their influence on his son. Gone were the occasional fits of fatherly cordiality when he would call his son Sasha, pat him on the back, and lavish him with compliments. He now addressed him formally as "Monseigneur," and praises were as rare as the smiles on his pale and morose face.

Alexander was absorbed by his Court and military functions, and by endless details connected with his administrative duties; extreme concentration was needed so as not to overlook any of the minute details of his work. Often his morning work tired him to the point that afternoons he rested until evening, when he again reported to the Emperor.

⋆ ⋆ ⋆

As time went by, even Alexander's strict subservience to his father did not seem to satisfy Paul's capricious moods. Of the two brothers, Constantine fared better because of his greater military stature. After a parade, Paul would shame Alexander, often in front of his fellow officers. "Your problem is that you lack a proper military attitude. You lack proper spirit. You are not cut out to be a soldier! You simply have no guts. On the parade ground you behave like a shy virgin on her wedding night. A Russian emperor must be a leader of men! Look at Constantine . . . how he commands the troops. . . ."

When Alexander sought to moderate his father's excesses, the Tsar responded, "How dare you protest my orders? You are disloyal to me."

Both at court and on the parade grounds Paul demanded strict exactitude in ceremonies. In his military tasks Paul was assisted by one of the few fully-trusted men from the Gatchina days, Alexander Arakcheyev. Arakcheyev was a descendant of minor nobility of very modest means, which had chosen a military career for him at an early age. During the last four Gatchina years, 1792–1796, Arakcheyev labored relentlessly at drilling, parading and maneuvering Paul's troop. He busied himself mainly with the modernization of the artillery entrusted to his exclusive command, and won continual praise from Paul. On his accession to the throne, the new Tsar poured favors upon Arakcheyev, who by that time had already reached the rank of colonel. Paul had Arakcheyev entered on the lists of the Preobrazhensky regiment and promoted him to the rank of major general. He was also presented with a landed estate, Gruzino, in the province of Novgorod, and two thousand peasant serfs. Overnight Arakcheyev became a wealthy man.

Naturally enough the rapid ascent of this self-made man did not endear him to the arrogant and snobbish Russian nobility. Arakcheyev's insistence on absolute, unquestioned obedience to the letter of his instruction and his refusal to discuss his decisions also aroused the hostility of his colleagues. They found his meticulous but crude habits of work, the methodical arrangement of his home and estate, and his spartan way of life all profoundly alien. Visitors to his estate at Gruzino said that the house was like a museum and the garden like a cemetery. It was, however, these very qualities which attracted Paul to Arakcheyev. "Here is a man after my heart," Paul would often repeat.

During the Gatchina period Arakcheyev had ingratiated himself also to Alexander. Their relationship began when Paul ordered Arakcheyev to instruct Alexander in the refinements of military service as practiced at Gatchina. Arakcheyev treated his young pupil with respect and kindness. In November 1796, when Paul appointed Alexander Military Governor of St. Petersburg, the young heir to the throne had almost daily contact with Arakcheyev, who was made the Grand Duke's deputy and advisor. Knowing the petty demands of the service better than Alexander, and often being able to shield him from Paul's anger, Arakcheyev soon became indispensable to the young Grand Duke. In return, Alexander grew more and more dependent on Arakcheyev's assistance. It was a strange symbiotic relationship; a refined and enlightened youngster became increasingly close to a narrow-minded and coarse martinet.

In early 1797, Arakcheyev was appointed Quartermaster General. Soon after, he was also given command of the Preobrazhensky regiment. Thus, Arakcheyev became one of the most important and powerful figures in the Empire. However, as a result of an incident during which he struck a colonel in the face and following which the colonel committed suicide, he was banned to Gruzino. However, Paul could not remain long without his henchman. Less than a year after his dismissal, Arakcheyev was back in St. Petersburg. He soon regained Paul's full confidence and was appointed Inspector General of his favored service, the artillery.

During Arakcheyev's absence, another man replaced him as Acting General of St. Petersburg. This was Count Peter von Pahlen, a Livonian aristocrat and descendant of one of the leading German Baltic families. Pahlen had entered the Russian army at a very young age and, during the reign of Catherine II, reached the rank of Major General and the post of Governor of Riga. He owed this promotion to the sponsorship of Plato Zubov. Some time after ascending the throne, Paul passed through Riga and was pleased with the discipline of the garrison and cleanliness of the city. Soon he ordered Pahlen to come to St. Petersburg. There the ambitious aristocrat again excelled in his devotion to duty. Efficient and ruthless, he was also a skilled diplomat who knew how to flatter his master and thus inspire him with confidence. Paul lavished honors and gifts upon this new favorite and presented him with large estates. Unlike Arakcheyev, Pahlen was a man of refinement and broad military and administrative experience and well suited for the task. Pahlen's close friend and fellow professional officer was General Levin Bennigsen, a Hannoverian in Russian service who had befriended Pahlen and soon became his most trusted associate.

To Arakcheyev and Pahlen, the brutal martinet and the refined Baltic aristocrat, Paul added a most bizarre and primitive individual as his personal servant. During the Gatchina days his mother had offered him a serf, a Turkish prisoner-of-war of uncertain origin, Ivan Kutaisov. He was to serve the Grand Duke as valet and barber, but his real purpose was to spy on Paul on Catherine's behalf. Kutaisov immediately grasped that it would be better to be on good terms with the prospective heir to the throne than with the aging Empress. After a few days of service Kutaisov fell to his knees and revealed to Paul the true nature of his mission. "I suspected this from the first," said the then Grand Duke. "Actually you could be most useful to me. Every week I shall dictate to you the report you will send to the Empress."

Paul soon took a fancy to this clever and subservient man. He sent him to Paris where Kutaisov perfected his hairdressing skills and learned quite respectable French. Upon his return, he became Paul's favorite—spy, confidant, and even political advisor—whose influence came to affect even personal relationships. This ambitious adventurer succeeded in so poisoning Paul's mind that he became resentful of the respect accorded to his wife by many courtiers and by her own children. Soon the resentment spread also to Paul's mistress of many years, Catherine Nelidova. Overnight, Paul flatly refused to speak to either of them. The double alienation isolated Paul, who became increasingly dependent on Kutaisov. As a consequence, Paul relied solely on the narrow-minded martinet Arakcheyev, the haughty Livonian aristocrat von Pahlen and the Turkish-born schemer Kutaisov.

* * *

Alienated from his father, Alexander longed for companionship. For some time he had been interested in Freemasonry. The mystery with which it was surrounded, the great antiquity of the

Order, supposed to have originated in the time of Solomon, its strange and mystical poetic ritual, its extraordinary names and titles, about which all manner of legends were related, had all aroused Alexander's romantic imagination. Alexander knew that in most countries of Europe, many highly placed people, even kings, were members of the order. He began to make careful inquiries of persons of high social standing whom his friends had identified as Freemasons.

One of them was Sir Charles Whitworth, the British ambassador in St. Petersburg. He informed Alexander that the lodges owing allegiance to the Grand Orient brought no good to the world and the French Revolution was largely their work. This branch of Freemasonry, argued Sir Charles, had been mainly responsible for the execution of Louis XVI and his wife, Marie Antoinette. That is why Catherine rightly ordered the immediate suppression of the Masonic lodges of this persuasion and the arrest of their leaders. He cited the fate of such Freemasons as Radishchev and Novikov, who were severely punished by Catherine because both were members of a lodge connected with the Grand Orient. "It serves them right. Perpetrators of regicide deserve no mercy. But our branch, the Scotish Rite is different, conservative." Sir Charles confirmed Alexander's information that several lodges of the Scottish Rite were active in Russia. The Grand Duke also learned that his own father had joined one of them, mainly to spite Catherine. The St. Petersburg lodge of the Scottish Rite comprised many aristocratic members. His bosom friends and aides-de-camp, Peter Volkonsky and Prince Adam, assured Alexander that unlike the radical, atheistic Grand Orient, the Scottish Rite was politically moderate, deist and accepted the Supreme Architect of the World as an object of worship. Their St. Petersburg branch had survived the reprisals of the years 1794–95, thanks to the protection of Sir Charles Whitworth, who arranged occasional meetings of the brothers at the embassy palace, technically a bit of British territory, hence outside Russian jurisdiction. Before long, Alexander was duly initiated into the order by Sir Charles himself.

* * *

The mental depression in which Alexander found himself after his forced separation from Marusha drove him briefly into the arms of his deserted wife. The second honeymoon was incomparably better than the frustrating first two years of their marriage, and these few weeks were, perhaps, the happiest of their married life. This was affirmed in a series of letters, in one of which Elizabeth wrote to her mother: "Oh Mama, I am so happy to be finally close to my beloved husband. He is so tender and affectionate." Another letter ended with the words, "He holds the happiness of my life in his hands. Therefore I will be unhappy forever if ever he ceases to love me." But having once known Marusha's fiery passion, Alexander soon became bored by Elizabeth's tepid passivity and with her inexperience in things erotic.

Some of the more enterprising French actresses and Russian court ladies diverted Alexander's attention from his marital duties, and soon the halcyon nights of tender intimacy with Elizabeth were over. She was left alone, often crying until the early hours of the morning. Her self-confidence was gone. The rock upon which she had built her life, her outwardly brilliant marriage to a powerful Grand Duke, heir to the throne of "all the Russias," had been shattered. She was unable to suppress the dark despair that overwhelmed her when she was alone. This she tried to conceal in letters to her family in Germany, mainly her mother. In solitude, she was haunted by bitter self-reproach. She felt that she had failed as wife and lover. Was she too passive, too timid for Alexander's ardent temperament? What could she do? Should she ask for a divorce or should she remain lonely, bitter and isolated from the court life that afforded ample opportunity to seek, and perhaps achieve, fulfillment through someone else? She did not enjoy good health, and the climate of St. Petersburg was unfavorable to her. The court doctor warned againt tuberculosis. She informed her mother of her melancholic state of mind and her husband's neglect. "Alexander does not love me as I need to be loved, as he would love me if he were able to understand me."

For a considerable period of time Elizabeth suffered Alexander's neglect in silence. Despite her misery she remained totally loyal and devoted to him, hoping that he would return to her. Elizabeth was a sensual being. For her, close companionship was essential. She required a minimum of intimacy with an abundance of tenderness. Yet, even a small amount of marital attention was denied her. Being the perfect lady, she kept up the appearance of harmony not only in public, but in private life. In public Alexander was full of seemingly tender attention and respect for his wife. But at night she was always left alone and suffered bitterly. An intimate detail which Elizabeth confided to her mother reveals in what a state of nervous tension she lived at that time: "Just think, Mama, what happened yesterday evening while my hairdresser was doing my hair. While she was combing it out, it made a crackling noise as if electric sparks were flying; she said that perhaps there were really sparks. We put out all the lights, and indeed my hair was all afire."

One day Elizabeth's dream of love and thirst for fulfillment underwent a strange twist. Her principal lady-in-waiting was Countess Varvara Nicholaievna Golovin, born Princess Golitzin, who was married to the Marshal of the Court, Count Golovin. Elizabeth and Varvara became close friends. As time passed both confessed that they had philandering husbands. They began reading, walking, and listening to music together, and grasped every opportunity to be with each other, and to exchange their thoughts and sentiments. It was Elizabeth who first began to confide in her companion. She admitted that Count Platon Zubov, undoubtedly guided by the instinct of the born gigolo and suborner, once attempted to seduce her, but she repulsed him with disgust. "How could I love a man who, while in his twenties, showered stale, forced, venal caresses on a woman of sixty-seven? Men like Plato who insist on lovemaking without love are disgusting."

Varvara was not surprised at this and remarked with the cynicism of a woman disappointed in her marriage, "Most men are like that. They are selfish and brutish and treat us as mere vessels, either as instruments of pleasure or as repositories of seed to produce their offspring, preferably sons. Once satisfied, they depart to chase younger and more attractive women, to drink, play cards or indulge in their obsessive bloody, beastly madness—those senseless wars. They are without deeper, tender feelings. They don't care about us as human beings or as companions. We women are more caring than men."

"I always suspected this was true," said Elizabeth, "but I hoped that Alexander was different."

"You are like most other women," Varvara continued. "Born into such a male-dominated society as Germany is, you accept this without question. Before now you didn't even dare to reveal your true sentiments, although we have been close friends for months. Actually, we are all raised to be hypocritical and to quietly accept our slavery, our subordination to the brute force of the domineering male. What is called 'marriage' is actually incorporation of the wife into her husband's personality. Real love ought not to be subordination, but an exchange of selves on an equal basis. Anything short of this is bound to restrict the other person. Actually, I found a more complete fulfillment in love with a woman than I have ever found with my husband. My adolescent love for a woman was the most sublime of my life. It led me to full self-realization."

Elizabeth was at first scandalized by this statement, but overcoming the first shock and gasping with excitement, she asked, "How did it happen? Please tell me all about it."

"My parents wanted a boy, and when I was born, they were disappointed. My father always said to me that what the family needed was a strong man to continue its tradition of military service. For my first twelve years or so my mother dressed me in boy's clothing. With my broad shoulders, narrow hips and slight bosom, they seemed to fit me well. In late childhood I went through a tomboy period. I rode horses astride and hunted quail, rabbit and deer with my father. He often called me 'my Diane the Huntress' or 'my Amazon.' For three years or so I had private tutors at home. They were both fetched from St. Petersburg. The first, Monsieur Dupont, had been a sailor, a petty officer, dismissed from the French Navy for reasons he never adequately explained. He was a drunkard and neglected his duties except for geography lessons. He enjoyed describing his travels, tracing them on a large map and a globe which he brought with him to our estate. One day my father surprised him, tipsy and slumbering on his bed while he was supposed to be having a lesson in French conversation with me. Angry, my father dismissed him and hired another French man, Monsieur Fragonard. He was an inspiring teacher, enthusiastic about French literature, especially Corneille and Racine, but he was also a compulsive womanizer. He made one of our laundresses pregnant and even tried to seduce me. When I reported this to my father, he was furious. He sent Fragonard packing and decided, 'Enough of French home tutors. The only place a bright girl like you can get a decent education is the Smolny Institute. Although it is mainly for the daughters of petty nobility, I understand they have excellent teachers for every subject.' And I was sent to St. Petersburg to Smolny to complete my education, that had been, until then, rather spotty, fragmentary and haphazard.

At the Smolny Institute I met Mademoiselle Paulette Girard, who taught us French. I was a bright, eager pupil and she immediately took a fancy to me. As a reward for my good grades—I was the top pupil of my class—Mademoiselle Girard gave me a private room next to hers. The winter was extremely cold. In our dormitories we had those beautiful, huge stoves, covered with blue Delft tiles, but that winter even they were not sufficient. One cold night Mademoiselle Girard came to my room with a hot water bottle. She sat on my bed and placed it tenderly under my feet. Then she began to caress me very gently, gently, while giving me a deep passionate kiss. It was a wonderful feeling that I had never experienced before. Throughout the winter she would call on me almost every night. With spring, our friendship continued. During the summer vacation I missed her, and we exchanged many letters. However, when I returned in September, I discovered that Paulette had tried to befriend many other girls. One of them did not like those nocturnal visits and her advances. She reported Paulette to the headmistress of the Smolny. There was a big scandal. Mademoiselle Girard was instantly dismissed and sent back to France. The headmistress summoned all the pupils of the Institute to the big hall and warned us against what she called 'unnatural sentimental friendships.' I wondered what was so unnatural in our relationship. For me it was a lesson in tenderness. It was the most wonderful experience of my life, and I treasure the memory of those days. Later, after my graduation with honors from the Smolny, I was given in marriage to Count Golovin. Actually I didn't want to marry at all, but it had been all prearranged by the two families in our childhood. What could I do? I had to obey."

"What became of Mademoiselle Girard?" asked Elizabeth.

"Well, we corresponded for some two years and then her letters suddenly stopped. During my visit to France, I went to Montpellier where she had lived with her sister. What a shock it was to learn that the idol of my adolescence was no more. Her sister told me she was ostracized and ridiculed by the petty, parochial, local society. She went through a period of deep depression, and one night drank a large bottle of iodine and died a terrible, slow death. The local doctors refused to help her."

★ ★ ★

The next night, seeing Elizabeth both depressed and crying, Varvara said quite frankly, "Let's be like two sisters, gentle, loving, and without paying the price that women pay for a moment of pleasure with men. Men are cruel beasts. Their treatment of us is sheer degradation. Shall we be like two tender, intimate friends?"

From that night on, the relationship between Elizabeth and her lady-in-waiting was charged with an increasing intensity of emotion. They tried to be together at all times. Any idea of separation was painful to Elizabeth. And yet such separations were inevitable. Count Golovin, as Master of the Court, had to travel with the Emperor during his frequent tours of inspection of the country and arrange for his master's lodging and entertainment. One day Vavara announced that her husband had to accompany the Tsar during his inspection of the Baltic provinces. Because of the numerous social functions included in the tour, he insisted that his wife accompany him.

"I will write you every day," she promised Elizabeth. And indeed she kept her promise. Elizabeth answered faithfully, and in one of her letters was a passionate declaration of tender friendship. "I miss you more than I can describe. I find no pleasure in life when I am separated from you. I implore you, come and dine with me on the day of your return." Another letter declared, "You are always in my mind. Your long absence makes me incapable of accomplishing anything. Ah! I cannot recapture the sweet thought that came to me this morning. It is cruel, cruel!"

The intimate friendship of the two women could not fail to be noticed by the servants. Soon gossip reached Alexander himself. Initially he was rather amused by the strange rumors, rumors being commonplace in court circles. Then suddenly he was summoned by his father for an urgent, strictly confidential, talk. Alexander was not at all surprised to see Paul agitated. It was a common occurrence. He expected another reprimand for some failure of discipline. But the subject of the interview surprised him beyond measure.

"Monseigneur," said Paul, "for several months I have been receiving reports of a strangely close relationship between the Grand Duchess Elizabeth and her lady-in-waiting, Countess Varvara Golovin. Are you aware of this? What is going on?"

"Of course, I am aware, Sire. But this seems to be only a sentimental girlish friendship."

"It is not!" exploded Paul. "You are trying to deceive me again! I have ordered them watched and their correspondence screened. Here is one of the letters which my people copied. Read what Elizabeth wrote a few months ago to Madame Golovin, 'Oh, if we could only pass those sweet evenings together as we did last autumn.' And in the next letter she confessed, 'My God, I am losing my head. My wits are going completely astray. If this lasts, I shall go mad.' And then another letter, 'I love you, I adore you. I miss you terribly! And yet I must live apart from you! All Petersburg is a burden to me if you are not here. God! God! How I love you'

"Is this normal sentimental girlish stuff?"

Alexander was dumbfounded and unable to provide a satisfactory answer. "I didn't know that things had gone so far."

"I want all this ended at once! I hold you responsible for terminating this strange relationship. Don't you know that you may one day succeed me on the throne? Don't you realize that one day you may be Tsar of all the Russias? An absolute ruler may be anything he wishes except the laughing stock of his subjects. We can afford an Ivan the Terrible but not an Alexander the Ridiculous. You may go, Monseigneur!"

"Sire," replied Alexander. "I have always obeyed your wishes."

While Alexander was executing as deep a bow as his bad back would permit, Paul added, "You try to deceive me by your apparent obedience and filial devotion. Like many others, you are trying to lead me by the nose. But, as you see, you are not successful. As you see, I have practically no nose. You think I know nothing. But I know everything. I will prove it. The day before yesterday, Sunday, at about 11:40 P.M., you accompanied that bloody whore, that aging tigress, Mademoiselle Chevalier, from the French Theater to her home. You did not leave until morning, around 6:30. That is why you were almost late for the morning drill and sleepy the entire day. What kind of heir to the throne are you? Look at your brother, Kostya. He is always on time, for every drill, every parade, and always alert. You are dismissed, Monseigneur."

The unusual intensity of Paul's fury frightened Alexander. Initially he approved of the friendship between Elizabeth and her favorite lady-in-waiting because it kept her busy and allowed him to continue his affair with Mademoiselle Chevalier, who amused him by her vivacity and sharp wit. She was as passionate as Marusha but, at the same time, so refined, so intelligent, so clever. Now, however, the situation was critical. Even after drinking a bottle of port, he could not fall asleep. Toward the morning, an idea suddenly occurred to him. Why not use Czartoryski to come between Elizabeth and Varvara? For a long time Alexander had watched Prince Adam cast admiring glances at Elizabeth. As a loyal friend of Alexander and his subordinate, aware of his precarious status as a virtual political hostage, Czartoryski had never dared to make any amorous advances toward Elizabeth. Yet his admiration for her was often reflected in his dark eyes and in his warm compliments on her appearance, dress, or hairdo. Alexander could not fail to notice this attraction of his bosom friend to his wife. The two men were bound together not only by their political aspirations and their liberal ideas but also by a brother-like friendship. And Elizabeth was moved by the seductive eloquence of the gallant Pole and felt the disturbing power of his attention, even while she was involved with Varvara. The perfect lady, she didn't dare take the first step. For some time her intimacy with Varvara seemed to satisfy her sentimental longings and physical needs.

Now driven by his father's anger, Alexander decided on a plan of action. He invited his friend to dine with him and Elizabeth. Soon after the dessert, he excused himself under some pretext and left his wife alone with his friend. He did this for several evenings in a row. All this was in perfect accordance with the grand tradition of elegant, prearranged adultery, but the timid Pole hesitated. When asked by Prince Adam why he neglected his beautiful and charming wife, Alexander answered, "I married Elizabeth in a hurry at my grandmother's behest when she was fourteen and I hardly sixteen. To tell the truth, I was never attracted to her physically. By now, my feelings for her are no more than those of a brother-sister friendship. The rose was dead when it seemed abloom. Are you, perhaps, interested in being her cavalier?"

Czartoryski gave no answer. Yet, his imagination was fired. His sleep was often interrupted by wild erotic dreams. He had felt lonely. For more than a year after his arrival at St. Petersburg, the cautious Pole had tried not to get sentimentally involved with high ranking Russian ladies of the Court, because of fear of personal and political complications. From the beginning, he had admired Elizabeth, but his sense of loyalty to his friend had prevented him from making any open advances toward her. However, Alexander's systematic arranging for the two of them to be left alone, and Elizabeth's increasingly ardent response to the Prince's complimentary words and tender affection, were most encouraging. Then came Alexander's offer, almost an order. What was he to do?

After five or six successive intimate dinners, with both hearts parched for romantic love, nature took its course. Elizabeth plunged into the affair body and soul. Yet her former attachment bothered her. After the first night spent in the arms of Prince Adam, she flew into the apartment of Madame Golovina, who lived on the floor above. Varvara was playing the harpsichord, and was most surprised to see Elizabeth after several days of unexplained absence. Bursting into tears, Elizabeth flung herself into her friend's arms crying, "Please forgive me, please forgive me."

"Forgive you? Forgive you for what?" asked Varvara.

When Elizabeth explained to her the reason for neglecting her "faithful friend and companion," Varvara tried to control her anger. She whispered, "I have always feared this might happen sooner or later. I had hoped it would be later."

⋆ ⋆ ⋆

For three years, the relationship between Prince Adam and Elizabeth continued under the approving eye of her husband. Elizabeth considered herself bound to her lover by ties which, though illicit, were not unusual by the standards of the time. On May 18, 1799, she gave birth to a daughter, Marie. The resemblance of the baby to Czartoryski was striking. The child had black hair and black eyes. After the baptismal ceremony, to which Paul had been invited to act as Godfather, the Tsar asked Elizabeth, "Madame, please tell me how a blond husband and a blond wife can produce a dark-haired child." After a moment of embarrassed silence, she stammered, "Sire, God is all powerful."

Paul was hardly convinced and burst into one of his notorious furies. His first impulse was to send Czartoryski to Siberia for life. "There have been enough bastards in the Romanov family, but at least they were Russian bastards. A damn Pole philandering with the Russian Grand Duchess—this is too much. Let him spend a long retreat in Kolyma. That will make him reflect on his arrogance and cool his ardor!"

Elizabeth was shocked and terrified. In despair, she flung herself at her father-in-law's knees, imploring, "Mercy, mercy, your Imperial Majesty. I am as much guilty as he is. If he goes to Siberia, I will go with him. I will. I will ask for a divorce and marry him, even if he is a convict."

The threat of a new scandal, and a certain lingering affection for his daughter-in-law, made Paul relent. When he calmed down, his harsh decision was altered; in a calmer tone he said, "The place of the wife of the Heir Apparent is in St. Petersburg, at the side of her husband. With the Italian campaign against France, the stakes are too great for us not to have a resident Russian diplomat at the Court of Sardinia. I will send Czartoryski to Florence to act as our Minister Plenipotentiary. His instructions will be drafted immediately. But he must leave at once, within twenty-four hours."

And indeed, Czartoryski was forced to leave without even saying goodbye to his beloved. For the third time since her marriage, Elizabeth was left alone.

CHAPTER 5

Am I My Father's Keeper?

In one respect Paul had agreed with his mother—they had both hated the French Revolution. Paul had called home those Russians who were traveling in France, and forbade the import of French books. He would admit Frenchmen into Russia only on a Bourbon passport. He banned clothing suggestive of revolutionary Paris, such as round hats, frock coats, and high collars. If worn on the streets, it was, on his order, snatched or torn away by the police. He went so far as to proscribe the words "society" and "citizen" as subversive. While Catherine used the Revolution as a pretext to fight its distant echoes in Poland and to absorb her eastern lands, Paul was ready to send Russian troops to assist Britain and Austria in fighting "the Jacobin hydra" in Italy and on the Rhine.

When a young general named Napoleon Bonaparte drove the Austrian toops from Lombardy, followed them as far as the Styrian Alps, and forced a humiliating peace on the frightened Habsburgs at Campo Fornio in 1797, Paul decided to act. Together with Austria and Britain, he joined the new anti-French coalition.

The incident that finally triggered Russia's actual military intervention against France was the seizure of the island of Malta. While launching an expedition to Egypt as a stepping stone to an invasion of India, Napoleon had captured the seat of the ancient crusading Order of St. John of Jerusalem, generally known as the Order of Malta. When its exiled members offered the Grand Mastership of this arch-Catholic body to Paul, he eagerly accepted the honor. He was most impressed by the magnificent ritual of the order and by the ceremonial dress: the black Maltese cloak with its white eight-pointed cross, the red and gold embroidered uniform and the plumed hat.

He created a Russian branch of the Order and decreed the formation of a new regiment to be called the Chevalier Guard; all officers had to be members of the Order. Paul granted to them enticing privileges that no other Guard division enjoyed; they would wear the plumed hats of the Knights of Malta, the likes of which were worn in the Russian army only by generals. The uniform of the Chevalier Guard included cuirasses and crimson tunics and, for Court receptions, a splendid red uniform with an insignia, a white enamelled eight-pointed Maltese cross, with lilies at the corners and a golden crown at the top. Paul's Chevalier Guard detachments were on duty at all times within Paul's residence and at all official ceremonies, including performances in the Hermitage Theater, where two officers of the Chevalier Guard stood behind the Emperor's chair. The Chevaliers considered themselves greatly superior to everyone else. This aroused indignation in the old Guard regiments, especially the Horse Guard, as the best soldiers and the choicest horses were taken from them for the Chevalier Guard.

When Paul began military preparation to fight "this vile revolutionary monster," as he called Napoleon, most of the veteran generals of Catherine's Turkish and Polish wars were in disgrace or in retirement, including the most famous of them, Field Marshal Alexander Suvorov. For having sent a mere captain with ordinary letters to St. Petersburg, Suvorov had received a public reprimand from Paul. Suvorov reacted by asking for a one-year leave of absence, but was refused. He then had begged to resign, and this was also denied. Instead, he was dismissed, put under vexing police surveillance and even forbidden to visit his friends or receive visitors. Suvorov then asked to enter a monastery, but this was also forbidden by the Emperor.

The shortage of competent commanders caused Paul to relent. He wrote a flattering personal letter to Suvorov, summoned him to the capital, and entrusted the sixty-eight-old hero with the command of the Russian expeditionary corps that was to go through Austria into Italy to rout Bonaparte's cohorts from Lombardy. On reaching Vienna, Suvorov showed to Emperor Francis II his mandate from Paul to conduct a war in the way he thought best. The Austrians, however, had their own plan and demanded the right of control over all the military operations. Suvorov was indignant. "We entered the fray to rescue them from a disaster of their own making and now they make arrogant demands of us."

Suvorov was an imaginative but prudent commander. His tactic was to reconnoiter carefully and then strike at the point at which a blow would be critical to the enemy. Fortunately, Napoleon was then in Egypt and the French troops were under the command of his subordinates. Moreover, Suvorov took advantage of the quarreling among the French commanders, and on arriving at Verona, he at once pounced on the confused French and captured Cassano. He entered Milan in triumph wearing an open peasant shirt and brandishing a whip. His triumphs were most spectacular.

Suvorov won the battles of Bassignano, and Marengo, and was in Turin by May of 1799. In June, the French general MacDonald hurried up the western coast and through the Apennines, defeating the Austrians at San Giovanni. Suvorov then advanced hurriedly and threw all of his troops into action. When his subordinate, General Peter Bagration, reported that he had no more than forty men in his decimated companies, Suvorov replied, "MacDonald has only twenty. We attack!" The French were driven back on the Trebbia, where Suvorov decisively defeated them again.

Meanwhile a reinforced French army advanced from the northern Apennines to Novi, where the Russians and the Austrians were outnumbered. Suvorov, following a day's scouting ahead of his front line, attacked before dawn on August 15. The French beat off several attacks, but Suvorov finally forced them to retreat in disorder. When asked his objective, he replied, "Paris."

The Austrians were becoming more and more jealous and uncomfortable with Suvorov's success. The Habsburgs wished to secure advantages for themselves from the recovered Italian territory and, to this end, played their usual chess game which they favored both in war and in diplomacy. They contrived to force a reshuffling of forces which would get Suvorov out of Italy and into Switzerland, a most difficult battlefield. He was expected to cross the Alps through the pass of St. Gothard and pursue the French into Switzerland. When most of the Austrian contingent of Archduke Karl von Habsburg had left, and before Suvorov arrived with his troops, the gifted French general Massena fell upon the smaller allied contingent, and on September 23, 1799, broke through the lines of General Korsakov. The Russian vanguard defended the passage until their ammunition ran out and, refusing to surrender, died where they stood. Massena then occupied Zürich, and General Soult defeated the Austrians once more.

After marching nearly fifty miles in three days, Suvorov reached the pass of St. Gothard with the bulk of his contingent. At the pass he was confronted by 9,000 French troops; attack was delayed for four days because the Austrians failed to supply the promised means of transport for the Russian troops. Finally, Suvorov forced the pass and scaled the heights behind the French, driving them to retreat. The route of their withdrawal passed through a short tunnel, where the mountain descended in a precipitous cliff to the torrent of a deep stream. Suvorov sent two detachments, one by way of the riverbed and another high up on the mountain, to capture the passage known as the Devil's Bridge before the French could destroy it. After another resounding success, the Russians reached Altdorf, where Suvorov learned that the road marked on his Austrian map did not exist. Boldly turning away over the side ranges, he crossed the Rostock Pass and reached the valley of Mutten. The journey was made single file through mountain mist, torrential rain, and hurricane wind. The commander was ever with his soldiers, sharing their hardships, sleeping at their campfires, eating their food, and singing their peasant songs. His subordinate, General Bagration, on reaching Muttenthal, surrounded a small French force, and his rear-guard repulsed two French attacks. Here, however, Suvorov learned of the Austrian defeat at Zürich.

By this time, Suvorov had lost all the cannon and was almost without food. Meanwhile, the French had closed the route behind him. Relying "on God and the wonderful devotion of the men," Suvorov again cut across the mountains, and by October 4, the Russians had reached Glarus. Once more in single file with many of the men without boots and half frozen, Suvorov's army made its way across the mountains to Chur in one day. In spite of the loss of one-third of his men, Suvorov was victorious again.

Paul was elated. He made Suvorov Generalissimo of the Russian army, one entitled to issue orders and decrees to the troops, like the Tsar himself. On the other hand, Paul was utterly dissatisfied with his allies, the Austrians as well as the British. He was angry because a Russian expeditionary corps, sent to serve under the Duke of York in Holland, had been defeated and had surrendered. Moreover, London refused to exchange French prisoners for Russians. Paul demanded the dismissal of the inept Austrian commanders. When this was refused, he decided to withdraw from the coalition and ordered the Russian expeditionary forces to return home. A triumphal reception was prepared for Suvorov in St. Petersburg. The Emperor's carriage was to meet him. For the homecoming of the great war hero, the streets were to be lined with troops, the city illuminated. But, by chance, Paul discovered a trifling breach of his regulations—Suvorov had employed a general in staff capacity. Furious, the Tsar cancelled the reception. Alexander tried to intervene on behalf of Suvorov, but to no avail. To Alexander's plea, Paul exploded, "You dare to question my decisions, Monseigneur? You are disloyal to me!"

"I am your most obedient son and servant, but loyalty sometimes calls for disagreements."

"Not with me! With me, disagreement amounts to treason! Look at your brother Constantine. He never questions my orders!"

By then, Suvorov was a sick man. From the time he left Prague, he had not been able to mount a horse and he was brought into St. Petersburg quietly by night on stretchers. He died a few months later, bitter and humiliated.

★ ★ ★

After his brilliant general, Massena, had saved France from invasion by his victory at Zürich, Napoleon, who had left his army in Egypt, returned to France. He found the inept and quarrelling five-man Directory (the collective leadership that ruled France after the downfall of Robespierre) so weakened by personal rivalries and so discredited by inefficiencies that he was able to overthrow it. Now, under the title of First Consul, he became a virtual dictator. Napoleon set himself to take advantage of Paul's change of mood toward his allies. He returned the Russian prisoners, loaded with presents and with their flags and arms and offered to make terms. Paul, fond of military glory above all else, was most impressed. Soon the two countries negotiated for peace, with Berlin as mediator. Napoleon acceded to all of Paul's requests—compensation to the King of Sardinia, restoration of the papal power in Rome, and acknowledgment of Paul as Grand Master of the Order of Malta. Paul was charmed, and gladly accepted all of Napoleon's concessions. In return, he renewed his Armed Neutrality League directed against Britain's naval supremacy. At Napoleon's request he expelled the French Bourbon pretender to the French throne, Comte de Provence, from his refuge at Mitau in Courland.

During the Italian and Swiss campaigns, Constantine participated in the difficult operations and was present at the battles of Trebbia and Novi. Suvorov had high praise for the Grand Duke and wrote in his report of August 25, 1799, to Paul that Constantine must be commended "for his courage and good example which inspired the entire army to greater effort." Paul was flattered by his son's military prowess and boasted, "You see what a son I have." A special decree declared that "in seeing with sincere satisfaction as Emperor and as father," the Grand Duke's "brave and exemplary deeds," the Tsar bestowed upon Constantine the title of *Tsarevich,* the title reserved for the eldest son as legal heir to the throne. Alexander's position became most awkward because there were now two Grand Dukes with the title of Tsarevich. Who would eventually mount the throne? Did he really want to compete for a crown which involved tremendous responsibilities he dreaded?

Alexander's old dreams of retiring were revived. Before the return of Constantine he had smuggled a secret letter to his former tutor Laharpe in his native Switzerland. The letter recounted Alexander's despair and unhappiness at being relegated to duties "which might just as easily be discharged by any sergeant . . . I hate despotism, and I bow to the spirit of freedom, the attainment of which is the aim of peoples." At the end of the letter Alexander alluded to his earlier plans of leaving Russia for good. He begged his former tutor to find him "a castle in Switzerland or, preferably, a plantation in Virginia where I could lead a safe and free life as a private citizen."

Meanwhile Paul continued his rapprochement with France. On the establishment of the consulate, he began to regard Napoleon as the restorer of law and order, a view which was very widely shared in Europe at that time. Paul was also impressed by Napoleon's benevolent attitude toward religion and his support of the reestablished French church. Initially, Paul had been anxious to lead a crusade for throne and altar, but found everywhere suspicion, jealousy and narrow self-interest. He believed that only he and Napoleon could restore peace to Europe. Paul's admiration for Napoleon grew still more when the First Consul settled the question of Italy with his brilliant victory of Marengo on June 14, 1800, and imposed another humiliating peace on Austria. Paul now suggested to Napeoleon that he should take the title of King.

Paul was also growing increasingly anti-British and favored the League of Armed Neutrality. By adhering to the League, Paul was echoing the common grievance of all continental powers against England, that she controlled all vital maritime trade routes. This, however, involved danger of war with Britain, which was a serious threat to Russia's economic interests. Now the Russian gentry was in an uproar. Their export of wood, hemp, tar, honey, wax and grain, all produced by large estates, was dependent on British trade. When Paul placed an embargo on all English shipping, trade was nearly paralyzed. Landowners grew increasingly restless because they could find no buyers elsewhere.

The estrangement of the gentry was deepened by the Tsar's domestic policies. Paul had granted individual serfs the right to petition the Crown against their masters' abuses—a right Catherine had suspended. The peasants could obtain redress from the Senate against Siberian exile ordered by their masters. Paul also prohibited the sale of landless serfs. The nobility was most unsettled by Paul's decrees that prohibited landowners from extending serf labor beyond three days per week, and gave merchants the right to buy serfs for use as factory labor. Many serf owners feared that the entire institution of serfdom might eventually be abolished. Their age-old, sacred right of absolute dominion over the serfs was threatened.

In trying to alleviate the lot of peasants, Paul had overlooked the danger of alienating the nobility, from which his Guard officers were chosen. Moreover, he had cancelled their immunity from corporal punishment, taxed their estates, and forbidden them to withdraw from government service without his personal permission which he usually denied. Furthermore, he had particularly offended the Guard Regiments by refusing to allow them to serve as his bodyguards. This task was now assigned to the most exclusive Chevalier Guards who increasingly held themselves above the rest of the officer corps.

Paul's policy of favoring France clashed with the changing mores and mood of the Russian upper classes. By the turn of the century the Russian aristocracy, under the impact of the Jacobin excesses, was becoming alienated from things French and was trying to rid itself of the nearly monopolistic hold of French culture. By that time, English ideas and manners had infiltrated Russian high society. The English lord, and not the French *seigneur,* came to be the arbiter of elegance, the model of gracious living, the supreme embodiment of refinement and feudal pride. While the changes in manners and morals were significant, the decisive factors were economic. The embargo on trade with Britain threatened not only the new fads and fashions of the Russian ruling classes, but their very livelihood.

Meanwhile, Paul and Napoleon were becoming closer. They went so far as to plot together to overthrow the still shaky British rule over India. A Russian force was to march through Central Asia by way of Khiva and Bukhara, to India's northern borders. According to Paul's plan, a corps of Cossacks was to start from Orenburg and march southeastward. At the same time a French force of 35,000 under General Massena was to sail down the Danube, across the Black Sea to Taganrog and then, via the Don and Volga Rivers, proceed eastward to Astrakhan and the Caspian. They would join the Russian force of equal size and march together toward the Himalayas, across them and into India. Paul's orders to General Orlov, commander of the Cossack advanced force, were rather casual, "I am enclosing all the maps that I have," he wrote. "My maps go only as far as Khiva and the Amu-Darya. Beyond that, send secret agents to contact the restless princes of India and organize a general uprising against British rule there." The only mention of transport and food was that each Cossack was to take an extra packhorse and be provided with rations for one week.

This was a fantastic plan, the product of a morbid imagination. Alexander tried to remonstrate with his father, stressing the futility of the Indian campaign. "Are you against me one more time?" asked Paul in a threatening tone. "I expected you to be a more loyal and obedient son."

Meanwhile, many more concrete dangers loomed. In the northern seas, where the League of Armed Neutrality soon was joined by Denmark and Sweden, joint fleets threatened British ships. To deal with this powerful League, Admiral Nelson was sent to seize the Danish fleet, and indeed Nelson did win a daring victory off Copenhagen in April 1801. Then Nelson was free to deal with Russia. But before he could muster the forces and reach Raval, decisive events took place in St. Petersburg.

★ ★ ★

The sudden reversal of alliances precipitated a dangerous domestic crisis. By 1800 the upper classes, the principal officials and the generals were convinced that the Tsar suffered from fits of folly and of mental aberration. Moreover, Paul's brutal ways made him the object of hate. Always capricious and cruel, he held arbitrary decrees constantly over the heads of his subjects and filled their lives with uncertainty and fear. To this constant dread, was now added an adventurous foreign policy that could mean a disastrous war with a great power, the economic interests of which were largely complementary to those of Russia.

Finally, by the spring of 1800, Paul had also alienated most of his personal friends and allies. In October 1799, his most loyal servant Arakcheyev was dismissed from service for the second time precipitated by a lie which he had told to shield his brother. A petty theft occurred in the arsenal while Arakcheyev's brother, an infantry major, was on duty. Arakcheyev concealed this fact when reporting the occurrence to the Tsar, and accused another officer who was promptly put under arrest. Kutaisov, Arakcheyev's jealous rival for the Tsar's favors, revealed the lie. Paul's anger knew no bounds and he dismissed Arakcheyev to his estate at Gruzino.

At the same time, Paul's relations with Alexander were further strained. One evening Paul surprised Alexander by a sudden visit to his studio. The Tsar's beady, shifty eyes observed that his son was reading Voltaire's *Brutus.* When Paul entered, the book was opened to the page describing Caesar's assassination, and ended with the words, "Rome is free. Let us render thanks to the gods." Paul said nothing, but ordered Kutaisov to bring to Alexander a history of Peter the Great, with the volume opened to the page describing Tsarevich, Alexis's story. Alexis was a studious youth, opposed to the radical reforms which Peter enforced by terror. Peter was furious and scolded his son, often in public. In 1716, Alexis first fled to Vienna, and then to Naples, for refuge from his irate father. This was considered treason by Peter. After long negotiations, Alexis was induced to return to Russia in exchange for a pardon; yet, after his return he was forced to renounce his rights to the throne, tried by the Senate and condemned to death in 1718 on a charge of conspiracy and rebellion against his father. Alexis was imprisoned and tortured to betray his alleged accomplices. One day he was found dead in prison after Peter the Great interrogated and tortured him for the last time. A hot iron had been shoved into his rectum by his mad father, to finish off the allegedly treasonous son.

After a week or so, Kutaisov reappeared to ask Alexander whether he had read the book presented by his father. Before leaving Kutaisov whispered a warning, "His Majesty has intercepted some of your treasonous letters to Laharpe. Your Highness's plans to settle abroad have greatly displeased His Majesty. Your plans are very, very dangerous. They are like those of Alexis Petrovich. The Emperor has said this to me several times. Beware."

* * *

All these events were carefully noted by the British ambassador in St. Petersburg, Sir Charles Whitworth. He was one of the most hardworking, skillful and experienced diplomatic agents at the disposal of the British Foreign Secretary, Lord Granville. Whitworth was bright, imaginative, and willing to take risks, all worthy attributes for an ambassador in a distant land in an age of slow communication. Moreover, Sir Charles had a great deal of personal charm, which he used both for his own gain and for the benefit of his government. His family had a tradition of service in Russia. Whitworth's great-uncle had been a much respected envoy to the court of Peter the Great. After spending some six years of Catherine's rule in St. Petersburg, Sir Charles was a veteran of the diplomatic corps. He kept detailed files on all the dignitaries of the Empire, and believed in having friends on all sides. He assiduously courted Platon Zubov, and was a lover of Zubov's sister, Olga Zerebtsov, whom he cleverly used as a source of Court gossip and information on governmental affairs. Having befriended the Empress's lover and sleeping with his sister, Sir Charles was the best informed diplomat in St. Petersburg.

When Paul ascended the throne, Whitworth established fairly good relations with him by flattering his military talents, while reducing his own contacts with Olga Zerebtsov to an absolute minimum so as not to irritate the new monarch, who hated the entire Zubov clan. Through Whitworth's skill, the British goverment was able to add to its payroll two of Paul's influential favorites—Catherine Nelidov, then Paul's mistress, and Kutaisov, his henchman. For the sum of 30,000 and 20,000 rubles, respectively, they were both instrumental in the signing of a commercial treaty on terms most favorable to Britain.

Whitworth was also a long-time friend of Count Nikita Panin, who became Russian Vice-Chancellor in the autumn of 1799. Panin was one of the earliest and most enthusiastic Russian Anglophiles. He believed that anything English was best; he imported from London practically everything—his clothes, his plum pudding, his whiskey and gin, even biscuits and his tea, which came originally from China in any case. Panin often railed against the French as bloodsuckers of Russia. Speaking in French to Alexander, he once said, "Don't you see that our country is as overrun with Frenchmen as with locusts. Most of our luxury trades and most of our skilled professions are dominated by Frenchmen. Tailors, milliners, cooks, dance masters are all French. Paris dictates our fashions, for women as well as men. Yet, English clothing is so elegant, so superior to the French. The French simply pick the Russian pockets. Russia resembles a big bear controlled by a small, but cunning French monkey." Then he added spitefully, "Englishmen should set the example for us. They prefer their own language, quite unlike our countrymen, who would rather speak French badly than talk to each other in Russian." Panin himself tried to set a good example, but often his French vocabulary proved to be richer and more colorful than his Russian and most of his letters were written in French.

Reporting to Britain's Foreign Secretary, Lord Granville, Whitworth listed Panin's attributes: "sound principles, good judgment, an uncommon facility in the dispatch of business, a thorough sense of the danger to which Europe is exposed by the Emperor's new policy as well as a rooted hatred for the principles and character of the French nation. But Panin is more of an intellectual than a leader of men. He talks too much; he is neither firm enough, nor is he ruthless enough. The Russians admire only those leaders whom they fear." As early as 1798, Whitworth began to look for more aggressive political allies as well as secretly working to prevent the breakup of the anti-French coalition. The main struggle within the Russian ruling circles was waged between Panin's faction, who favored continuation of the war against France, and that of Count Theodore V. Rostopchin, a young man who, having been unpopular with Catherine, soon became Paul's favorite aide-de-camp and political advisor. The count advocated an independent Russian policy which inclined more and more toward accommodation with France and against the continental ambitions of Austria as well as the maritime encroachments of Britain.

By the beginning of 1800, observing Russia's growing cooperation with France and fearing the worst, Sir Charles decided to act. He began to gather around himself a group of trusted men, and to forge a plot against Tsar Paul. The central pillar of the conspiracy, however, was to be, not the vocal and unstable Panin, but Count Peter von Pahlen. Pahlen was a tall, broad-shouldered Livonian magnate, with a high forehead, broad smile, and confident steely eyes. He had been a coronet in the Guards at the age of seventeen, and enjoyed a reputation as one of the heroes of the Prussian campaign of 1759. His advance was spectacular; by 1781, he had been already promoted to the rank of major-general. His brilliant services had been rewarded, while Catherine still reigned, by the gift of the huge estate of Eckau in Courland, and by his appointment as military governor of Riga and then of all the Baltic provinces. Pahlen seemed to take life lightly, and lived in an easygoing manner. He was witty and genial, and projected a carefree and happy-go-lucky nature. Yet, his bonhommie and joviality were but a mask under which he concealed a different personality. Indeed, under that attractive, lighthearted exterior there was an iron will, a reckless audacity, and boundless ambition.

Under Paul, Pahlen's talents as a brave military commander and efficient administrator assured his further meteoric rise. His posts of Civil Governor of the Baltic provinces, of Military Governor of Riga, and of Inspector of the Livonian Cavalry and Infantry, were soon relinquished when he became Acting Governor of the capital, appointed to assist the Grand Duke Alexander, who was a novice in administrative matters. Pahlen's rise continued, and he seemed to triumph over all rivals. And indeed, after the second dismissal of Arakcheyev, Pahlen became Paul's right arm as well as his eyes and ears in the capital. To this end, he was also appointed Postmaster General. In this capacity he could intercept most letters of the Russian establishment.

Sir Charles knew that Pahlen had the reputation of being one of the most daring, cunning and ambitious men in Russia. Whitworth admired Pahlen's courage and flexibility and, in a dispatch to Granville, compared him to "these dolls which you may upset and place head downward, but which always right themselves." Pahlen had no equal in overcoming difficulties and surmounting obstacles.

Whitworth and Pahlen understood each other well. They were both apprehensive about Paul's pro-French policy and anxious to foster close relations with Britain, Austria and Prussia. At Sir Charles's suggestion, Pahlen began to meet with various disgruntled officers and officials. All these seemingly accidental encounters took place not at the British embassy, which would be suspect by Paul, but at Olga Zerebtsov's house, under the guise of balls and musical evenings. Between drinking and dancing, serious matters were discussed and the nucleus of a conspiracy was formed. All the conspirators agreed on one point. They feared that the Tsar's unpredictable, erratic behavior and adventurous policies were threatening Russia's external security and domestic stability. What they needed was a strong, unifying leadership. Pahlen, as Acting Governor General of the capital, actually controlled security matters in the capital. After some persuasion by both Whitworth and Panin all agreed that Pahlen should lead the plot.

★ ★ ★

In March 1800, Whitworth felt that a British break with Russia was impending, and that he would have to leave St. Petersburg soon. One night he sent a secret message to Pahlen: "Come discreetly, and alone, to dine with me at 8 P.M. next Sunday at the embassy." When Pahlen appeared that evening, the host received him not in the main dining room hall, but in his private studio. The dinner was served by Sir Charles's trusted valet, an old Scotsman, Ian MacDuggal. After several glasses of brandy and two bottles of claret, port was served. Then Sir Charles proceeded to explain the purpose of the meeting.

"I invited you alone because I agree with the saying that wherever there are three Russians at least one must be a spy. Moreover, you are an honest to goodness Livonian Protestant and a member of our Masonic lodge. Therefore, I can trust you completely. For weeks we have been talking. Now we must act, and act quickly. His Majesty is mentally unstable and totally unpredictable. He has to be put aside, at least temporarily, to save Russia from a disastrous war as well as bankruptcy. The Russian Empire is very rich and productive but it is on the verge of ruin, for it has little industry, and can only maintain its place in the European community by its exports to Britain, which have been wiped out by prohibitive custom tariffs." After a moment of silence, Sir Charles asked Pahlen, "Are you ready to cooperate?"

"Your excellency, this is a tricky, nay, a most dangerous proposition. I have gathered some 50 to 60 men, but most of them still hesitate. To raise our hand against our legal ruler would be a most daring step. Moreover, the Emperor is our fellow Freemason."

"Of course, I wold not suggest regicide. No, God forbid. I am no Jacobin. I have in mind setting up a regency on the pattern of those which the mental aberration of King Christian VII in Denmark and King George III in England made necessary in their realms. In Russia, as in my country and in Denmark, the regency would fall to the Heir Apparent. It is, therefore, necessary to secure the cooperation of Grand Duke Alexander. The young prince is highly intelligent and, I hope, fairly popular. The favor with which he is regarded by most people should grow, as the hatred of his father increases. It was said that when Alexander threw himself at the Tsar's feet imploring mercy for a victim of his anger, Paul repulsed him and kicked him in the face! The Emperor accused Alexander of being a weakling, coward and traitor. He threatened Alexander with the fate of Alexis Petrovich."

"Yes, yes. I have heard about these threats from Kutaisov."

"As for our Freemasonic brotherhood," continued Sir Charles, "the Emperor has excluded himself from our community by accepting the Grand Mastership of the Roman Catholic Order of Malta. He is not only fascinated by the Maltese uniforms and ceremonial, but he also spreads some monstrous Roman superstitions. This is disgusting. Look at him consorting with those damn black devils, the Jesuits. They have swarmed all over Russia like locusts. They keep proselytizing and have converted many people of high standing to the papist heresy. They have acquired enormous wealth, so many large estates, buildings, colleges. It has been calculated that they already own some 32,000 serfs, or 'souls' as you call them. What you should do is force the Emperor to renounce the crown in favor of His Highness Grand Duke Alexander, who would act as regent. After the abdication, the Emperor can keep the title, a generous allowance, and whatever estates he wishes to keep. Maybe he would like to return to Gatchina. Let's have another glass of port."

After they drank it, Sir Charles resumed his argument. "Maybe the Emperor would like to settle abroad. Britain and her overseas domain are at his disposal. After all, the Royal Navy has captured Malta; perhaps he would like to restore his pet order and run the island as he wishes. There he would be a sovereign ruler."

"Let's keep all these options in mind but it would not be prudent to attempt anything without being assured of the firm consent of the heir to the throne," interjected Pahlen. "Alas, such a commitment is still lacking."

"Of course. But you are in a better position than I to persuade him without arousing the Emperor's suspicions. After all, being the Acting Governor General of the capital, as a part of your duties, you see the Grand Duke almost daily."

"That is true. As a matter of fact I had already sounded out his opinion when we were in the bath together a few weeks ago. Yet, he was reluctant to commit himself, because he still fears for his father's life, and for his own, of course. I tried to present to His Highness all the dangers to which Russia is exposed under the present rule. I tried to impress upon him that it was his sacred duty to assume power and rule Russia in an enlightened, statesmanlike way, that he must not sacrifice the welfare of millions of people to the extravagant caprices of a single man, even if that man were his father. I reminded him that his mother's liberty, and perhaps her life, were also threatened by the growing morbid aversion of the Emperor to his wife. Their marital relations were upset soon after the birth of their fourth daughter Catherine in 1788. That aversion and threats grow now from day to day. In a fit of rage the Emperor is capable of the most outrageous acts."

"I fully agree, and this is another reason to act promptly," insisted Sir Charles.

"When I approached Grand Duke Alexander again, a few days ago," continued Pahlen, "His Highness told me, 'You want me to be like a giraffe; you want me to stick my neck out. Am I to raise my hand against my father? I have my plans on how to get out of this country, settle down and live peacefully as a private person in a free land.' I tried to reassure him, 'Your Highness, I guarantee the Emperor's life and safety.' But the Grand Duke was still suspicious and noncommittal. Again he asked, 'Can you swear that my father's life will be spared?' "

I reassured him, "I swear it on my honor. But he still voiced his doubts and assigned his adjutant, Peter Volkonsky, as his liaison with us, as his observer."

"Before we part," said Sir Charles, "let us establish our plan of action. The most important thing is to keep working on the Grand Duke, to encourage him to be more firmly committed to our plan. Without his consent, his Semionovsky soldiers would not be able to act as we wish. They must be on duty at the Emperor's new palace at the critical moment. We also must have Kutaisov on our side. He should persuade the Tsar not to recall Arakcheyev to the capital. At present, I don't have much money at my disposal. But here are 40,000 rubles to keep him happy. I repeat, Kutaisov must persuade the Emperor to do two things: keep Arakcheyev at Gruzino as long as possible while recalling Platon Zubov to the capital. The Emperor must be made to believe that Platon has undergone a change of heart; that in exile he not only had time enough to atone for his sins, but has become an enthusiastic admirer of the Emperor's new field artillery regulations; that Platon is willing to serve, if the Emperor so desires, as even a simple cannonier in one of the batteries, just to be near such a great military leader. At the same time, we must make Kutaisov believe that Platon would like to marry his daughter. Being a miserable social climber of low birth, he is sure to fall for this. But may I repeat once more by far your most important task is to continue working on the Grand Duke Alexander. Constantine would be no good. He is too much like his father and is devoted to him, body and soul."

As Pahlen was leaving, Sir Charles shook his hand and warned, "Two things are necessary—complete secrecy and quick action. Lost is he who speaks, brave he who acts."

There was no trouble with Kutaisov. Forty thousand rubles combined with the prospect of a wealthy aristocrat such as Count Platon Zubov marrying his daughter made Kutaisov a firm ally. And, indeed, Kutaisov soon received a formal letter from Platon Zubov asking for his daughter's hand in marriage. Delighted with the honor, he carried his message to the Emperor, together with Zubov's words of admiration for the Tsar. At first the suspicious Paul hesitated. Kutaisov, throwing himself at the Emperor's feet, begged him not to put any obstacle in the way of his daughter's good fortune. "Your Imperial Majesty and my little father, don't refuse. Zubov is now your great admirer. He would be your slave." Paul mellowed and accorded this favor.

For the moment things seemed to develop smoothly. Yet, at the end of 1800, Pahlen's plans were upset by changing circumstances. Nikita Panin, one of the most important members of the conspiracy, was exiled to his estate, because Paul had sensed his silent opposition to war with Britain. Of more significance, the conspirators' detailed plans were complicated by the Tsar's move to a new residence. Paul hated the Winter Palace because of its association with his late mother. Consequently, he ordered construction of a new imperial residence to be called Mikhailovsky Palace. Actually more a fortress than a residence, it was hastily completed by February 1801, well ahead of schedule because Paul's increasing fear of a plot against him.

While moving, Paul established strict security mesures. Like a cornered animal, Paul sensed danger everywhere. He went so far as to order a small kitchen near his own apartments, where he planned to have his meals prepared by a trusted servant to prevent an attempt to poison him. Armed sentries were placed at all entrances and kept watch on all approaches to the castle. Twice a day one of the two drawbridges was lowered to give passage to fresh sentinels, food supplies and mail. Surrounded by deep moats, with the drawbridges and gates guarded by hand-picked Chevalier Guards on round-the-clock duty, Paul gradually developed some sense of security.

Paul ordered his reluctant family to move into the new residence and share his voluntary prison, although the freshly plastered walls were still damp, and not all the necessary furniture had been provided. His new mistress, Princess Anna Gagarin, established herself in a suite of apartments, connected with those of the Emperor by a secret staircase. It was rumored that Paul was at the point of repudiating his wife in order to marry his concubine.

Soon after his relocation, Paul began to ponder new dynastic plans. On February 6, 1801, Prince Eugene of Würtemberg, the thirteen-year-old nephew of the Empress Maria, arrived in St. Petersburg. Initially, when Paul invited him to stay with his aunt in Russia, it appeared to be inspired by one of the occasional phases of kindness that alternated with the brutality with which he treated the Empress. But the Tsar's fancy was soon more deeply engaged. To please his uncle, the boy had presented himself to Paul in a Russian dragoon uniform; the boots were so large that when he tried to kneel before the monarch, he lost his balance and fell on the floor. The Tsar overlooked this mishap, picked him up and placed the boy on his lap, lavishing him with tender words and caresses, unprecedented behavior for Paul, who was always stern and morose. The young prince was told by Paul that he was to marry Paul's daughter, Catherine, and be made his heir to the throne.

⋆ ⋆ ⋆

After the beginning of March, Paul lived in complete seclusion and did not leave the castle, even for short walks. He avoided his wife. Having borne him eleven children, she was a spent, prematurely aged woman. The Court doctors had forbidden her to have marital relations with her husband, because another pregnancy could threaten her life. As an eighteenth-century princess, she was accustomed to monarchs having official mistresses, but the manner in which her husband treated his lawful wife was rather humiliating. For instance, Paul had ordered her to arrange the furniture and bedding of his mistress's apartment in the new castle. Although Princess Gagarin's bedroom communicated directly with Paul's by way of a secret staircase, he ordered the access from his apartment to the Empress's rooms barricaded.

Meanwhile, rumors of the plot against him were reaching the Tsar. On March 10, an anonymous letter informed Paul that there existed a plot on his life involving some fifty to sixty people, including Pahlen himself. Enraged, Paul summoned Pahlen immediately. So as not to arouse his suspicion, Paul pretended the occasion was a small private dinner to honor his loyal servant. Like Peter the Great, he firmly believed that only when drunk are people completely sincere. The dinner was arranged in one of the small drawing rooms adjacent to the Emperor's quarters. Paul appeared to be carefree and cordial. Before dinner, many drinks were served in large glasses from two different decanters. While Paul's contained plain water, Pahlen's glass was continually filled with strong vodka. By Court etiquette, Pahlen could not refuse any of the numerous toasts lavishly proposed by his imperial host. After five or six glass-emptying toasts, Paul was convinced that Pahlen was ready to be confronted with a searching cross-examination.

"I have been informed that a conspiracy is being concocted against me, and you, the Acting Governor of St. Petersburg, did not inform me of it! Are you ignorant of this?"

"Pardon me, Sire," Pahlen answered calmly, "I am not only not ignorant of it, but I am a part of it."

"What? You participate in a plot against your sovereign?!"

"Yes, Sire," continued Pahlen, with the same air of self-confidence. "I am a part of it. I joined the plot for your sake, to protect your life. By now all the members of this conspiracy are known to me. I assure you on my word of honor that the guilty ones can escape neither my vigilance nor the justice of Your Imperial Majesty."

"Who are these damned traitors?" shouted Paul.

"Sire, prudence forbids me to name them. Moreover, the list is very long, much longer than sixty names. After all that I have had the honor to reveal to Your Majesty, dare I flatter myself that you will accord me your entire confidence and rely upon my zeal to guard your life?"

This puzzling talk had the effect of further arousing the Tsar's curiosity. "Who are they? At least who are their ringleaders?"

"Sire," answered Pahlen, respectfully bowing his head, "caution prevents me from revealing the illustrious names."

Paul, poisoned by mistrust, immediately fixed his suspicion on his wife and his sons. "I understand," snarled Paul in a voice choked with emotion. "Is it my wife, the Empress Maria Fedorova?"

Pahlen did not reply. His eyes riveted on Pahlen, Paul continued his interrogation. "Is it the Grand Duke Alexander, or perhaps Constantine?"

Pahlen bowed his head, as if in acquiescence, but kept his ambivalent silence.

"As for the Empress Maria," said Paul in a menacing tone, "I will dispose of Her Majesty myself. Meanwhile, the Grand Dukes are to be strictly watched."

"Your orders will be executed in due time, Sire. However, please allow me at least forty-eight hours to apprehend all the plotters."

"Good and loyal Pahlen," exclaimed Paul, "I leave everything to thee." Then he embraced Pahlen cordially, kissed him on both cheeks and said, "Even my wife and sons are miserable traitors! You are the only man I can really trust."

"Actually, your list, Sire, is far from complete. Many officers of your trusted Chevalier Guard, now watching the Mikhailovsky Palace, are among the conspirators. I would remove them from the palace at once. The only fully reliable troop is the Semionovsky regiment. They are body and soul devoted to Your Majesty. Why not summon them?"

At first Paul expressed his doubts, but by the end of the interview, impressed by Pahlen's devotion and efficiency, entrusted all the security arrangements to him. He gave Pahlen handwritten permission to enter the Mikhailovsky Palace at any time of the day or night and to arrest anybody he saw fit, including the Grand Dukes. "Keep this document with you at all times." Then he revealed to Pahlen that he was determined to divorce his wife, send her to a nunnery, arrest both his sons, and try them for treason. For this he needed time to conduct the investigation personally. He ordered that the Chevalier Guard leave the castle and that the barricade separating his bedchamber from that of his wife be reinforced and that she, as well as Alexander and Constantine, be kept under close surveillance. He ended by snapping, "In a few days, many heads shall fall."

After leaving the Tsar, Pahlen quickly summoned the other conspirators, sending to them his trusted officers as messengers. Having assembled some fifty plotters, he said, "The secret is out. There is at least one traitor, one informer among us who sent a denunciation to the Tsar. However, the tyrant is still ignorant of the names of most of us involved in the plot. But who can tell if another traitor may not have revealed our whole plan to him? If life is dear to you, we must hasten to finish our work."

Pahlen's stratagem was to send the plotters to the palace under the command of General Bennigsen, an adventurous cavalry commander who had been dismissed from the service by Tsar Paul and still nursed a deep grudge for his dismissal, while he stayed behind. Pahlen had actually contrived a double intrigue and was ready to betray either his master or his accomplices according to the denouement. If at the decisive moment fate worked against the plotters, his plan was to arrest those culpable and say to the Tsar, "Sire, I provoked the conspirators to act in order to arrest them all. You are saved, Sire. I have proved, once again, to be your most loyal servant."

After taking leave of the conspirators, Pahlen, armed with the order which Paul had given him, went to Alexander's apartment located just below that of the Tsar. Immediately brought into the Grand Duke's presence, Pahlen bowed profoundly and informed him of his father's threats and of the Tsar's determination to act quickly and mercilessly. Pahlen also informed Alexander of his mother's prospective fate. "Here is the order of your arrest. What is your decision?"

Alexander had hardly glanced at the paper when he exclaimed, "And my brother, too!"

"The Senate," added Pahlen, "and the entire Empire wish to throw off this intolerable yoke, and confide its destines to you. I am here only as the faithful interpreter of that wish. We must act at once, Your Highness. There is no time to lose."

When Alexander hesitated, Pahlen tried to make him understand how the universal exasperation among all classes against the Tsar was to be feared. "Look at England. There the royal family disposed of King George III and entrusted the direction of the goverment to the Prince of Wales, although the mental condition of the King was less alarming than that of our Tsar. And it all happened in a country where sovereign authority is more restrained and is limited by law, where the sense of legality is much stronger than anywhere in the world."

"You, Your Highness," continued Pahlen, assuming the same air of moderation, "could, without mounting the throne, take the reins of governemnt as Regent, always being ready to return them to your father when his health is restored and he has recovered the composure necessary for the performance of his duties. Such are the views of the Senate, of the army, and of the whole nation."

Despite Pahlen's arguments, Alexander was hesitant. "If we fail, my father will surely treat me as cruelly as Peter the Great treated Alexis."

Pahlen became impatient and blustered out: "Monseigneur, the next two days will without a doubt decide the fate of Your Imperial Highness, your august mother, and of all Russia. Now is the time for action, not for moral or legal reasoning! Lost is he who hesitates, victorious he who acts!"

On leaving Alexander, Pahlen posted six guards at his door with an officer in charge and ordered that the Grand Duke not be let out without a written order. Once again, assembling the conspirators at Platon Zubov's residence, he addressed them, "Let us not hesitate to show ourselves worthy of Russia in acting as her liberators! One cannot make an omelet without breaking an egg!"

Invoking Brutus, the conspirators swore to kill the tyrant. To bolster their courage, they gulped large draughts of champagne. Only Pahlen, his second-in-command General Bennigsen, and Peter Volkonsky, Alexander's adjutant, abstained, in order to be in full control of the situation.

Pahlen saw the Emperor once more and persuaded him that the conspiracy was under surveillance, and the Grand Duke Alexander under house arrest. His success in calming the Tsar was complete.

That night Paul went to relax with his mistress, Princess Gagarin. After his talk with Pahlen, he was fully reassured and finally enjoyed a sense of safety and full control of the situation. "Let tomorrow take care of itself," he said while kissing the Princess.

★ ★ ★

At midnight the conspirators made their way in small groups toward the Mikhailovsky castle. Dark clouds obscured the March skies, while wet snow covered the ground in sharp contrast to the reddish walls of the still unfinished castle. The drawbridge was the first obstacle. Two sergeants guarding it hesitated to honor Pahlen's pass, but finally did agree to lower the bridge and open the gate. The conspirators entered the fortress. As the band crossed the garden surrounding the palace, a flock of crows roosting on the trees was startled up. The croaking birds, considered a bad omen, frightened some of the more superstitious conspirators and, for a moment, caused some of them to reconsider their plans, but both Pahlen and Bennigsen insisted they continue on. At all times Pahlen and Volkonsky remained behind watching the behavior of the conspirators, listening intently to each sound while urging them on.

Pahlen had removed the Chevaliers guards and in their place stationed officers of the Semionovsky regiment. One sentinel who had been overlooked, saw the approaching group, and was about to alarm the Tsar's personal servants when he was silenced by the conspirators. Having reached the interior of the palace without hindrance, they mounted the steps of the grand staircase.

Paul, after passing the evening with Princess Gagarin, slept peacefully in his bedroom. Just as the conspirators were about to enter the Tsar's bedchamber, Paul's personal servant, who was dozing in the armchair at the door, suddenly perceived the intruders and jumped in front of the conspirators, shouting, "Stop! Who goes there? I say stop!" When they refused, he drew his pistol. They fell upon him and cut him down. The loud noises woke Paul. He sprang out of bed and ran to the door which led to the apartments on the ground floor, forgetting that he had ordered that door locked and barricaded the previous night to secure his apartment from his wife's intrusion. Furiously he kicked at the door, but to no avail. He was trapped. What could he do?

The principal door to Paul's bed chamber crashed open. The conspirators rushed in shouting, "Down with the tyrant! Abdicate! Abdicate!" Paul had only time to hide behind a Cordovan leather fireplace screen. The plotters first looked toward the bed. It was empty. They searched the room, but found no one. Then one of them saw bare feet under the screen. "Here he is! Here he is!" Paul was dragged to the center of the room. One of the conspirators called for Pahlen. But Pahlen did not answer. He was outside the room, closely watching the outcome of the struggle. He was ready to arrest his fellow conspirators should the plot fail. The conspirators, with swords and pistols, surrounded Paul. Gathering all his courage, he pleaded, "Don't you respect your sovereign? Beware! You are facing your Tsar!"

"Paul Petrovich," shouted Platon Zubov, "you see in us the authority of the Senate. Take this document, read it, and decide your own fate. Sign the act of abdication!"

Mortally frightened, and with trembling hands, Paul took the paper from Zubov. By the light of the nightlamp, which flickered upon his pale, contorted features, and upon the ferocious, drunken faces of the conspirators, Paul read the document. He loudly protested the accusations of tyranny and the details of his faults, follies and crimes. His pride and his dignity as sovereign were mortally wounded. He threw the paper down, shouting, "No! Death before dishonor! I will not abdicate! Never ! Never!"

Seeing that most of the conspirators were half-drunk and unsteady, Paul had decided to fight. While Platon Zubov stooped to retrieve the act of abdication from the floor, Paul jumped toward his bed where two pistols and a sword were hidden under the pillow. But the leaders of the band, Bennigsen, and Platon and Nicholas Zubov, leaped on him from three sides and overwhelmed him. Paul's sword was torn from his hand and he was thrown to the floor. The Zubov brothers grasped Paul's officer's scarf, wrapped it around his neck, and attempted to strangle him. Paul resisted furiously, but in vain. The furious assailants were too much for him. Even as the limp body seemed to stir for a moment, Platon Zubov stomped on the Tsar's belly with both feet, shouting "Let's drive out his cruel soul from this miserable body! Let's finish him off!"

Paul breathed his last as Pahlen entered the bedchamber, sword in hand, followed by two adjutants and a dozen soldiers. He had still not decided whether to denounce the traitors and rescue the Tsar, or proclaim the triumph of the plot. The sight of the Emperor's massacred body shattered him. He leaned against a pillar and did not move for several seconds. Then he uttered, "Thank God the tyrant is dead. We are saved. . . ."

Stifled cries and groans had reached the Empress Maria through the barricaded door. She rushed out of her apartment and ran up the staircase which was filled with conspirators. Bennigsen, who was one of the few able to maintain some composure that night, stopped her from entering the Emperor's chamber saying, "Your Majesty, this is not a sight for a lady."

And Alexander . . . what was he doing that fateful night? He and Elizabeth occupied a suite on the ground floor of the Mikhailovsky palace, some distance from the room where the Emperor slept. From Pahlen Alexander had learned that this night would be critical; he was aware that his father would be called upon to abdicate, and that he would be asked to assume supreme powers. In his uniform he had thrown himself on a sofa, full of anxiety and doubt. He was fully aware of the smallest details of the plot, and had had himself selected the third battalion of the Semionovsky regiment to stand guard that fateful night of March 11/12. Although Elizabeth had been alienated from him for a long time, at this crucial moment she took pity on her husband, consoled him and tried to inspire him to courage. His passivity and helplessness amazed her. Did he not hear the tumultous rushing of the conspirators, or the shouts and screams of the victim?

★ ★ ★

When the Empress was informed by Bennigsen that the Emperor was dead, she did not cry. A strong and ambitious person, she recovered her composure very quickly. In the days when she and Paul were close, when he was only Heir Apparent, he had always spoken of entrusting the Regency to her if anything were to happen to him. She was not much of a politician, but was not disposed to accept the position of mere dowager, and thought that, at last, she had gained a chance to assert herself, to be Regent. Both Bennigsen and Pahlen failed to dissuade her to inspect Paul's bedroom.

She ranged throughout the imperial apartments. Meeting some grenadiers, she quizzed them repeatedly, "Did your Emperor die a victim of treason? Now I am your Empress. I alone am your legitimate sovereign!" But though she was generally respected, she did not inspire feelings of enthusiasm and devotion which attract men to a cause. Her confused appeals to the soldiers, made half in broken Russian, half in German, had no effect. After some quarter of an hour of fierce contention they forced her to return to her room. Guards were placed at her door to prevent her from leaving once more. Frustrated and exhausted, she collapsed.

The only member of the Imperial family who retained her presence of mind was the Grand Duchess Elizabeth. She did her utmost to keep Alexander calm during the sleepless night. She gave him courage and self-reliance. Moreover, in this night of tragedy and horror, she sought for a few moments to soothe her mother-in-law and to persuade her to remain in her rooms, and not expose herself to the fury of the drunken conspirators. At half-past one in the morning, Pahlen entered the antechamber of Alexander's bedroom and asked the chief valet, "Is the Grand Duke asleep?"

"No, Sire," answered Ivan Melnikov.

Pahlen commanded, "Go tell him that I am here."

Melnikov knocked on the door and entered to find Alexander sitting on the sofa next to his wife. When the trembling Alexander appeared in the antechamber, Pahlen saluted him with his naked sword and said, "It is all over. Your Majesty, you are the Tsar of all the Russias. Come with me and receive the allegiance of the troops."

Alexander was on the verge of collapse. The first impulse of his evasive nature was to shirk even the accomplished fact. Then Pahlen seized the Grand Duke roughly by the arm and barked, "You have played the child long enough. Go and reign! But first come and show yourself to the Guards."

When finally Alexander left the palace, mounted the horse and, accompanied by Pahlen, reached the Senate Square, he saw the parade ground crowded with troops. On the right was a batallion of the Preobrazhensky regiment in blue and white uniforms, on the left a batallion of the three Izmailovsky Guards in green and white attire; and in the middle the Semionovsky soldiers in the familiar green and red. Behind them were the Horse Guards and the artillery men with their cannons. All had been efficiently arranged by Pahlen, who purposely spurned the Chevalier Guards, as he was unsure of their loyalty. He wanted the regiment whose officers were most prominent in the plot to first swear the oath of allegiance, to set the example for other units of the St. Petersburg garrison.

A large crowd of people had assembled around the assembled troops. They cried for an explanation of the rumors circulating throughout the capital. Was the Tsar murdered? Did he die of apoplexy? Would he not appear in a moment with his angry face and his uplifted cane as always on the parade ground? What were they to think? What was being hidden from them?

When Alexander confronted this mass of humanity he could find no appropriate words. His obvious confusion immediately affected the mood of the soldiers, some of whom became defiant and even arrogant. Paul had been fairly popular with the common soldiers because he did not show much favor to the officers and was lenient and fatherly to the rank and file. At heart, they had taken vicarious pleasure in seeing their superiors humiliated, scolded, slapped on the face and caned by the mad Tsar. Pahlen spoke a few words to General Tylzin, commander of the Semionovsky regiment, who was involved in the plot. The general reassured him concerning the mood of his soldiers, although their defiant attitude belied his optimism. Alexander remained petrified and speechless. At this tragic moment he could not deal with the surprising defiance of the soldiers. His obvious inability to cope with what had happened perplexed them. Pahlen hurried the new Tsar to the quarters of the Semionovsky regiment where Alexander was fairly popular among the officers and hence should feel more at ease. Though he was nominally in command of the whole brigade of the guards, this regiment was regarded as particularly his own because he was its honorary colonel. Pahlen turned to the soldiers and shouted in a calm, steady voice, "Men! His Majesty the Emperor Paul died last night from a stroke. You must take the oath of allegiance to his son and heir, hitherto Grand Duke and now Emperor, Alexander Pavlovich. Here he is. Long live Tsar Alexander I!"

There was deadly silence. General Tylzin was dumbfounded. Pahlen, perplexed, took off his hat and wiped his forehead with his handkerchief. The soldiers remained silent. Then one of the old sergeants of the Preobrazhensky battallion shouted, "Why did he die? He was all right yesterday. Show us his corpse!"

Another soldier cried out angrily, "Why should we take the oath without reflection? Why should we swear allegiance to anyone? We all have to serve for twenty-five years, while you officers come and go at will."

"Of course, it's all the same to us," barked an old sergeant.

The desperate Pahlen tried to appease the soldiers and shouted "There will be no drill today! It is a holiday to celebrate the accession of the new Tsar. You will each receive a ration of vodka!"

Only then did the Semionovsky men begin to react more positively and one by one they voiced their approval. Scattered shouting, "Hurrah, hurrah, hurrah! Long live our Tsar Alexander!" was heard. The officers vigorously joined in and soon the whole company shouted, "Long live the new Tsar! Long live Tsar Alexander!" Other units followed the lead of the Semionovsky men, and the applause became more spontaneous. Alexander relaxed somewhat. He reviewed all three detachments of soldiers on the parade ground, accepted their ovation, and thanked God it was over.

After that he returned to the palace and entered the large hall adjoining the fateful bedchamber. The Dowager Empress, forgetting her former humiliations, and, with a true German sense of duty, was trying to restore some order to her late husband's rooms. Alexander avoided her glance. Two Court doctors were preparing the battered, barely recognizable body of his father for embalming. When Alexander asked them on whose orders they were acting, they answered, "General von Pahlen told us to complete this task as soon as possible." Alexander then learned that Pahlen also had commanded the servants to build the traditional *castrum doloris* in the palace chapel and had instructed the capital's metropolitan to prepare his clergy for the solemn funeral of the deceased Tsar.

Alexander did not wish to linger at the scene of the crime, and moved promptly to the adjacent oval chamber, the wardrobe of his late father. The room seemed empty, but soon he noticed Princess Gagarina seated on a stool in the corner, her head leaning against the stove. She was sobbing and moaning disconsolately. She was, perhaps, the only person who quite sincerely regretted Paul's death. Only last night he swore to her that, after divorcing his wife and sending her to a convent, he would marry her, proclaim her Empress and crown her solemnly in the Kremlin.

Without speaking a word to the Princess, Alexander went up to the huge dining room, now the scene of particuraly noisy revelry. In the center of the hall, surrounded by a group of courtiers and drunken officers, stood Platon Zubov, with his usual cynical smile, holding a half-empty bottle of champagne. He was telling obscene stories about his duties with his former imperial lover. The stories were greeted with loud bursts of laughter from most of the equally drunk company. "You see how hard I had to work. And all this for patriotic reasons."

His brother Nicholas was also quite drunk. He sported a large bruise on his swollen face which he had suffered while strangling the Tsar, who fought back with his fists and feet; before breathing his last, Paul had kicked Zubov in the face. Nicholas bragged that he had greater strength in his hands than Alexis Orlov, who had had a similar encounter with Catherine's husband, Peter III, at Ropsha.

While the drunken orgy was going on, Pahlen, cool as always, appeared at the door and shouted, "Silence, Silence! Have you no respect for the dead Emperor? I have an announcement to make. His Imperial Majesty Emperor Alexander has just ordered official Court mourning for thirty days."

No such order had been issued by Alexander, who was still in profound shock, and confused beyond measure. Like a ghost, he continued to wander throughout the palace. Finally, without undressing, he fell on his unmade bed. Thoroughly exhausted, he slept until early afternoon.

CHAPTER 6

Reforming Russia

Although the real cause of Paul's death was suppressed by censorship, few well-informed people in St. Petersburg believed that Paul had died of apoplexy any more than Peter III had died of colic. Various accounts of the murder began to appear in foreign newspapers. The chronicles of Imperial Tsarist Russia had too often resorted to the euphemism of cerebral hemorrhage. Talleyrand, Napoleon's foreign minister and a leading European wit, hit the mark when he concluded, "The Russians need to invent another disease to explain the mortality among their emperors; the Russian government is an absolute monarchy tempered by assassination."

For the Russian upper classes, Paul's reign had been a nightmare. The nobility's privileges were threatened by his reforms; the military feared a senseless war against Britain; the bureaucratic apparatus was confused by an avalanche of contradictory decrees. Merchants were infuriated by the ban on trade with Britain. No wonder, therefore, that Paul's death was met with a sigh of relief by most of the establishment. For a few days, the drawing rooms, as well as the taverns of the capital, saw an orgy of drinking and merrymaking. By the evening of March 12, there was not a bottle of champagne left in St. Petersburg. It did not take long for the news of the Tsar's death to filter down to the masses, who understood little of what had actually happened on the fateful night of March 11/12, 1801, yet passively accepted whatever had transpired at the top.

Hasty preparations were made for the funeral. The Tsar's body lay in state in the chapel, dressed in the uniform of a Horse Guards general. His face had been carefully made up, and a huge, black plumed hat had been tilted on his head so that it almost covered his crushed left eye, while his mangled throat was hidden under a high collar. On March 12 in the afternoon, the entire Imperial famly had come from the Winter Palace to the Mikhailovsky Palace. Elizabeth declined to attend, claiming ill health. First to enter the funeral chamber were Alexander and the widowed Empress Maria Feodorovna. Her fat, round face was covered with red blotches, and from time to time she sobbed hysterically. As the Dowager Empress approached the body, she stopped and exclaimed theatrically, "How tragic! How tragic! God help me to bear it." She moved on, but, before she reached the catafalque, staggered back, turned towards her son, and said to him in strongly accented Russian, loud enough so all could hear, "I congratulate you, my dear son. You are now the Emperor!"

Alexander bowed toward her, took a step forward and kneeled at the catafalque. His face was somber, and deathly pale, and his jaw trembled convulsively. He made the sign of the cross three times and prayed for a few minutes, crossing himself several more times. Then he rose and kissed his father's bruised forehead.

The day following the publication of the official death notice, on March 13, many people went to the Mikhailovsky Palace, ostensibly to pay their last respects to the Tsar, but in reality to celebrate and gossip. Many visitors paid no attention to the mangled corpse, but laughed and joked quite freely, sharing their versions of the mad monarch's last days and the circumstances of his death.

While preparations for a solemn funeral were going on, Alexander suffered a fit of deep depression and bitter remorse. Memories of the tragic night of March 11/12 took a heavy toll on his nerves. Despite a mask of calm, inner turmoil was reflected in his haggard looks. The child-like smile disappeared from his face, and his bright blue eyes dimmed and projected sadness and turmoil. For days his physical and mental energy were sapped by self-condemnation for his conduct during the period preceding the assassination. He was obsessed with questions: Would it have been possible to spare his father's life? Should he have taken more vigorous precautions against the unavoidable oversights in a dangerous undertaking? Did he display enough determination while negotiating with von Pahlen? Should he not have demanded stricter guarantees from him?

Alexander was painfully aware that he was not ascending the throne in the way that he had expected. Pahlen's promise to spare Paul's life—which Alexander had made a condition of his adherence to the plot—had not been kept. Would the wily powerbroker respect his oath of loyalty and obedience to Alexander as Tsar?

While Alexander was struggling with his personal trauma, Pahlen grasped the reins of government and held them firmly. It was he who cancelled the ill-starred, senseless expedition to India and thus saved the remnant of its Russian forces from almost certain death. It was he who negotiated with Admiral Horatio Nelson, whose powerful fleet hovered off Riga and threatened the naval base of Kronstadt with bombardment. It was Pahlen who unearthed a liberal accession manifesto that Czartoryski had drafted for Alexander as far back as 1797. All the while he treated the confused and hesitant young monarch as his puppet. In private conversations with the Zubov brothers, Pahlen called Alexander "infantile," and "spineless."

In addition to Pahlen's domineering and arrogant posture, another threat to Alexander's supremacy was the attitude of some of the Guards regiments. The reluctance of the Preobrazhensky and Izmailovsky Guards to take the oath of loyalty to Alexander was proof of the common soldier's attachment to the late Tsar, whom they still recognized as their protector against the abuses of the officers. The fact that it was mainly Pahlen's vigorous intervention that swayed the mood of the two key regiments frightened Alexander. Would Pahlen be so bold as to use his authority to place some other, more pliable, prince on the throne? Could he not now plot with the great aristocratic families—the Vorontsovs, the Dolgorukys, the Golitsyns, the Razumonovskys, the Rumiantsevs, the Stroganovs—to establish an oligarchy behind the veil of the much debated Charter of the Russian People?

* * *

Torn by doubt, Alexander met with his favorite adjutant and bosom friend, Peter Volkonsky, who, as a member of the conspiracy, was well informed about the plans of its ringleaders. Recovering from his initial anguish, Alexander opened his soul to his friend. "Look at my predicament, Peter. I did not want the crown. It was tossed on me by fate. I agreed to the plot to save our poor Russia, and perhaps my own head, from the cruel caprices of a madman who was leading all of us to ruin. But now what am I to do with this crown that has been forced upon my head?"

"I understand Your Imperial Majesty's troubles, but here I am of little use. I am not a politician, but merely a soldier. However, since you, Sire, have honored me with your august friendship, may I be allowed to express my personal opinion frankly?"

"Yes, of course. It is your duty to do so, especially at this critical moment."

"Since you ordered me to join the plot to report everything of importance to you, I have been watching von Pahlen and his clique rather closely. Do you authorize me to continue this task? After all, my chief duty is to be at your side as your adjutant and act as your private secretary."

"You must continue to be in close touch with Pahlen's clique. Actually I am most anxious to hear your opinion of his plans."

"Sir," Volkonsky stressed, "despite the objections of some of the conspirators, namely Pahlen, Panin, and the Zubov brothers, you have been proclaimed, not a constitutional monarch, but 'the Supreme Autocrat of all the Russias.' The oath of allegiance sworn by the troops and the officials uses this very title and it is officially binding. Yet, from the confidential whispers I have overheard, Pahlen and his henchmen aim to limit your power and eventually make you their puppet. They speculate much about the Senate acting as the future legislative chamber, but actually they want to use it as a cover for their plans. They thirst for more privileges for their oligarchic clique. As an autocratic Tsar, you can do anything. You may even decide to share your power with some sort of advisory chamber of council, whatever its title would be, but this should be an act of Your grace and not the result of pressure from such amibtious men as Pahlen, Panin or Bennigsen. Giving ground to them would only invite new concessions. Be firm. Those bastards respect only strength. Actually, the least dangerous of the whole group is Panin. He talks, talks, talks, but there is more bark than bite in his monologues. For instance this idiotic Anglophile would like to see a British parliamentary system established here. How ridiculous! Can you, Sire, imagine this sort of thing in Russia? But Pahlen and his coterie, like Bennigsen for instance, are vicious men. They take Sweden's oligarchy as a model. Moreover, they are not mere talkers, but men of action. Pahlen is as cunning as he is ruthless. He already considers himself a grand vizier, and you a weak, impotent sultan. I have overheard Pahlen several times; he dared to talk about you in a way no Russian subject should ever speak of his Tsar. I trust that Your Majesty will allow me not to mention the adjectives he used while speaking of you."

Remembering Pahlen's behavior the critical morning following the assassination, Alexander had no doubt of Volkonsky's veracity. There was a long pause. Then Volkonsky continued his analysis of the precarious position in which he found his master.

"What I suspect is that Pahlen *et consortes* will press you to carry out your casual promises to establish some sort of constitutional regime. You ought to resist them. You should act promptly and decisively to neutralize the plot. First of all divide the plotters. Banish the ringleaders from the capital. At the same time, make yourself better known to the capital's garrison, especially to the oficers and noncommissioned men of the Guards. They are mainly scions of the nobility, whether sons of aristocracy or of poor squires, yet they all feel threatened in their privileged status by your late father's various decrees. Remedy this. Restore the traditional rights of the nobles: no taxes, no flogging, no compulsory state service. Under the pretext of inspecting various units, visit their garrisons, their casinos, their barracks; talk not only to the officers but also to the rank and file. Each of your regimental inspections should be followed by some kind and generous gesture toward the officers, as well as the rank and file. For instance, give them additional allotments of vodka, grant more ample rations, etc., etc. But don't neglect the aristocratic officers of the old Guard regiments. They resent the privileges of the Chevalier Guardsmen, their gaudy uniforms, their plumettes, their superior horses. But be careful! Don't withdraw those honors from the Chevaliers. They are your father's creation and right now they are in a sulky mood. Rather consider what new privileges you can extend to the old guardsmen. Sire, as your most humble servant and devoted friend, may I urge you to begin a fight for power at once. Call your own shots. Be daring and be quick. Be ruthless if necessary. Everything is at stake! You must gain more friends among all ranks of the military. Remember your clever grandmother's tactics when she was fighting for the crown that, after all, didn't belong to her. You are fighting for what does belong to you by right, by heredity."

* * *

Alexander was frightened by the implications of Volkonsky's words. Taking to heart his warnings, he set to work at once. He summoned Arakcheyev, who had arrived at the capital soon after Paul's assassination. Arakcheyev wept, but took an oath of allegiance to his new master and placed himself at his disposal. Alexander's instruction to him was, "Count Pahlen, General Bennigsen and the Zubovs must be watched discreetly day and night. You are charged with the task of organizing the surveillance. Pahlen's every suspicious step must be reported to me. I trust you completely."

A few days later, after hearing Arakcheyev's report of Bennigsen's extended, nightly visits to von Pahlen's residence, Alexander made the first step to split the conspirators and appointed Bennigsen Governor General of Lithuania. When informed of the Tsar's order for him to leave for the new post within forty-eight hours, the embittered Hannoverian sneered, "The ingrate! He forgets that to raise him to the throne I risked the scaffold!"

After Bennigsen's departure, Alexander proceeded to methodically implement other parts of Volkonsky's scheme. With his and Arakcheyev's help he prepared a detailed program for inspecting, during April and May, all regiments stationed in and around the capital. This included the naval base at Kronstadt. Meanwhile, he drafted a series of decrees that rescinded some of the harsh measures imposed on the nobility by Tsar Paul. Alexander reaffirmed Catherine's Charter of Nobility, which Paul had violated repeatedly by infringing on noblemen's property, security and dignity. He decreed that, once again, no nobleman could be deprived of his life, property, or title without a trial and a formal verdict by his peers. The squires' right to form provincial assemblies and to elect Marshals of Nobility was reinstated. The members of that estate were free to travel abroad and to enter the service of friendly states; they were exempt from poll tax and from flogging, a punishment often used by Paul, even on senior officers.

Alexander's visits to the militia included not only parades and field exercises but also a great deal of socializing, dining, drinking and merrymaking. The strenuous timetable affected his health and upset his digestion. At the end of the tour of inspection he was compelled to spend several days in bed. But, in a few months he had learned the names, characters, and even hobbies of most of the commanders above the rank of company, squadron or battery. After each visit he dictated his observations to Volkonsky, now in charge of the Tsar's private files. The inspection tour convinced Alexander that he could rely on the garrison of the capital and surrounding region. Consequently, he felt that he was no more a snail without a shell. Pahlen remained the only man who, by his skill, daring and ambition, could be a serious threat to the throne.

By the end of May, Alexander had decided to challenge his arrogant rival. On June 17, at 5 A.M., Pahlen was awakened from sleep by his valet. It was Volkonsky, who brought to Pahlen an urgent order from the Tsar to appear at once at the Winter Palace. The surprised kingmaker questioned the reason for so urgent a message, delivered at such an early hour. Volkonsky replied, "It is not my task to discuss with Your Excellency the reasons behind His Imperial Majesty's wishes." When Pahlen, barely shaven and without having taken any nourishment, reported to Alexander at his studio in the Winter Palace, he was shocked by the Tsar's icy reception and words. "It is our will that you leave the capital immediately for your estate in Curland. You are to remain there indefinitely and await my further orders."

The command was so blunt and so unexpected that Pahlen was speechless. As he bowed to the Emperor, Alexander was already leaving the studio. That evening, without packing even the most necessary belongings, Pahlen left the capital for Riga and then for his estate. The next day, two of the three Zubov brothers, Platon and Nicholas, were also exiled indefinitely to their respective estates. Thus the conspiratorial clique was split and neutralized. Alexander was now firmly in control.

* * *

From the beginning of his reign, Alexander had established a fairly steady daily routine. At 6 A.M., still in his morning gown, he took his tea and ate a hearty breakfast. After dressing, and weather permitting, he went for a short walk in the park of the Winter Palace or Tsarskoye Selo. There, the gamekeepers would often direct his attention to their deer, swans, ducks and geese; and the gardeners, their fruit and flowers. Occasionally, he fed the animals and gave orders to the park personnel. At 7:30 or 8 A.M., he was at his desk, looking over official papers and reports. At 10 A.M., he sometimes ate fruit ripened to perfection from the palace greenhouses. Shortly before noon he liked to get on his horse and review the mounting of the guards. Then he changed clothes, and either continued to work on state documents or received his ministers and other high officials. At 4 P.M., he dined, and after tea he worked in his study until 9 P.M., or met with his advisers. Around 11:00 or 11:30 P.M., he had a light meal of cheese or fruit and went to bed.

Long before the coup d'etat, Alexander had gathered around him a hand-picked group of men whom he could trust explicitly. He called them his "Secret Committee" because the suspicious Paul disapproved of such gatherings, and discretion was a must. During his father's reign, the activities of the Committee were extremely limited. They consisted of translating some seminal foreign books into Russian. Many works awaited publication, since Paul permitted few books on politics and philosophy to be printed. Now the Secret Committee began to meet openly, but the name remained. All of its carefully chosen members were united by a single idea. Peter the Great, they believed, shook Russian out of her timeless torpor only temporarily. After his death, the Empire lost its momentum and its impulse for progress. While expanding territorially, domestically Russia remained in the bog of barbarism and superstition. What was needed, therefore, was a vigorous push to reform the country in the spirit of the Enlightenment. For this, dedicated co-workers were needed and detailed plans prepared.

After his proclamation as Tsar, one of Alexander's early directives was to recall Prince Adam Czartoryski from the Sardinian court then in Turin. Immediately after his return to St. Petersburg, the prince became a member of the Committee. On his arrival in the capital, Czartoryski was shocked to find that Elizabeth's feelings had changed radically. She was now in the arms of a young officer, Lieutenant Gregory Ovechnikov of the Horse Guards. She refused to see the prince and his letters remained unanswered, a humiliating end to the great love affair of his life. In desperation, he sought relief in hard, systematic work. More reserved and taciturn than ever, he avoided the frivolous St. Petersburg court and plunged into the numerous tasks assigned to him by his master. Work became for him the narcotic he needed to compensate for the loss of his great love.

On Czartoryski's return, the Emperor had a long conference with him which lasted for nearly six hours and dealt with an urgent task facing the Secret Committee, its composition and the procedures to be followed. In addition to Czartoryski, there were three other members of that body. The first was Nikolas Novosiltsev, an able jurist and adroit courtier who served as the Tsar's main personal secretary. Novosiltsev had a brilliant mind, but a weak character. His desire for distinction and for amassing a fortune to cover his lavish expenses made him opportunistic, and eventually corrupt. Novosiltsev introduced to the Committee his cousin, Count Paul Stroganov. Twenty-three years old, Stroganov had been tutored by Gilbert Romme, former president of the French National Convention, who made Stroganov a librarian at a Jacobin club in Paris. There he wore revolutionary garb, long loose trousers, a loose jacket and a Frigian cap. All this shocked Empress Catherine, and she summarily ordered him home.

The fourth member of the Secret Committee was Count Victor Kochoubey. The nephew of Count Bezborodko, Catherine's foreign minister, he was sent to the embassy at Constantinople. While in Turkey, Kochoubey acted with skill and acquired considerable diplomatic experience which Alexander planned now to use in the office for foreign affairs.

This small group of gifted and reform-minded men was to provide Alexander with concepts on which to base his plans to modernize the Empire. They belonged to a generation nourished with the ideals of the Enlightenment, and believed its doctrines to be a sort of philosopher's stone, a universal remedy, which would remove all obstacles, moral and political, to the regeneration of society.

An occasional associate member of the Committee was Laharpe, who had come to visit his former pupil. Laharpe, at that time about forty-four years old, was a member of the Swiss Directory, and proudly wore the uniform of that office. He did not take part in the regular meetings of the Committee, but during the morning walks in the garden he conversed privately with the Emperor. He also frequently presented to Alexander long memoranda which meticulously reviewed all branches of the Russian administration. These papers were first read at the Secret Committee meetings and afterwards passed on from one member to the other to be considered at leisure, as they were very long and required detailed, written comments. The radical and impatient Stroganov dismissed most of Laharpe's remarks, often writing on the margin of his memoranda: "Too long and confusing. What a bore!" Other members of the Secret Committee were more tactful, but they also considered him rather dull. But Alexander continued to show considerable respect to his former tutor, often repeating, "I owe him so much, so much. He was the mentor of my youthful years."

★ ★ ★

One evening at the end of June, after an informal early light dinner, Alexander opened the Committee's first session with a short speech: "My late father, when he ascended the throne, wished to reform almost everything. He began brilliantly, but the promise of the first few months was not maintained because of his harsh methods and his self-centeredness. Everything was to be decided by him and him alone. This was impossible. Consequently, things were turned upside down. It would be a waste of time to tell you of all the contradictory and capricious measures that he undertook. I am sure you remember that there was severity without justice in state affairs and irrationality combined with inexperience. Appointment went by favor; merit had no impact. The peasants, though taken under the protection of law, were burdened by excessive taxes and conscription. Commerce was first impeded and ultimately strangled by the embargo on our exports to England. Eventually individual liberty and comfort were at an end." He stopped for a moment and then continued.

"We must now resume the reform begun by my illustrious ancestor Peter the Great. But our methods must be different, more civilized and humane; our timing more measured, dictated by circumstances and proper reflection, not by the whims of one man. The target, however, remains the same: to make Russia a part of Europe, an enlightened, civilized country. This is still our goal. Our most urgent and critical problem is determining what shall be done about the overwhelming majority of our population, the serfs, their welfare, their education and eventual emancipation. Then we have to deal with the central administration, so antiquated, so inefficient, and, alas, so corrupt. We must also alter our educational structure. I hope, gentlemen, that you will assist me in carrying out the arduous task of reform."

Then Alexander raised his glass of champagne and proposed a toast. "I drink to the success of our common endeavor and to Russia's enlightened progress." Applause and a tumultous exchange of opinions followed. Around midnight, members dispersed, resolving to meet once a week and charging Stroganov to prepare an agenda for the next meeting and a paper on the serf problem as urgently requiring attention.

And indeed serfdom was Russia's number one problem, enormous and frightening. In 1801, of a population of some forty million people, fewer than five per cent lived in towns and cities. Free peasants formed another five per cent or so, leaving about ninety per cent of the population indentured in one way or another. Roughly half were the property of the Crown, while another half were owned by private landowners. All members of the Secret Committee were aristocratic serf owners, yet they understood that serfdom must first be limited, and eventually abolished altogether. The first question necessitated immediate steps to alleviate the intolerable burdens borne by the serfs and thus prevent the increasingly frequent peasant mutinies which threatened the stability of the Empire. And the second question concerned the time in which the entire delicate process might be accomplished.

Yet the problem of eventual emancipation was so complex and so dangerous in its implications that most members of the Secret Committee hesitated to tackle the issue. The Committee's only radical abolitionist was Paul Stroganov. To one of the first sessions of the Committee he brought the book *Journey from St. Petersburg to Moscow,* work of early reformer Alexander Radishchev. Published in 1790, it had been immediately suppressed on Catherine's order. She was frightened because the booklet portrayed the barbarous condition of the serfs. Radishchev was charged with treason and sentenced to death. Fortunately, Catherine's more reasonable advisers persuaded her to commute the sentence to ten years of exile in Siberia. Paul immediately reversed his mother's verdict and allowed Radishchev to return to the capital to take part in the work of the codification commission in which he passionately defended the peasant cause. Yet, disillusioned by the negligible impact of his efforts, in despair he committed suicide. Stroganov later read long passages of Radishchev's book and a chaotic discussion followed into the night, but without any conclusion.

The second session of the committee was more structured than the first. It was opened by Stroganov with a speech on serfdom. After a short introduction, outlining the magnitude and seriousness of the problem, he reread passages of Radishchev's work to illustrate his argument. "Many landowners are miserly and cruel," stressed Stroganov. "Some of them are our friends, or perhaps even relatives, but this should not blind us to their inhumanity and barbarity. Some squires force serfs to work seven days a week in the fields, take away all their land and often will buy livestock at a price which they themselves arbitrarily determine. The serfs are not allowed to marry or travel outside the estate without the master's permission. Lest the serfs starve, the masters feed them but poorly and not infrequently only once a day."

Stroganov continued. "Apart from the duty to work on the landowner's fields, which the serfs owe their masters or the Crown, they also face numerous demands from the State. The most formidable of these are the poll tax and military service. Each village is called upon to furnish a requisite number of conscripts for our armed forces. The wars of the Empress Catherine, her campaigns against Turkey, Poland and Sweden, required thousands of soldiers annually. As the gentry has been exempt from conscription and the merchants could always buy themselves off from the draft, the full burden of these wars fell on the peasants. Exempted were only those who were lame, deaf, blind or maimed. Healthy young men had to serve for twenty-five years if selected by lot and this law is still binding. The long, harsh service frightens many youngsters. Frequently the draftees cut off a finger or even a hand as the time for recruitment approaches. The conscripts often cry while they take leave of their parents or sweethearts, whom they may never see again. It is shameful."

Here Stroganov received the half-hearted applause of his colleagues. He continued. "In reality our serfdom amounts to slavery. Slavery similar to that which exists in most European colonies and in the American South. No wonder that the Russian peasant avoids work, because he never knows what it is to work for himself, for his own profit. He realizes that he can never enjoy the fruits of his labor beyond his needs for subsistence. He has no interest in anything because he possesses nothing. Since he has been treated inhumanely and brutalized by centuries of harsh treatment, how could he be human? It is hardly surprising that he seeks to escape from this intolerable existence in drunkenness and wild outbursts of hatred. These are the primary reasons for our frequent peasant mutinies. Do you remember that of Pugachev?"

Stroganov ended his speech by quoting Radishchev's words, "Oh strange law of our land! Your wisdom exists too often in your words alone! Is this not an open mockery? And worse, is it not a mockery of the sacred name of liberty. If only the serfs, crushed by their heavy bonds, inflamed by despair, were to smash our heads, the heads of their cruel masters, with the shackles that hinder their freedom, and cover their fields with our blood! What would the country lose thereby? Soon from their midst would arise great men to replace the slain generation. This is no fantasy. My gaze pierces the thick veil of time which hides the future from our eyes. Let this barbarous bond of serfdom vanish forever!"

★ ★ ★

Stroganov's speech profoundly shocked the other members of the committee. After a moment of deep silence, a long stormy discussion ensued, lasting well beyond midnight. Again Stroganov was the most outspoken of the group.

"While we are not yet ready to debate the Constitution and establish a Bill of Rights, similar to that which the recently free North American colonies voted for their people, or something resembling the French Declaration of the Rights of Man, thousands of our serfs suffer in degrading misery. While we wine, dine and discuss endlessly, thousands of 'souls' are sold and bought like cattle. Even old serfs who have served on one estate for several generations are separated from their families and sold to other squires. Serfs, accused often of imaginary crimes, are judged and punished by their masters with no recourse to law. Some of them linger in the mines of Siberia for alleged crimes or even small misdemeanors. The great majority of landowners accept the system from which they benefit or, if they deplore its abuses, persuade themselves that any changes might threaten the very foundations of the social order. That is why they call the peasant lazy, arrogant, and rebellious. I would like to give you a few examples of the way many of our landowners treat their serfs."

While speaking these words, Stroganov brandished a packet of newspapers which he had taken from his pocket, and began to read an advertisement: "For sale, a fine girl, 18-years-old, can dress hair and has been taught everything she needs to know; moreover she is very pretty; in assurance, thereof, she can be given to a prospective buyer for three days' inspection; inquiries can be made on the St. Petersburg side near the Sytny Market opposite Piskunov's public house at the corner."

Despite the shouts of Novosiltsev and Kochubey, "This is illegal! This has been forbidden by Tsar Paul," Stroganov continued his harangue. "It is illegal but it is widely practiced. I have in my desk many more such examples, collected at random, but I don't wish to bore you by quoting them further. You know for yourself the real situation of our peasants, whom some want to proclaim 'citizens' by issuing another piece of paper that you call Charter of the Russian People. This is mockery! This is hypocrisy! Its sponsors thirst for personal power, for oligarchic power for their clique and not the Russian people. While complete abolition of serfdom requires a great deal of study and preparation, and may take years, we ought to limit its worst and most shocking abuses as much as possible. We should proceed immediately! The first measure I propose is to grant the peasants inviolability of their personal, private property, including their cattle and implements, so often arbitrarily confiscated by their master. The second immediate decree should be to forbid buying and selling of peasants, and to allow them to marry without permission of the master. The third urgent measure is to enforce effectively the late Emperor's decree limiting the serf's work on the master's land to three days per week, with no work on Sundays and holy days. These are most urgent steps, to be taken at once. Meanwhile a commission of legal experts should be set up to prepare total emancipation of the serfs from their barbarous bondage. Let us petition our august Emperor to appoint such a commission as soon as possible."

Exhausted, Stroganov stopped, sat down, took a lace-trimmed handkerchief from his pocket and wiped his sweat-covered forehead. His speech made a profound impression on the members of the Committee. The tension thus created was somewhat relieved by servants who, on Alexander's order, served brandy. After a brief exchange of views among his colleagues, Stroganov resumed his argument. "We are all hypocrites, alas. We speak refined French, wear English fashions, listen to Italian operas, and in so doing we pretend to be civilized Europeans. But toward our peasants we behave like barbarians. Our practice differs so much from our laws. Take, for instance, the institution of torture, that shame of our country. Despite its abolition by the Empress Catherine, it is still being practiced on a large scale by our police." Turning toward Alexander, Stroganov challenged him, "Abolition of torture ought to be finally enforced under your enlightened rule, Sire! This and the emancipation of serfs would mark your reign with eternal glory!"

After a break it was Czartoryski's turn. He spoke more calmly but with equal firmness. "I basically agree with the speech of my friend, Count Stroganov. Serfdom is an anachronism. Our final objective should be to turn the present-day serfs into free, rent-paying tenants working on their masters' land, as in England for instance. But I think it would take not years, but generations, to achieve such a goal. I advise caution, prudence. We have to bear in mind that Russia is like a large ship. It takes a long time to build up speed and a still longer time to turn her around without capsizing the huge vessel."

Novosiltsev and Kochubey applauded the argument of Czartoryski, who acknowledged this and then continued, "Before emancipating our peasants we must educate them for freedom. Our problem is how to turn illiterate serfs into responsible, enlightened citizens. An enormous, and lengthy task. To responsibly exercise political rights and to wisely discharge the obligations implicit in free citizenship, one must be prepared, which means one must be properly schooled. People who can neither read nor write cannot act as responsible citizens. Therefore, while agreeing with my friend's proposed measures limiting serfdom, I would suggest, first of all, that we focus our attention on public education. Our most immediate task should be widespread education. I mean education starting with primary parochial schools. How many do we have now? I don't know. The same with advanced schools. If we are to believe our bureaucrats, we have only twenty or thirty and one truly Russian university, that of Moscow. Here, of course, I don't count the institutions of higher learning existing at the fringes of the Empire, in the Baltic and Polish-Lithuanian lands, for instance the University of Vilna or that of Riga. But these institutions are patronized mostly by the German, Polish and Lithuanian youth, not by the Russians. Yet, to properly administer this huge Empire, to provide it with well trained officials, we have to have more Russian schools and more Russian universities. Moreover we must broaden access to our advanced and academic schools, now available only to noblemen. What about our merchants, what about the Jews?"

Kochubey supported Czartoryski's argument and raised another issue, that of modernizing the bureaucracy. "Besides being better educated, our officials and teachers should be better paid. Their miserably low salaries are one of the sources of corruption. Everybody steals or, at least, receives bribes, and the dividing line is very, very thin. How can you rule a country where there are practically no honest, reliable officials? As a matter of fact, dishonesty and financial irresponsibility filter down from the top. The verbs most conjugated at the Court are 'to borrow' and 'to be in debt.'

I am in debt
Thou art in debt
He is in debt
We are in debt
You, Ye are in debt
They are in debt.

If our dignitaries, mostly people with immense fortunes, act in such a lighthearted way, what can you expect from underpaid petty officials who can barely make ends meet on their meager salaries?"

Discussion on the three topics, serfdom, bureaucracy and education, went on until the early hours and was resumed at the next meeting. In fact, endless debates continued for about two years, with limited results. Education and bureaucracy were easier to deal with and attention was, therefore, focused on them. The highly controversial problem of the abolition of serfdom was repeatedly neglected.

Some details of the Committee's deliberations leaked out and created a great deal of controversy and opposition, especially among the conservative members of the Russian political elite. The poet Gabriel Derzhavin and the historian Nicholas Karamzin protested against the idea of altering even slightly the traditional social structure. Liberalism and autocracy are incompatible bedfellows, Karamzin maintained. For Russia autocracy was like religious dogma; its abandonment would spell her ruin. People like Stroganov or Kochubey, let alone the foreigner Czartoryski, Karamzin argued indignantly, were so alienated from their native country that they should be treated as strangers and not allowed to direct its course. "They know Russia as well as an educated well-to-do Russian knows Paris," he declared contemptuously. He also objected to the plan to admit Jews to Russian public schools. This had been forbidden by Catherine and the measure should stand.

Czartoryski was the chief target of Karamzin's vituperations. Karamzin considered him a dangerous man, a representative of a recently conquered enemy nation, a "Jesuitic hypocrite, a treacherous papist." His very presence among the governmental elite of St. Petersburg was regarded as a provocation to Russian patriotic sentiments. Karamzin was supported by Prince Peter Dolgoruky, who maintained that Czartoryski was "the most hated man in Russia." As Dolgoruky once remarked, "The proper place for such people is Siberia and not St. Petersburg."

★ ★ ★

Of course, the masses of the Russian people were not aware of the Secret Committee's meetings, let alone the details of its deliberations and the controversy that surrounded the debate among the intellectuals. Most of the subjects of the Tsar were too preoccupied with their daily chores, with bare survival, to be bothered with rheoretical discussions which they didn't understand anyway. They also missed the spectacular parades so often staged by the late Tsar Paul. Consequently, when in September 1801, the twenty-four-year-old Alexander rode in great style to his coronation at the Moscow Kremlin, he was greeted with enthusiasm by the masses of people. By that time, his popularity was beyond a doubt. Here was a young, handsome prince, riding a gilded coach, surrounded by his brilliant Chevalier Guards—men in shining helmets and breastplates, mounted on splendid, prancing horses. What a spectacle!

Alexander and Elizabeth were robed in traditional vestments of gold brocade. The Metropolitan of Moscow, Platon, presided over the ceremony with great dignity. He handed the Imperial crown to Alexander. The young Tsar held it for a moment and placed it firmly on his head. Alexander next crowned Elizabeth and then both received the Metropolitan's blessing. The couple returned to the throne to accept homage from the members of the Imperial family and high dignitaries. Finally Alexander was formally presented to the people by the Metropolitan. At once the bells of the Kremlin towers and the ceremonial roar of a twenty-one-gun salute announced to Moscow and all the surrounding countryside that Alexander was, indeed, the crowned Emperor and Autocrat of all the Russias—Great, Little and White, European and Asiatic—and that the Tsar, the Father, was marrying Mother Russia.

On the evening of the coronation there were fireworks and illuminations, banquets for a thousand guests, a huge open-air feast for the townfolk, plays, concerts and military parades. After the most solemn part of the coronation ceremony was safely over, Alexander's spirits and self-confidence began to rise. His good humor spread to his attendants and friends. The future looked bright. The country was at peace and reform seemed to be within reach.

CHAPTER 7

From Domestic Reform to Foreign Adventures

On his return from Moscow, Alexander sought to continue his collaborative efforts with his liberal friends, although his sentimental liberalism began to ebb somewhat. His lofty ideas were not dismissed at once. They were, however, considerably modified by the harsh realities of everyday life and by all sorts of diversions. He became aware of the obstacles which fundamental changes would encounter in a tradition-bound society, burdened by the inertia of its bureaucratic establishment. Conscious of the frightening extent of his tasks, he was like a man who preferred to amuse himself with the diversions of childhood, but must leave his favorite recreations and return to the tasks of adult life.

Nevertheless, a few issues raised by the Committee were cautiously acted upon. For instance, in December 1801, Alexander decreed that landed property could be acquired not only by the gentry and the merchants, but by any legally free person, even by Crown peasants. The serfs of the Baltic provinces gradually became free tenants. Another important result of the Secret Committee's work was the reform of the central administration.

Hitherto, it had been in the hands of collegial boards established by Peter the Great. They were unwieldy, costly and inefficient, torn by personal rivalries and red tape that often paralyzed them. In September 1802, Alexander replaced these collegial bodies with seven ministries, each headed by an individual who was personally responsible to the Emperor. These were the Ministries of Interior, Foreign Affairs, War, Navy, Education, Finance and Justice. Later, a Ministry of Police was added. Nevertheless, Alexander was reluctant to follow the Committee's recommendations for establishing a central executive body, which could evolve into a cabinet and would share responsibility with the sovereign.

Another field in which some real progress was achieved was education. Alexander fully agreed with Czartoryski and Kochubey that, before any constitutional charter could be proclaimed, people had to be educated. That is why Alexander promoted schools on all levels: primary, advanced and university. An Institute of Pedagogy was founded in St. Petersburg; later it became a university. Six other academic institutions and over forty new advanced schools were founded in Russia under his rule.

Alexander's serious work was frequently interrupted by his active social life and his military preoccupations: parades, inspections, maneuvers. There were also some frivolous and surprising incidents. One morning he was dressing to attend the mid-day changing of the guard. The uniform included white elk-skin breeches, and it was essential that they be very tight and have not the slightest crease. To this end they were dampened before being put on. The operation called for the help of at least two vigorous servants. In the midst of this tricky operation, there was a sudden knock at the door. An obviously embarrassed Peter Volkonsky entered the room.

"I beg your indulgence, Sire, but a sensitive situation requires Your personal intervention. The Chief of Police has just reported that His Highness, Grand Duke Constantine, is roaming the public garden dressed in his general's uniform minus his breeches. He hides in the bushes and when young ladies pass by, he jumps out and shocks them by exposing himself. His status and his dignity prevent the police chief from arresting him. What shall we do? What is Your order, Sire?"

"I see that my brother is saving a lot of time not struggling, as I do now, with these tight breeches. Now I realize that before reforming Russia, I must reform my brother first of all. What a bizarre man he is! No wonder that his wife despised him. We will have to find him another spouse, not an easy task. While some people are occasionally shocked when caught with their pants down, Kostya likes to shock."

"What is your order, Sire?" asked Volkonsky impatiently.

"Peter, convey to my brother my order to retire to his apartment at once. Here is my cape. Take one of my carriages and this cape to cover him while you take him home."

⋆ ⋆ ⋆

After his return from the coronation ceremonies Alexander also became increasingly involved in the social life of the capital. Under his father, all court functions, including official balls and state dinners, were dangerous affairs because of Paul's rigidity as to proper etiquette and dress. Not only drills and parades but also court functions and festivals were arenas where each man risked his position and even his liberty. All who approached Tsar Paul were in fear of being addressed by the irascible Tsar with some insulting word. Paul had consistently fancied that sufficient respect was not shown to his person. No one was sure that he would retain his status by the end of an evening.

Alexander was resolved to project a new image of the Emperor, not as a tyrant but as a benevolent, enlightened ruler. And indeed, the first years of his reign seemed promising. Both his look and his manner radiated serenity, grace and good will. Unlike his ugly father, he was physically very attractive—tall, blond and majestic. He had a classic forehead and bright blue eyes which gave him the appearance of amiable simplicity. He wore no jewelry and was the first Tsar to dispense with imperial pomp. He was invariably courteous in his dealings with people. He liked to wander among his guests and patterned his behavior on that of an ordinary gentleman. He often used such phrases as, "Will you permit me to remark," "I beg to be excused," or "I hope you don't mind if I disagree with you." With ladies he was consistently gallant, bowing to them while asking, "May I have the honor of dancing with you?" He would kiss their hands while thanking them for a dance or for helping him with a dish. He could charm anyone when he wished to.

Until Alexander's coronation, a strict mourning was observed by the Court. But after his return from Moscow, he decided to relax the strict rules of official mourning, and to revive the social life of the capital. The 1802 St. Petersburg season started on New Year's Day with a reception at the Winter Palace, given by the Emperor for the diplomatic corps. This gala was held in the vast St. George Hall, decorated with marble Corinthian columns and six huge chandeliers. There, Alexander, seated on his red and gold throne with the Imperial coat of arms embroidered on the velvet tapestry behind him, received the good wishes of the assembled representatives of foreign powers. Thereafter, until the beginning of Lent, elegant society moved through a whirl of balls, concerts, banquets and private parties.

Alexander sponsored two balls. At the White Ball, unmarried girls between the ages of fifteen and eighteen were introduced to society. Dressed in white, the debutantes were accompanied by their sweethearts or friends, but carefully watched by vigilant chaperons, usually mothers, aunts or older cousins. While the young people were enjoying themselves, their chaperons sat on the sofas and chairs arranged along the walls of the ballroom and gossiped, exchanging the latest court rumors and spinning intrigues. Meanwhile the young couples swirled until the early hours of the morning, enjoying quadrilles, and Russian, Hungarian and Polish dances and even the waltz, hitherto considered as "lascivious," but now accepted by polite society.

The second great occasion of the season was the Pink Ball for married couples. The Winter Palace was the setting for both balls, with most of its 1,100 rooms opened to as many as 2,000 guests. The grand palace was furnished with art treasures, mirrors, chandeliers, paintings, Persian rugs, and mahogany and rosewood furniture upholstered in fine silks. The Golden Hall was walled with mosaics in the Byzantine style, the splendid Malachite Room decorated with marble columns and tables and huge urns of rich green malachite. The ballroom stretched 200 feet long and sixty feet wide, with shining floors reflecting a myriad of candles. For very important events the hall was decorated with huge jardinieres of laurels and rhododendron, a profusion of flowers in porcelain and silver basins, and baskets of orchids. Invitations to both balls were most coveted and a summons to one of them was considered a great honor, an indication of high social status.

Through the halls of the Winter Palace, an army of lackeys silently moved—all in court livery—knee breeches, powdered wigs, white stockings and silver-buckled patent leather shoes. Along the Grand Staircase with its enormous columns and steps of Carrara marble stood troopers of the Chevalier Guards with gleaming silver breastplates and helmets topped by double eagles. At the top of the Grand Staircase, at the main door, stood two crimson-turbaned oriental servants, whose function was to open the doors to the entering dignitaries while the Master of Ceremonies grandly announced their names and titles.

★ ★ ★

A court ball usually began at 9 P.M., when the Master of the Court appeared and tapped the floor three times with his cane crowned with the golden imperial double eagle. The tapping brought immediate silence. The Master called out, "Ladies and gentlemen, Their Imperial Majesties!" The main doors opened and an imposing procession began. First came the Grand Master and Mistress of the Imperial households, followed by the Emperor and the Empress, who were accompanied by their suite and their pages. Then followed the Grand Dukes and Duchesses in order of seniority. During this time, the national anthem was played by a military band.

The dress rules were strict. For all official ceremonies, the ladies of the court had to wear court dress. Over a white silk or satin underskirt with gold braid or embroidery around the hem and down the front, the body and train of the dress were of crimson, green or blue velvet embroidered in silver and gold. Hair was coiffed low and caught in a net of gold. Over it was worn the traditional Russian diadem of matching velvet, richly embroidered and studded with jewels, from which draped a veil of tulle or lace over the shoulders. The Empress and the Grand Duchesses wore the same costume, only more lavishly decorated, and with a longer train sewn with diamonds or pearls. For less formal receptions, the ladies wore low-cut gossamer-light dresses of their own choice, and flat-heeled slippers. While there were some civilian guests at the balls, most of those attending were from the military and were in uniforms of one sort or another.

In the main dance hall were two projecting balconies where two orchestras alternately played. Court balls always opened with a polonaise. This was actually not so much a dance as a promenade, a graceful procession of exquisite dignity. The participants formed two lines, leaving an aisle down the middle of the ballroom. Then the orchestra played a slow, majestic tune and the promenade would begin, led by Alexander and Elizabeth. As the cortege proceeded, each gentleman offered his hand to the lady of his choice, and couple after couple joined the march. Gradually the dancing couples formed a brilliant kaleidoscope, constantly changing in colors and shape. They made a tour of the hall, and returning, formed again, first a double and then a quadruple line. Then the ladies, dipping their heads, passed under the raised arms of the men. Following the polonaise came quadrilles, cotillions, waltzes and the vivacious, imaginative mazurkas, bold, lively dances with intricate, swift yet smooth sliding footwork! In mazurkas improvisation played as great a role as the established rules. Alexander, who liked the dance very much, used to say, "Show me how you dance the mazurka and I will tell you what kind of person you are."

About 11 P.M., the Emperor led the way into the dining rooms where tables were set for supper. As the Imperial couple stepped over the threshold, innumerable candles were lighted. At supper, the Emperor and Empress, and the Grand Dukes and Duchesses, seated themselves at a large table on a dais. Towering above the gilded Imperial armchairs were enormous sprays of camellias and roses. Other tables were laid around the base of palm trees or rhododendrons brought from the hothouses of Tsarskoe Selo. Many servants walked up and down the dais serving delicacies. As many as a thousand people were seated at such suppers, at fifty or sixty tables set in the rooms adjoining the main dining hall. On all the tables were great vases of elaborate floral arrangements and silver candelabras. The menus were an epicurian delight. As many as twelve courses were served, including fish, fowl and various roast meats, all accompanied by choice wines. In addition to imported liqueurs, domestic vodka and Crimean and Caucasian wines were also offered. The gold and silver lustre of ornate salt cellars, forks, knives and spoons shimmered in the light from the crystal chandeliers. In several rooms adjacent to the dining hall round tables were laden with desserts, tea, champagne, lemonade and cakes. Throughout the night, ices in the shape and color of fruits were served by the liveried servants. The great Court balls lasted until 7 or 8 in the morning, and ended with a white mazurka, so called because it was danced in broad daylight. Even before that traditional dance, most guests were exhausted, but to leave the ball earlier was regarded as bad manners or evidence of lack of stamina.

Other kinds of entertainment were the Court masquerade balls arranged just before the Lenten season. Again the main halls of the Winter Palace were opened to accommodate the guests. The masquerade began at six in the evening and continued till the next morning. Many of those invited wore fancy costumes or elaborate masks. For the first of these masquerade balls, Alexander wore a Grecian costume that represented Zeus, while Elizabeth was dressed as Pallas Athena. The couple and group dances were interspersed with Italian chamber music. After midnight, Cossack, Tartar, Circassian and Gypsy dances were performed by folk ensembles in native dress.

Like the orgiastic Roman Saturnalia, the last days of the Carnival were a real pandemonium, as if to make up for the coming lean and austere Lenten season enforced by the Orthodox Church. Even the frivolous courtiers had to submit to these traditional rigors. Wearing their finest jewels, wealthy members of the society rushed to countless lunches, dinners and balls. The theaters performed morning and evening. After Ash Wednesday, however, all such affairs came to a halt. School was suspended and public offices closed. The seven-week Lenten fast was the most important fast of the year and was, on the whole, strictly observed, though often reluctantly. No meat of any kind, nor eggs, butter or sugar were permitted. Instead, rich and poor alike subsisted on black bread, mushrooms, cabbage, fish, potatoes, and tea or coffee with milk. The most devout excluded even fish in the first and last weeks and ate nothing at all on Wednesday and Friday of those weeks before Easter.

★ ★ ★

Another significant aspect of the life of St. Petersburg were military parades. Like his father, Alexander paid a great deal of attention to drilling and reviewing his troops. But, unlike Paul, he was not obsessed with parades, and reduced somewhat the scale and frequency of military displays. Every day, there was, of course, a routine changing of the guard; at noon, a fresh batallion of infantry or a cavalry regiment marched through the city, with banners flying and bands playing, to take over the sentinel duties at the Imperial palaces and other important public buildings, such as the ministries and the Admiralty at the Senate Square. This spectacle was a daily routine. But, from time to time, on special occasions, such as the anniversaries of the great victories or on his name's day, Alexander solemnly reviewed his troops on a grand scale. The Field of Mars or the Senate Square were the usual choices for these grand parades. The parades provided free entertainment and most of the capital's population crowded to watch them. Elegant coats and dresses of the nobility and prosperous burghers mingled with the red, blue and yellow skirts and scarves of peasant girls and the caftans of coachmen and poorer merchants, craftsmen and servants.

The most spectacular parade was staged on May 28, 1803, (or May 16 of the old Julian calender) when the city of St. Petersburg celebrated the centennial of its founding. The celebration began with a solemn religious service at the Cathedral of SS. Peter and Paul. Then the Tsar went to the Senate Square. Tall and impressive, he stood next to the equestrian monument of the city's founder, Peter the Great, surrounded by dignitaries and his equestrian officers. The national anthem was played by the massed military bands. Then the Emperor rode past the troops. The soldiers crisply presented arms and the spectators uncovered their heads. The Emperor greeted each unit with the traditional words, "Good day, my lads! Good health to you!" The soldiers replied with the regulation answer, "We wish good health to Your Imperial Majesty!" Then, accompanied by martial music and the stirring ruffles of drums and trumpets, thousands of men lined up in rows, proceeded to march; lances and bayonets were shining in the sun, pennants were fluttering in the wind. It was a magnificent spectacle.

The public's favorite was the cavalry. The parade was led by two regiments of Cossack Guards, one in blue, the other in red uniforms. All wore low boots and high sheepskin hats from which hung long, ornamented tassels. The Cossacks were followed by the Chevalier Guards, who surpassed everyone, even the Horse Guards, with their splendid attire and martial looks. The Chevaliers were dressed in white uniforms and red capes. Their tight jackets gave them a wasp-waisted look and they had high, stiff, patent leather jackboots and silver breastplates as well as helmets surmounted by a shining double edge. They trotted by on their gray chargers, their sabers glinting in the sunlight. The lancers wore blue jackets with red facing, while the hussars draped over their shoulders their fur trimmed scarlet pelisses, embroidered in gold. Drums rattled. The infantry batallions marched past like robots, the sharp steel tips of their bayonets glimmering in the sun like reflecting mirrors, while the regimental bands, each in turn, played exhilarating martial music. Batallions of engineers followed. Finally came the crunch and scrape of both heavy and light batteries of canons rumbling over the cobblestone, followed by the horse artillery with their shiny brass caissons. They were greeted with a fresh outburst of stormy applause, and shouts of "Long live our brave artillery men! Hurrah, hurrah, hurrah!" After the parade the Emperor again rode past the troops and cried, "Thank you, my lads!" Again the thunderous reply bursting from a thousand throats was, "We thank Your Imperial Majesty."

The May 28, 1803, parade was a memorable, splendid display of Russia's military might. Such spectacles, on a smaller scale, were repeated at least a dozen times a year. They provided welcome entertainment for the populace, while keeping their patriotic pride alive and their thirst for pagentry satisfied.

* * *

Though occupied with military matters and affairs of state, Alexander never neglected affairs of the heart. The supportive, cool-headed attitude of Elizabeth during the horrible March days of 1801 cemented their friendship. They continued to attend most of the formal functions together and she became his confidante in important matters; a tender brother and sister-like friendship replaced marital intimacy. Elizabeth herself, occupied with her young lover, Gregory Ovechnikov, ignored Alexander's numerous infidelities, even those involving her own ladies-in-waiting. This strange, mutually agreed upon arrangement lasted for years.

While most of Alexander's affairs were fleeting, in 1804 he became involved in a serious romance. One evening, at a Pink Ball, Alexander was chatting with Czartoryski in a chamber adjacent to the main ballroom. The band was playing a mazurka, the sounds of which mingled with the murmur of a fountain occupying the center of the chamber. The talk suddenly stopped when Alexander noticed two ladies leave the ballroom and pass through the chamber. One of them was a young girl, another a woman in her late twenties. Seeing the Emperor, they made deep curtsies and exited hurriedly. Both were elegant and very refined, but Alexander was instantly attracted to the more mature of the two. Her statuesque slender figure, her marble-white shoulders revealed by a low-cut gown, her mass of black hair and dark eyes at once fascinated him. He asked Czartoryski who she was.

"The woman with the black hair is the wife of Dmitri Lvovich Naryshkin, Your Majesty's Great Huntsman. She was born Princess Maria Sviatopolk-Czetwertynski. Her father was hanged in 1794 by a Polish revolutionary mob because he belonged to the pro-Russian faction opposing the new 1791 Constitution." Then Prince Adam added casually, "The Czetwertynskis, like the Czartoryskis, are both princes of Lithuanian origin, descendants of Gedymin, Grand Duke of Lithuania, and of his son and successor. Olgierd. We are distant cousins."

Alexander was so impressed with Maria Naryshkin that, at the next Court reception, he approached her and said directly, "Madame, I was so struck by your charm and beauty at the Pink Ball that I have reproached myself for not taking the opportunity to meet you earlier. Could I see you more often in greater privacy?"

Flattering words slipped off Alexander's lips like water from the leaves of waterlilies, but his directness obviously surprised Maria. Wrinkling her brow and fluttering her long black lashes, pretending to be offended by Alexander's directness, Maria haughtily answered. "My husband and I would be most honored to have Your Imperial Majesty attend any of our musical evenings. During the winter we receive at our residence at Fontanka every Wednesday at six. Dinner follows our concerts. During the summer, also on Wednesdays, we entertain at our villa on Stony Island."

Alexander was greatly disappointed by this formally correct, but rather cold reply. Thus far, his experience with women was one-sided. His marriage had been arranged in the old patriarchal tradition. With Marusha, Mademoiselle Chevalier and other actresses, as well as ladies of the Court, he was not the hunter but the hunted, not the predator but the prey. It was enough to approach one of his wife's ladies-in-waiting, pay her a few standard compliments on her good looks, and express his desire to see her "more often," and she would curtsy and whisper, "I am your Majesty's humble servant." In more private encounters, many Russian ladies would fall to their knees and say, "I am your slave. I am all yours."

Maria was the first woman who seemed unimpressed by his position and not attentive to him as a man. "How odd, how unusual," he thought. "What shall I do?" He had no experience in the art of seduction. But from innumerable French romantic novels that he had devoured, Alexander had learned that no woman can resist indefinitely a well calculated onslaught of gallant compliments and properly chosen gifts from a young, good looking man. Yet he considered that, in the case of a proud Polish lady, he had to be very tactful, astute, and patient.

So every Wednesday evening at about six o'clock, the Naryshkin residence at Fontanka, situated on the canal of the same name, would witness a recurrent event. A huge, shiny, black carrige, with plate-glass windows and ornaments of brass around the cornice, driven by four gray horses, would draw up to the entrance. Two lackeys, in court livery, would jump off the footboard, let down the steps of the carriage and assist its occupants out, while respectfully raising their three-cornered hats with their left hands. Civilian passersby stopped, bowed and removed their caps, while officers stood at attention and saluted. The lackeys, bowing subserviently, conducted their master to the entrance, opened the door wide as he entered the mansion. Behind Alexander marched Peter Volkonsky, carrying a huge basket of orchids or roses and a box of chocolates. Such visits were repeated for several weeks. Alas, all in vain.

For Alexander, who was hard of hearing, the musical concerts were ordeals he could barely endure. The only redeeming feature was that, being seated in a comfortable soft chair in the first row, he could doze discreetly and thus rest a little from his busy official schedule. Charmed by Maria, he was ready to put up with all sorts of inconveniences to be near her. The dinners that were served after the concerts gave him an opportunity to chat with the hostess. He paid her compliments not only on the high quality of her musical program, but, above all, on the classical symmetry of her features and her charm. Maria was too clever not to notice the mesmerizing effect she had on Alexander. But all his advances and efforts to arrange for a secluded rendezvous were rejected politely but firmly.

"Your Majesty forgets that I am a happily married woman. Do you want me, Sire, to be another of your numerous courtesans or concubines, like Mademoiselle Chevalier or those loose actresses and ladies-in-waiting at the Court?"

As Maria continued her stubborn and haughty attitude, Alexander's exasperated passion grew ever stronger and eventually became an obsession. He persisted in his courtship, applying all his remarkable theatrical aptitude, every imaginable trick of dissembling and simulation. After several months of systematically devised stratagems, he began to feel that some sort of obscure bond of affection, some unspoken link, began to develop between him and Maria. Could Maria really be quite so immune to the compliments and adoration of a young, attractive man and the most powerful monarch of Europe? Was Maria's haughtiness real or merely contrived? Was there some mysterious inhibition that made her deny him those moments of tender intimacy that, since the beginning of time, daring and enterprising young males were supposed to enjoy with attractive women?

The more Alexander pondered these puzzling questions, the more he became convinced that the game of seduction involved not only skill and astuteness but also a great deal of patience. Didn't the perennial battle of the sexes consist of a persistent match of two cunning, adversarial wits squared against each other, watchfully waiting for the proper moment to reveal their real intentions?

And indeed the long expected moment came suddenly after one of those seemingly interminable, boring musical evenings. During the dinner, while helping Alexander to the smoked salmon, Maria whispered, "Sire, I have just learned from a lady friend that my husband is unfaithful to me."

Alexander grasped her meaning immediately: "When may I see you alone?"

"Please come the day after tomorrow, late in the afternoon around four o'clock. My husband pretends to have a card party that day with his friends."

The eager Alexander arrived at Fontanka twenty minutes early. When he entered the drawing room and sought to proceed further toward the bedchamber, a fat, red-faced chambermaid tried to stop him, saying, "I beg your pardon, Sire, but the Countess is still in her bath."

Alexander brushed her aside, and, without knocking, entered. In a zinc bathtub shaped like a shoe was Maria. She shouted protests, ordering her guest to wait for her in the drawing room. Alexander ignored her protests. Eyeing her simple bathtub he said: "A Venus de Milo in a zinc bathtub? This is unworthy of even merchant women. For shame! I shall order you a luxurious bathtub from Italy, one made of white Carrara marble."

* * *

The love affair with Maria Naryshkin immediately absorbed much of Alexander's time and attention and became a serious drain on his work of reform. At first kept secret, the romance soon became public knowledge. For a year or so, at least two or three evenings a week, Alexander visited Maria, either at her Fontanka palace or at Stony Island. Before long the frequency of his visits increased and the two places became as much home to Alexander as the Winter Palace and Tsarskoe Selo. Eventually the lovers openly received foreign and domestic guests together, and officially entertained on a large scale. Having surrendered to Alexander's ardor, Maria enjoyed the romance. She was proud of her position as the chief mistress of the Tsar, and was determined to keep him attached to her as long as possible, perhaps forever. The fact that most courtiers began to pay more attention to her than to the Empress flattered her vanity and pride. While in public she preserved all the appearances and addressed her lover as "Your

Imperial Majesty;" in private she called him "my young Greek god" or simply "Sasha."

The romance with Maria did not prevent Alexander from occasionally frolicking with other ladies. As he said, "I love women too much to be satisfied with only one." Fortunately for Maria, Count Naryshkin proved to be an understanding husband, who privately admitted that he was highly honored by "the devotion and admiration that His Imperial Majesty bestowed on my lovely wife." Once he surprised Maria in the midst of a rather tender moment with Alexander. Closing the door of the bedroom into which he had unwittingly intruded, the tolerant husband admonished his wife most tactfully, "Madame, please! Be more careful! What if, instead of me, one of our servants had opened the door?"

Maria remained Alexander's official companion for more than fifteen years. The liaison of Alexander and Maria did not disturb Elizabeth unduly. She gracefully withdrew into the background and consoled herself with the discreet affection of numerous other men, mostly younger than she, such as Ovechnikov. Actually she was glad that her husband was involved with a distinguished but rather distant lady, rather than with one of her own ladies-in-waiting. Such affairs, carried out in her own milieu, were embarrassing to her, although she did tolerate these indiscretions.

Eventually, Maria bore three children to Alexander, two daughters and one son. The eldest daughter, Zinaida, died as a child, in June 1810. The second, Sophia, whom Alexander adored, and who inherited her mother's beauty, died of consumption at the age of seventeen in 1824. After each birth Elizabeth had congratulated Maria and sent her appropriate gifts.

Despite's Maria's intellectual limitations and her rather compulsive narcissism, Alexander, for many years, was seldom bored in her company. Realizing her inability to satisfy her lover's craving for an intellectually stimulating relationship, Maria tried to use her sense of dramatics to provide him with relaxing and entertaining companionship. Endowed with her statuesque figure, and certain inborn dramatic talent, she favored Greek or Roman-style dresses made for her by the best courtiers in Paris. Having discovered Alexander's strong interest in Greek mythology, she would appear one day dressed as Hera, another as Pallas Athene, still another time as a Bacchante or a nymph. She would often play the harp or flute. Her poses and gestures, the color and arrangement of her dresses, all were plotted to anticipate Alexander's mood. Adorned in rather transparent gowns and carefully draped cashmere shawls, she would let down her lovely, long, dark hair and perform well rehearsed dramatic scenes, serious or sad, playful and erotic. Being a born actress, she would amuse him with her dancing, singing or performing, whichever seemed to suit his capricious mood.

After the birth of the two daughters came the long-awaited son, Emmanuel. This increased Maria's pride and self-confidence beyond measure. A few weeks after her confinement, she unleashed a long-thought-out tirade on Alexander. Speaking with her strong French accent, she ranted: "Darling, as you see, Elizabeth is unable to provide you with a male heir. I can. Don't you want the crown to be inherited by your direct descendant? Look at Emmanuel, what a lovely Grand Duke and heir to the throne he would make. You should divorce Elizabeth and make me your legal wife, your Empress."

Alexander protested. "The Holy Synod would not agree to such a divorce. And then what should I do with Elizabeth. She is one of my best, most trusted friends. Would you have me send her back to Germany?"

"Couldn't you force those bearded bastards of the Holy Synod to grant you a formal divorce? After all, you are the head of the Orthodox Church. The bishops sat like dumb dogs when Peter the Great divorced his wife, despite the fact that she had borne him a son, Alexis. Why can't you confine Elizabeth to a nunnery?"

This was too much for Alexander. He exploded, "The Russian people would never, never tolerate a Polish woman on the throne again. Don't you know what happened two hundred years ago to Dmitry the Pretender and his Polish wife, Maryna Mniszek? Do you want to have me murdered while you and Emmanuel starve in a dungeon?" It took him a long while to calm down. Then he closed the subject saying, "I don't want this ever to be mentioned again. Ever!"

Yet, Alexander could not hide even from his wife the pride he felt in fatherhood. He acknowledged Emmanuel and reared him with paternal care and tenderness. Elizabeth accepted this with equanimity and again congratulated Maria on the birth of her son. Emmanuel grew to manhood and eventually held many high offices in Russian service.

★ ★ ★

Alexander's romance with Maria increasingly distracted him from his official duties. The sessions of the Secret Committee continued, although they became more infrequent as Alexander gradually disassociated himself from his youthful dreams of reform. He rejected various proposals of Stroganov for at least a partial emancipation of the serfs. On the other hand, Alexander accepted a measure by which landowners might voluntarily free their serfs, if they so desired. In March 1803, a decree allowed squires to sell freedom and land to serfs who could afford the price. Moreover, special law courts were set up to oversee the process and make sure that the price of emancipation was not exorbitant. The district Marshals of Nobility, as well as the local courts of law, were to testify that the terms of the agreement were negotiated freely and that the price was equitable. Moreover, Alexander vowed not to grant away any more Crown peasants into serfdom, as his grandmother and father had so often done. What was most significant was that he kept his promise.

Actually, from the time of his coronation, Alexander's attention was shifting from domestic matters to foreign affairs. At the time of Paul's death, the war of the Second Coalition against France, which had begun in 1799, was dragging its way to an inconclusive end. By the end of 1800, Napoleon's victories against the Austrians at Marengo and Hohenlinden reestablished his control over northern Italy. The humiliated Austrians were forced to again sue for peace. In the closing months of his reign, Paul was cooperating with Denmark, Sweden and Prussia to form the League of Armed Neutrality, a grouping of powers calculated to limit Britain's dominant position in the Baltic. But this alignment was short-lived. Five days after Paul's murder, British naval action destroyed most of the Danish fleet anchored at Copenhagen. The Baltic Straits, so vital to Russian trade, were under the control of the British Navy. Immediately after his accession to the throne, Alexander offered to reach a compromise agreement with London.

The Anglo-Russian Convention of June 1801, ended all hostilities in the Baltic and laid the groundwork for further negotiations. Alexander, however, did not trust Britain's intentions, and much that Bonaparte was achieving in post-revolutionary France appealed to his own political instincts. Provided Napoleon had no territorial ambitions in the vital areas of Central Europe, the Balkans or the eastern Mediterranean, Alexander could see no conflict of interest between France and Russia. By October 1801, a treaty formally restored peace between the two countries. The French recognized Russia's interest in the Levant and conceded the principle that Alexander should be consulted over any major reshaping of the territorial boundaries of the German states. When, a few days later, Panin was forced to retire to his estate and hand over responsibility for foreign affairs to Victor Kochubey, most people believed Russia would pursue a policy of external peace and internal reform, as did Kochubey. He underestimated, however, Alexander's growing ambition and thirst for glory.

On his return to St. Petersburg from the Moscow coronation, the Tsar received a letter from King Frederick William III of Prussia, an ally of Napoleon, proposing that the two monarchs meet at the Baltic port of Memel in Prussia, just across the Russian border, to discuss the affairs of Germany. Alexander accepted the invitation without informing his Foreign Minister. Understandably, Kochubey was angry, "Imagine a Minister for Foreign Affairs who is given no knowledge of such an escapade by his Monarch!"

Although Alexander had never met Frederick William, there had been a close cooperation between the royal families of Berlin and St. Petersburg since the division of Poland, which created a community of interest between the co-partitioning countries. Moreover, both were concerned with Napoleon's increasingly flagrant encroachments on the rights of several German states. Curiosity also played its role. Alexander had heard so much about Prussia that he was eager to see the country for himself. Moreover, Alexander, brought up by his father in the cult of glorification of everything Prussian, wondered about the merit of the army of Frederick William III. Was it still the army of Frederick the Great? On the other hand, Frederick William believed that the Tsar could have some influence on Napoleon because of the clause in the Franco-Russian treaty of the previous October which allowed joint mediation by both countries on the future of the German lands.

Alexander arrived at Memel on June 10, 1802, and spent nearly a week at the ancient Hanseatic port on the Baltic Sea, a former outpost of the Teutonic Knights. Memel held a special fascination for him. It was the first foreign town he had seen in his entire life. He was much impressed by the order and cleanliness of its streets and the solid look of its buildings. But the attraction of his visit was Queen Louise, the wife of his host. Then twenty-five, and thus a year his senior, she was a great beauty as well as a compulsive seductress. She combined a vivid intellect and strong will with an elegant, slender figure, delicate features, and magnetic charm. Would these have an effect on the exotic prince from the North? Queen Louise was determined to test her refined coquetry and her insatiable thirst for fascinating company. Her fatuous, pedantic husband was wearisome to her and she openly ignored him as an old bore.

Success came sooner than expected. At their first encounter, the Queen bewitched Alexander. He was captivated by her rare amalgam of intellectual brilliance and mature but radiant beauty. He enjoyed flirting with Louise, and she, for her part, was overwhelmed with admiration for his kindness and charm. She systematically flattered his vanity, calling him "my young Apollo" and "the most charming young gentleman I ever met." In a few days they had advanced far along the path of intimate friendship. Every evening there was a ball, and the Tsar danced with the Queen more than with any other lady. But the Arcadian nights did not crowd out the daily political discussions. Every morning the Tsar would ride out beside the King along the Baltic beaches, deep in serious conversation about the future of Europe.

Alexander was greatly impressed by all he saw around him, including the clean and orderly military barracks, and the solid municipal buildings, but most of all by the royal guard regiment marching and countermarching on the parade ground with the rigid precision which Paul and himself had vainly tried to impose on his soldiers.

After his return from Prussia, Alexander confessed to Volkonsky, "I found small, provincial Memel much superior to our own cities. The town is built for human beings to live in and not merely for ostentation and display of wealth, like our St. Petersburg. Even in the lower parts of the town the streets are paved. The Prussian villages are also attractive. The houses, though often small, are solid, tidy and well built. Everywhere in Prussia you find factories, and industry flourishes. The rivers are well regulated and alive with ships and other vessels. The German coaches have fine horses and the English carriages they use are excellent. One sees landscapes that, by their beauty, are not unworthy of the brush of the Dutch masters. I entertained the very highest opinion of Prussia and its people."

So pleased was Alexander with the attentions paid to him at Memel that he would certainly have championed Prussia's claims to leadership in Germany, had the First Consul been prepared to accept it. Yet, the consistent French military successes ensured that it would be Napoleon who would first draft any new frontiers of Central Europe. Moreover, the other German princes preferred to settle directly with the victorious Bonaparte. Consequently, "joint mediation" became a hollow phrase for what the French had already determined to impose on the Germans, while Russia had simply to accept the *fait accompli*.

* * *

Alexander's impromptu Prussian visit provided Kochubey with a valid pretext to resign his post as Minister of Foreign Affairs in the autumn of 1802. Alexander turned to Count Alexander Vorontsov, an ailing sexagenarian, to take over the post of Chancellor as well as that of Foreign Minister. Meanwhile, in March 1802, the Treaty of Amiens ended hostilities between Franch and Britain, while three months later peace was concluded between France and Turkey. For a few months Europe enjoyed a respite from war, the first time in a decade. The future seemed serene.

Vorontsov, like Nikita Panin, was an inveterate Anglophile. Both realized that Russia's economy depended on trade with Britain and on free passage through the Baltic Straits. That is why, despite his master's pro-French leaning, Vorontsov would rather have opted for a British connection. For the moment, however, he preferred to steer clear of foreign entanglements and declined to respond to tentative proposals from London for closer cooperation against Napoleon. Alexander shared Vorontsov's desire for peace but, while respecting Vorontsov, the Tsar preferred to work privately with his friend Czartoryski, whom he appointed as Vorontsov's deputy. That appointment was a risky move. Both the Tsar and Prince Adam were well aware of the hostility which the presence of a Pole in such a high position would arouse among many Russian dignitaries. What was objected to most was that Alexander was on more friendly and familiar terms with Czartoryski than with any of his Russian aides, with the exception of Peter Volkonsky, who remained the Tsar's most intimate and trusted friend.

Among Czartoryski's fiercest enemies was the proud and energetic Prince Peter Dolgoruky, descendant of one of Russia's oldest aristocratic families. As the Tsar's principal adjutant, he often attended meetings of the Council of State. One of the controversial points between them was the future of Russo-Prussian relations. Dolgoruky suspected the Pole of being anti-Prussian, as the lion's share of Poland was given to the Prussians by the Third Partition. Dolgoruky viewed as a risky proposition Czartoryski's suggestion of depriving the Prussians of their mastery of Central Poland, including Warsaw, in order to reestablish a Polish state in alliance or even in personal union with Russia. When Czartoryski tried to explain why it would be advantageous for Alexander to oppose Prussia's inordinate growth and her appetite for more Polish lands, Dolgoruky interrupted, "Please, Prince, may we hear rather less about these Polish affairs? Have you forgotten that you are still in the service of the Tsar of Russia? Are you still dreaming of rebuilding your old Poland?"

In his defiance of the Prince, Dolgoruky was not alone. Other Russian dignitaries, many of them of German origin, like most Baltic barons, publicly denounced Czartoryski as a potential traitor who could, at any moment, prove false to his duties in order to advance the cause of his native country. Everything in Prince Adam's behavior, his manners and even his meticulous dress, seemed an affront to his Russian critics. His reserve, his haughtiness, and his cool politeness were derided as "Jesuitic hypocrisy." "He pretends to serve us well in order to betray us more easily later on," Dolgoruky would say. "Honey on the tongue and ice under the tongue."

Czartoryski's numerous enemies were backed by the Empress Dowager, Maria, whose influence on Alexander increased after Paul's assassination. The young emperor, tormented by a sense of guilt, hardly found the moral courage to oppose many of his mother's requests, one of which was to dismiss Czartoryski immediately and send him packing to Poland. Here, however, Alexander took a firm stand and refused to give in. "My dear mother, his collaboration is indispensable to me. How am I to carry out my task of revitalizing Russia without the help of honest, hardworking and impartial people such as Adam?"

In addition to Czartoryski's nationality, his powerful, passionate and domineering personality was another factor that made him highly unpopular. A hard worker himself, he made his subordinates at the Ministry labor for longer hours than they were accustomed to under his permissive predecessors, often beyond the call of duty. Punctuality and meticulousness discharge of assigned tasks was strictly enforced by the Prince at the Ministry of Foreign Affairs. This shocked many high officials, most of whom were of aristocratic descent and regarded their posts at the Ministry as their privilege, a sinecure which should carry much prestige but little work. As an official, dismissed by Czartoryski for drunkenness and laziness, complained to his protector, Prince Peter Dolgoruky, "That damn Pole doesn't understand our open Slavic nature. He is haughty, secretive, hard as a rock and cunning as a snake. It is a shame our Tsar tolerates such an alien in such a sensitive post."

* * *

Initially, Alexander and most of his ministers were committed to an isolationist policy for the sake of peace. Yet, the problems of Germany and Italy, and the future of Malta—held since 1800 by the British but promised to be restored to the Knights of St. John—testified to the hollowness of the Treaty of Amiens. Even had he wished to do so, Alexander could not ignore the crisis precipitated by Napoleon's continual encroachments on the rights of the German princes, as well as the position of the Emperor in Vienna. All the while Napoleon ignored Russia's right to mediation in the German affairs. But when the details of the new German settlement were ready for presentation to Vienna, at the end of 1802, Napoleon found he needed Alexander's support in order to persuade the Habsburgs to accept such a diminution of their traditional rights as Holy Emperors of the Germanic Nation. Alexander, for his part, was prepared to follow the French lead, provided that Napoleon would treat generously those German principalities which had close dynastic links with Russia, such as Baden, the homeland of his wife. Napoleon was willing to offer Baden the towns of Heidelberg and Mannheim, and he also presented additional territory to Alexander's first cousin, Frederick of Würtemberg. But the First Council was not inclined to admit that the Tsar had any right to protect the interests of the King or Sardinia, nor to concern himself with the affairs of Switzerland, so dear to Alexander because of Laharpe. Moreover, the Russians continued to show what was to Napoleon a tiresome obsession with Malta. Since the Knights of St. John had conferred the Grand Mastership of their order on his father, Alexander claimed to be the rightful protector both of the Knights and their little island.

Britain tried to take full advantage of these Franco-Russian clashes of interests. London also opposed Napoleon's growing ambition in the eastern Mediterranean, and feared the consolidation of his domains, from which their goods were excluded by the continental blockade, resulting in a growing economic depression in England. At first, the Maltese question brought France and Russia closer together, for it was in both their interests to encourage Britain to evacuate the island. But in the first weeks of 1803, there were widespread reports of intrigues by French agents in the Levant and in the Balkan peninsula. The possibility that Napoleon might establish French hegemony in these regions which Russian regarded as her natural sphere of influence made Alexander modify his original attitude toward Malta. Better the British remain on the island than that it should become an advance French base, the jumping off spot for possible Napoleonic expansion into the Slavic Balkans.

When war was resumed between Britain and France in May 1803, Alexander accepted the fact that he might have to abandon Russian isolationist policy. Advised by Czartoryski to stand firm in defense of Russia's position in the areas adjacent to Russia, Central Europe and the Balkans, he was increasingly ready to pursue a vigorous line in foreign affairs. "Grasp the opportunity. Encourage formation of a league of European states, a European federation," urged Czartoryski. Yet the Tsar was uncertain how he should tame Napoleon, whether by friendly persuasion or by joining another coalition against him. Whatever the case, the Tsar wished to make sure that, should war come, the Russian army would be able to hold its own. Anticipating that sooner or later the drums would roll once more, Alexander resolved to prepare the Russian army for battle. On May 26, 1803, while appointing Arakcheyev Inspector General of Artillery, Alexander instructed him, "It will be your prime task to build up gunnery and establish effective systems of supply and command in that vital branch of our armed forces. If it comes to war, the formidable firepower of the French should be answered by our new, improved guns from the Tula arms works. Our cannons will be the most effective reply to Bonaparte's claim that he has the greatest artillery in the world."

CHAPTER 8

Austerlitz

The issue precipitating the break between St. Petersburg and Paris was the execution of the Duke of Enghien in the spring of 1804. Louis de Bourbon Condé, Duke of Enghien, was a nephew of Philippe, Duke of Orléans, who was head of the junior branch of the Bourbons. After the outbreak of the French revolution, the Duke of Orléans sided with its radical wing, renounced his title and assumed the name of citizen Egalité (Equality). When, during the Reign of Terror, his uncle was nevertheless executed, his son, Duc d'Enghien, joined a force of emigrés ready to fight for the royalist cause. With the declaration of peace of Amiens in 1801, the young Duke retired to Baden. In spite of the fact that he was quietly residing in neutral territory, early in 1804 he was seized by French agents on Napoleon's orders for alleged complicity in an anti-Bonaparte plot. He was brought to the fort of Vincennes near Paris, summarily tried by a court-martial, and shot as a traitor to France. On hearing the news, Alexander, whose wife Elizabeth was daughter of the Prince of Baden, became furious. He immediately denounced the crime, ordered his Court into mourning, and refused to receive the French ambassador.

Napoleon's reaction was not long in coming. Under the signature of his Foreign Minister Talleyrand, the First Consul inserted the following note in the official *Paris Monitor:* "When England mediated the assassination of Paul I, if the Russian government had known that the authors of the plot were not more than a league from the frontier, would it not have promptly seized them?" In this allusion to the death of his father, Alexander saw a personal insult and decided reprisals. The first was to break diplomatic relations with France. But what next? Alexander was torn between the need to continue his domestic reforms and the desire to take revenge on Napoleon, which meant costly war. "His soul has not yet acquired a definite color," noted Czartoryski of Alexander to his family in Poland. "It is all the colors of the rainbow, with amisty gray predominating. The idea of war weights upon his mind and torments him."

In a way his rival's behavior determined Alexander's action. On May 18, 1804, Napoleon proclaimed himself Emperor of the French. The coronation ceremony was full of symbolic innuendos. Pope Pius VII was forced by Napoleon to come from Rome to dignify the ceremony. Thus, what Leo III had refused Charlemagne, Pius VII consented to do for the son of a sacrilegious revolution. The majestic ritual of the coronation was spoiled by Napoleon, who snatched the Imperial crown from the trembling hands of the Pope and put it on his own head saying, "God has given it to me. Let he who touches it beware!"

To Alexander, the proclamation of Napoleon as Emperor was an intolerable offense, a challenge to the monarchical order of which he was a pillar. Correct relations with the head of the French Republic, General Bonaparte, could be tolerated, but that a revolutionary parvenu, a Corsican upstart, should appropriate the Imperial rank and put a crown on his head was for Alexander a profane masquerade. Upon learning of the coronation at Notre Dame, he exploded, "Napoleon will not be satisfied to reign over France. He will soon aspire to extend his rule over all of Europe. His aim is a universal empire. He is eager to be a new Caesar, as well as a new Charlemagne. Thus far there have been two emperors, a Habsburg in the West and a Romanov in the East. Europe is too small for a third."

As if to support Alexander's apprehension, Napoleon proceeded to Aix-la-Chapelle to kneel before the tomb of Charlemagne. There he seized the most precious relic of the basilica, a fragment of what was believed to be the cross of Calvary, set in a talisman of sapphire and gold, which Charlemage had received as a gift from the Caliph Haroun-al-Rashid. Then on May 26, 1805, in St. Ambrose Cathedral in Milan, Napoleon placed on his head another crown, the Lombard crown of Italy. It was called The Iron Crown because the Byzantine goldsmiths who had fashioned it in 625 for the Lombard kings had set upon it in a circle of enamel one of the nails which was reported to have pierced the hands of Jesus Christ on Golgotha. No one since Charles V had dared to wear the crown. Then, acting as the King of Italy, Napoleon presented to France the republics of Genoa, Venice and Tuscany, and the Papal States and the Kingdom of Naples.

"Where is he to stop? Master of all the Occident, he would next lay his hands on the Orient, on Constantinople, Georgia, Persia and India. He is insatiable! His ambition knows no bounds! We need no longer hope for any moderation from Bonaparte," said Alexander to Czartoryski. "We must therefore show him that 200 thousand Prussians, 200 thousand Russians and 300 thousand Austrians are ready to stop him. . . ."

In St. Petersburg, a council composed of all ministers and the chief military leaders began to analyze carefully the new international situation. Their *tour d'horizon,* however, was not too optimistic. "Although her King, George III is already on the verge of insanity, we can count only on Britain. Frederick William III of Prussia is Napoleon's ally, almost his satellite. Furthermore, he is a weakling, and he would give way at the slightest pressure from Paris; Francis II of Austria is obtuse and solemn, obsessed with the antiquated, Spanish court ceremonial. Actually he is a fool in full dress. Thus, our potential allies are imbecile puppets in the hands of inept ministers." Alexander thus summed up the reports of his advisors.

"Thank God King George has a brilliant Prime Minister, William Pitt," interjected Czartoryski. "Moreover, let's hope that

Chancellor Kaunitz left some pupils at the Austrian chancellery. And let us also hope that the Habsburgs understand that their position is endangered not only by Bonaparte's greed, but also by Prussia's ambition to rule Germany. . . ."

Indeed, the ceremonies that had taken place in Paris, Milan and at Aix-la-Chappelle alarmed Vienna more than any other capital. The fact that, after having usurped the Imperial Crown of France, Bonarparte added to it the crown of Lombardy, was a provocation for the Habsburgs. The Treaty of Luneville formally stipulated the independent status of the north Italian Cisalpine Republic. Moreover, Austria was eager to regain her position in Italy, though she had not yet recovered from her participation in the wars of the first two coalitions and from all the disasters which she had suffered since the French invasion of the Appenine Peninsula in 1796. Yet, the treasury in Vienna was empty and Austria was unable to reconstitute her shattered army. That is why, when Alexander suggested to Vienna that it should unite with him in taking measures against Bonaparte, a frank confession was heard from the Austrian Minister Kobentzel: "We are at the mouth of the French guns and we'll be blown to bits before you are able to save us!. . ."

However, what Kobentzel did not tell Alexander was that the Austrians remembered Suvorov's plundering and pillaging troops on their soil, and dreaded Russian aid almost as much as the French menace. Moreover, Kobentzel was not unaware of the gist of Czartoryski's memorandum on Russian foreign policy that suggested rebuilding of Poland in union with Russia. One of its copies had been sold to the Prussian ambassador in St. Petersburg by a Russian official. The Prussian, short of funds, traded it for 45,000 rubles to his Austrian colleagues. Kobentzel grasped the meaning of the memorandum. The idea of seizing on the impending conflagration in Europe as an opportunity to restore Poland, by reassembling under the scepter of the Romanovs all the provinces which had been appropriated by Empress Catherine, together with Frederick II and Maria Theresa, frightened Vienna almost as much as Berlin. Moreover, calculated Kobenzel, the Polish plan alienated Prussia, the main benefactor of the third partition of Poland and a potential member of the coalition. Prussia was then mistress not only of Danzing and Thorn, but also of Warsaw and a large chunk of central Poland. Consequently, Frederick William was puzzled and bewildered when Alexander sent a note that tried to lure him away from the association with France and attract him to the alliance then being formed against Napoleon. He whispered to his secretary, "Either Alexander is a fool or a hypocrite. Our alliance with France is the best shield of our security, of our intergrity. Czartoryski's plan is a deadly threat to the very existence of our state."

Perceiving the dangers of joining the shaky coalition against Napoleon, the awkward and timid King Frederick William took refuge in dilatory shifts and excuses. Despite repeated Russian pressure, he chose neutrality. He saw no incompatibility between French expansion and the existence of a strong Prussia that could profit from the further disintegration of the Habsburg Empire and acquisition of new territory in Germany. Yet Frederick William was somewhat ashamed of his subservience to Napoleon and tried to cover it with brave gestures. Drawing himself erect, he exclaimed to the Russian envoy in Berlin, "My principles are unshakable. I fear nobody. I await events with a firm heart!"

★ ★ ★

Having thus failed both in Berlin and Vienna, Alexander addressed himself to London, the perennial antagonist of France, now menaced by her not only in the Mediterranean but also on the continent, where Hanover, the hereditary principality of British monarchs, was theatened by Napoleon's renewed aggressiveness. For several months Britain had been relentlessly working at St. Petersburg and Vienna to get the two countries to confront France, dangling the spectacle of additional financial subsidies and more lucrative trade. Alexander hesitated and procrastinated, but Napoleon's expansive drive finally caused Alexander to view the British overtures with greater favor. After consulting Czartoryski, he decided to open negotiations with Britain. A secret diplomatic mission to London was entrusted to Novosiltsev, Alexander's secretary and Czartoryski's secret rival. What Novolsiltsev lacked in diplomatic experience, he made up for with his fertility of mind and aptitude for intrigue, which fully justified his nickname "Mr. Weathervane." No one could guess and better implement the real intentions of his master. At the end of October, 1804, Novolsiltsev was dispatched with detailed instructions based on Czartoryski's memorandum—a fundamental reconstruction of Europe, sponsored jointly by Russia and Britain, as the best way of containing Napoleon's expansive drive.

When Novosiltsev presented the plans to William Pitt, the Englishman was surprised and irritated. Instead of an offer of a straightforward military alliance against France, which he had expected, he saw a vague, idealistic scheme for redrawing the map of Europe, turning it into a loose confederation of States, and establishing an international body to mediate conflicts between its component members. Bored by Novosiltsev's long exposition, Pitt interrupted bluntly, "How many soldiers could you muster against Napoleon?"

"About 200,000 men." was the answer.

"What subsidy would you require to keep such an army fighting?"

"At least four million pounds per year."

"This is much too much. We can't afford it. We would grant you the utmost that the state of our finances allows us at this time, or some two million. As for the rest of your overambitious, chimeric plan, we would have enough time to examine these complex problems after the war. Do you wish to divide the skin of a bear that is still very much alive.?"

Then Pitt summoned his private secretary and ordered him to prepare for dictation of a draft of a treaty of alliance between Great Britain and Russia. The draft provided for a subsidy of two million pounds per year, allowing Russia to supply an army of at least 200,000 men to face the French forces in central Europe by late summer. Detailed military consultations between the two partners were to start at once. Czartoryski's plan for Europe was ignored altogether, as "a piece of daydreaming and visionary nonsense," as Pitt referred to it in private. The Anglo-Russian treaty was the nucleus of the Third Coalition against Napoleon. On August 9, 1805, Austria reluctantly acceded to the pact. Sweden, threatened in her vestigial Pomeranian possession by Napoleon's encroachments on North Germany, joined the coalition later on.

On paper, the military plans of the Third Coalition were spectacular. A four-pronged offensive was to be launched against France on land as well as on sea. In the Mediterranean, a Russian naval squadron was to cooperate with Admiral Nelson's fleet in his planned invasion of Naples, then a French dependency. On the northern flank, Swedish forces, reinforced by a Russian contingent of 20,000 men, were to operate from Pomerania against Stralsund. In central Europe, apart from the Austrian troops facing Italy, the main Habsburg army of 80,000 under General Mack was to march toward Ulm to threaten the French on the Rhine. At the same time, some 70,000 Russians were to reinforce the Austrians and bar Napoleon's road to Vienna.

Yet, soon after the signing of the treaty of alliance with Britain, Alexander had second thoughts. Following a careful review of the situation, he felt that he had flung himself, with a light heart and with inadequate resources, into a dangerous adventure. He had dreamed of leading a huge crusade for the fundamental reconstruction of Europe and now saw himself dragged into a war that had actually more to do with defense of Habsburg dominance in Germany and in British trade than with his original plans.

At the time his romance with Maria Naryshkin was in full bloom and he was reluctant to wrest himself from her arms and lead his forces to the Austrian lands. He suddenly became aware of how unprepared he was for a distant war. His army was essentially that which had been shaped by his father. It had been drilled by him for parades, not for actual fighting, certainly not for facing Napoleon's seasoned veterans on the field of battle. Armaments and supplies provided by the neglected Russian arsenals were deficient. Munitions, equipment, provisioning and transport were either lacking or insufficient.

There was also the problem of leadership. Who was to command the Russian contingent? From among the pupils of the great Suvorov, only the aging and ailing Michael Kutuzov remained. Count de Langeron, a French emigré in the Russian service who knew him intimately, drew the vignette: "No one could have more intelligence than Prince Kutuzov, and no one could have less character. No one could combine so much poise with so much astuteness. No one could display more talent and exhibit more depravity. A prodigious memory, extensive knowledge of military matters, powers of conversation, both agreeable and interesting—such are Kutuzov's good points. Extreme violence; a peasant-like coarseness when he is angry or when he has no need to fear the person he is addressing. He is the ablest of Suvorov's pupils."

It was true that Kutuzov did enjoy a great military reputation because of his past achievements. He had taken part in the Turkish wars in Catherine's reign and under Suvorov's command he had captured the fortresses of Ochakov and Ismail, but during these campaigns he was seriously wounded and lost an eye. Moreover, Kutuzov was already more than sixty years old, fat and ailing. The wounds of his previous campaigns left him exhausted, and occasionally made him inert and somnolent. He could barely mount a horse and traveled usually in a comfortable calash drawn by four horses. He walked with difficulty and had little stamina. Having displeased Alexander in the post of Governor General of Petersburg, for three years he had been living in the country with his mistress, a stout Moldavian peasant woman who dominated him completely and did not hesitate to berate him in the presence of others. Now, despite his advanced age and his numerous shortcomings, he was recalled to lead the Russian army.

★ ★ ★

On September 21, 1805, on a cold, misty morning. Alexander set out from St. Petersburg accompanied by his staff, including Czartoryski, who rode on horseback next to his master. Soon after they passed the city limits, lightning flashed across the murky sky. A heavy storm was approaching from the Gulf of Finland. Thunder rumbled on the horizon and heavy rain pelted the ground. "A bad omen," whispered an old Cossack captain from the Tsar's personal escort. He crossed himself three times. "A very bad omen. . . . We had better turn back. . . . This is no proper time to embark on such a devilishly risky venture. . . . A winter campaign in a strange land is a damn difficult enterprise. One should start a venture like this only at dawn on a sunny spring day after a new moon."

Czartoryski himself was filled with foreboding. In supporting Alexander's war plans, the Prince had hoped that his master would follow through on the Polish segment of the strategem. "If Pitt persisted in ignoring our total plan, so much the worse for Britain's long term position. But Russia must act, even if left alone," reasoned Prince Adam. "Our scheme was firmly agreed upon when I discussed with the Emperor my memorandum on the policy that Russia should follow; stop Napoleon's aggression, contain Prussia's cancerous growth, rebuild Poland in personal union with Russia and then reshape Europe along confederate lines."

And indeed, while his troops moved slowly through Poland on the way to Bohemia, Alexander seemed to remain firmly supportive of the Polish plan. He entered Puławy, the ancestral estate of Czartoryski on the middle Vistula. Prince Adam took great care to prepare the ground for the Emperor's visit. By the end of September 1805, the Puławy palace was crowded with that part of the Polish aristocracy who was willing to side with Russia, should Alexander turn against Prussia they would favor an armed resistance; oppressive Prussian rule over most of Poland constrasted with the fairly liberal administration of the provinces annexed by Russia. In his informal chats with the representatives of the leading Polish families,Alexander let it be known that, as soon as he subdued Bonaparte, he would restore Poland under his aegis, while preserving the existing social status quo. What he expected from the Poles was wholehearted support in the format of a national uprising against Prussia. He was so kind, charming and persuasive that few of the audience doubted his sincerity.

Polish landowners feared the radicalism embodied in Napoleon's code of laws. Equality of all citizens before the law and the abolition of serfdom was the last thing the serf-owning Polish nobility wanted. Consequently, they favored Prince Adam's pro-Russian policy and were willing to cast their lot with Alexander. Polish lands united under an enlightened Romanov prince who, the Polish aristocrats hoped, could preserve the old constitution of May 3, 1791, which simply took the peasants under "the protection of law" without giving them the land they cultivated. When Czartoryski read to the assembled crowd Alexander's planned manifesto, summoning Poles to take arms against the Prussian oppressors, the enthusiasm knew no bounds. Poland's resurrection seemed to be only a matter of time. At a gala dinner given by the Czartoryskis, Prince Adam proposed the toast: "To the future King of Poland!"

At the same time, however, Russian opponents of Czartoryski's scheme were not asleep. Under the influence of his chief rival, Peter Dolgoruky, Alexander secretly looked for an alternative plan. He sought to detach Prussia from the French alliance and to use the Prussian army to supplement the forces of the coalition against Napoleon. Yes, when King Frederick William III was lured by the Russian ambassador in Berlin to join Russia, Austria and Sweden, he hesitated. Again he promised only neutrality. Meanwhile, French troops crossed Prussia and marched toward the Danube to face the approaching Austrian army under General Mack.

"This is a flagrant violtion of Prussian neutrality!" exclaimed Alexander. "This should push Frederick William into our arms and reinforce our coalition by 200,000 Prussian troops! Such a contingent, combined with our forces and the Austrians, should give us overwhelming military superiority against Bonaparte. . . ."

It was in the hope of exploiting the French violation of Prussia's neutrality in winning over Frederick William that Alexander decided to send Prince Dolgoruky to Berlin with a personal message to the King, urging him to join the coalition. Despite most pressing arguments and offers of generous territorial gains in Germany,

Dolgoruky returned with only reluctant permission for the Russian troops to cross Prussian territory to join the Austrians. But Alexander would not take "no" for an answer. He decided to use his personal influence on the King and Queen Louise. Abruptly quitting Puławy, he hastened to Berlin, where he arrived on October 25.

Czartoryski, still at his side, was in despair. His monarch's policy was the opposite of that which Prince Adam had advised him to follow. In Berlin King Frederick William, while overwhelming the Tsar with flattery and honors, again refused to commit himself militarily and consented only to a series of clauses defining, in complex terms, Prussia's possible mediation between the belligerents. Only the rejection of that mediation could cause Berlin to act. Queen Louise, who continued to call Alexander "my angel of consolation" and "my divine friend," feared that this evasive attitude of her weak husband might cause an estrangement between the two courts. To safeguard the badly shaken friendship, she devised a demonstration designed to bind her husband to her lover by creating at least a symbolic bond between Russia and Prussia. France should either grant Hanover to Prussia or face her joining the Third Coalition, she calculated. On November 3, at the stroke of midnight, both rulers proceeded through the deserted streets of Potsdam to the garrison church. There, lighted by the flame of a torch, they approached the crypt containing the remains of Frederick the Great. Standing beside his tomb, the Russian Tsar and the Prussian King clasped hands and exchanged an oath of eternal friendship. Queen Louise, pale and enveloped in a black cloak, was the presiding genius of that vow. "Any violation of the oath would be a sacrilege," she proclaimed.

Alexander's relationship with the Prussians shocked Czartoryski, not because of the romantic aspect but, because the whole affair finally detached Russia from his pet scheme. While abandoning his Polish plan, Alexander had become involved in a vague, noncommital friendship with an uncertain partner who still oscillated between Russia and France. Should Napoleon be more insistant, situated at the northern flank of the main theater of war,

Prussia was a potential danger despite her king's platonic gestures toward Alexander. Against whom the Prussians would eventually fight was uncertain because Napoleon could still bribe them with Hanover. Czartoryski did not hesitate to implore his master, in frank terms, not to get involved in a problematic friendship. "Your grandfather's attachment to the Prussian court was just as disastrous to him as to Russia. Prussia in control of central Poland would, sooner or later, attempt to seize other lands in Eastern Europe, including Lithuania, as well as Russia's Baltic provinces. . . ." Even Volkonsky, certainly no friend of the Poles, didn't hesitate to support Prince Adam in his plans and was most critical of the Potsdam visit and wondered, "Are we witnessing a repeat of the Anthony and Cleopatra story?"

On returning from the Potsdam church to Berlin, Alexander took leave of his hosts, got into his carriage and departed. His journey was leisurely, however. On his way he stopped at Weimar to meet Wolfgang Goethe and to discuss with him at length his literary works. Only afterwards did he proceed to join his soldiers marching toward Bohemia.

★ ★ ★

While the allies, deluded by the prospects of Prussian help, procrastinated, Napoleon acted with his usual dispatch. Even before he learned that Admiral Villeneuve's squadron had given up its attack across the English Channel and gone to Cadiz to be smashed at Trafalgar by Nelson, Napoleon had abandoned his plan to invade Britain. Immediately he turned his assembled army from Boulogne toward the Rhine to confront the Austrians under General Mack. Surrounding the Austrian contingent, Napoleon cut off Mack from Vienna, smashed his force and compelled him to surrender on October 20, 1805, at Ulm. Following this victory, Napoleon marched at a breakneck pace toward Vienna.

Meanwhile, Kutuzov's contingent proceeded at a sluggish pace toward Moravia, and around Russian Olmütz, a fortress some forty miles north of Brün (Brno). By that time the exhausted Russian forces were in poor shape; there was no adequate commissariat and the famished troops were often reduced to pillage. On November 13, Alexander received a disquieting report of Napoleon's capture of the Habsburg capital. This prompted the Tsar to send another urgent message to Frederick William; "Things are in a much more alarming state than we imagined when I left Berlin. Every moment is precious. The fate of Europe is in your hands." Alexander's appeal remained without answer, however.

At last, on November 18, he reached Olmütz where the Austrian Emperor Francis I was anxiously awaiting him. They held a council of war. There was to be no supreme command because the mistrustful Austrians insisted on their contingent remaining an autonomous entity. At one point, distressed by the loss of his capital, Emperor Francis was ready to withdraw from the coalition and begin negotiating with Napoleon for an armistice. Alexander, still deluded by the hope of attracting Prussia to the coalition, vigorously vetoed this and pressed for immediate military action. "Our first truimph on the battlefield would force the hand of Frederick William."

All the while there was a great deal of friction between the allies. The Russians grumbled at the scarcity of supplies, promised by the Austrians but seldom delivered. These quarrels created a gloomy mood among the allied leaders. As a result, Kutuzov suggested avoiding a decisive battle as long as possible. He considered even the joint Russo-Austrian forces inadequate to face Napoleon. Kutuzov urged his master to withdraw and thus lure the French away from their supply bases. "Let Napoleon exhaust his troops by chasing us. Then he will fight." Alexander, however, insisted on an immediate showdown. Kutuzov accepted Alexander's plan reluctantly. While its details were discussed, he slumbered at the conference table, only pretending to pay attention to the bitter technical controversies between his staff officers and their Austrian counterparts.

On November 20, Napoleon entered Brün, provincial capital of Moravia, and started to reorganize his forces while waiting for reinforcements from the Third Corps of Marshal Davout, who was still in Vienna. The Russian and Austrian troops limited themselves to scouting the countryside around Olmütz, Austerlitz and Brün. Olmütz, a small town, was grossly overcrowded. Distribution of food was erratic, and water supplies were inadequate as well as unsanitary. Alexander and his troops suffered from stomach disorders and the Tsar himself was forced to spend a few days in bed. Before he was struck by illness, however, he carried out several inspection tours and even drove fairly close to the French advance posts. Through his field glass he could observe that there seemed to be a great deal of confusion and that the enemy seemed to be withdrawing from its commanding positions on the road from Vienna to Olmütz.

Could it be that Napoleon was anxious to abandon the ground he was unable to hold? Was he hesitating concerning what to do next? If so, the allies should take advantage of his loss of nerve. To split the coalition, or at least to lull the enemy into a sense of false security and gain time to gather reinforcements, Napoleon had dispatched an envoy with a letter to Alexander assuring him of his good will and suggesting a personal encounter to arrange for at least a temporary truce. The Tsar's reply was negative. Furthermore, it was addressed not to "the Emperior of the French," but to "the Head of the French government, General Bonaparte." To Dolgoruky, who carried the message, Napoleon appeared "a little fat figure, remarkably dirty and ill-dressed,"and his troops dislocated and in disarray.

Dolgoruky returned to Olmütz elated and submitted a grossly exaggerated report about Napoleon's being nervous and his army preparing to withdraw toward Vienna, news which Alexander was hoping to hear—that the fear of defeat by superior forces had prompted Napoleon to put out peace feelers designed to save his troops from an impending defeat. As a consequence of this assumption, Alexander offered Napoleon the choice of immediate withdrawal from the Austrian lands and the Italian peninsula, or of a renewed war "which would only end when the French retired behind the frontiers of 1789." Hearing this ultimatum, Napoleon exploded with fury and rejected the Tsar's offer brought to him by "an impertinent perfumed young puppy. . . who spoke to me as he would have to a serf whom he wished to send to Siberia." The die was cast.

The Russians and the Austrians were stationed on the elevated ground overlooking a vast plain stretching between Brün and Austerlitz. At the fortress of Brün, the road from Vienna turns eastward at a right angle, then forks, one road leading to Olmütz, the other to Vienna. Yet after capturing that fork, Napoleon had ordered his advanced right column to retire closer to Brün. He seemed to be yielding an advantageous position, running north to south along the Pratzen plateau. Thus, the allies saw their supposition that Napoleon was a hesitant, discouraged man confirmed. As a consequence, the allied troops were ordered to advance beyond the Pratzen Berg, thus abandoning the formidable defensive position, which Kutuzov favored. The plan was to break Napoleon's withdrawing right wing, reach the road from Brün to Vienna, and cut him off from his line of retreat and supplies.

It was exactly to invite such a move that Napoleon had left the right flank almost open. At the same time, he had hurried troops from Vienna to bolster his apparently vulnerable wing. But while the allies were bickering and confused, Napoleon was in top form. On the evening of December 1, he expressed his satisfaction at the course which his operations had taken, and indeed planned for a quick, decisive battle the next day, December 2, the first anniversary of his coronation. For Napoleon immediate decisive victory was a must. It was true that his lines of communication were indeed dangerously extended. His finances were in a precarious state and the danger of another attempt to overthrow him was always present in his mind. On December 1, he said to Davout, "The Prussians will ultimately abandon their neutrality and come down from the north to attack our rear. We must beat the Russians and the Austrians as soon as possible before Prussia intervenes. Tomorrow is the day. . . ."

On the eve of battle, as usual, Napoleon mixed freely with his soldiers. Beside a bivouac fire he chatted with his general about Corneille and of the revival of the arts which he hoped to see in his own time. "It is the drama of politics which should provide the theater with a modern equivalent for the fatalism which we see in the classical plays." He also reminisced about the ups and downs of the Egyptian campaign. "I should have taken to wearing a turban. I should have dressed my army in baggy trousers. I should have accepted Islam . . . I should have relied on Arabs, Greeks and Armenians to win a war against the Turks. I should have proclaimed myself Emperior of the Orient and made my return to Paris by way of Constantinople!. . . ."

★ ★ ★

The battle of Austerlitz was fought on December 2, 1805. The morning was chilly and misty, the ground covered with a thin layer of wet snow. Napoleon's stratagem was simple—to wait until the mid-day sun dispersed the mist and dried the ground somewhat; he wanted to lure his enemies to make the first move by continuing to withdraw his troops on the right flank. Thus, he encouraged the allied troops to descend from the hilly position which they held, and planned to turn his infantry and, supported by artillery fire, pounce on them. Kutuzov grasped the gist of Napoleon's stratagem and ordered his troops to wait until the French made the first move. He would attack them while they were storming the hilly Russian positions on the Pratzen plateu Alexander, however, was eager for a quick, easy triumph. The allies, enjoying a numerical superiority, were bound to crush their confused opponents, he calculated.

In his red and green uniform, white chamois leather breeches and high boots, riding a bobtailed chestnut stallion, the Tsar cut a magnificent figure. Accompanied by the Austrian Emperor Francis, Alexander galloped toward Kutuzov who stood on the top of the Pratzen hill, carefully examining the enemy positions through his field glass. Kutuzov warned his elated master of Napoleon's suspected trick and begged him to wait until the fog lifted and the French began their advance. But Alexander was eager. "Why aren't you starting the battle?" asked the Tsar impatiently. "Let us fall back and lure the French away from their bases instead of abandoning ours," cautioned Kutuzov. "We should not march straight into Napoleon's trap."

Kutuzov was urged by the excited Tsar.

"Let's begin," insisted Alexander, "Let's attack!"

"We should rather wait, Your Majesty," Kutuzov stubbornly maintained. "Not all the columns have formed up yet, Your Majesty. Let us wait until we are sure of Napoleon's intentions. . . ."

The angry Tsar did not like Kutuzov's reply. He shrugged his round shoulders as if resenting Kutuzov's sluggishness, and sneered. "You know, Michael Ilarionovich, we are not in the Mars Field in St. Petersburg where a parade does not begin until all the troops are perfectly formed."

"A battlefield is not a parade ground, Sire. It is a serious business that costs human life. That is why I do not begin," retorted the obstinate Kutuzov in a resounding voice. "That is exactly why I do not begin, because we are not on a parade ground."

The Tsar resented Kutuzov's arrogant reply, and ordered immediate attack in full force. Kutuzov submitted to his master's will and with obvious reluctance sent his adjutants one by one to the divisional commanders. At the order to attack, the Russian troops shoulted, "Hurrah! Long Live the Tsar!" and moved forward. Encouraged by the example of their allies, the Austrians fell in. The Russo-Austrian troops in four columns also descended into the valley, attempting to turn Napoleon's apparently weak right flank in order to cut him off from Vienna. Napoleon, who had concentrated most of his strength in his center, was waiting with the bulk of his forces for just such a move. When the Russians came down from the heights of Pratzen, their dispersed regiments were at the disadvantage. The Russo-Austrian columns were first decimated by Napoleon's guns and then cut to pieces by the French infantry in a bayonet charge by the veterans of Marshal Davout's reserve corps. The Russians fought bravely, but found themselves outmaneuvered and outgunned.

Recognizing the plight of their allies, the Austrians threw into the fray their last reserves, but they were stopped and beaten back. The cautious Kutuzov had been holding back for emergency a few battalions of infantry and eighteen squadrons of cavalry under the command of Grand Duke Constantine. Seeing the desperate plight of the allies, trying to snatch victory from the jaws of defeat, Constantine ordered his cavalry reserve to charge. In his silver helmet and breast plate he led the desperate counterattack himself. Shouting "Hoorah," some two thousand horsemen, the flower of the Russian cavalary, galloped to stem Marshal Soult's victorious advance. Initially, the sheer impetus of the charge broke the line of the French infantry. But behind the infantrymen were the massed batteries of the French artillery. When the guns began to speak, a terrible carnage began. The charge broke down.

Napoleon, who was watching the great sweep of the charge through his field glass, and was astonished by the dash of the Russian attack. He always admired courage, even if displayed by the enemy. When the charge turned into a massacre, he said to one of his adjutants, "There will be many ladies in St. Petersburg soon weeping when they learn of the fate of their lovers and husbands."

The battle of Austerlitz lasted only two hours and ended in a complete French victory. The Russian retreat turned into a rout. A motley of confused soldiers streamed past Kutuzov and his staff and threatened to stampede Alexander, his adjutants and Czartoryski, always on horseback at his master's side. Eventually, they were carried away by the panicky retreating mob, unable to grasp what was happening. Kutuzov himself was wounded. At one moment, there was a danger that the Russian commanders would be captured by the fast advancing French cavalry vanguard. The rout was so complete that Alexander was separated from Czartoryski who was acting as his personal aide and guide.

⋆ ⋆ ⋆

When the Tsar's suite had ridden about two miles from the battlefield, Alexander, a poor horseman, was confronted by a deep ditch. His horse stopped suddenly, refused to jump and started kicking and snorting. Turning the horse sharply, Alexander vigorously goaded his mount with his spurs and riding stick to force the horse to jump. The horse responded by arching his head, rearing and throwing off its rider. The humilitated Tsar had to cross the ditch on foot, knee-deep in the mud. He was shivering with cold; his eyes were hollow, his cheeks sunken and pale. Exhausted, he sought to rest. He slumped down under an old, hollow apple tree trunk, covered his eyes with his hands and wept. He now realized that his own pride and rashness were the main cause of the defeat. His dream of being a great leader of men was shattered. After a time of plaintive meditation, he remounted and rode to join Czartoryski and Volkonsky, discreetly waiting for him a distance from the apple tree.

"We are babies in the hands of a giant," said Alexander to his companions. "We are helpless babies. . . ."

The flight continued for two days, almost without a break. Kutuzov, although wounded, revealed his cool organizational skill. Thanks to his presence of mind, the retreat of the bulk of the troops was carried out slowly. Yet, because it was difficult to reassemble the dispersed and disorganized Russian units, some detachments blindly wandered for days east of Austerlitz and south of Olmütz. Separated from his officers and his equipage, accompanied only by Czartoryski and three Cossacks, Alexander was half-dead with fagitue and shame. When forced to stop from time to time to rest the horses, Alexander warded off sleep until the third day when there was no longer any danger of being captured by the enemy.

In the evening of the third day he fell sick. Fortunately his English doctor, James Wylie, was at his side and provided him some ease for violent intestinal cramps. Leaving Volkonsky and Czartoryski with the Tsar, Wylie rode to the nearest Austrian command post and secured a bottle of red wine to warm his patient's stomach. After a restless night crowded by haunting nightmares, by seven the next morning Alexander was able to mount his horse and continue the flight at a less hurried pace, until he reached the safety of Russian territory. Riding between Czartoryski and Volkonsky, Alexander received frequent reports from various sources, both military and diplomatic. Two days after the battle, on December 4, the Emperor Francis had agreed to a suspension of hostilities. Then he agreed to Alexander returning to Russia with his army. The ill-starred campaign was over. The magnitude of the Austro-Russian defeat was reflected in the casualties: about 15,000 killed and wounded, 11,000 captured. Napoleon had lost about 9,000 men total.

Czartoryski, analyzing the new situation, remarked sarcastically, "The battle was the climax of the preceding confusion. Because of the divergent field reports which reached Your Imperial Majesty, we often passed in the course of one day from the depth of dejection to excessive assurance." Then he added a still more bitter observation: "At Austerlitz your presence, Sire, was of no advantage. It was precisely at the point where you were stationed that the rout was most immediate and complete. Your Majesty yourself took part in it. Your departure augmented the stampede and the general discouragement. . . ."

Alexander arrived at Gatchina at midday of December 21, 1805. He dreaded the ordeal of a public return in daylight. He exchanged horses and proceeded through the night to the Winter Palace. He talked to Elizabeth of the disappointing outcome of the campaign, and condemned bitterly "the infamous conduct of the Austrians, always cowardly and not infrequently even treacherous." As always, when he was frustrated he found his spouse a good listener and received from her kind, warm words of consolation. He carried his sorrows silently to his bedroom. Only four months earlier he had boasted to Elizabeth and Maria Naryshkin of returning in triumph and now he had to face them both, a broken, humiliated vanquished man. "I must raise a new army of at least half a million to take revenge on this damn upstart from Corsica. I must, I must. . . , I have nothing left but my honor, and to renounce it is to cease to be a monarch." Then he stopped, reflected for a while and said philosophically to Elizabeth, "After all, the young Peter the Great also suffered defeats at the beginning of the Great Northern War. The triumph of Poltava did not come at once. . . , It was preceded by the catastrophe of Narva. . . ."

CHAPTER 9

Tilsit

Napoleon called Austerlitz "my finest battle." As time passed the far reaching consequences of the defeat became more and more apparent. The peace signed by Emperor Francis at Pressburg (Bratislava) imposed great sacrifices on Austria and put an end to the Holy Roman Empire after more than seven centuries. Now a confederation of Rhenish states was formed and put itself under French protection. After Austerlitz, Napoleon wrote to Pius VII, "I am now like Charlemagne, for I unite the crowns of France and Lombardy, and my empire marches toward the Orient." And, indeed, he soon redoubled his diplomatic pressure on the Ottoman Empire. On May 2, 1806, he appointed as his ambassador to Constantinople one of his ablest officers, General Sebastiani. For his guidance, the Emperor dictated the following instructions: "1) You must work for a triple alliance between me, the Ottoman Porte and Persia against Russia and England. 2) The Bosphorus must be closed to the Russians. I have no intention of sharing the straits with anyone. 3) I wish to consolidate the Ottoman Empire and make it serve me as a center of opposition against Russia."

When this threat became known in St. Petersburg, Alexander concluded that Russia must resume hostilities with France to defend her vital interests not only in central Europe, but also in the

Balkans and the Mediterranean. He was counting on fresh British subsidies and the Prussian resistance to Napoleon's new encroachments on German pride, the formation of the Rhenish Confederation, a smokescreen for the French hegemony over Germany. "The fact that he annexed Hanover, which he had promised to Prussia as the reward for its neutrality, must eventually compel Frederick William to act in defense of his own interests, as well as his honor," calculated Alexander. "Napoleon's plans in the east must be frustrated since they threaten our interests in the Balkans." On this point both the Tsar and Czartoryski showed no hesitation, "We must make Bonaparte understand that we are ready to resume the war rather than consent to his designs on Turkey and permit Bonaparte to gain a dominance over the Ottoman Empire," they concluded. To support that resolution they drafted a declaration stressing that Russia would occupy the Danubian principalities of Moldavia and Wallachia to safeguard her interests and oppose Napoleon's eastern scheme.

The Prussians, who had failed to side with the Russians and the Austrians when they could be helped, before Austerlitz, still remained inactive. Although encouraged by the upsurge of German national sentiment and goaded on by his bellicose wife, Louise, Frederick William hesitated. He was paralyzed with fear by Napoleon's lightning-quick victories over the Russo-Austrian coalition. Yet Queen Louise persisted and pressed for a military showdown with the French. As a weighty argument she used Alexander's promise of help contained in a personal letter to Frederick William on March 10, 1806. Forgetting the two-faced Prussian stand during the first phase of the war, the Tsar had written, "Now an intimate alliance between Prussia and Russia seems to be more than ever indispensable. In moments of danger Your Majesty should remember that you have in me a friend ready to fly to your aid. In all that you say and decide you can confidently rely on our full assistance, which Russia is prepared to send you whenever you judge it necessary."

When Queen Louise read the letter, elated, she urged her husband, "Do you, a successor of Frederick the Great, commander of the army trained by the finest officer in Europe, and inspired by the finest tradition to his victories, still hesitate to act? What kind of man are you?"

Lured by Alexander's promise of military aid, and his own wife's hysterical pleas, the hen pecked King capitulated and declared war on France. Napoleon was furious. "For too long I have treated the Prussians with kindness, and now they betray me. A treacherous King, a treacherous nation."

Alexander was indeed willing to help the Prussians to resist Napoleon's onslaught, but his resources were limited and he needed time to muster his reserves. Before Alexander could join his Prussian ally, Napoleon acted with his customary speed. By a remarkable turning maneuver through the Thuringian Mountains, Napoleon cut off Frederick William's army from Berlin, and then destroyed it in twin battles fought on October 14, 1806, at Jena and Auerstadt. This catastrophic defeat produced a chain reaction. The remaining Prussian units panicked and surrendered, mostly without fighting. The Prussian fortresses yielded one after another and Napoleon entered Berlin in triumph. He was greeted by servile city notables who offered him the sword of Frederick the Great. He refused scornfully saying, "I don't need it. I have my own."

In the royal palace of Charlottenburg Napoleon's agents carefully searched the bedroom of Queen Louise. There, in one of the drawers, they found a portrait of Alexander and his love letters to her, hidden among perfumed bits of lace and ribbons. Napoleon fumed "I will send this wretched whore, this she-devil, back to the Seventh Hell where she belongs." He ordered the French press to publish the letters, together with his comments. "The Queen of Prussia is with the army, dressed up like an Amazon, wearing the uniform of her dragoons, writing twenty letters a day to stir up trouble on all sides. We will teach her a lesson. She demands blood and she will get it."

From Berlin Napoleon advanced into Poland. During the late autumn he captured Poznan and Warsaw, which the Third Battalion had given to Prussia. In both cities he received an exuberant welcome. In Warsaw on November 27, 1806, Napoleon proclaimed the establishment of a rump Polish state to be called the Duchy of Warsaw. While attending a ball in the city shortly thereafter, Napoleon met the fugutive blond Countess Maria Walewska, who soon became his mistress. Thus, at one time, the two rivals for the mastery of Europe had Polish mistresses, both named Maria. In each case, the romantic liaison lasted for about fifteen years.

★ ★ ★

Among the people most disappointed by the turn of events was Czartoryski. His advice had been ignored, and all his long-range political plans were in ruin. Consequently, he tendered his resignation as Acting Foreign Minister in July 1806. While submitting his resignation, the Prince could not help but remark bitterly. "We should have forestalled Napoleon by proclaiming a Polish kingdom while issuing a guarantee of Polish liberties, and linking the crowns of Russia and Poland in a dynastic union similar to the link between the Habsburgs and Hungary. Now the Polish trump card is in the hands of Napoleon." The resignation was accepted by Alexander, though reluctantly.

After his return to St. Petersburg, Czartoryski learned from Novosiltsev that Elizabeth had continued her romance with a young lieutenant of the Chevalier Guards, Gregory Okhotnikov, and that she was pregnant. He tried to reestablish contact with her, but all of his letters to her were returned unopened. In October 1806, moreover, another piece of news reached the Prince. After attending an opera performance, Okhotnikov was stabbed in the back with a stiletto. The crime was never investigated properly by the police, while all sorts of wild rumors circulated as to the perpetrator. Elizabeth, who meanwhile gave birth to a daughter, visited Okhotnikov several times and was at his deathbed. On his grave she ordered a marble statue erected that represented a weeping angel. Those who knew her recognized that the angel had Elizabeth's features.

After months of patient waiting, Prince Adam wrote another

letter, begging Elizabeth to see him. In reply he received a short, blunt note: "Before leaving for Sardinia, you swore your eternal love for me. Yet, one of the first reports that the Emperor received from Florence from your own private secretary, described in great detail your affair with Queen Clotilda. When Alexander showed me the report I almost collapsed. It took several days to recover from the shock. Then I met Gregory at a New Year's masquerade ball. He paid with his life for his love for me. I love him still and will remain faithful to his memory to the end of my days." The letter was signed simply "E."

While Prince Adam was recovering from the shock and depression that followed, the strategic situation of Russia worsened considerably. The hopelessly belated Prussian intervention lured the French armies closer to Russia's western frontiers and threatened Lithuania and the Baltic provinces of the Empire. While the Prussian army was being smashed by Napoleon's veterans, Alexander made a supreme effort to mobilize all the available resources of his Empire. He was encouraging a national crusade against the forces of evil threatening Holy Russia. The Orthodox clergy was ordered to preach against Napoleon, who was denounced by the Holy Synod as " a renegade, the French Anti-Christ," who "had sold himself to the Jews and claimed to be their Messiah." The regimental chaplains were provided with copies of the Synod's proclamation describing Bonaparte as "the Servant of Satan and the worshiper of whores and idols," as well as friend of the "perfidious Jews."

Since Kutuzov was still recovering from the wounds he had suffered at Austerlitz, Alexander, after considerable hesitation and soul-searching, appointed as Commander-in-Chief, General Benningsen, previously disgraced and removed to Lithuania. With 67,000 men and 276 cannons he was sent to Poland to stem the French cohorts who were pursuing the remnants of Frederick William's armies into Poland and East Prussia. The first clashes with the French resulted in Russian reverses. Deprived of effective support on the part of the dispersed and demoralized Prussian troops, Benningsten retreated northward and fought stubborn rear-guard action at Pultusk on December 26, 1806. One of the most bloody battles of the campaign ended in a draw.

With the beginning of the year 1807, Benningsen advanced with fresh reinforcements in an attempt to outflank Napoleon's left wing. The two armies clashed on February 7 at Prussian Eylau, south of Königsberg in a terrible battle fought in a blinding snowstorm. When the 63,000 Russians surprised the 41,000 French, it seemed that Benningsen finally had the upper hand. Both armies fought with desperate tenacity. Fortunes changed from hour to hour. When Marshal Augereau's attacking corps lost its direction in the storm, it was decimated at close range by powerful Russian batteries. As a result, the Russian center, advancing in a compact mass, almost smashed the French. Napoleon tried to stem the Russian advanced by a cavalry charge, but failed. Throughout the course of the protracted battle, outlying French detachments proceeded to the field of action and Napoleon was saved from defeat only by the concentrated mass of his artillery. The clash ended late at night with no definite result. Benningsen retired and Napoleon kept the field of battle, proclaiming himself victor. Each side lost between 18,000 and 20,000 men. It was the first serious deadlock of the campaign and both sides needed to pause to lick their wounds, while waiting for reserve forces to bolster decimated ranks.

In the spring the contest was resumed. On June 14, 1806, Napoleon believed that he had caught Benningsen off guard in his march toward Königsberg. Yet, Benningsen proved more alert than Napoleon had anticipated, and threw his army of 58,000 at Napoleon's 80,000 at Friedland, twenty-seven miles south of Königsberg. Here Napoleon once more showed his mettle. Brilliantly, he swerved his marching columns round to face the Russian onslaught. The Russians were first stopped, then were pushed back into the village of Friedland. Benningsen defended the village stubbornly from house to house. Close-packed, the Russian soldiers mounted several desperate bayonet charges to repel the French attacks. Finally, the Russian troops were forced into a small compact space and mercilessly cut down by volleys of grapeshot fired by the massed French batteries at close range. The Russians were almost all either killed, wounded, taken prisoner, or driven into the nearby river Alle, where many of them drowned. The Russian army lost some 19,000 men, while the French casualties amounted to less than 9,000. Six French and nine Russian generals were wounded. General Michael Barclay de Tolly, who personally led a hopeless final cavalry charge to allow the remnants of the Russian troops to withdraw, also suffered severe wounds and barely escaped capture.

While the French medical services were well organized, the Russian ones were in a deplorable state; there was an acute shortage of medical personnel, antiseptics and bandages. Access to medical treatment depended a good deal on rank, chance, and favor. Only lighter cases were taken. Men who might have been saved, but who would have been unfit for future service, were left behind. Most of the wounded who were shunted aside died.

The Prussian allies, still with a hard core of some 25,000 soldiers around Königsberg, did not assist the Russians in their predicament. Eventually Prussian troops abandoned the city and retreated eastward toward Tilsit to the Russian frontier, while the French promptly occupied Königsberg and made themsevles undisputed masters of East Prussia, thus menacing Alexander's Lithuanian provinces stretching just east of the Niemen River. Reinforcements did not arrive in expected strength. Russian supply services were in monumental disorder. Alexander's troops were discouraged, famished and exhausted. Even bread rations arrived most erratically and the soldiers were forced to live largely off the impoverished land. Despite the great levy, which was to have yielded a militia of about 600,000 men, Alexander was left with hardly more than 30,000 poorly trained reserves. Moreover, he was most dissatisfied with the absence of financial help promised by Britain. There was nothing more he could expect from the cowardly Prussians.

Were the Russians to face Napoleon's cohorts alone? Under the circumstances, Benningsen and most generals declared peace to be an urgent necessity. By June 1807, Alexander accepted their advice and decided to ask for an armistice. The Russian officers who were sent to Tilsit to negotiate with the French were instructed to be civil, to remember Napoleon's imperial title and not to refer to him as "General Bonaparte." Napoleon, whose army was also exhausted and far away from its supply bases, eagerly agreed to the proposed armistice and offered to meet Alexander at Tilsit.

★ ★ ★

The setting for the historic meeting of the two rivals at Tilsit was a masterpiece of Napoleon's stage management. Throughout the night of June 24/25, French engineers worked to construct a barge supporting a wooden pavilion draped with canvas. During the morning of June 25, it was towed to the midstream of the Niemen River and secured to the piles of a ruined bridge. The pavilion was decorated with Imperial eagles and monograms, painted in the only color available, green. The letter "N" faced the left bank, the letter "A" the right. The scene arranged by Napoleon was supreme proof of his ability of improvisation. One of the secrets of Napoleon's virtuosity in the field of showmanship lay in adroitly playing upon popular imagination. "Nothing is to be left to chance. . . ." he often repeated. "Success lies in the preparation of small details." His goal was always the same—maximize his power and his prestige as an invincible yet benevolent ruler through image building.

Alexander, in his parade uniform, arrived on the right bank of the Niemen at eleven o'clock, accompanied by his brother Constantine as well as by General Benningsen and his aide-de-campe Count Paul Lieven. They were forced to wait for almost two hours for Napoleon's arrival, a blatent reminder of who was the master of the situation. Shortly before one o'clock, the victor boarded the raft amidst the excited sounds of cheering crowds heard from both banks of the river. Then Alexander and his retinue were rowed across the water. Napoleon, accompanied by Marshals Berthier and Duroc and General Armand de Caulaincourt, welcomed Alexander, embracing him with effusive cordiality and calling him "my brother."

Alexander's first impression of Napoleon was a shocking disappointment. How was it possible that this dwarfish man, with pasty complexion, bilious and puffy face, could be a great leader of men, a master diplomat, as well as victor in numerous battles? Only when Napoleon fixed his scrutinizing gaze on his guest and began to talk did Alexander begin to grasp Napoleon's charismatic power. Although a foot shorter than any of the others, Napoleon dominated the meeting from the beginning. He embarrassed his guest and sought to disarm him by a show of generosity. When offered the Grand Cross Order of the Legion of Honor, Alexander objected saying "But, Sire, after all, I have been defeated. The Grand Cross is awarded only to victorious commanders." "Yes," answered Bonaparte, "I know, but being defeated by Napoleon is almost equal to a victory."

The meeting between Napoleon and Alexander was a memorable event. The two emperors, only a few days before bitter enemies, exchanged compliments, embraces and assurances of eternal friendship. On either bank of the river, drawn together as though in an amphitheater, stood the soldiers of the armies, which only eleven days earlier had been slaughtering each other with rare ferocity. Now, as if miraculously transformed, they were cheering and looking on the historic spectacle. The scene was sketched, drawn and painted by several artists whom Napoleon summoned for the occasion. A special medal was to be struck to commemorate the meeting of Tilsit. While honoring and flattering Alexander, Napoleon did his best to humiliate the King of Prussia, Frederick William III. Although the negotiations took place on his territory, he was not invited to attend. During the long deliberations he meekly stood with his generals and courtiers on the bank of the Niemen, like a punished schoolboy. In passing by him and his wife, Napoleon had barked, "How did you dare to declare war on me?" Then to soften his harsh remark and to appear gallant, he turned to Queen Louise and complimented her on the design of her gown. He touched the silk of her dress with his fingers and asked, "What stuff is this madame? . . . French or Italian?"

"Sire, how can you talk of fripperies at such a solemn moment?" she answered him with tears in her eyes.

In the afternoon, Alexander and Napoleon withdrew to Tilsit

for secret talks. Alexander opened the interview with the words, "Sire, I hate the English as much as you do." To which Napoleon replied, "Then all else can be arranged. Let's work together to bring to their knees this nation of shopkeepers and swindlers. The American colonists taught them their first lesson. I will finish them off." During the talks, Napoleon received a dispatch from his ambassador in Constantinople that informed him of the assassination of the Sultan Selim during a revolt of the Janissaries. He showed the message to the Tsar with the comment, "This is an act of Providence, telling me that the Turkish Empire cannot survive!. . . . The road to the East is opened."

After the meeting Napoleon personally decorated two dozen selected Russian officers with the red-ribboned order of the Legion of Honor. When the Tsar asked Napoleon to award a Legion to the Russian Commander-in-Chief, General Benningsen, Napoleon smiled ironically and refused. The expression on Alexander's face suddenly changed from one of elation to gloom. He understood the refusal to decorate the man who on a tragic night in March 1801, was the first to break into the bedchamber of Paul.

Despite the unpleasant incident, fraternization was the order of the day. Napoleon, wearing his customary black hat with a tricolored brocade and a simple green uniform open over a white vest, mounted his white Arabian horse and rode side by side with Alexander to the town square. One battalion of the Preobrazhensky regiment was facing a battalion of Napoleon's Old Guards. The battalions presented arms and almost simultaneously shouted "Hurrah!", "Vive l'Empereur!" and "Love live our Tsar!" Then both sovereigns dismounted and inspected the two detachments together. Approaching the right flank of the Preobrazhensky battalion, Napoleon made a request: "Sire, I ask your permission to present the Legion of Honor to the fifty bravest of your soldiers and officers, those who have borne themselves most valiantly in the last campaign." Alexander agreed, and then consulted the Lieutenant Colonel commanding the battalion as to whom the orders should be awarded. The ceremony proceeded for the next hour or so during which Napoleon insisted on chatting with those officers who spoke French, and embraced them with effusive cordiality.

Then Napoleon invited the entire battalion to dinner with soldiers of his Old Guards battalions. He insisted that the two units should break ranks and mingle. The French officers as well as enlisted men were ordered to be friendly and outgoing to their Russian counterparts. All guests were served by trained French butlers. The Tsar intended to return the hospitality in equal style, but the Russians had not enough proper cutlery and, despite Alexander's readiness to pay a high price, none could be obtained. Moreover, Russian food supplies were limited, barely adequate for the meager daily rations of the troops.

The next morning, Napoleon demonstrated to Alexander the discipline and skill of his troops, especially the mounted couriers, called Guides, of whom he was very proud. These men were rigorously trained to deliver messages on horseback and defend themselves with pistol and sword while riding, or running or swimming to their destination, if left without a mount. "Without their courage, speed and initiative, I couldn't command my troops spread over miles and miles of territory often alive with enemy soldiers." On Napoleon's order two of these Guides jumped into the Niemen, swam across the Russian bank of the river and back. Then they mounted their horses and demonstrated their ability to jump over ditches and hedges, and made a show of their skills in acrobatics, fencing and target practice.

The next day a great parade of the French elite units was held. Alexander was fascinated by the spectacle, meticulously choreographed by Napoleon himself. Accustomed as he was to reviewing troops, Alexander was impressed by the sight of so many splendid soldiers perfectly drawn up, row after row in impeccable alignment. The Guards looked especially impressive in their white breeches, gold-buttoned waistcoats, and dark-blue jackets crisscrossed with white bandoleers supporting ammunition pouches. On their heads they wore huge bearskin busbies with scarlet pompons angled down over their eyebrows. The grim faces of the veterans, all of them at least six feet tall, were made even more martial by their long bushy mustaches. Nowhere in Europe, even in Prussia, had Alexander seen a more imposing body of troops.

Equally impressive were the Mounted Guards on splendid steeds. In silver-embroidered jackets, sky-blue crimson collars and shoulder straps they rode jet-black horses in rigorously straight columns behind their officer. Cuirassiers constituted the bulk of Napoleon's heavy cavalry. They looked most spectacular in their shining silver breast plates and helmets, all mounted on their huge dark beasts when they galloped past. But the most colorful of all was Napoleon's personal bodyguard, the squadron of dark-faced Mamelukes whom Napoleon had recruited in Egypt. In their plumed turbans, red pantaloons, multi-colored sashes, into each of which was thrust two pistols and a dagger, they dazzled the Russian spectators. "What an army! No wonder, Sire, that you smashed the Prussians to pieces!" exclaimed Alexander with a mixture of admiration and envy.

After the spectacular parade Napoleon dismounted and personally congratulated each unit of his troops on its performance. He carefully inspected each detachment with the concern of an expert to whom no detail was unimportant. He stopped before several veterans, questioning them in a warm cordial tone. He often mentioned battles in which they had been wounded or decorated. Having attended hundreds of similar functions in Russia, where soldiers were treated with harshness, more like forced labor than as warriors, Alexander was startled by Napoleon's close, almost paternal, relationship with his soldiers, his good humor with the men, his care for their well being and respect for personal dignity. Alexander was especially astonished to hear Napoleon addressing individual soldiers in the familiar second-person singular, often calling them by their first names.

★ ★ ★

On July 7 at Tilsit, the former enemies signed a series of treaties of friendship and cooperation. By one of them, Alexander agreed to abandon his allies—Prussia, Britain and Sweden—while Napoleon promised to disengage himself from his ally Turkey. He had already begun measures which led to the Continental Blockade, by which British goods were to be excluded from Europe, and "the nation of the shopkeepers" strangled economically. Now Alexander vaguely promised to join the blockade and ban English ships from Russian harbors, though he purposely avoided formal commitments. Moreover, Alexander had to accede to the French control of the gulfs of Cattaro and the island of Corfu because Napoleon insisted that Russia had no business in the Mediterranean. He had no doubt that he would soon chase the British squadrons from it. Consequently, only the Balkans were left for Alexander's expansive designs. "You can claim, if you wish, the Danubian principalities of Moldavia and Wallachia. They are your natural sphere of expansion. So is Finland." As for the Black Sea straits, the Dardanelles and the Bosphorus as well as Constantinople itself, Napoleon refused to grant them to Alexander. "Mastery of Constantinople," he said, "means mastery of the world." It was in the eastern Mediterranean that he hoped to undermine the British hold in the middle sea which he, in turn, considered a sphere of French influence since the time of the Crusades.

At Tilsit, Prussia lost her share of central Poland. This chunk of territory was to become an autonomous state under French protection and to bear the artificially concocted name of Duchy of Warsaw. At one moment Napoleon was ready to cede it to Alexander, but Alexander refused the gift. "I don't want to act as jackal and grab territories that had belonged to my former ally, the King of Prussia." Yet, Alexander insisted that Napoleon should not expand the duchy by giving Danzig to the Poles. Napoleon denied any such plan. "I have no intention of being the Don Quixote of Poland. The Polish state that I will create will bear the modest name of the Duchy of Warsaw. I need to keep the Prussians and Austrians in check. So don't worry. . . . I will not allow the Poles to threaten your realm." Alexander did worry, however, because, despite Napoleon's promises to the contrary, he considered the duchy a French military colony, as well as the nucleus of a potentially larger state.

At Tilsit, Prussia was not only despoiled, but also compelled to host a large French army of occupation. When Alexander, mindful of the Potsdam oath of friendship, interjected that Frederick William, who was formally still the Sovereign master of Tilsit, should be consulted before the fate of his lands was determined by a one-sided mandate, Napoleon repeated, with emphasis, "No, no! A nasty king, a nasty nation, a nasty army. It was only because of your pleas, and for the sake of your friendship that I spared them from utter destruction. Isn't that enough?" The existence of the Confederation of the Rhine, founded under the French protectorate after Austerlitz, was now reaffirmed, thus reasserting Napoleon's hegemony over Germany.

All this was done in one day. As Napoleon said rather boastfully, "In a few hours we have done more than our ministers accomplished in several days."

After the signing of the Treaty of Tilsit, Napoleon invited Alexander to a splendid banquet. Although the host was a thousand miles from his country, the dinner could match any meal of a monarch at home in his capital. The Emperors, as well as members of their personal suites, were seated at a separate table on the dais. Twelve black men, dressed in the Mameluk style, with white twisted turbans and green gold-braided jackets and wide red pantaloons sashed with cashmere belts, attended the main table, serving elaborate dishes and wines. Once more, Alexander was nonplussed by Napoleon's organizing skill and his masterly stage managing. "How was it possible to prepare such a Lucullan dinner so meticulously and at such short notice?" he asked himself enviously.

For the moment, Napoleon seemed to be elated by his apparent conquest of an ally whom he so much needed if he was to bring the British to their knees and arrange the fate of the world in accordance with his imperial vision. Yet, a few days afterwards, he confided to his staff and later to the Austrian Ambassador in Paris, Count Clemens Metternich, "It would be difficult to have more intelligence than the Emperor Alexander, but I find that there is something lacking in him and I have not managed to discover what it is. He is a Sphinx, a Talma of the North. Is he a sincere man or a virtuoso of duplicity?"

Alexander's fascination with Napoleon vanished as soon as the Tsar left Tilsit and removed himself from his rival's hypnotic spell. On his way back to St. Petersburg, chatting with Dolgoruky, Alexander tried to justify his behavior." I am not a fool. . . . For Russia the Tilsit treaties were concluded at a heavy price. There are, however, some compensatory features. We are now free to pick a quarrel with Sweden and annex Finland, and thus better protect our capital which is, after all, a frontier city. After that Moldavia and Wallachia will be wrested from the Turks. Thus, we will firmly hold the mouth of the Danube. And not least, we have halted Napoleon's eastward drive. He learned at Eylau and Friedland that his striking power was not effective so far from home. Should he ever forget this lesson, we have gained time to prepare ourselves. He laughs best who laughs last."

CHAPTER 10

"Napoleon's Prefect in Russia?"

Alexander's return to St. Petersburg on July 4, 1807, after Tilsit was much more depressing than his return from Austerlitz. Then there was at least a valid excuse for the shameful defeat: Austria's cowardice and treachery. Moreover, there was a hope of reversing the upset with Prussia's help. Now Prussia was not only hopelessly defeated but torn to pieces, occupied by Napoleon's armies and, for all practical purposes, his satellite. The Russian position was, of course, better; the Empire had lost no territory and there were no French garrisons on her soil, but the Tilsit agreement chained Alexander to an erratic giant with a dream of supremacy over Europe.

Napoleon's assent to Russia fighting the Swedes and Turks and subjugating Finland and the Danubian principalities of Moldavia and Wallachia was a mere sugar coating that would allow Alexander to swallow the bitter pill and present to the outside world the Tilsit agreement as a mutually advantageous compromise. Harsh economic realities, however, worked against the Franco-Russian alliance. At Tilsit, Alexander had promised to break diplomatic relations with Britain, ban British ships from the Russian ports and to eventually join the Continental Blockade. Yet, it was to Britain that Russia sent most of her exported materials: grain, hemp, wood, flax, tar, tallow, potash, leather, wax and horsehair. Of a total of 30 million rubles' worth of merchandise that left the port of St. Petersburg at least 17 million rubles' worth went to the British, while only about 1 million rubles' worth went to the French. That same year, of 986 merchant vessels that entered the port of St. Petersburg, 477 were British and only a dozen French. This disproportion explained the anxiety of Russian merchants when trade with England was banned in 1807. Soon after Tilsit the French made an effort to increase their purchases in Russia, but even by their tripling trade in 1810, it was impossible to make up for the large deficit in the Russian balance of trade. Flooded with paper money, Russia was on the brink of economic disaster.

To this one should add the psychological aftereffects of the downfall of Tilsit. The Russian people had become accustomed to Suvorov's great victories, and could not come to grips with the recent double defeat, which they blamed on Alexander's rashness and ineptitude. People asked themselves: Did Peter the Great or Catherine the Great ever ask another power for permission to assert Russia's might over her neighbors? When a small child asked an officer why everyone was cheering the returning troops since the army had been defeated, the answer was that they were fortunate to be alive.

Within the politically-minded circles of St. Petersburg and Moscow, whispered abuse was showered on the ruler who had lost two crucial campaigns in a row and submitted to the ignominious Treaty of Tilsit. Opponents of his policy accused Alexander of prostrating himself at the feet of the victor and fraternizing with the Conqueror whom a year ago he had denounced as anti-Christ and defender of Moslems and Jews. Did Alexander convert the French Anti-Christ to Christianity? Did he baptize him in the Niemen?

Among the promoters of the widespread campaign against "the

abominable treason of Tilsit" was the Dowager Empress, traditionally second to the Tsar in the court hierarchy. Protected by her position, she became a focal point of the opposition to the treaty that drastically curtailed Russian exports and made the country "a province of France." French royalist emigrés who had enlisted as officers in the Russian elite regiments fanned the flames of discontent. "It is certain," wrote one of them, Roger de Damas, "that today Bonaparte runs his Empire and directs its affairs as if Russia were only one of the provinces of France. The Tsar is no longer anything but his prefect in Russia."

Among Napoleon's opponents must also be counted Alexander's Baltic barons, who, though Russian subjects, had retained sentimental ties with Germany, and the Prussian officers who had enlisted under the banners of Alexander after the dissolution of the army of Frederick William III. In September 1807, when the Tsar decided to change the uniform of his troops, replacing the tight Prussian-type tunics with more comfortable ones modeled on those of the Napoleonic army, they muttered against "the French livery."

Even Elizabeth, usually loyal to her fickle husband, was critical of the Tilsit agreement. She ascribed it to a magic spell Napoleon cast on Alexander. This was reflected in the letter she wrote to her mother, the Margravine of Baden: "To me, Bonaparte is like a charlatan or magician who by all sorts of tricks, or by force, succeeds in winning the hearts and minds of his victims. Russia has resisted for a long time, but she has now taken the final step like the others. The Emperor apparently feels an irresistible attraction towards this seducer."

Supported and encouraged by the Dowager Empress, the intrigues in high Court circles took on the pattern of a conspiracy. Sinister and subversive slogans were hatched by anonymous persons: "The blindness of the Emperor is the Empire's ruin," or "The Emperor should bear in mind how his father died." This deep current of dissatisfaction was noted and duly reported by foreign diplomats. "To escape from this dangerous situation," wrote Count Joseph de Maistre, the Sardinian representative in St. Petersburg, "many people see no hope except the Asiatic remedy. . . ."

While maintaining an outwardly impassive calm, Alexander was deeply wounded by this harsh criticism. He sought consolation in the bosom of Maria Naryshkin. Almost every evening the Imperial carriage was seen driving the Tsar to her villa on Stony Island. But, now even she became indifferent to his fits of self-pity and recriminations. Her coldness, however, was not politically motivated; she was engaged in one of her numerous secret affairs with a young officer of the Chevalier Guards. A few weeks after his return to St. Petersburg, from Peter Volkonsky, his eyes and ears in the capital, Alexander learned of her numerous love affairs during his absence at the front. It was too much for him. He exploded to his bosom friend Volkonsky, "For years I trusted this woman completely! And yet she is just as treacherous as other beautiful women. She is a voluptuous mare who only pretends to be a great lady and a refined intellectual to keep me at her feet." His first reaction was to break with her. After a moment he calmed down, turned to his friend and ordered him, "Peter, this is between us. You are never to repeat my words to anyone." And he decided to forgive Maria her infidelities, mainly for the sake of their daughter Zinaida whom he adored.

* * *

In his depressing isolation, Alexander turned to the only human being he considered to be a loyal, trustworthy friend: his younger sister Catherine. The strange bond that united them had its roots in childhood. Alexander was the eldest in a large brood of four boys and five girls. During his childhood and adolescence, he had had little opportunity to interact with his family, except for his brother Kostya because of his grandmother's strict orders regarding their presence at Gatchina except his military training and occasional short ceremonial visits. The situation changed dramatically when Paul ascended the throne and moved with his family to the Winter Palace in November 1796. Since that time, Alexander displayed a great deal of affection toward all of his brothers and sisters, but from the beginning he took a special fancy to his fourth sister Catherine. Born in May 1788, she was eleven years his junior. Dark, slender, but not beautiful, she was, however, vivacious and highly intelligent.

Normally, sexual attraction between brothers and sisters is blunted by familiarity. This was not the case with Alexander and Catherine; they were, for all practical purposes, strangers to each other. When Alexander ascended the throne, she was thirteen years old, and an exceptionally precocious girl of brilliant mind, fertile imagination and unbridled temperament. She had been strictly educated by her German mother, who tended to substitute rigid discipline for affection and tenderness. Sometimes when Catherine wanted to caress her "dear mama" and tried to climb on her lap, she was rejected and ordered to get down. "Don't wrinkle my gown," she was told. Catherine was also reprimanded and reminded by her governesses that her mother favored her sisters because they had better manners and did not rebel against the rigid etiquette prescribed for the Grand Duchesses. "You are a little devil," her mother would say to her. The same was the case with Catherine's governesses, who had been instructed by the Empress to train the children to be slavishly obedient and to fight any "undue tendency toward overindulgence and sentimentality." She was to be a perfect lady, a future wife and mother of royalty.

Paul was still more strict with the children. His occasional gestures of tenderness were overshadowed by outbursts of terrible temper, often lasting for days. Deprived of motherly affection himself, he tended to project his orphan complex, a mixture of shame, guilt and rejection, to his progeny. Consequently, Catherine was completely deprived of an emotional refuge in both mother and father. Alexander, practically kidnapped by his grandmother at the age of five, had spent his adolescent years under the overprotective wings of an authoritarian old woman who desperately tried to substitute for both his parents. It was she who determined what her grandson was to read, what kind of tutor he was to have and whom he was to marry. Her wish to train her grandson as a future monarch, nay, as a mythical hero, clashed with her occasional desire to play with him as with a puppet. There was, however, no real warmth in her caresses, only pride in having a bright good-looking pet.

The adolescent Catherine had no contacts with young men of her age, except for weekly dance lessons. Her instructors in French, German and English music and horseback riding were all elderly, unattractive men, and she was considered too young to participate in the Court receptions and balls until she was fifteen. Alexander was the first attractive male who treated her as a real woman. He offered her flowers and danced with her as if she were a grown-up lady—an intoxicating and exciting experience that fed her vivid imagination.

Catherine's mind was shaped not only by the experiences of her childhood but also by her reading mostly sentimental novels. One of the first novels she read was a story of unhappy love, *Die Leiden des jüngen Werther (The Sufferings of Young Werther).* The author was the very celebrated but sill youthful, Wolfgang Goethe. Then came Rousseau's *Emile.* The first English drama she read was *Romeo and Juliet,* lovers of about her age. The books made a profound impact. Girlish fantasy caused her to identify with Juliette. "But where is my Romeo?" she would ask herself.

Early on, Catherine displayed remarkable social gifts and established varied contacts. For instance, she befriended the poet Vasily Zhukovsky, who submitted to her for critique his ballad entitled "Ludmila." She was also interested in history and, at the age of fourteen, she read Voltaire's *History of Charles XII* from cover to cover. She inherited her temperament, intelligence and ambition from her grandmother and namesake, Catherine, and scorned the artificial aura of domestic respectability displayed by her stiff, pompous and forbidding mother. Her rebellion was stimulated by the rumors of the old Empress's innumerable amorous excesses and those of her father's increasingly frequent love affairs. The lively young girl's desire to outshine others and to command attention challenged her parents' demands for respect and obedience.

By the age of fifteen, precocious Catherine was in full rebellion against society's image of femininity. She insisted on riding horseback astride and wished to take fencing lessons. Only her mother's furious veto thwarted these attempts. Her repressed longings for independence and adventure were thus only intensified. She waited anxiously for an opportunity to reassert herself. The reading of works of Marquis de Sade and of de Banthome's *Vies des Grands Capitaines et des Dames Galantes* fired her imagination and cost her several sleepless nights. Although the latter book was intercepted by her French governess, Catherine never forgot the frivolous adventures of its heroines, emancipated women three centuries before the word "feminism" entered daily vocabulary. To be free, independent, bold and adventurous, such were her secret dreams. She would often say, "I don't want to marry; I want to live."

Thirsting for affection in an emotional Sahara, the precocious Catherine, temperamental and flirtatious by nature, saw in Alexander a tender, captivating participant in her games and practical jokes. In her teen years, he became the companion with whom she walked, talked and read her favorite books. Long conversations and solitary promenades alternated with pranks and madcap games. Soon they persistently sought each other's company and would often ask each other what actually bonded them so closely. They began to exchange kisses and caresses, though it was invariably Catherine who initiated these "small innocent tokens of sisterly affection," as she called them.

Initially, Alexander tried to repress his impulses, but his moral scruples proved weaker than his mounting passion. What started as brotherly cordialities gradually turned into an intimate attachment. Alexander made a point of visiting Catherine on her birthday and on her nameday, always with baskets of flowers, and showered her with expensive gifts. With time, the attachment became an obsessive passion that eventually came to rival his steady romance with Maria Naryshkin.

Elizabeth became aware of this new involvement of her husband. While she showed an amazing tolerance for his other peccadillos, including affairs with some of her ladies-in-waiting, she could hardly tolerate Catherine's presence, and avoided her during Court functions. In private, Elizabeth referred to her as "that arrogant nasty girl," or "that aggressive vicious sister of yours. . . ." Catherine was, perhaps, the only person toward whom Elizabeth, always an impeccable lady, could be really rude.

In the spring of 1803, the Dowager Empress, Maria Fedorovna, found what she considered a possible suitor for Catherine's hand, the Habsburg Archduke Joseph, Palatine of Austria. Catherine protested, "Am I to be sold like a stupid calf at the marriage market?" Despite these protests, the wily Maria Fedorovna insisted on the match and invited the Palatine to St. Petersburg for an extended visit. When Alexander learned the real purpose of the visit, he supported Catherine in her opposition to the prearranged marriage. He became uneasy, sulky and irritable. When the Archduke revealed an attraction to Catherine, Alexander became ill-tempered with him. The idea of Catherine marrying and leaving Russia was unbearable. So disturbed was he at the thought of losing his beloved sister that he took to his bed and remained unwell for nearly a week. He criticized the proposed marriage and put forward all possible obstacles: age, religion, etc. Eventually, the discouraged and offended Archduke Joseph returned to Hungary. This near loss of Catherine further deepened Alexander's tender feelings for his favorite sister. She had become for him a "vital companion," "the brightest light of my life," as he put it in one of his numerous letters to her.

At the time Alexander ascended the throne, he was paying more and more frequent visits to his sister's apartment. No doubt her maids of honor were well aware of what was going on. To reach her rooms, it is true, he had to pass through that of her governess. But they had other concerns. Most of the maids of honor had their own visitors. Nevertheless, eventually these nocturnal visits were reported to the Dowager Empress. Maria Fedorovna summoned Alexander and reproached him for his scandalizing behavior. He denied any impropriety.

"Mother! My friendship for Catherine is purely platonic. Her sisterly affection is indispensable to me. She understands me better and cheers me more than Elizabeth or even Maria. Catherine is more sensitive and intelligent than any woman I know. I need her companionship and warm friendship."

Soon, however, even the intimate friendship was not enough to satisfy the growing ambition of Catherine. Like her grandmother, she was thirsty also for power. "Last night I had a dream," she said once to Alexander in May of 1802. "We were sitting beside each other on a golden throne while foreign ambassadors knelt in front of us, begging us to accept gifts from their masters. . . ."

Alexander was shocked and reacted vividly: "This was an insane dream, Cathy. . . . You should control your wild imagination!"

"What is so wild in my dream? The Persian rulers and the Ptolemaic dynasty in Egypt provide examples of marital ties between brothers and sisters. None of these dynasties made any secret of doing in public exactly what was forbidden to commoners. It was a prerogative of royalty, a means to consolidate power. In a book which you yourself gave me on my last birthday, I read that Queen Cleopatra of Egypt was the issue of several generations of intermarriage between brothers and sisters. Actually both her husbands were her brothers. . ."

★ ★ ★

The feelings which Alexander had for his sister were extraordinarily intense. This was reflected in their correspondence which, again, was initiated not by Alexander, but by Catherine. In one of her first letters to him, written in April 1801, she said, "Dear Sasha, now when we are both orphans, I must admit that I consider you not only my brother, but also my warmest and most affectionate friend, by ties of both blood and affection." To this Alexander replied, "My dear, I cannot tell you how much your letters please me . . . It is indispensable to my happiness to be loved by you, because you are the most beautiful creature that has ever existed in this world. I adore you and am only afraid lest you will eventually despise me. . . . Alas! I cannot use my former rights to press most tender kisses in your bedroom. . . ."

In another letter, Alexander wrote to Catherine, "My good friend, your letters are each more charming than the preceding one and I cannot tell you what real pleasure they give me. If you say that you are mad, at least you are the most delightful crazy girl who has ever existed. I must declare that you have completely conquered me and that I am mad about you. I adore you. . . . Good-bye, charm of my eyes, adoration of my heart. . . . All my heart and soul is yours."

Catherine answered Alexander's letter in a no less tender way. "Dear Sasha, when taking my pen to write to you, I felt somehow like a schoolgirl appearing before her teacher. She scratches her head, not knowing fully her lesson, and especially not being aware in what sort of humor her master is. However, I say to myself, if he wants it, all is well. If not, he will tell me his reasons and then we shall see. Anyhow, I say to you now, let us be friends, Sasha. It is I who invite you to this! . . . Good-bye, Dearest, I am all yours."

After his return to St. Petersburg in July 1807, the depressed Alexander alienated from most of his friends, went to see his sister. The visit to Pavlovsk, where Catherine then resided, was to seek a balm for the criticism from his mother and the indifference of Maria Naryshkin. His presentation of Tilsit as his personal triumph found a rather cool response even from Catherine. "God has saved us," he said. "Instead of having to make sacrifices, we have emerged from the combat with a sort of luster. What do you think of all these happenings? Imagine my spending days with Bonaparte and talking for hours quite alone with him! . . . Doesn't it strike you as being all rather like a dream! . . ."

His rationalization for the concessions he had made to Napoleon were scornfully rejected by Catherine. "All this is a trap. Your pact with the French is a pact with the Devil. It is damaging not only to you as a sovereign monarch but to Russia's vital interests and to her prestige," she blurted out. "All the charm Napoleon has used on you is only so much deceit, for the man is an upstart, a combination of cunning, ambition and pretense. . . ." Then she added in a quieter tone, "You have to remember that you made huge sacrifices, but for what? I wish to see our Motherland respected not only in words but in reality. Our dear Russia certainly has the means and the right to be a leader of the world and not a French dependency. While I live I shall not get used to the idea that you submitted to Bonaparte."

"So even you, my favorite sister, condemn me. . . ? Don't you have even one word of encouragement for me. . . ?"

"Forgive the flow of my angry words, dear Sasha, but it is only from the well of my heart that the mouth speaks. My sincere devotion will end only with my life. You can count on my love and friendship always. But beware of Bonaparte."

The night Alexander spent at Pavlovsk somewhat calmed his nerves. The next morning, while relaxing in Catherine's bathtub, he meditated on the strange constellation of women that surrounded him. "I have a consort who is my legally wedded spouse, but actually no more than my friend, warm and understanding, but merely a friend. Maria is my de facto wife, mother of my children, but not my friend, only my lover. . . . My mother wanted to be Regent. Brushed aside, she is frustrated and covets my power. She encourages those opposed to me and trys to undermine my authority. Actually she is now the focus of the opposition to me. And, here am I with a sister who is everything I could possibly desire: a passionate lover, an understanding friend, a delightful companion. What a pity I am not an Egyptian pharoah, what a pity. . . ."

While being helped to dress by his servant, Melnikov, Alexander mused, "The most usual figure in a man's life is a triangle: husband, wife and his or her lover. But I have to deal with a female quadrangle: my mother, my wife, my mistress and my sister. I am dependent on each of them for different reasons. What a strange situation. What an emotional maze. . . ."

★ ★ ★

Napoleon was aware of the unpopularity of the French alliance. His ambassador General Savary, former chief of Gendarmes who commanded the firing squad that executed the Duc d'Enghien, was barely tolerated by Alexander and totally snubbed by St. Petersburg society. Consequently, Napoleon soon replaced him with a descendant of an old aristocratic and essentially royalist family, General Armand de Caulaincourt. To overcome Russian society's coldness toward him, Caulaincourt gave a series of dinners and entertainments of various kinds. His sumptuous tables were open to all and attracted many guests. He spent more than his salary of 600,000 francs and started to borrow money. "Must I sell my shirt to pay my debts?" he wrote Napoleon. Yet, even this lavish entertainment could hardly dispel Russian distaste for the French connection.

While facing the opposition to his new foreign policy, Alexander tried to deal with domestic issues; finances especially, undermined by the war and plagued by the issue of paper money that had debased the value of the ruble, needed much attention. He realized that internal reforms, interrupted by hostilities, had to be resumed in order to prevent the antiquated bureaucratic mechanism from being run into the ground. The large sums of money required for the war made it difficult to support his initially rather generous subsidies to establish several universities and advanced schools. Gone were Stroganov and Czartoryski, his idea men and the administrators of broad bold vistas. Novosiltsev, subservient, even servile, as ever, did not share Alexander's passion for reform and grew increasingly opportunistic. Though ready to carry out his master's orders, he seldom put forward ideas of his own. There remained Kochubey, then Minister of the Interior, but his reforming zeal had cooled down considerably by then and he was also more of a "yes" man than an independent voice. Of course, Arakcheyev was always there, still obsessed with military matters, still the martinet-in-chief.

Despite the dispersal of the Secret Committee, Alexander felt morally committed to continue his search for a government based on law and, perhaps, for some sort of consultative institution that would strengthen his authoritarian rule. What he missed was an intelligent, energetic, efficient instrument to carry out some of the dreams of his youthful years.

In this quest for a loyal co-worker, Alexander was helped by an accident. One day in 1807 Kochubey, then Minister of the Interior, was to report to him in person on the affairs of his ministry. Being unwell, he sent to the Emperor one of his deputies, Michael Michailovich Speransky. Alexander expected to see a servile, obsequious *chinovinik,* a narrow-minded bureaucrat. Instead he observed a tall, well dressed and well mannered man with long nose, thin lips, deeply penetrating eyes and a balding head. Briefly yet precisely, he presented his ideas and astonished the Tsar by being ready to defend his logical arguments. Alexander was so impressed with the report that he made Speransky his personal assistant. Soon he became the Emperor's trusted co-worker and advisor, his right hand.

Speransky's career was most spectacular. He was born in 1772 in Cherkutine, a village in Vladimir province, son of a parish priest, a member of the lowest stratum of free men. Yet, the clerical status of his father opened to Michael opportunities that were closed to most Russians without noble birth, namely education in one of the diocesan seminaries. And indeed, at the age of twelve Speransky had entered a seminary at Vladimir and emerged from it at the top of his class. In 1790 he was selected to enter the newly established seminary in the Alexander Nevsky Monastery in St. Petersburg, recently established as a model for other institutions. This seminary offered as solid an education as one could receive anywhere in Russia at the time. The young Speransky studied classics, history, French, German and the philosophical and scientific thought of the Enlightenment, as well as the more traditional subjects of an ecclesiastic training. Here, as at Vladimir, he proved to be an outstanding student; in 1792 he was selected to teach mathematics, physics and rhetoric, and in 1795 he became an instructor in philosophy.

An ecclesiastical career was clearly open to Speransky, but he rebelled against the tradition that a son of a priest ought to become a priest, and in 1796 accepted a secular position as secretary to Prince Aleksei Kurakin. Yet, his inferior social status made him shy and self-conscious, evidenced by the fact that he took his meals with the servants and not at the master's table. Soon, however, he attracted attention and respect for his penetrating intelligence and fanatic devotion to every task to which he was entrusted. Tsar Paul appreciated such qualities. Within a few months the Tsar appointed Kurakin Procurator-General of the Senate, and Speransky found himself at the hub of Russian political life. When Kurakin was relieved from his position, Speransky stayed on in the chancery of the Senate and within a year had reached the eighth rank in the government service, which automatically brought him hereditary noble status. From then on his behavior changed. Feeling more secure, he rejected his humble ways, began to dress like a gentleman and was driven in luxurious four-horse carriages.

In 1798 he fell in love with and married an English woman, Elizabeth Stephens, but after giving birth to a daughter a year later, she died. Speransky never fully recovered from this blow and never remarried. The tragedy probably reinforced a natural inclination to aloofness, hypersensitivity, suspicion of rivals and proneness to invective. Thereafter he led a lonely life, which left him socially isolated throughout his career. He combined his native cunning and his gift for clear exposition of complex problems with an immense appetite for work and tried to impress his ideas on his new Imperial master, Alexander, during their long conversations. In his paper entitled "On the Fundamental Laws of the State," he maintained that even an all-powerful monarchy cannot govern without public spirited people and an educated group of propertied citizens.

Alexander replied: "But Michael Michailovich, you are playing with fire. You want to confront me, or my successors, with a sort of Russian National Convention. As a young man I was inclined to share Count Stroganov's enthusiasm for the French experiment. But we all saw how it ended. . . ."

"I understand perfectly Your Imperial Majesty's apprehensions. As a matter of fact I share them myself. It would take at least one generation. But we must plan far beyond that and prepare for the abolition of serfdom. . . ."

"Your idea of abolishing serfdom is premature. More than that it is dangerous. My friends, Stroganov and Czartoryski, were right in saying that we should educate the peasants before we turn them into free tenants. An outright emancipation would spell revolt of the nobility against the State and result in anarchy. Can we afford such an experience in the near future?"

Speransky retreated immediately and said, "I agree with Your Imperial Majesty, I fully agree. . . . My plan is a long-range one. Of course, we should not hurry. But even the longest journey begins with a single step. I also fully agree with you, Sire, that education should precede emancipation. That is why I am pushing for the spread and reform of schools, especially the parochial schools. They should teach our peasants how to read, write and count."

Speransky, who in his heart admired Napoleon and his reforms, realized how the Russian economy was essentially dependent on trade with England. A way in which to reconcile the French alliance with the needs of the Russian economy was difficult. He suggested to the Tsar that custom officials simply close their eyes to the contraband carried out under Swedish and American flags. "Should the French challenge us, we could always claim ignorance. If they insist, we can then promise to cope with future violations of the blockade. . . ."

Another of Speransky's proposals was to increase the domestic production of such basic goods as sugar and cotton. "Why do we have to smuggle them from Britain's colonies?" he asked. "Let's replace cotton with our native hemp or develop cotton and sugar beet plantations in our southern provinces, the Black Sea regions of the Ukraine or the Crimea. Why not borrow money from the French, the Swiss and the Dutch?" However, the Russian landowners and merchants, for generations accustomed to relying on State patronage, refused to seriously consider Speransky's far-sighted plans. As for Alexander, his social and sentimental involvements, as well as his predilection for miltiary display, did not allow him time to deal with fundamental domestic issues, another reason was the complex diplomatic situation in which Russia found herself by 1808–1809.

* * *

Napoleon, who had an extensive intelligence network in Russia, was well aware of the Tsar's domestic difficulties. To consolidate the Franco-Prussian partnership Napoleon contemplated a marriage with one of Alexander's sisters, either Catherine or Ann. To attain this objective he was ready to offer the Duchy of Warsaw as a reward. Not trusting Caulaincourt to negotiate so delicate a matter, and relying more on the spell he had so successfully cast on Alexander at Tilsit, Napoleon suggested another personal encounter in September 1808 at Erfurt. The very choice of this town was significant. Although it had belonged to Prussia, Napoleon's whim declared it a single "special preserve of the Emperor," *le domaine reservée à l'Empereur."*

As soon as the St. Petersburg Court learned of Alexander's intention to go to Erfurt, all hell broke loose. The Dowager Empress, Maria Fedorovna, once again was in the vanguard of fierce opposition to the visit. "Stay away from Erfurt for the sake of Russia's honor. Napoleon treats Europe as a pirate treats a captured vessel and you as his slave! He shifts monarchs as our landowners shift their serfs from one estate to another," she raged. "The bloody tyrant has recently compelled the Spanish king to abdicate and replaced him with Joseph Bonaparte. Stay away, I repeat. Stay away, my child."

"Not to go to Erfurt," argued Alexander, "would reveal my hand much too soon. It would make me, defenseless and at the head of a country torn by internal dissent, an open enemy of the most powerful monarch in the world. Laharpe was a wise teacher. He once told me the story of Machiavelli's last agony. When the author of *The Prince* was dying, the priest who came to hear his confession, suspecting him of devil worship, asked, 'Have you renounced Satan?' Machiavelli replied, 'It is too early to make enemies. . . .' "

Maria Fedorovna was deaf to such arguments. "This is a good story, whether true or false. As the Italians say, *Si non e vero e bene trovato.* I am convinced that by responding to Napoleon's summons you humiliate both yourself and our dear Russia. Erfurt for you may be what Bayonne was for the Spanish king. Erfurt is a trap!"

Alexander remained silent while his mother continued hysterical supplications. "Sasha . . . Stay away! You will ruin your empire, and your family. Turn back, there is still time. Listen to the voice of honor, to the prayers and pleas of your mother."

Alexander respectfully reiterated his argument, "For the moment I must pretend to share Napoleon's views. Let us not hasten to declare ourselves against him. We would run the risk of losing everything. Rather, let us appear to consolidate the alliance so as to lull him into a sense of security. Let us gain time to prepare. Time works for me. While Napoleon's greed grows, his resources do not. His Spanish adventure is a bottomless pit. Germany, especially the humiliated Prussians, are seething with hatred, and thirst for revenge. Let's wait."

Alexander left St. Petersburg with only a small retinue which included Grand Duke Constantine, Chancellor Rumiantsev and Speransky. During the October days of 1808 the roads that led to Erfurt were thronged with long lines of vans, barouches and other carriages bringing dignitaries, chamberlains, maids of honor, pages and servants from every corner of continental Europe. They carried with them their finest dresses, their jewels, their gold and silver plates, their best cooks and liveried footmen. On the way to Erfurt, Alexander decided to stop at Königsberg, where he met the King of Prussia and Queen Louise. After listening to their grievances he was even more convinced that Prussia also was playing for time and contemplating revenge. This did not prevent him from telling Marshal Lannes, who welcomed him to Friedberg, "I have much affection for Emperor Napoleon and I shall prove it to him at every opportunity."

Napoleon met Alexander at the gates of Erfurt. On seeing him approach, Napoleon dismounted and embraced the Tsar with effusive cordiality. Then an equerry led to Alexander a gift from his host, a splendid black horse named Eclipse, with Russian harness and caparison of white bearskin. The two sovereigns made their entrance into Erfurt riding stirrup to stirrup. Drums rolled, trumpets sounded, bells pealed, and the artillery fired a salute. The crowd of spectators applauded. Napoleon rode calmly on his white Arabian stallion. He sat rather carelessly, one hand holding the reins, the other patting the neck of his mount. He paid no attention to the acclamations of "Long live the Emperor!" as if taking them for granted. Alexander rode beside Napoleon, tense and uneasy. He was irritated and jealous that most of the cheers were directed towards Napoleon and not to him. He felt ignored, neglected in the shadow of his host.

★ ★ ★

The meeting at Erfurt marked the apogee of Napoleon's glory. All the pageantry was designed to impress the subject princes of Europe with the power of the new Charlemagne. The day following Alexander's arrival was devoted to public ceremonies. Most impressive was the opening of the meeting at the princely palace occupied by Napoleon. Officers of the Imperial household gathered in the main hall and the Lord Chamberlain stood motionless at its monumental staircase. Tapping his silver-embossed baton the Master of Cermonies announced in resounding voice the titles of the entering guests. The order and form of these announcements were planned by Napoleon himself, based upon rigid etiquette and a strict protocol, and with careful regard for dramatic effect. First came the ambassadors and ministers. They were succeeded by minor royalties, like the Duke of Weimar and the Duke of Mecklenburg. Then came the Kings and Queens, starting with those of Saxony, Westphalia and Bavaria. And then, after a noticeable pause, the Lord Chamberlain shouted, "His Imperial Majesty, Emperor of All the Russias, Alexander the First!" Reading discreetly from a small card which he held in his left hand, the Lord Chamberlain spelled out a dozen or so feudal titles that the Russian Tsars had abrogated for themselves, by either inheritance or conquest. Finally, after a prolonged silence that increased the tension among the audience, the Lord Chamberlain tapped his baton three times and uttered a single loud cry, *"L'Empereur."*

Unlike other bemedaled potentates, most of them covered with gems and decorations, Napoleon appeared in the austere green uniform of his Chasseurs of the Guards, adorned only by the red ribbon of the grand Cross of the Legion of Honor. He radiated the supreme self confidence that assumed the validity of the command "Thou shalt have no other gods before me."

All heads bowed, while ladies made deep curtsies and remained immobile in the posture until he passed by. Again Alexander felt ignored. Wasn't he, the Tsar of all the Russias, the honored guest of Napoleon, who should have been the last to enter the august gathering?

In the evening Napoleon and Alexander attended a sumptuous banquet, followed by a great ball at the castle of Weimar. The Tsar tried to hide his irritation behind a mask of good manners. He danced with the ladies while Napoleon watched him, motionless, an ironic condescending smile on his lips. Together they talked to the Kings of Bavaria, Westphalia, the Grand Duke of Würtemberg and other reigning princes of Germany who had hastened to pay homage to their protector. All these petty princes trembled before the man on whom their survival depended. In the course of the gathering, as King Maximilian Joseph dared to raise his voice to interject his opinion on some trivial matter, Napoleon snapped at him, "Hold your tongue, King of Bavaria!"

The following days were divided equally between private conversations and public ceremonies. Together the two Emperors watched the maneuvers of the French occupation army stationed in Germany. Together they visited the battlefield of Jena, scene of the defeat of Prussia. Goethe himself was summoned to Erfurt, bowed before Napoleon, and was rewarded with the Cross of the Legion of Honor.

One evening, having dined at Napoleon's table, the princes and their entourages met again at the theater. The most celebrated actors of the Comedie Francaise appeared before the distinguished guests. Talma, acting in Voltaire's *Oedipus,* turned toward Alexander and recited a line inserted by Napoleon, "The friendship of a great man is a gift of the gods!" At these words, Alexander rose, shook the hand of Napoleon, who was seated beside him in the box, and then they embraced each other, as if repeating the performance on the Tilsit raft. The audience responded by a spontaneous ovation.

The Tsar was particularly impressed by the actress Antoinette Bourgoin, nicknamed "the goddess of joy and pleasures." He mentioned his interest in meeting her in private to Napoleon, who replied, "I do not advise you to make advances to her."

"You think she would refuse?" said the Tsar.

"Oh no!" explained Napoleon. "Quite the contrary. She would be delighted. She would use your visit to blackmail her manager to double her salary. Moreover, in a couple of days all Paris would know the details of Your Majesty's anatomy from head to toe. . . . And then, I take an interest in your health. As a matter of fact I am interested in the health of the *entire* Romanov family," he added enigmatically.

The surprised Alexander pressed him for an explanation. Napoleon replied, "About my sincere interest in the Romanov family we should, perhaps, talk in private tomorrow. Now let me say that my Minister of Police, Fouché, intercepted an interesting contraband package sent from a London pharmacy to Mademoiselle Bourgoin. It contained a powder used for making potions against the disease which you foreigners call French, while we Frenchmen call it either Spanish or Italian. Whether it was brought to Italy by the crusaders, or to Spain by the sailors of Christopher Columbus, I will not argue."

The next day, from their first conversations, Napoleon noted that Alexander was not so accommodating as he had been at Tilsit. Having an urgent need to send his armies from Prussia to Spain, Napoleon wanted a formal pledge that the Tsar would join him should Austria take advantage of his Spanish involvement. Alexander, however, found varied pretexts to avoid committing himself. The talks dragged on and grew acrimonious. During one dispute, stormier than the others, Napopleon flung his hat on the ground and stamped on it. Unimpressed by the display of temper, Alexander said, "You are violent; I am stubborn. So anger will get you nowhere with me. Let us talk, let us reason, or I shall leave." Napoleon calmed down.

"Sire," resumed Alexander, "you assure me of your peaceful intentions toward Russia, yet you maintain strong garrisons in the countries adjacent to my realm, in Prussia and in the Duchy of Warsaw. I beg you to demonstrate your friendship toward me by evacuating your troops from both these countries. . . ."

"At Tilsit, as I am sure you remember, I offered you the Duchy of Warsaw, lock, stock and barrel. You refused it since this was a piece formerly belonging to the King of Prussia, your bosom friend and ally. Now I need the Duchy to keep the restless Austrians, as well as Prussians, in check. If you are my sincere friend, you should not mind this."

"I don't. But the Poles sent spies and agitators into my western provinces. They covet these western domains—Lithuania, Podolia, the Ukraine. . . ."

"Their appetites are platonic. Without my aid they can do nothing."

Alexander remained silent, while Napoleon was nervously pacing the room, arms clasped behind his back. After a while he resumed his bluster, "At Tilsit, I was most generous toward you. I agreed to your annexing Moldavia and Wallachia. I consented also to your conquest of Finland. Isn't that enough to prove my benevolence toward Russia?"

"Yes, Sire, but this means diversion of my country's resources toward the north and the south, and away from the vital region of central Europe which you dominate, and from which the main threat to my country may come. Don't you toy with the idea of reestablishing the old Polish-Lithuanian state at our expense?"

"If you wish I will put in writing the firm resolve that I voiced several times at Tilsit, never to create a greater Poland. I established the Duchy of Warsaw from the Prussian share of Poland's partitions, not yours. You even profited from the arrangement as I ceded the Białystok region to Russia. I repeat, I need the duchy to keep both Prussia and Austria in check and weak enough not to menace your mighty Empire. Prussia was crushed by me and is no menace, but the Austrians are still sulking, plotting and secretly rearming. At any moment they may take advantage of my involvement in Spain. Should this happen, would you prove your friendship and help me? Would you at least refrain from attacking my eastern flank, protected by the Duchy of Warsaw?"

"Should Emperor Francis be foolish enough to attack you, I will be at your side. I will never take arms against you."

Following these words, Alexander made a gesture with his right hand toward his left hip, as if to draw his sword, and noticed that he had forgotten it. Napoleon, who had just drawn his own, grasped the meaning of his guest's intended gesture, picked up his sword from the table and offered it to Alexander. "Please accept this as a small token of my friendship for you and my good intentions toward Russia. Together we should be able to bring the English shopkeepers to their knees."

"I accept your sword as a token of your friendship. Your Majesty can be very certain that I shall never draw it against him."

Having thus duped each other, the two rivals signed a series of agreements, some open and some secret. In an official communiqué they declared themselves satisfied at the consolidation of the Russo-French ties. In a secret agreement France accepted, in advance, Russian annexation of both Danubian principalities, Moldavia and Wallachia, as well as Finland. Another secret convention provided for military cooperation against the Austrians, should they begin hostilities against France or one of her allies.

⋆ ⋆ ⋆

At the time Alexander expected Napoleon to explain his intriguing reference to his interest not only in Alexander's health, but that of the entire Romanov family. But his host avoided the subject. When pressed by the Tsar to tackle it, he cut the conversation short by saying, "This is a very delicate matter. I charged Talleyrand with it. He will see Your Majesty before your return home."

And indeed, two days before Alexander's departure from Erfurt, Talleyrand did ask for an audience with the Tsar. Talleyrand had been dismissed from the Foreign Ministry in August 1807, but had retained considerable power as Grand Chamberlain and Vice-

Grand Elector, the third highest dignitary of the Empire. Napoleon brought him to Erfurt because of his diplomatic experience.

"My Master," said Talleyrand, "wishes to divorce the Empress Josephine because, being forty-six years old, she is unable to bear children, and he is longing for a male heir. Is there any chance, Sire, of your younger sister, Catherine, now nineteen years of age, to be offered in marriage to my master?"

The shocked Alexander was at a loss as to what to say. He was horrified at the very idea of his beloved Catherine leaving Russia. After a moment of hesitation, and mastering his fear, he replied, "I am greatly honored by the Emperor Napoleon's proposal, but it is not for me to decide. I will have to consider it after consulting the Dowager Empress, my mother, as well as my sister."

Talleyrand used the confidential encounter with Alexander to warn him against Napoleon's plans and his boundless ambition. "Sire, what are you doing here, among all these petty, servile princes? It is in your power to save Europe, and you will not succeed by giving way to Napoleon. Europe cannot be saved except by close cooperation between Russia and Austria. The French people are civilized; their sovereign is not. The sovereign of Russia must therefore be the ally of the people of France and not of their adventurous and irresponsible master. By destroying the last vestiges of Austrian power in central Europe you endanger your own Empire, which may be next on the list of Napoleon's conquests. The lion has pulled in his claws, but not all the way. Beware. . . ."

Alexander took to heart Talleyrand's warning, which actually amounted to treason. After this crucial conversation he said to Rumiantsev, "Talleyrand's services should be rewarded. I will send him money through our Swiss banker. If he accepts, he is ours. In the future, we may need a man of his rank. Perhaps Speransky should be put in touch with him."

What puzzled Alexander most was Napoleon's marriage proposal. During his journey back, the Tsar calcuated, "Catherine can't` remain single any longer. To keep her at home I should marry her to some elderly, tolerant harmless man who would reside in Russia, either in or near one of the capitals. The problem is to find such a candidate, a man who would be acceptable to such a temperamental, capricious and strong-willed girl."

Catherine, when informed by Alexander or Napoleon's proposal, was livid with rage. "What happened to you, Sasha? Suddenly you talk like our mother. Can you imagine me away from Russia, in the arms of this dwarf of a vampire?"

"The very idea is odious to me. But you should marry, sooner or later."

"I don't want to marry. I want to live." She reiterated her standard argument, ". . . I am not a calf to be sold on the market!"

"But your marriage is a necessity for at least two reasons. First, a proper marriage would enhance your social status while protecting your reputation. Second, as a Romanov Grand Duchess you must serve our Empire. Our grandmother used to say that Grand Dukes and Grand Duchesses are State property and she was right. Our marriages are a part of our diplomatic game."

When Catherine calmed down, they sat on a sofa and began discussing Alexander's stratagem. "Since we live not in Egypt but in Russia, we must act accordingly. Let's draw up a list of foreign princes that would be politically advantageous to us, while personally acceptable to you." They moved to Catherine's studio where a large table served as the desk on which she usually wrote her letters and on which she kept her favorite books. Among them was a copy of the *Gothaischer Hofkalendar,* popularly known as the *Almanac of Gotha,* a gold mine of information on most of the aristocratic families of Europe. After studying the thick volume, they concluded that Duke George of Oldenburg, heir to the throne of that duchy, and only a dozen years older than Catherine, would be the most suitable candidate.

"I met him once casually. He is shy, awkward and not very good looking, but I set no value on appearance," concluded Catherine.

"Since his domain is threatened by Napoleon's ambition and his situation as heir is rather precarious, we should be able to persuade him to settle in Russia," scolded Alexander.

"Provided you would give him a position prestigious enough to satisfy his vanity and fill his empty pocket," interjected Catherine.

"I could always find him some post at the Court or make him a governor of one of our provinces."

"What about Tver? It is on the way from Peter to Moscow. Every time you travel to the old capital or back you could stop to see me for a day or two."

"This would be a wonderful arrangement!"

Tver, an old city on the upper Volga a hundred miles along the Petersburg road from Moscow, also suited Alexander's purpose politically because it needed a good administrator. Soon a special Russian envoy was sent to Oldenburg and the marriage was promptly arranged.

Although Alexander understood the rationale of Catherine's marriage and insisted on it, its prospect affected his health profoundly. The day after the wedding ceremony, he took to his bed, and again before the couple's departure to Tver, where George was to reside as governor. On August 26, 1809, Catherine left Petersburg amid scenes of tearful farewell, as though passing into distant exile.

Unable to obtain the hand of Catherine, Napoleon renewed his attempts to marry a Romanov Grand Duchess, this time the younger sister Anne, who was barely fifteen. Alexander again avoided a straight answer, again pleading the necessity of seeking his mother's counsel. "If Napoleon insists, how is he to be answered?" he asked his mother. "The consequences of a refusal will be acrimony and ill will." The Dowager Empress exploded hysterically, "Must my poor Annette be sacrificed for the good of the State? What a miserable existence the child would lead with a man who knows no restraint because he does not even believe in God! . . . What would she do in Paris, in that school of wickedness and vice? . . . Shall I, Annette's own mother, dictate her unhappiness? . . ."

For several hours Alexander and the Dowager Empress debated various replies that might be given to Caulaincourt.

After an extended family council, Caulaincourt was informed that as Grand Duchess Anne was barely nubile, this precluded her marrying during the next year or two, until she would reach puberty. How could she be given in marriage to Napoleon, who was already forty years old? Nevertheless, to avoid an open quarrel between the two courts, it was hinted that in a couple of years, when Anne had reached full development, the situation could be reconsidered.

Napoleon was furious on learning that he was being turned down for the second time. Russo-French relations reached another critical point.

★ ★ ★

In the spring of 1809, taking advantage of Napoleon's embarrassing involvement in Spain, the Austrians pounced on his forces in Germany and invaded the Duchy of Warsaw. Napoleon instructed Caulaincourt to invoke the secret Franco-Russian convention concluded at Erfurt that obliged Russia to assist France if she were challenged by Austria. Alexander responded with apparent firmness, "We have done everything to avoid war. Since the Austrians have provoked it and begun it, you will find in me an ally who will march boldly. I shall do nothing by halves." However, he spoke quite differently to the Austrian Ambassador, Prince Schwarzenberg, who reported to Vienna, "The Emperor assured me that Russia would do everything humanly possible to avoid striking blows at us. He added that his position was so strange that although we found ourselves in opposite camps, he could not help but wish for our success."

Reluctantly, the Tsar gave the order for 60 thousand men to cross the Bug River and enter Austrian territory. By devious means, the Russian army avoided contact with the Austrian troops they had come to fight. Russia's true adversaries were not the Austrians but the Poles, who had rallied to the French cause. Caulaincourt was repeatedly instructed to urge the Russians to act more vigorously. "We are slow, said Chancellor Rumiantsev to Caulaincourt, "but we are sure." Prince Poniatowski, commander-in-chief of the Polish forces, wrote Napoleon, "I am loath to accuse the Russian generals of perfidy, but I cannot conceal from Your Majesty that there is perfect accord between them and the enemy. The Russian casualties in the entire campaign amounted to two Cossacks killed and two officers wounded, one of them accidentally, as a result of a drunken brawl."

Napoleon was furious and vented his wrath on the Russian ambassador in Paris, "One of your peasant weddings may result in more casualties than your entire campaign in Galicia. What kind of an ally are you? Report my profound dissatisfaction to your master and do it at once. . . ."

After brilliant victories in Bavaria, Napoleon again occupied Vienna on May 13. The hard-fought battle of Wagram settled the outcome of the war, to Alexander's great disappointment. He was officially on the side of the victor, yet he deplored the downfall of the vanquished. By the Treaty of Vienna, signed on October 14, 1809, the Duchy of Warsaw was enlarged at the expence of Austria. To keep up appearances Russia was given the district of Tarnopol in southeastern Poland. Russian opinion was outraged at this pittance. "Napoleon has humiliated His Imperial Majesty, Tsar Alexander," wrote one of the St. Petersburg courtiers to the Dowager Empress, "by giving him from the lands taken from Austria, not some province, but 400,000 souls, as much as Peter the Great once gave to his drinking companions or Catherine her lovers."

Without waiting for the promised "definitive answer" of the Russian court concerning his possible marriage to Grand Duchess Anne "in a couple of years," Napoleon announced his intention to marry Marie Louise of Austria. From then on events moved quickly. Pope Pius VII was taken prisoner, and Holland and the Hanseatic cities were annexed. Among the territories swept up by Napoleon was the little Duchy of Oldenburg, and the father-in-law of Alexander's favorite sister was dethroned. "It is a public insult," said Alexander, "a slap in the face of a friendly power." Moreover, he could not afford to be complacent about the economic ills of his Empire, which were affected by the Continental

System. Inevitably the Russian merchants and their credit institutions were hit by the failure of several German banks, which resulted in the commercial panic throughout the Continent. Moreover, the old resentment at French interference with secret Russo-British trading arrangements was revived under the guise of it being interference in Russian domestic matters. There was much talk in St. Petersburg of seeking release from the Continental System, which prevented Russia from openly exporting hemp, grain, lumber and flax, or from receiving English manufactured goods, while permitting the Empire to be flooded with French silk, perfumes and wines.

The Council of State considered ways of gradually easing Russia out of the Continental System, and the question was also discussed between Alexander and his ministers. Rumiantsev opposed any change in tariffs, primarily because he did not want to force a diplomatic crisis with the French. Speransky favored freer trade carried on under the American flag, and the Minister of Finance supported him, but Alexander was unable to make up his mind. Speransky maintained that the Continental System was stimulating industry within Russia and helping the merchants to find new markets, but few found his arguments convincing.

⋆ ⋆ ⋆

After the return from Erfurt, Alexander had charged Speransky with various diplomatic tasks of a clandestine nature. One of these was to oversee the Russian intelligence net in Europe, especially in France, where Talleyrand was the key figure. By 1809, Speransky became one of the most powerful men in Russia, a rival of Arakcheyev. This rise to power by the orphaned son of a poor clergyman aroused a great deal of jealousy in aristocratic Court circles. The fact that he had access to the Tsar more easily than anybody else, and dined with him frequently, was unbearable to the jealous courtiers. For about four years, from 1807 until the Spring of 1811, Speransky enjoyed confidence comparable to that of Alexander's old aristocratic friends of the Secret Committee.

What was still more irritating for the nobility was Speransky's suggestion to sweep aside the cherished privileges permitting more rapid advancement of members of the nobility within the civil service. And indeed, the Tsar decreed that applicants for the higher ranks of State services should be appointed only after sitting for a written examination. The decree ordered that henceforth the titles of nobility awarded to those who had served the State would be purely honorific and would not confer any rank in the civil service. Another decree provided that promotion to the higher ranks of the service would be dependent on a certain level of education. Many noblemen were indignant over this restriction which aimed at the traditional preferment granted to birth and not to education. There was grumbling that Speransky advised abolition of serfdom, that he wanted to tax the nobility and to establish a high custom tariff on luxuries. Both of these measures aroused furious indignation among the squires. Members of the petty nobility still on the lower rungs of the social ladder would be prevented from climbing to greater eminence because they could never pass an examination in Russian language and mathematics, let alone in the stricter disciplines of Latin and French. Only an obsessive pedant, would seek to mortify honest Russian boys in such a way, argued Speransky's opponents.

Gradually a coterie formed, welded together by jealousy and vested interests, bent on toppling the arrogant man who dared to rise from the dust of a provincial parish to a ministerial rank. Scandal-mongers scoured Speransky's private life for juicy morsels, but they did so in vain. Then his enemies tried to implicate this "sneaky crook," as they called him, in an affair involving smuggling of English goods into Russia aboard an American vessel. This intrigue failed also because the documents used to prove it were a crude forgery.

Speransky's enemies, unable to oust him from his position through fabricated gossips, used one last weapon. They smeared his reputation by alleging he was a foreign agent, a "disguised Jacobin." This particular accusation had begun as soon as the Tsar returned from Erfurt, for it seemed to some in attendance of Alexander that Speransky was unduly impressed by the institutions of French government and customs. He was quoted as calling Napoleon "a new Justician," "a great legislator." Such overheard words of praise were sufficient for jealous rivals to maintain that Speransky had been bribed to introduce into Russia alien ideas and innovations based upon French constitutional usage. He was guilty of treachery to the old Russian values and it was essential for someone to expose to the well-intentioned Tsar, a "viper," a "Judas."

As the Russo-French relations became more and more tense, attacks on Speransky as a leading Francophile multiplied. He defended himself by stating, "I see the Emperor of the French not so much as the victor of Wagram but as restorer of religion, the author of the Civil Code, the reorganizer of the country, the creator of an administration that is unequaled in the world." This defensive explanation was denounced as cover for his morbid Francophilia and an act of treason.

What also irritated the aristocracy was that this son of a humble parish priest, after his appointment as Minister of the Interior, jettisoned his early modest manners and began to behave as if he were one of them. He began to import his clothing from the leading Paris tailors, went riding on a thoroughbred horse with a short-cropped tail, and gave receptions as sumptuous as allowed any boyar. When he suggested taxing the nobility, indignation in the Court circles knew no bounds. "This bloody upstart wants to be equal to us. Worse than that, he wants to ruin us."

One of Speransky's chief critics was Karamzin. He took great care to befriend Grand Duchess Catherine. He visited her quite often in Tver and flattered her by calling her "the most brilliant woman in Russia, a worthy granddaughter of our Great Catherine." During one of the numerous visits by Alexander to Tver, Karamzin denounced Speransky's criticism of native institutions. "One of my friends—I am not going to reveal his name to Your Highness—reported to me the following statement by Speransky: 'There is little difference between the peasant's subservience to the landlords and the nobility's subservience to the Monarch. Only free men are creative and productive. I find in Russia only two estates, the slaves of the sovereign and the slaves of the landlord. The former are called free in relation to the latter, but in fact there are no free men in Russia, except beggars and philosophers. . . .' "

"That is scandalous, indeed!" reacted Catherine.

"How do you like such a vilification of our system? If our leaders don't believe in our way of life, how are we to face the impending French invasion?"

"This upstart wants to undermine the ancient foundation of the Muscovite-Russian state. His reforming schemes are a Pandora's box, out of which fly all the ills that are overwhelming Russia," raged the historian Karamzin. "Russia does not need a constitution. Fifty vigorous, efficient governors would be enough." Then he added, "The Tsar should, perhaps, study Machiavelli's *The Prince,* instead of listening to such foggy-minded people as Speransky." Pretending to believe that Speransky aimed to abolish serfdom, he expounded, "I do not know that it would be difficult to return freedom to them. It is less dangerous for the security of the State to enslave men than to free them at the wrong time."

During the visit at Pskov, Karamzin submitted to Catherine a memorandum which included the following passage: "Since Peter the Great we have become citizens of the world, but we have ceased to be citizens of Russia. . . . The Frenchmen have taken control of our education; our court has forgotten the Russian language. Fascinated by European luxury, our nobility has allowed itself to be driven to ruin. . . . It is dangerous to meddle with the structure of an old State. . . . Russia has existed for a millenium as a great empire, not a savage horde. Yet still the reformers speak to us of new institutions and new rules, as if we had just emerged from the virgin forests of America." Even publication of a code of laws, modeled after the French and proposed by Speransky, was condemned by Karamzin. "Russia really does not need to solemnly admit her stupidity before all of Europe and to bend her graying head over a book concocted by a few crooked lawyers and

Jacobins. Our political principles are not inspired by the Napoleonic Code of Laws or an encyclopedia published in Paris but by another encyclopedia infinitely older, the Bible."

* * *

While talking to Catherine and reading Karamzin's memorandum on Ancient and Modern Russia, Alexander realized how isolated he was from the powerful conservative forces that opposed Speransky. He realized that behind the attacks on Speransky, there was some sort of plot, but he was reluctant to denounce it as such, aware that he would challenge those very forces that he needed to mobilize the country's resources and to defend it in case of an external danger. Was it sound to pursue a policy of reform that was unacceptable to those privileged in terms of wealth and birth? Was this a good time to be occupied with internal changes when Napoleon was mustering his forces for a possible invasion of Russia? Was it prudent to rely on one man, who was without a power base and highly unpopular?

At the head of the open opposition was Araksheyev, who constantly protested against Speransky's suggested reforms. For a long time Alexander tried to keep a balance between his two confidants, who hated and despised each other. Speransky, the cultivated, enterprising, imaginative and flexible liberal looked down on the uncouth, semi-literate bugbear with coarse manners and the primitive mentality of a drill sergeant. Araksheyev, on the other hand, suffered from an acute inferiority complex and refused to rub shoulders with Speransky, whom he considered an interloper, intriguer and upstart. As a result of this clash of personalities, Alexander shaped his policy balancing the advice of these two rival characters. Being a past master of playing double games, he would meet them separately in great secrecy and hide from one what the other had said. He pretended to believe the one who had spoken last, and waited for circumstances to determine his course of action.

What proved to be a deadly blow to Speransky was the discovery that, once charged with keeping in touch with Talleyrand and other Frenchmen willing to serve Alexander, he had begun to expand his intelligence network and infiltrate some high Russian offices. After establishing his secret agents not only in several European capitals, beginning with Vienna, he began to bribe employees of the Ministry of Foreign Affairs to procure for him secret files of their office. When informed of this, the Minister of Police, General Balashev, immediately reported it to the Tsar.

On Sunday, March 17, 1812, a messenger from the Winter Palace brought Speransky an order to present himself before the Tsar at eight o'clock that evening. A general and two high-ranking police officers were waiting in the antechamber when Speransky arrived. He was ushered into the study and remained there for two hours, alone with the Tsar.

"Mikhail Mikhailovich," said Alexander, "It has been reported to me that you have committed a series of most injudicious indiscretions. Your enemies call them acts of treason. Knowing your previous loyalty and devotion to the throne and to me personally, I refuse to believe that you have acted in bad faith. Yet copying confidential files from our Ministry of Foreign Affairs, is a serious breach of security. . . ."

"But, Sire, at Erfurt you charged me with being a liaison between Talleyrand and similar friendly people in France. Moreover, you channeled through me money from various banks to pay for their services. . . . You, yourself, asked me not only to advise you on domestic matters but also on foreign affairs. Didn't you tell me to use 'all means necessary' to be well informed on the activities of our own diplomats abroad, to supervise their doings and report to you confidentially my observations about any impropriety? Whenever I asked His Excellency Minister of Foreign Affairs for official files, so indispensable for my work, he refused me. He treated me like an intruder and imposter. His behavior was so haughty, so rude that I, his ministerial colleague, had every right to challenge him to a duel. At one point I was determined to do so and I began to take fencing lessons. But, Sire, I had to give up this insane idea. . . . How can I, son of a poor parish priest, learn enough about dueling at the age of forty to match an aristocrat who started fencing and shooting as a child? This would be suicidal. . . ."

"I sympathize with you, with your plight, Mikhail Mikhailovich, but you must also understand my position. The enemy is knocking at the gates of my Empire. I know that the accusations made against you are at least grossly exaggerated, but in the situation in which you have been placed by the suspicions you have drawn upon yourself by your conduct and the remarks you have permitted yourself to make, what can I do? You have to realize that it is important that I don't appear weak in the eyes of my subjects by continuing to place my trust in a person suspected of state treason. . . . In a critical situation even an autocratic ruler must listen to the voice of public opinion. . . ."

"But Sire, these accusations are not exaggerated. They are entirely false, fabricated. . . . They are slanderous. . . ."

"Perhaps. . . . I would say even most probably, but what is at stake here is not only your fate, but the fate of the Empire. I am extremely sorry, my dear Mikhail Mikhailovich, but I must sacrifice you for the sake of unifying Russian public opinion to face a mortal danger. . . . I hope you understand my motives. . . . One cannot judge sovereigns by standards of private morality. Politics dictates to them duties that repel the heart. . . ."

"Sire, is this the way you repay as devoted and selfless a servant as you have probably ever had? . . ."

"I am most grateful for your loyal services, Mikhail Mikhailovich," answered Alexander, and hugged him with exuberant, exaggerated cordiality. "Statesmen, however, must determine their steps not by emotions, not by sentiments, but by *raison d'Etat*. Politics requires me to perform this surgical operation, as unpleasant as it may be, in cold blood, even when my heart condemns it. Nevertheless, my severity, alas necessitated by the situation, will be mellowed by my generosity. You will reside at Nizhny Novgorod, not an unpleasant city, on the banks of the Volga. Your pension will be sufficient to cover the expenses of a household worthy of your former ministerial position. You may take with you all your belongings, including your splendid library. Farewell, my dear Mikhail Mikhailovich. When the circumstances change, I may need your services again. . . ."

The two police officers who had accompanied Speransky to the Imperial studio were waiting in the anteroom for the end of the audience. At last the door opened and the two appeared on the threshold. Both Speransky and the Emperor himself had tears in their eyes. Each seemed greatly shaken. Speransky held his green Morocco leather portfolio nervously clutched against his chest. Alexander said with emotion, "Once again, farewell."

When Speransky reached home he found a police carriage and four Cossack officers waiting for him. His official papers were placed under seal. In the middle of the night, Speransky left St. Petersburg under escort to go into exile in Nizhny Novgorod. The same day the two officials of the Ministry of Foreign Affairs who had communicated secret documents to Speransky were placed under lock and key.

Speransky's disgrace was greeted by the public as a great victory. "What a great day for the country and for us all," wrote a contemporary writer. "God has shown us his benevolence, and our enemies have fallen. An outrageous crime, an infamous piece of treachery has been discovered in Russia. . . . Speransky was ready to deliver up our country and our Emperor to our worst enemy."

* * *

With Speransky in Nizhny Novgorod, the shaken Alexander gradually began to regain his composure. The congratulations he received on the occasion of this step soon allayed his moral scruples. He had the feeling that by sacrificing his close associate he had rebuilt national unity around himself. In his conscience he justified his step by the alarming intelligence he received both from Paris and from his agents in Poland. Napoleon was concentrating his troops in Prussia and the Duchy of Warsaw. Danzig was rapidly becoming a huge military depot. Austria was urged to supply a larger continent of her soldiers to serve in a great "European crusade" against "the perfidious giant of the North." In May 1812, Caulaincourt, a vigorous proponent of Franco-Russian co-operation, was recalled for "health reasons."

On the morning of May 18, the day before his departure, Caulaincourt was received in a farewell audience by the Tsar. Alexander treated Caulaincourt as a personal friend and warned him, "Should the Emperor Napoleon make war on me, it is possible that we, at first, shall be defeated. But this will not give him peace. . . . We shall make no compromise agreements. We have plenty of open spaces in our rear, and we shall preserve a well organized army. . . . I shall not be the first to draw my sword, but I shall be the last to sheath it. I should sooner retire to Siberia and even to Kamchatka and cultivate potatoes there than yield my provinces and sign a treaty in my conquered capital that would spell surrender."

When Caulaincourt reached Paris, he attempted to convince Napoleon that he was no longer dealing with the naive charmer of Tilsit and Erfurt but with a determined and resourceful opponent. "You speak like a Russian," Napoleon barked at Caulaincourt. "One good battle will see the end of your friend Alexander and his castles of sand."

CHAPTER 11

War Without Peace

***B**y* the middle of May Napoleon's splendidly equipped 554,000 troops had been deployed on the left banks of the Niemen and the Bug, along the line from the coast of the Baltic to Volhynia and Podolia. What was called the Grand Army, however, was composed mostly of his allies—Germans, Italians and Poles—around a hard core of French troops. Among the Old Guard regiments a popular marching song had a threatening stanza:

From the North to the South
The warlike trumpet sounds
Tremble the enemies of France.

Napoleon left Paris in a hurry to join his army. On his way, leading through Derezno, Danzig, and Warsaw, he carefully supervised the logistics of the Russian campaign. He was most anxious to ensure that his troops would be properly supplied not only with the best weapons, but also with foodstuffs and munitions, which were to be transported to the Russian frontier in heavy ox-drawn wagons and then transferred to the lightweight horse-drawn carts especially designed for the primitive Russian roads. A part of the supplies of flour, oats, rice and wine was sent by sea to Danzig and

Königsberg, the main depots of the Grand Army in the East. At Napoleon's side rode the gloomy Caulaincourt, now his main advisor on Russian affairs, who warned of the risks of the invasion, "Because of its geographic position, its expanse and the rugged nature of its terrain, Russia may be thought of as immune from the threat of invasion. Her enemies may have no better luck than the Romans had against the Visigoths, the Scythians or the Parthians."

"You are too frightened of the barbarians," Napoleon snapped at him. "Russia is a giant with feet of clay. You disregard my soldiers' prowess, their toughness and courage. When drums begin to beat it is like a thousand heartbeats striking in unison to weld our soldiers into a powerful hammer, ready to smash any enemy in one decisive battle west of the Dnieper. You are not taking my leadership into consideration."

"As far as the art of war is concerned, Sire, the barbarians have often been more creative, more inventive than civilized people. Do you remember the Tartar methods of scouting and fighting? They were adopted by the Cossacks. For instance, they pretend to flee to lure their enemies into a trap, and they use the terrain masterfully. Remember also the new methods of command and warfare pioneered by the Visigoths. While Roman officers shouted their orders, which were often lost in the noise of battle, the Visigoths used flag signals, that made their command much more effective. The stirrup is another Visigoth invention, and made cavalry what it is today. The Romans used horsemen only for message-carrying and for reconnaissance, but the stirrup allowed the use of cavalry in great numbers as an attacking force. Thanks to the stirrup, the Visigoth horsemen, seated firmly in their deep saddles, could use the lance and the sword freely. This was demonstrated at the battle of Adrianople in 378 A.D., if my memory doesn't fail me. At that battle no fewer than three legions of Roman infantry were wiped out by a numerically inferior horde of Visigoth horsemen."

"You know your ancient history well, Caulaincourt. So do I. You have to bear in mind that the Roman Emperor Valens was a nonentity. He was no match for the victor of forty battles."

Despite all this boasting, at heart Napoleon was convinced that he would simply terrify Alexander into submission by threatening him with invasion. He still nursed the hope that everything would be settled at the last moment "over a private meal together among the advance posts." Thus, Napoleon acted as a man, who, while jumping over an abyss, begins to doubt whether he should have jumped at all.

Wishing to make it easier for Alexander to make the first move, Napoleon sent to him one of his aides-de-camp, General de Narbonne, whose instructions were to go to Vilna, where the Tsar was stationed, and to remain there as long as necessary to persuade the Tsar that Napoleon was still desirous of a peaceful compromise. To Narbonne's advances, Alexander responded, "Tell your Emperor that I shall not be the first to draw the sword. In the eyes of the world I do not wish to have the responsibility for the bloodshed in this war. But I shall agree to nothing that is contrary to the honor of my country. Russia will never shrink from the threat of danger. All the bayonets in Europe would not alter my resolution."

Then, spreading out a map and pointing with his finger to the farthest extremity of his Empire, the Siberian peninsula of Kamchatka, Alexander warned, "If war should break out and fortune should go against me, the Emperor Napoleon will have to pursue me as far as this to obtain peace." Narbonne, who had intended to stay for several days, was politely informed the next morning that "his post horses would be ready at six o'clock that evening."

On June 22, Napoleon's army crossed the Niemen without opposition and began its advance toward Smolensk along the route that Charles XII of Sweden had taken almost a century before during the Great Northern War. On June 27, the 113th anniversary of Peter the Great's victory over the Swedish army at Poltava in 1709, Alexander issued a proclamation which exhorted his soldiers to display similar indomitable spirit and to take revenge on the invaders. Then he sent a special envoy to open negotiations with the Swedes to assure their neutrality. This would allow the Russian troops, on garrison duty in recently annexed

Finland, to be withdrawn to reinforce the modern army of Prince Michael Barclay de Tolly.

Initially the Russian forces numbered no more than 120,000 men, but they were gradually reinforced by five divisions commanded by Kutuzov, withdrawn from the Daubian principalities after a peace treaty had been hastily signed with Turkey. Another deal that Alexander made with his northern opponent Sweden allowed him to withdraw some 14,000 of the Russian forces from Finland. Moreover, new militia battalions were hastily formed and added as the hostilities progressed. The Russian troops, constantly swelling in number, were divided into two separate armies, one commanded by Barclay de Tolly and the other by Peter Bagration. Later a third army was formed in Podolia under General Tormassov to observe the Austrian corps of Prince Schwartenberg that formed the right, southernmost wing of the Grand Army. These three, even if united, could not match the superior forces of the invaders. Yet, to prevent that possibility was one of Napoleon's objectives. He wanted to defeat each of the three armies separately.

The Russians realized this and on the advice of Barclay de Tolly they decided to lure the invaders deeper into hostile country while avoiding Napoleon's attempts at encirclement of each of the three armies. Refusing to wage decisive battle, the Russians constantly harassed the enemy, draining his resources. Evading Napoleon's grip, the Russian forces retired by forced marches towards the Dvina and the Dnieper. Thus the hope of a decisive battle faded away. Napoleon could not believe that the Russians would abandon all Lithuania to him without a shot. He assumed that they would do battle before Vilna or soon after that. With no doubt that he would score a brilliant victory, he kept repeating to Caulaincourt, "As soon as I have beaten him, Alexander will sue for peace." While withdrawing the Russians destroyed everything that could be useful to the enemy: military installations, houses, peasant cottages and food stores, while evacuating whatever could be saved eastward, beyond the Volga. Thus the invaders, who had expected to live off the country, were facing the limitless stretches of the Russian countryside stripped of practically everything: food and shelter; and even the water was often poisoned.

To these difficulties one must add the unexpectedly harsh and capricious climate. Within a few days after the crossing of the Niemen and throughout the month of July, first dreadful heat and then torrential rains followed. Moreover, long stretches of primitive roads paralyzed transports while lack of food and forage had much enfeebled Napoleon's troops. As the Grand Army advanced, its ranks were thinned by desertion, disease and attrition in numerous skirmishes. In exhausting marches during which the columns dragged endlessly along, the unpaved sandy roads were filled with stragglers, the artillery and the cavalry lost a third of their horses, and no trace of food was found in the charred villages.

Meanwhile, the Russians put forth an extraordinary show of national zeal. Everything that could be useful—horses, arms, equipment, provisions—was poured into the army. Old and young, over and under regulation age, flocked to the colors. Hastily organized militia made remarkable marches to reach headquarters. Partisan bands harassed the advancing invaders. Fathers of families, many seventy years of age and upwards, placed themselves in the ranks, and faced fatigue as well as peril with remarkable patriotic ardor.

At the end of June the news was brought to Napoleon that an aide-de-camp of the Tsar, General Balashov, had arrived with a personal letter from Alexander. Immediately Napoleon's face lit up. "My brother Alexander is already suing for an agreement. He's frightened. My stratagems have routed the Russians. Before a month has passed they will be begging for mercy."

Alexander's letter stated, "If Your Majesty will consent to withdraw your troops from Russian territory, I shall regard what has passed as if it had never been, and an agreement would still be possible between us." After a first glance at it Napoleon exclaimed, "To ask me to order a general retreat of my army. . . , what a demand to make of the victor of Austerlitz and Friedland

. . . Alexander is making a fool of me!"

The interview with Balashov turned into a wrangle, an altercation. With burning eyes Napoleon flung the question at his guest, "Which is the main road to Moscow?"

Balashov retorted, "To reach Moscow one takes the road one fancies. Charles XII set out by way of Poltava."

Napoleon treated the answer as a bad joke. His idea was still to defeat the enemy in one great decisive battle, and penetrate to the heart of Russia to dictate peace to his adversary. He anticipated that the decisive battle would be waged between the Dvina and the Dnieper, between Vitebsk and Smolensk. But from Vilna to Smolensk was 250 miles, and from Smolensk to Moscow was another 250 miles of scorched, desolated land.

★ ★ ★

Since the beginning of the hostilities, Alexander had spent many agonizing hours. Despite his efforts at mobilization, the Russian forces were still inadequate to challenge the invader in the open field. Moreover, his headquarters were filled with bitter quarrels, intrigues and rivalries. Barclay de Tolly, Bagration and Tormassov squabbled continuously, accusing each other of indecision, cowardice and even treasonous plotting.

On July 27, just before Vitebsk, the Russians seemed ready to accept combat. But by dawn next morning, the enemies had disappeared without any indication of the road they had taken. The disappointed Napoleon said, "Both Russian armies have probably decided to give battle at Smolensk. I'll attack them together. . . ," and, indeed, on August 17, the two armies clashed at the gates of Smolensk. The battle was short and chaotic. In the evening the Russians withdrew after having set fire to the city. The relatively easy victory at Smolensk made Napoleon decide to push immediately toward Moscow. He said to Caulaincourt, "Before a month is out we shall be in Moscow, and in six weeks we shall have peace."

The thought of 250 miles through a devastated, scorched country with swarms of Cossacks on his flanks didn't frighten him.

What worried him most was that he would have to further extend his lines of communication. He was 300 miles from the banks of the Niemen along which his chief supply bases and arsenals were moved, 650 miles from the Oder, 1100 miles from the Rhine and 1300 miles from Paris.

The battle of Smolensk brought about a major crisis in Russian public opinion. The French were irresistibly pushing toward Moscow, while the Russian political establishment clamored for a firm stand to stop the Russian retreat and face the enemy in defense of the Old Capital. Serious criticism of Barclay de Tolly's leadership was expressed, including accusations of treason. From the beginning of the campaign Alexander wrestled with the thorny problem of supreme command. Painstakingly he went over the reports sent to him by field commanders, read letters full of grievances against Barclay de Tolly's "indecisive" leadership and military "incompetence," and listened to verbal complaints of his alleged "treacherous contact with the enemy." Similar accusations were also directed against Bagration. As foreigners they were surrounded by suspicion on the part of the native Russians, jealous of their high rank. Alexander was at a loss about what to do. By this time everyone was clamoring for Barclay de Tolly's dismissal on the grounds that he was a traitor as well as a fool. But who was there to replace him? Alexander had no doubt of Bagration's personal courage but he had never placed much faith in his understanding of broad strategic matters. He mistrusted and disliked Bennigsen for the role he had played in Tsar Paul's assassination. Besides, Bennigsen, born a Hanoverian, was even less Russian than Barclay, who could at least claim to be a product of Livonia, a Russian province for the century since Peter the Great had wrested it from Sweden in the Great Northern War. At one time Alexander hesitated about whether he himself should assume the functions of Commander-in-Chief. Yet, he realized how little he knew of the art of war. As was often the case, discouraged, depressed and confused, he retired from the front and went to Tver to see his favorite sister, Catherine.

By that time, Catherine was already advanced in pregnancy,

moody and irritable. Despite her pregnancy, which had affected her good looks, and despite her nasty temper, Alexander was still fascinated by Catherine's inner strength and her indomitable will. Now he regretted having forced her into a loveless marriage that placed so many physical and psychological obstacles between him and his closest, most understanding and perceptive companion. He tried to be polite to her husband, the meek, complacent George. At times, however, rage overcame Alexander. He became infuriated at his own deplorable decision. His frustration to allow this nonentity to stand between him and his favorite sister surfaced and was now directed against his poor brother-in-law. In a peevish way Alexander scolded him for not supplying enough militiamen, for not training them personally and staying too close to home. Just before his departure he sent George to personally inspect the stores of oats to be sent to the front for the Tver dragoons, then about to leave for the front. He wanted to be alone with Catherine. Alarmed at her brother's seeming intention to play a part for which he was quite unfit, Catherine implored him to give up any idea of directing military operations. "For God's sake," she said, "do not attempt to command the army in person! Don't try to meddle with military operations. Remember Austerlitz. What we need is a new and competent commander-in-chief in whom the troops have confidence, and you inspire none."

"I know this but whom shall I appoint?"

"Overlook all those foreign mercenaries, all those Protestant Germans and Scots, Bennigsens and Barclays. To bolster the morale of the troops you must have more Russians at the top. Proclaim the war as a fight to the finish, a national crusade. Only a true Orthodox Russian, such as Kutuzov for instance, will inspire the confidence of our people in such a patriotic war."

"I trust and pray that your confinement will be easy, without complications." Then he kissed Catherine's forehead and whispered, "Whatever happens to us and to our country, you must remember that I have loved you more than anyone else. Farewell, my darling." Resigned and heavyhearted he climbed into the barouche that was to take him to Moscow. When the carriage was in motion, despite the presence of Peter Volkonsky, he broke into tears and wept bitterly. Only after an hour or so did he manage to control this spasm of despair. He regained his composure enough to study the latest reports from the front. This did not improve his mood, however. Retreat and defeat everywhere; successful French advance all along. New depression overcame him. "How is this damn war going to end?" Then mastering his bad mood, he dictated to Volkonsky the order appointing Kutuzov as Commander-in-Chief of all the armed forces of the Empire.

At that time, Kutuzov was already sixty-seven. He was fat, flabby and somnolent, and suffering from arthritis and gout. He had only one eye; the other had been ravaged by an enemy bullet. He could mount a horse only with great difficulty; the aid of two or more adjutants was usually required to place him in the saddle for a brief time to review the troops. At other times he traveled in a comfortable, cushioned barouche. Unable to forgive him his humiliating behavior at the battle of Austerlitz, Alexander had treated him coldly ever since. Yet he had to recognize Kutuzov's experience and the confidence he enjoyed among common soldiers as well as staff officers. "His power over them is unique," he admitted to Peter Volkonsky. "That is why I decided to appoint him to lead all three armies."

Actually Kutuzov was in full agreement with Barclay de Tolly's Scythian strategy of retreat combined with small diversionary battles and the scorched earth policy. Yet, to justify his appointment and to please the Tsar, as well as to appease the public, Kutuzov decided to wage a major battle west of Moscow. The problem was the choice of the best site for such a stand.

* * *

Alexander felt duty bound to visit Moscow and inspect its defenses. He was greeted at the Kremlin by the Governor-General, Count Rostopchin. During his two months in office he had managed to goad with frenzy the patriotic spirit of the people and their hatred of Napoleon. Rostopchin accompanied the Tsar to a religious service held at the Cathedral or the Dormition led by the

Patriarch, during which Alexander had a profound experience. The Patriarch, addressing him, said, "You are the living icon as well as the instrument of God on earth. To your hands He entrusted not only the destiny of Russia, but, indeed, of the entire world. You are the Almighty's shield and sword." Alexander was dazzled by these words, transfigured in heart and mind and soul. The rapture which he felt, as he gazed at the tombs of the former Tsars and Patriarchs at the Kremlin, restored his spirit. It was like an act of grace. He felt that he was an instrument chosen by Providence to bring salvation to his people.

Until that fateful day religious emotions had counted for little in his life. The interminable ritualistic incantations of the Orthodox services often annoyed him. Suddenly they gained a new meaning as an expression of something deeper. What was behind them was still enigmatic, yet memories of these experiences opened to him new metaphysical vistas. Since that memorable visit to Moscow, Alexander, hitherto a skeptic, a practicing non-believer, began to doubt his doubts. His mind was in turmoil. If he could experience such regenerating grace after a few moments of prayer and meditation, perhaps religion was something more than a vestige of the barbarous past, more than an instrument by which to manipulate a primitive people, as his grandmother and Laharpe had taught him in his youth.

When Alexander returned from the Cathedral of the Dormition to his quarters at the Kremlin he felt a sudden strong impulse to study the Bible for the first time in more than twenty years. He owned an English version, given to him by his religion teacher, Reverend Samborsky, on his tenth birthday. But Alexander had been discouraged by Laharpe from reading it. His mentor assured him that Greek mythology was more colorful, entertaining and instructive than "the bizarre biblical legends." Sheer curiosity made him reach for the thick, richly bound Russian volume, which he had noticed on a top shelf of the Kremlin library. He tried to grasp the heavy book and it fell to the floor. When Alexander bent to pick up the volume he saw that it was opened to the Proverbs, 41: "I will say of the Lord: He is my refuge and fortress, my God. In Him will I trust." Alexander was deeply impressed. Was the opening of the Bible at this very place a mere coincidence? Was it perhaps a personal message from above at this hour of danger? Feverishly he perused the book, and in St. John's Book of Revelations read: "I looked down, and before my eyes was a white horse. Its rider carried a bow and he was given a crown. He rode out conquering and bent on conquest . . ."

Fascinated by the passage, he continued to read from both the New and the Old Testaments. For the rest of the evening he devoured the Bible, finding that its words gave an unknown peace to his heart and quenched the thirst of his soul. He meditated deeply about the words. "Trust in the Lord with all thine heart and lean not unto thine own understanding." The more he read the more absorbed he was in his study. About 4:30 A.M., he fell asleep, exhausted. He slept uneasily, disturbed by a nightmare of the rider on a white horse who clashed with him in bloody duel. The prediction of the old Gypsy came to his mind.

He awoke in early afternoon, shaking all over, and was informed by his servant, Melnikov, that two gentlemen, Generals Rostopchin and Balashov, had been waiting for well over two hours to present their reports and ask for instructions. Alexander dressed hastily with Melnikov's help and had a four-hour conference with the visitors. After that he returned to his rooms to meditate. He came to the conclusion that it would be a good thing to read the Bible more often to compare the two versions, Russian and English, and to make marginal notes of his personal reflections. But the good resolution was soon swept aside as he was overwhelmed with military and bureaucratic duties, signing orders and decrees, inspecting new units being dispatched to the front and negotiating with foreign diplomats.

Saying good-bye to Moscow and its Governor General Rostopchin, Alexander gave him full authority to act as he saw fit, whatever might occur. "Who can predict events? I rely on your wisdom and energy entirely."

Rostopchin replied, "Sire, you can depend on me." And indeed he immediately set to work to fire still more the patriotic sentiments of the inhabitants, issuing a proclamation that summoned them to "supreme sacrifice to defend our Holy City against the infidel and cruel Frenchmen, the locust and scourge of Europe. Hell must be repelled with hell!"

The response was overwhelming. A fever of self-sacrificial emulation gripped the people of Moscow. Representatives of the merchant class made voluntary contributions totaling 2,400,000 rubles for the war effort. Count Mamonov alone offered 800,000 silver rubles and a casket full of diamonds worth hundreds of thousands more. Some nobles let it be known that they were going to give up their private orchestras, choirs, and actors and allow the members to volunteer for the citizens' militia. Others declared that they were going to reduce the number of footmen, grooms, and retainers in their employ, also to be trained as soldiers. Human nature being what it is, however, a number of Moscow merchants decided to make the most of this patriotic frenzy. Overnight the cost of a saber, hitherto valued at about 5 to 6 rubles, soared to 30 to 40 rubles. A pair of pistols which had cost 8 to 10 rubles was hawked at 40 to 50 rubles.

* * *

Alexander slipped into St. Petersburg on September 2 at 2 A.M. after a long journey which had been interrupted by several stops and hasty inspections of the newly formed militia. In some cases these were peasants from northern provinces; in other cases the militia included detachments of Bashkir or Tartar horsemen brought from central Asia and the borders of Siberia. Many of them were seated on small, shaggy-footed ponies; not infrequently their equipment consisted of long pikes, bows and quivers of arrows. Only the centurions of these exotic units were armed with pistols or muskets slung across their backs. In their clenched fists they held curved, oriental sabers with which they saluted their "white Khan," about whom they had heard wild, fantastic tales. In some cases these strange soldiers did not understand a word of Russian. When the Russian commander of a Bashkir squadron shouted, "By platoon, to the right wheel!" the squadron didn't move. Only when the native deputy-commander repeated the order in their own tongue did the unit carry out the maneuver. As the squadron passed by, saluting Alexander, he noticed that some of the ponies were not much larger than large Siberian dogs. "They are small but hardy," explained Volkonsky. "They can survive on straw and conifer twigs for weeks."

The Tsar's return to the capital had not come a moment too soon. In his absence and the absence of reliable news from the front, wild rumors had begun to circulate. From Riga came reports that its governor had lost his nerve, ordered the evacuation of the city and set fire to the seaport's suburbs instead of preparing to defend the vital fort. Even more upsetting was the news that Napoleon, after having occupied Smolensk, headed straight for Moscow. Immediately Alexander ordered most of the remaining garrison of St. Petersburg to march south to join Kutuzov, who was preparing for a major battle west of Moscow. For the inhabitants of the capital this meant that St. Petersburg was being abandoned to its fate, with no more than a few battalions of the newly recruited soldiers to protect it. In view of that, Dowager Empress Maria Feodorovna issued orders that some of her most valuable belongings be packed in case the Imperial family had to leave in a hurry. Many government offices began to destroy vital state documents. Huge files of these were burning in the Senate Square.

Despite the Napoleonic invasion, the French theater in St. Petersburg continued its performance as usual. Many inhabitants of the capital felt that it was an outrage. They believed that, at such a moment, French actors and actresses should not be tolerated in the city's only public theater. To show their disapproval, some of the Petersburgers imposed a boycott. The British military observer, Sir Robert Wilson, discovered, when he went to watch the celebrated Mademoiselle Georges play the lead role in Racine's "Phedre," that most boxes and benches were empty.

To bolster the morale of the Court and the public at large Alexander solemnly swore "to retreat to the Kazan and to fight on the shores of the Volga, to let my beard grow and eat potatoes in Siberia like the poorest peasant rather than to sign a peace." But, while alone in his studio, he occasionally doubted his own words and wondered if, despite the reinforcements dispatched to the front from St. Petersburg, Kutuzov would be able to stop the invaders at the gates of Moscow. As a "Te Deum" was chanted in the Cathedral of Our Lady of Kazan on the anniversary of Alexander's coronation, crowds maintained a hostile silence, and only the church choir continued to sing. "One could have heard a pin drop," noted Elizabeth, "and I am sure that a single spark would have put this crowd aflame." On his knees, the anxious Alexander prayed to God for strength to stick to his resolution. The Sardinian Ambassador, Count de Maistre, wrote to his King that "nothing but a miracle can now save Russia."

★ ★ ★

After Kutuzov's appointment, everyone expected the Russian strategy to be reversed overnight, a firm stand taken and the enemy smashed in a single, decisive battle. Yet, after assuming the supreme command, the new Commander-in-Chief ordered an immediate withdrawal from the Smolensk region westward. Patriotic Russians were disappointed once more. While Alexander passed his days gloomily meditating on God and his mysterious ways, Kutuzov was regrouping his forces, and mobilized thousands of peasants, including women, ordering them to build extensive earth redoubts along a vast field flanking the village of Borodino. The village was situated astride the road from Smolensk to Moscow, some seventy-five miles west of the old capital and on the left bank of the Kolcha, a tributary of the Moskva. Napoleon's troops, by then numbering only slightly over 135,000 men, had to capture Borodino if they wanted to march along the Smolensk road to Moscow.

Kutuzov concentrated more than two-thirds of his forces on the northern or right wing. The Russian position beyond the Kolcha River was protected on that flank by the Moskva River and strong earth fortifications, and by equally powerful redoubts on the left flank. Thus, if Napoleon wished to take the shortest way to Moscow, he had to fight his way through this series of powerfully fortified positions. Thus, Kutuzov hoped that the enemy would be forced into a frontal battle. His goal was two-fold: he wanted to bleed the enemy out while retaining for himself enough strength to assure the defense of the old capital. By that time, the forces of the two adversaries were approximately equal. The Russian army numbered about 132,000 men and 624 guns, and the French army, about 135,000 men and 587 guns. But whereas the whole French army consisted of regular soldiers, in the Russian army there were about 21,000 insufficiently trained and poorly armed militiamen and 7,000 irregular cavalrymen, mostly Cossacks. Napoleon was expected to rout the Russian forces, and intended to break through the center of their position, bypass its left flank and cut off the road of retreat to Moscow.

On the night of September 6, the two armies faced each other across a narrow expanse of plowed fields. The flickering lights of campfires threw up eerie shadows in the darkness. When Napoleon inspected his troops, the Russian officers could hear cries of "Vive l'Empereur" as he passed down the lines and chatted with the soldiers of the advanced posts. On both sides the night was too tense for sleep.

At dawn cannons began to rumble menacingly. The battle began at about 6 A.M. with an attack by troops led by Eugene Beauharnais on the village of Borodino across the Kolcha River. The French drive was repulsed with heavy losses. The attacks by the Polish troops commanded by Prince Joseph Poniatowski also failed, but they pinned down part of the forces of one Russian corps for several hours. The assault of Napoleon's main forces on the two redoubts guarding the flanks of the Russian defenses lasted for more than six hours without interruption. One of the major obstacles for the attackers was the fort known as the Rayevsky redoubt, so called because of the valiant general who commanded it. He kept up the spirits of his men by walking among them with his pipe in his mouth, his boots shining and his uniform impeccably clean. To protect the redoubt, the commander put his cannons deep behind his infantry while filling the forward trenches with bayoneted fusiliers. To charging cavalrymen the redoubt resembled a huge porcupine bristling with the steel of its bayonets, over which their horses had to leap. The French cavalry attack, a superhuman attempt, was preceded by a fierce bombardment of more than a hundred guns. The redoubt was so badly battered that its parapets were turned into a mass of shapeless mounds of overturned earth, enveloped in a thick cloud of dust and smoke, broken by the reddish glow of spouting Russian cannons.

Seeing that the redoubt was still resisting, Napoleon ordered a second attack by his cavalry. The task was assigned by the Second Cavalry Corps, commanded by General Mountbrun. During the charge he was knocked from his horse by grapeshot that sent a piece of metal through his kidney. The charge again failed to achieve its goal and only decimated the flower of Napoleon's cavalry. To replace General Mountbrun, Napoleon appointed General August de Caulaincourt, the younger brother of Armand, former ambassador to St. Petersburg. August was ordered to resume the attack at whatever cost. The tactics of the new assault were to be changed. Cavalry was to outflank the redoubt on both sides, while the frontal attack was to be carried out by three infantry divisions, some 30,000 men led by Prince Eugene de Beauharnais, and supported by nearly 300 cannons.

The assault was launched by 3 P.M. Now hell broke loose. Through the volley of artillery fire, the avalanche of grapeshot, and the hail of musket fire, the French infantry forced its way into the redoubt, only to be eventually beaten back. Then followed the two-pronged cavalry charge. The fight was terrible. Men and horses fell backwards down the steep slopes of the redoubt. Cries rang out as men tried to extricate themselves from under their wounded mounts. Those horsemen who managed to leap over the bayoneted fusiliers trampled everything underfoot, dealing death and destruction to the remaining defenders. Riders who had been knocked from their horses continued a savage attack on foot, wrestling foes with their sabers, fists and even teeth. It was the task of the second wave of cavalrymen, largely Polish and Saxon, to proceed simultaneously from the left and the right to finish the terrible carnage.

At the end of the battle the redoubts and the surrounding area were covered with dead and wounded, and wandering riderless horses added to the chaos. Those who suffered lighter wounds tried to make their way back to the ambulance carts. The battlefield was strewn with upset wagons and the corpses of dead horses, their stiff legs sticking up into the air. Everywhere rifles, sabers, helmets and breastplates of the cuirassiers were intermingled with shattered fragments of human bodies and dismembered limbs. The battlefield resounded with wild cries of severely wounded men, cursing their fate or imploring surviving comrades to summon scarce stretcher bearers to fetch them to the nearest hospital area. Alas, in only a few cases could these pleas be satisfied. Most of the survivors were so exhausted that they could barely take care of themselves.

Distant from and perhaps unsure of the situation on the smoke-obscured battlefield, Napoleon had anxiously watched the seesawing of the clash. Despite the urging of his marshals he refused to commit the 20,000-man Imperial Guard. "At such a distance from France I can't risk losing my veterans," he retorted. Thus, by his hesitation, Napoleon forfeited the chance of gaining a decisive, rather than narrow, victory since Kutuzov had committed to the battle every available man. Consequently, the outcome of this carnage was, in fact, indecisive. Yet, since the Russian army abandoned the field and withdrew eastward, Napoleon claimed the victory. To enhance the disappointing result of that bloody encounter in the eyes of the world, he referred to it in his annals as The Battle of Moskva, though it actually took place on a tributary of that river. In the Battle of Borodino, Napoleon was surprised by the Russian army's tactical skills, such as maneuvers by reserves from the rear and along the front, sustained utilization of cavalry and active defense with combined infantry, cavalry and artillery forces.

The battle was the most bloody of the entire campaign, a Pyrrhic victory. The French army suffered irreparable losses of more than 30,000, including 47 generals. The Russian troops lost 44,000 men and 23 generals, among them Prince Bagration, commander of the 2nd Army. Caulaincourt accompanied Napoleon as he rode on horseback to inspect the battlefield. "Horrible, Sire!" shouted the disgusted Caulaincourt. "Bah!" retorted Napoleon. "Remember the words of the Roman emperor, 'The corpse of an enemy always smells good!' "

★ ★ ★

Seven days later, at midday on September 14, the advance guard of the French Army approached Moscow. Marching in open order, Napoleon's troops mounted Sparrows Hill under a brilliant sky. Struck with awe at the majestic sight, the soldiers stopped and cried, "Moscow! Moscow!" Napoleon approached the top of the hill at a gallop, dismounted, took his field glass and contemplated the spectacle. From the summit of Sparrows Hill he beheld the legendary city, with its thousand churches and monasteries crowned with golden and azure onion domes, glittering copper spires and cupolas. Less than a mile away the red towers of the Kremlin were visible. Around it spread a multitude of white-washed palaces and mansions of the nobility, as well as those of prosperous merchants, many of them surrounded by parks and orchards. Transported with joy, Napoleon exclaimed, "So this is the famous city!" Then he added, "And it is high time, too!"

His joy lasted but a moment. When informed that the Russians were hurriedly evacuating the city and trying to burn it, Napoleon turned to Caulaincourt and said, "The barbarians are trying to destroy their ancient capital. Is this possible? Caulaincourt, what do you think of it? Tell me, can you believe it?"

"Your Majesty knows better than anyone what I think of it," was the reply.

When Napoleon's advance units entered the city, it was deserted and fires were visible at several points. Not a single representative of the old capital, not even a policeman, was to be seen. Only a few thousand of the very poor inhabitants remained; some of them had seized the opportunity for looting and were roaming the streets. On the third day of the French occupation massive fires, carefully planned by Rostopchin, began to devastate the city.

Napoleon ordered an end to the arsonists' activities by decreeing summary executions by hanging for all those caught redhanded. Undeterred by this, the arsonists continued their work. Some went about their business with torches, others with baskets filled with incendiary devices of all kinds. Any house occupied by a senior French officer was in danger of destruction; panic spread. General Grouchy, commander of the Third Cavalry Corps, escaped being roasted in his bed when an arsonist was caught about to put a torch to his blanket. Marshal Davout had to change his residence three times as each was set on fire. Some houses were found cunningly booby-trapped, with a charge of powder calculated to ignite at the moment a door was opened.

On the morning of Friday, September 18, rain began to fall, leading to a downpour later in the day, which extinguished most of the fires, but turned the ravaged city into a sea of mud. Columns of dirty smoke rose from the charred skeletons of burned out houses, covering the city with a pall which enveloped it like funeral crepe. In the midst of the ruins emaciated horses wandered aimlessly about, as well as packs of famished dogs. The air was foul, and one could not escape the smoke and putrefaction. Standing on the red brick Spasky tower of the Kremlin, Napoleon contemplated the enormity of the catastrophe, and sighed, "All this augurs great misfortune for us!"

Since the main body of the Russian army had been evacuated from the old capital without a fight, Napoleon was convinced that Alexander would have to sue for peace. To pass the time, the restless Napoleon kept himself busy with administrative and literary pursuits. The Statute of the Comedie Francaise (still in effect, by the way) was conceived at the Kremlin to pass the time between one round and another of frustrating attempts at negotiation with Tsar Alexander.

On the 20th of September he wrote to Alexander, "The proud and beautiful city of Moscow is no more. Rostopchin has had it burned down. Four hundred arsonists were arrested in the act. All have declared that they acted on the orders of their Governor. It is the same policy which has been pursued since Smolensk. This is uncivilized behavior. Humanity and the interests of Your Majesty and of this great city demand that it should be handed over to me in trust. The administration, the magistrates, the policy should have been left in place. That was the case in Vienna, Berlin and Madrid. . . ." Again, no answer.

Napoleon was in a frenzy of rage. But how was he to take revenge on his rival? Here, in the heart of Russia, he was not hampered, as he had been in Lithuania, by the need to cater to the native aristocracy. Suddenly an idea flashed through his mind. What better means could be found to force Alexander's hand than to threaten his landowners with civil war? Napoleon had been persuaded that the threat of a French decree emancipating the country's serfs would suffice to spur Russia's landowners to pressure Alexander to sue for peace. But, after lengthy hesitation, Napoleon abandoned the idea. "An emancipation decree would mean general anarchy and we would be engulfed in it."

★ ★ ★

After the loss of Moscow, Kutuzov tried to explain his line of reasoning in a lengthy report to the sulking Tsar. "After the bloody battle of Borodino, I was obliged to withdraw from our position there. The army was in a state of chaos." Only two days later Alexander felt confident enough to let his subjects know the bitter truth. He had Kutuzov's personal apology published with only minor changes in the text, along with an official governmental proclamation in which the Generalissimo's decision to abandon Moscow was defended on the grounds that it was designed to "turn the enemy's short-lived triumph into an eventual inescapable disaster." The proclamation ended by invoking the aid of Almighty God on behalf of the Russian people's righteous struggle against the enemy. For in triumphing over Napoleon "and in saving itself, it will save the freedom and independence of rulers and their realms."

By the end of September 1812, Alexander's popular support had reached its nadir. He cloistered himself in his palace on the Kammenoy Ostrov in the loop of the Neva and took long solitary walks, meditating over his predicament. He was ill, burning with fever, and refused to see anyone but Arakcheyev and Balashov for the dispatch of current business. He left the administration of the empire to Arakcheyev, the army to Kutuzov, and prayed fervently for God's help. Worn down as he was by depression, his will to resist remained unbroken. He consoled himself by the incoming reports that Kutuzov's army, posted outside the city, was reorganizing, regrouping and getting ready to take up the offensive at an opportune moment.

The most painful and bitter wound was that inflicted by the renewed reproaches of his sister, Catherine, who again berated him for lack of courage and resolve, actually for betraying the trust of the Russian people. "Moscow is taken," she wrote to him. "The loss of Moscow has brought the general exasperation to a head. Popular discontent has reached a climax and it does not spare you. If this is apparent to me, you may judge how it must appear to others. You are openly blamed for the miseries of your Empire, for its ruin, and finally for having lost your country's honor and your own. One of the chief accusations is that you failed in your word given to the people of Moscow who awaited you with desperate impatience. You give the appearance of having betrayed them. I leave you to judge the state of things in a country where people despise their ruler. Think of your honor!"

Nevertheless, there were some voices supporting his stand. The French emigré opponent of Napoleon, Madame de Staël, who took refuge in St. Petersburg, wrote to him applauding his determination to continue the struggle. The British diplomat, Sir Robert Wilson, and Freiherr Karl von Stein, an exiled Prussian, also offered their best wishes, and congratulations for his refusal to negotiate with Napoleon. To those who, like his brother Constantine, advised him to seek peace, Alexander replied, "Vast space and time are on our side. If Napoleon wants peace, he must make it in Kamchatka."

Meanwhile, Napoleon's mounting troubles made him wonder about the feasibility of making his winter quarters in Moscow. How long could he stay in the devastated, burned city? By October the food found in the cellars of the burned houses was all but consumed. How was he to provide for his troops? How could he maintain his extended lines of communication through Poland and Germany? Might not the Russian partisans, who were growing in strength every day, cut off his retreat? And finally, might not his Austrian and Prussian allies, whose task was to protect his flanks, take advantage of his discomfiture to change sides? The defeated but not destroyed enemy forces just outside the city were growing daily in strength and confidence.

On October 4, Napoleon renewed his conciliatory gestures and sent General de Lauriston to Marshal Kutuzov with an offer of armistice. The offer was forwarded to the Tsar. In Napoleon's messages Alexander saw nothing but a desperate avowal of impotence. No reply was returned. The Tsar instructed Kutuzov to inform his troops that the war would continue as before, without mercy, so long as one French soldier remained on Russian soil. "Either Napoleon or me. We can no longer rule together. I have come to know him. He will not trick me again!"

"Alexander is certainly obstinate!" Napoleon cried when Lauriston returned. "He will repent of it! He will not get better conditions than those I offered him today. He doesn't see where this may lead him, with a man of my character!"

By mid-October, however, after having lost two weeks in frustrating negotiations, the long delayed order of retreat was finally given to the French troops. On October 19, at dawn, Napoleon's army began to leave Moscow. The former Grand Army now had shrunk to only 87,500 infantry, 14,750 cavalry and 533 guns, burdened with a train of some 40,000 carriages and wagons loaded with loot and baggage. Behind them came a caravan of camp-followers, including French women and children, as well as servants acquired during the city's occupation. The result was a slow and cumbersome convoy of enormous length. Napoleon had issued orders that needless vehicles must be left behind, and burned one of his own as an example. It proved impossible, however, to stop others from decamping with theirs. After all, he himself had grabbed some of the Kremlin's treasures, including the great cross from the Bell Tower of Ivan the Great, which he intended to erect over the Hotel des Invalides.

The retreat from Moscow was, perhaps, the most humiliating and tragic period in Napoleon's career. Even nature seemed to conspire against him. The winter of 1812 had arrived by the end of October; by the beginning of November temperatures fell well below freezing. The demoralized soldiers, most of them overloaded with loot, suffered as much from want of food and fuel as from the lack of proper winter clothing. Moreover, in the scorched and desolate countryside, they had no cover from night's bitter cold and had to bivouac on the frozen soil and sleep in the snow, barely covered with rugs or straw snatched from ruined cottages. The constant danger of Cossack and partisan raids made careful sentry duty imperative for both officers and common soldiers. As a result, their snatches of sleep were usually limited to a few hours, more often than not to an hour or two. The corpses of those who had fallen during the Battle of Borodino still littered the fields and roadways. Yet, until the passage of the Berezina, Napoleon's magnetic personality still exercised its dominance over his soldiers. From time to time he would leave his sleigh to ease his numbed limbs. Dressed in fur, a staff cut from a birch tree in his hand, he would chat with the freezing and starved men who constituted his proud Old Guards. Some of them would drop beside him on the road, still shouting "Vive l'Empereur!" Then he would return to his carriage. As it glided across the snow he would talk to Caulaincourt of his former glories and his future plans, and of the fresh, young armies he planned to raise on his return to France. At times he was jubilant, at other moments his voice would rise in screams of hatred. "It was England that made my friendship with Alexander impossible. The perverted English poisoned his mind and frustrated all my efforts at conciliation. I must have revenge on England first of all!"

From day to day the once Grand Army was dwindling at an alarming rate. The nightmarish crossing of the Berezina on November 28 was a final blow to the fleeing invaders. After that they resembled a motley rabble of frozen, starved and tattered stragglers. Napoleon himself owed his escape to the devotion of his engineers who, waist deep in icy waters, constructed a second pontoon bridge across which the Emperor's carriage managed to muddle, almost miraculously.

On December 5, at Smorgoni, Napoleon was informed of the suppression of General Malet's revolt in Paris. He decided to abandon the pitiful remnants of his army and rush through Warsaw to Paris post haste. "In the current situation, I cannot rule Europe except from the Palace of the Tuileries." Aside from the driver, he took with him only Caulaincourt and a Polish interpreter. The road before him was covered with carcasses frozen in contortions of cruel agonies.

How to present France with a tale of defeat, and thus prepare the country for new sacrifices, occupied his mind at all times. At his temporary quarters in Warsaw, located in the English Hotel, was outlined the famous Bulletin Number 29. It appeared in *Le Moniteur* of December 16, 1812, two days before the arrival of the Emperor in Paris. In dignified words filled with tragic pathos, the commander of a non-existent army described its struggle to force Russia into his European system. The final defeat of his heroic efforts came not as a result of the superior skill and overwhelming might of the barbarous enemy, but because of "nature untamed by man." Each word of the Bulletin was selected with great care. Succeeding scenes of the heroic struggle added to the impression of inevitability, and blended into one gloomy, mournful panorama. As in a tragedy of Sophocles or Shakespeare, there was the uncontrollable and mounting perversity of an all-powerful Fate. The snow-covered plains of Byelorussia were described with heaps of corpses, both human and animal, abandoned wagons, soldiers struggling under heavy burdens, generals commanding platoons, and colonels battling in bayonet charges as if they were simple privates. And in each phantasmagoric scene, worthy of the brush of a Goya, stood the figure of the fearless Emperor, surrounded by the indomitable remnants of the Old Guards, fighting to the last round of ammunition. The Bulletin, despite its description of apocalyptic events, stressed the supreme tranquility and self-control of the leader. During the whole ill-starred odyssey, the Bulletin pointed out, he did not for a moment lose his nerve, but, by superhuman effort, rose above the unconquerable. The Bulletin ended with the words: "The health of His Majesty the Emperor was never better."

* * *

When informed of the final disintegration of Napoleon's forces, in the first rapture of his miraculous victory, Alexander wrote to his sister Catherine. "This is the work of God. It is He who has so suddenly changed our whole perspective by bringing down on Napoleon's head all the disasters he had planned for us."

She replied, "Yes, let us render thanks to Providence, but it is you who have forced Fortune to be propitious by refusing to sue for peace. And it is your firmness that assures you of a glorious immortality."

Yet Alexander's glory in the War of 1812 was only secondary. His actual contribution to the military victory was small. His firmness merely reflected the Russian people's determination to fight to the end. It was the common people who saved Russia by their stubbornness, courage and spirit of unlimited sacrifice. It was the people who destroyed almost everything that was of value to the enemy, burning their homes and their beloved Moscow. The harsh climate did play its role, but it was the staid resistance of the Russian people that finally determined the outcome.

Pursuing the retreating remnant of Napoleon's army, Kutuzov had reoccupied Vilna on December 10. There Alexander joined him on December 23, on the eve of his birthday. The Tsar's nose was frozen because he had traveled for three days in an open sled, and the icy wind penetrated even the thick fur collar of his great coat. His return was triumphant. The facade of the Vilna town hall was illuminated and displayed a silhouette of a doubleheaded black Russian eagle clawing the many tentacled heads of the Bonapartist hydra. The Tsar celebrated his return by decorating Kutuzov with the Order of St. George, First Class, expressing eloquent thanks for his services during the campaign. The next day, Alexander's birthday, Kutuzov gave a sumptuous and carefully staged banquet for the Tsar. When he appeared at the door, several captured French banners were flung down on the parquet floor for him to tread on. During the ball that followed the dinner, the Russian officers were forced by Alexander to dance with the Polish and Lithuanian ladies even whose menfolk had joined Napoleon's armies. Meanwhile he summoned Czartoryski and revived his former plans for joining Poland to Russia under his scepter.

Alexander's next step was to negotiate the defection of the Prussian army commanded by General York, whose task was to cover the left flank of the French retreat. York, however, avoided fighting the Russians and thus saved most of his troops practically intact. This was an invitation to negotiate a formal cooperation of the two armies. It was formulated in the Russo-Prussian convention of Taurogen, signed on December 30. The convention of Taurogen was followed by the formal Russo-Prussian treaty which Alexander signed with Frederick William III at Kalisz. The agreement provided that Prussia surrender to Russia most of the territories Berlin obtained as a result of the second and third partitions of Poland. In return for these cessions of Polish lands, Alexander vowed to compensate Prussia with Saxony, an ally of France. Both signatories pledged to continue the war until all Germany was liberated from French occupation. The convention was another blow dealt to Napoleon's system of alliances. The patriotic enthusiasm unleashed throughout Germany by the French defeat and the Taurogen convention did not augur well for the French hegemony over Central Europe. Alexander remained in Vilna for three weeks intoxicated by the completeness of his triumph. Elated, he plunged himself into a world of social entertainment. Yet, between one ball and another he deliberated with his generals and civilian advisors on the future. Some urged peace; some advised him to continue the victorious campaign. Having accompanied him to Vilna, Baron Heinrich von Stein, whom Napoleon chased out of Prussia as a militant promoter of German unity, kept bombarding Alexander with memoranda imploring him to undertake the deliverance of the German lands from Napoleon's despotism. Thus, Stein argued, would be inaugurated in Europe a great beacon of enlightenment and progress, a fount of music, literature and philosophy. "What nobler task could be conceived for you, a magnanimous Liberator of Germany?"

Despite his mounting self-confidence, Alexander was still hesitant about the course of action he should take. The cautious Kutuzov voted for cessation of the war. Chancellor Rumiantsov, Arakcheyev and Rostopchin were of the same mind. After the supreme effort which the Russian soldiers and the Russian people had just sustained, the country had every right to think solely of its own interests and abandon further ambitious plans of helping others. Therefore, they urged the Russians to incorporate the Duchy of Warsaw and then make peace with Napoleon with little concern for Prussia, Austria and England. Russia's most urgent task ought to be rebuilding the devastated western provinces of the Empire and consideration of her international position. The chief stubborn spokesman for immediate peace was Kutuzov. "Why do we have to meddle in the European mess? Our brave boys defended our sacred Motherland heroically. The rest of the world admires their bravery. Isn't that enough glory? They should not be now forced to make new sacrifices. We would be foolish to fight any longer, mainly for the sake of the Germans. Let Europe stew in her own juice. What do we seek in Europe anyhow? Our officers will return home with nothing but silly ideas and syphilis."

But this was not Alexander's view. Enraptured by the dramatic reversal of his fortunes, and elated by his triumph over his rivals, whom he hated and admired at the same time, he listened more to the alluring and eloquent suggestions of Baron von Stein. Russia ought to bring about the final downfall of Napoleon's hegemony.

He would take vengeance on Paris for the profanation of Moscow, for Austerlitz, Friedland and Smolensk. He would inscribe his name in the annals of history as the savior of Europe, beginning with the German people.

While meditating on the mortal danger from which he had just escaped, and the prospects that the military victory opened to

Russia, Alexander again reached for the Bible. On opening it, the first sentence he noticed was from the second letter of St. Paul to Timothy: "The Lord stood with me, strengthened me and I was delivered from the lion." Alexander was always interested in astrology. Aware that Napoleon was born on August 15, i.e. under the sign of Leo, Alexander was again amazed at how the Bible seemed to be full of prophetic statements applicable to Napoleon and to him personally. The Erfurt memories of "a lion riding a white horse" flashed through his superstitious, impressionable mind and caused him to make a decision. The next morning he ordered the Russian army to cross the Niemen and advance into East Prussia and Poland. The war then must go on, its aim being to liberate Germany from Napoleon's hegemonial rule.

After the end of the Russian campaign, Kutuzov, thoroughly exhausted and ill with pneumonia, had collapsed and took to his bed. When Alexander learned of his illness, he visited the sick room. Lying in his field bed, Kutuzov resembled the thick trunk of a big, old tree that had fallen during a violent storm. When he saw his master enter the room, he tried to raise his upper body, but his strength failed him and he collapsed. With the courage of a dying man, Kutuzov asked the Tsar, "Why did you send our soldiers to shed blood for those damn greedy, haughty Germans who look down on us Slavs as if we were savage barbarians?"

"I trust, Mikhail Ilarionovich, that you will forgive my differing, once more, with you."

The dying Kutuzov whispered, "I will forgive you, but the Russian people never will."

CHAPTER 12

The Triumph

The failure of the Russian campaign destroyed the myth of Napoleon's invincibility. The immediate sequel to his retreat from Moscow was the convention of Taurogen. The Russo-Prussian agreement found immediate backing in London, which promised generous subsidies for the continuation of the coalition's war against Napoleon.

Initially, the Austrians did not support Russia and Prussia. Emperor Francis, as father of Marie Louise, still had some regard for his son-in-law. Besides, as severely as Napoleon's prestige had been damaged, he still commanded formidable resources. Once back in France he promptly recreated his army with vigor, and it was no longer certain that he had made his last mark on the battlefield. Metternich, therefore, tried to gain time and to maneuver in such a way that the Habsburgs might, in due time, pass from the tactical alliance with France against Russia to a firm association with Russia and Prussia against France, without provoking Napoleon prematurely. Meanwhile the situation was rapidly changing to the French leader's disadvantage. The French army in Spain was beaten by Wellington at Vittoria, followed by the evacuation of Madrid and the flight of King Joseph Bonaparte back to Paris. The road across the Pyrenees was left open to the

British. As Napoleon's vulnerability became obvious, on August 10, 1813, Austria declared war on France.

Meanwhile, the German campaign was developing. Despite a few brilliantly won battles by the outnumbered and outgunned Napoleon, his situation was becoming critical. On October 15, seeing himself in danger of being encircled at Leipzig, he resolved to fight an all out battle. He was confronted by 349,000 allied men while he could mobilize 155,000 soldiers at most. To counterbalance that enormous disparity he grasped the initiative and attacked vigorously to prevent the impending concentration of his enemies and destroy each allied army separately. At decisive moments of the battle Alexander behaved with consummate courage. He had bravely risked his life by rushing to the sector where the Russian army was most perilously threatened and several times flung his escort of Cossacks into the fight. For two days it was a touch-and-go affair. But at the peak of the battle, Napoleon's Bavarian and Saxon allies deserted him. As a result, he lost the Battle of Nations after four days of slaughter. By October 18, it was no longer a retreat for Napoleon's troops; it was a rout. On November 4, he recrossed the Rhine at Meinz with the remnants of his battered contingents.

The allies followed on his heels. Between December 21, 1813, and January 1, 1814, with 250,000 men they pressed across the Rhine between Koblenz and Basel. With reinforcements streaming from Austria, Germany and Russia, they soon had 420,000 men, divided into three armies. Schwarzenberg commanded the principal force, the Army of Bohemia, that advanced by way of Switzerland and the Jura mountains. Blucher led the Army of Silesia, which passed into France through Alsace and Lorraine. A third army, the Army of the North, was concentrating in the Low Countries under Jean Baptiste Bernadotte, a former Marshal of France, but now a newly elected Prince-Royal of Sweden. At first encountering no resistance, the allied troops confidently advanced straight toward Paris. Thus began the French campaign of 1814. Napoleon fought with grim determination and with the ferocity of a predator at bay. By January 26, when the three armies had reached the Seine, the Aube and the Marne, respectively, Napoleon counterattacked and again won a series of unexpected, brilliant victories against the invaders.

The surprised allied leaders panicked and were considering peace negotiations. Alexander rejected any compromise and declared himself in favor of a march on Paris. "We must not make peace with Napoleon. Peace with Napoleon can never be anything but a truce. I shall not make peace as long as Napoleon is on the throne."

The three armies regrouped and resumed their offensive on Paris. By March 22, the indecisive battles of Caronne, Laon and Arcis-sur-Aube had further drained Napoleon's resources and somewhat reestablished the military position of the allies. Napoleon could be saved only by a miraculous reversal of fortune. He had a brilliant idea: he would steal between the disjointed armies of his enemies and attack them from the rear. Then he would fling himself upon their lines of supply, and cut them off from the Rhine. He was aware that by this stratagem he would leave Paris exposed. Yet, he calculated, the allies would hardly dare to advance on his capital because they would be forced to redeploy their troops to face the new situation in their rear. Fate, however, conspired against him, when on the evening of March 24, a crucial report reached Russian quarters. A Cossack patrol had managed to seize a messenger dispatched from Paris to Napoleon. The messenger carried a packet of letters and confidential messages from Fouché, the Minister of Police, who complained of the general unrest in the capital, the increasing misery of the populace and the discontent in the provinces. Fouché concluded that the exhausted state of the treasury and the arsenals, as well as the widespread desire for peace made continuing the war impossible.

Alexander reflected on the report that night and on March 25 decided, "We must rapidly march straight on Paris with all our forces and dictate our conditions there.

Barclay de Tolly protested, "Napoleon will see that we aren't following him. He'll turn on us and attack our rear as we make our way toward Paris. The lion isn't dead yet. It's too early to piss on him. Beware!"

Alexander replied, "My decision is firm. We shall march on Paris at once."

And indeed, by March 29 the allies were at the city gates. The next day, about one o'clock in the afternoon, while the battle was still raging on the northern sector, Alexander galloped to the summit of the hill Chaumont, from whence his eyes beheld the spectacular panorama of the city claiming to be the capital of Europe. An irresistible euphoria filled his soul, while he repeated to himself, as if in a trance, "So Divine Providence in its sublime wisdom has permitted that this should be done by me—*by me!*"

★ ★ ★

On March 31, 1814, at two o'clock in the morning, Paris surrendered. Assuming the role of the magnanimous victor, Alexander decided to spare the Parisians any sort of reprisal for the sack of Moscow. The delegates of the municipality could not believe their ears when he told them, "Fear nothing, neither for your private dwellings nor for your public monuments. I come here as your friend and liberator. The soldiers will not be quartered with you. You shall merely have to furnish them with food. Your police and your National Guard shall continue to maintain law and order. There will be no revenge for the invasion of my country. I take the whole city under my protection. I have no enemies in France, except Napoleon Bonaparte."

At eleven that morning, preceded by a squadron of his Cossack escort in their red tunics and black Persian lamb hats trimmed with the golden doubleheaded Imperial eagle, Alexander, accompanied by his second younger brother Grand Duke Nicholas, made his triumphant entry into Paris. He was wearing the green and red uniform of the Semionovsky Guards and the blue ribbon of St. Andrew Grand Cross. Symbolically, he was mounted on the dark Arab mare named Eclipse, which Napoleon had given him at Erfurt. To the left of the Tsar rode the King of Prussia, and on his right Prince Schwarzenberg, representing his master the Emperor Francis of Austria, who remained at Chaumont, having excused himself from taking part in the victory parade in the capital of his vanquished son-in-law and his daughter Marie Louise. Behind the three leaders marched some 30 thousand men. In the vanguard were Alexander's soldiers: Russians, Tartars and Circassians; then followed various German units, mainly Prussians; then came Austrians, Croats and Hungarians, representing the nationalities of the Habsburg Empire. They all had fought the day before against the French, but were now applauded by the Parisians as their liberators from the Napoleonic dictatorship. The rays of spring sun lit Alexander's face and a glint of pride flashed in his blue eyes. He was at his pinnacle, his day of sweet triumph over his rival.

A silent reception in the working class district of Saint-Martin alarmed the victors. Few people were to be seen at the windows and on the pavements and those who did appear displayed angry faces and clenched fists. The French workers did not like Napoleon's dictatorial ways, but they could not forget that he reestablished the revolutionary principles of equality before the law and equality of opportunity. Beyond the gate of Saint-Denis, however, in the bourgeois districts, the crowds became more dense. There were cries of "Long live our liberators!" and here and there, a bold voice dared to shout, "Long live the Bourbons!" while the white flag waved.

Alexander's reception became increasingly jubilant as he progressed toward the center of the city. There the houses were decorated with carpets and flowers. From balconies and windows, white Bourbon banners were unfurled as the spectators frantically acclaimed the passing march of their invaders. In order to have a better look at the handsome Russian Tsar, several young women forced their way through the Cossacks' escort. The more adventurous ones even climbed onto the rumps of the Cossack horses and rode embracing the victors. Alexander, seeing them, remarked to Schwarzenberg, laughing, "I hope my Cossacks do not abduct these Parisian Sabines!"

Alexander entered Paris as conqueror, yet to judge from the

enthusiasm of the crowds which assembled along his route and from the benevolent countenance of the victor, he appeared to be a Henry IV or a Louis XIV reentering his capital upon return from a successful campaign to receive the homage of his subjects.

However, Napoleon was not yet beaten. He remained at Fontainebleau, with some 60,000 men still loyal to him, and could counterattack at any moment. The question facing the allies concerned their next move. Alexander's feelings for Napoleon were summed up in his words at the allied council: "The final defeat of Napoleon is not merely a political necessity. It is required by the Christian conscience as a testimony to the world of justice and morality. No dealings are possible with Napoleon!"

While the allies hesitated, on April 5 Schwartzenberg informed the Tsar that Marshal Marmont's reserve army, on which Napoleon depended to reinforce his contingent to Fontainebleau, had crossed the Austrian lines and surrendered. Alexander exclaimed, "This surrender is manifestly the will of Providence." When asked what he intended to do about establishing a sovereign in France, he answered, "A regency is impossible. Bonaparte's son, 'The Eagle' is too young. Moreover, the father is an insurmountable obstacle to the reign of the son. The Bourbons, alas, are the only solution."

Yet once more Alexander's ambivalence toward Napoleon surfaced. This was, he argued, another moment to show magnanimity. He fought a hard battle against the French Provisional Government and his allies to obtain for Napoleon the sovereignty of the Island of Elba. The vindictive Talleyrand, Hardenberg and Castlereagh would have liked to deport him as far from France as possible, preferably to the Azores, over a thousand miles off the coast of Portugal. Alexander's attitude toward Napoleon and his love of the generous gesture moved him to defend his former rival, whom he hated and admired at the same time. "I have been forced to go to war. Now that Bonaparte is defeated, I forgive him all the ill he has done my country. I forget his misdeeds and can again become his friend. I wish him to retain his title of Emperor. We shall give him the island of Elba in absolute sovereignty, with two million francs a year. His family will be granted ample pensions. If he refuses to accept Elba, and can find no asylum elsewhere; let him come to my country. I shall give him a magnificent welcome. I shall do all in my power to mitigate the defeat of a man so great, yet so unfortunate."

While insisting upon leniency toward the vanquished enemy, Alexander supported the Bourbon restoration. At his suggestion and that of Talleyrand, the Senate on April 6 proclaimed that "the people of France freely called to the throne Louis-Stanislas-Xavier of France, brother of the late king, as Louis XVIII." His return to France was delayed, however, as he was detained in London by an attack of gout and did not arrive at Compiegne until April 29, where the following day he met Alexander.

Previous to the encounter the Tsar had sent a message of warm felicitations to Louis, concluding with the admonition to govern France with moderation and "husband the memory of twenty-five years of glory." Louis, very sure of his privilege and regarding the divine right of kingship as sacred dogma, had taken that suggestion as a piece of impertinence presented to him by an arrogant barbarian. At Compiègne, he received the Tsar with studied condescension, as if to belittle this benefactor to whom he owed the crown. To begin with, the King, without rising from his own ornate, gilded armchair, upholstered in red damask, motioned the Tsar to a very ordinary one. Icy smiles and banal, conventional amicabilities followed. Astonished by the King's ingratitude, Alexander took a profound dislike to him and barely concealed his anger from his escort. "Louis XIV could not have received me more coldly at Versailles in the days of his greatest power! One would think that it was he who had come to place me on my throne!"

Despite his anger toward the new ruler, Alexander was convinced that a strong France, under a legitimate, constitutional king, was necessary for the equilibrium of Europe. He refused to agree with Castlereagh, Metternich, Stein and Hardenberg, that the allies should exploit their victory to the fullest and make the French pay for their twenty-two years of conquest. The peace treaty of May 30, 1814, was a compromise. It inflicted painful losses on France, since it deprived her of all her territorial acquisitions since 1792 and confined her within the boundaries of the old monarchy. But it imposed no military restriction and no indemnity upon her. The problem of France seemed to be settled.

However, the Allies had not been able to agree on the fate of other territories which were now free of Napoleon's rule. What was to be done with Poland, Saxony, Hanover, the Rhineland, the Netherlands and all of Italy? Having voiced their disagreement, and being aware of their mutual hostility, they decided to postpone the consideration of these problems until a congress which was to meet at Vienna.

CHAPTER 13

The Victors Amuse Themselves

*I*t was at the insistence of Austria's Foreign Minister Count Clemens Metternich that Vienna was chosen as the spot where the peace congress was to gather the following September. The choice was symbolic. Austria was the first to fight against revolutionary France and suffered most for her persistence. Alexander hated Metternich because the handsome Austrian actually had dared to compete with him, not only in politics, but in various gallant affairs. Alexander was now determined to take his revenge. He resolved to grasp and to retain for himself the direction of the approaching congress, the role which Metternich believed should be reserved for himself as host. Moreover, Metternich opposed Russia's rule over the whole of Poland because he considered it dangerous for Europe, and for Austria, especially. Alexander's real intention, he suspected, was to reconstitute the kingdom of Poland under the scepter of the Romanovs, which in itself would destroy the new European equilibrium established after Napoleon's downfall. "The entire Poland united with Russia is bound to dominate central Europe and thus to become the mistress of the European continent," he argued. Soon the rivalry turned into a personal diplomatic duel.

Metternich, who followed Alexander from Paris to London, had no difficulty exploiting the distrust of Russia growing in the mind of Britain's austere and suspicious Foreign Secretary Robert Castlereagh. Only a close alliance of Austria and England could restrain Russian ambitions, argued Metternich. His work in London was made easier by Alexander's lack of tact and arrogant behavior. His dining table conversations with the wife of the Prince Regent soon developed into an intense flirtation that resulted in a series of secret meetings, duly reported to the husband. Moreover, Alexander quoted right and left the satirical epigram which he had heard from one of the Whig politicians:

> Some by religion cure their grief,
> By dissipation some,
> A Princess in water seeks relief,
> The Prince takes it in the rum.

All this made the Regent angry and turned the initially triumphant visit of the Tsar into a source of friction by arousing Britain's mistrust of Alexander's ambitious plans. His departure from London was marked by coldness on both sides.

* * *

After this disappointing visit, Alexander embarked at Dover on June 20, crossed Belgium and took a short rest at the Court of Baden, where Elizabeth was staying with her mother. There a deputation from the Holy Synod and the Council of the Russian Empire appeared, humbly imploring Alexander's consent to be known by the title of "Blessed" and begging his permission to erect at the Senate square in St. Petersburg a monumental column bearing the inscription, "To the restorer of kings, from a grateful Russia."

After a short visit to St. Petersburg, Alexander left for Vienna on September 12. On the way he stopped at Prince Adam Czartoryski's palace at Puławy. By this he wished to show the Poles that they could count on his good will in spite of their participation in the invasion of Russia in 1812. By then the establishment of a great Slavic Empire under his scepter had become an obsession with him. While flattering the Poles and promising them a liberal constitution, Alexander avoided promises and refused to be pinned down concerning the Polish frontiers he would be willing to accept. "This will be decided in Vienna, at the Congress."

While promising to champion the restoration of Poland in a personal union with Russia, Alexander had no illusions about the difficulties he would have in ruling that nation of cantankerous individualists. During the Congress, he wrote to Laharpe: "The Poles will take advantage of every opportunity to recover their political existence as a nation, but I shall have to condemn myself to a perpetual mistrust in their regard, to take inquisitional measures." The new Polish army was to be commanded by his brother, Constantine.

Twelve days later, on September 24, Alexander made his solemn entry into Vienna surrounded by a group of his trusted advisors. To represent his Empire at the Congress, Alexander had chosen a most varied group of delegates. They included his former ambassador in Vienna, Prince Andrew Razmovsky; his current ambassador there, Count Stackelberg; his acting Minister for Foreign Affairs, Count Nesselrode; his diplomatic advisors Barons Anstedt and Stein; his two aides-de-camp, Pozzo Di Borgo and Capo d'Istria; and finally, as a specialist on Polish affairs, Prince Adam Czartoryski. Of that brilliant phalanx selected to defend the cause of Russia, there were four Germans, a Corsican, a Greek, a Frenchman from Alsace, and a Pole; only one delegate, Prince Razumovsky, was Russian. Although nominally a ranking representative, he did not take an active part in the work of the delegation. "Perhaps I was appointed for the sole reason that at least one man of Russian blood was needed."

By the beginning of September 1814, sovereigns streamed into the Austrian capital from all over Europe. The kings of Prussia, Bavaria, Württemberg, and Denmark, the Grand Dukes of Hesse-

Cassel, Hesse-Darmstadt, and Saxe-Coburg, and all the princelings of Germany rushed there to involve themselves in the diplomatic intrigue. The Congress of Vienna was the greatest gathering of crowned heads ever assembled. Although the Congress did not formally open until October 1, by the middle of September the Austrian capital was crowded with a host of distinguished visitors. The dethroned and dispossessed princes whose lands had been seized by Napoleon eagerly anticipated the restoration of their territories and rights.

Among all the rulers present, Alexander alone excited general attention. While the other monarchs and diplomats confined themselves to following the everyday work of the Congress from a dignified distance, Alexander flung himself directly into diplomatic combat. From the first, his ambitious Polish scheme encountered three redoubtable antagonists, all of the great exponents of the art of diplomatic fencing, one more intelligent and wily than the other—Metternich, Talleyrand and Castlereagh.

Alexander feared and hated all three, but Talleyrand he despised most because of his aggressive greed. The Prince of Benevento, so celebrated for his diplomatic skills and his refined taste while protesting "the most sincere and tender attachment" to him, constantly alluded to the need for increasing the secret Russian subsidies which had been issued to him since Erfurt. When the Tsar, who needed no more intelligence reports, stopped the flow of money, Talleyrand switched his allegiance, countering his former benefactor at every step. Alexander was informed that Talleyrand had promised Metternich and Castlereagh to oppose the Tsar's Polish plans as "an attempt to dominate the continent of Europe." It was also reported that in order to get into the good graces of Louis XVIII and be forgiven for his countless apostasies, his services to the Revolution and to Napoleon, Talleyrand told the King that the Romanovs were actually a "bunch of miserable bastards," because the dynasty dated only from 1613, while the Bourbons were infinitely more ancient.

Alexander's position was difficult, indeed. Rebel though he was against many traditions, he could not ignore the duty laid upon him by the Russian establishment: the army, and the nobility, the central pillars of his realm. After each victory, they believed, it was the duty of the Tsar to compensate for the wartime sacrifices by an expansion of territory. This was traditionally the one tangible symbol of military triumph that the Russians appreciated. Territorial growth was a must for each Tsar of Russia. Once he decided to continue a war he must bring home the spoils. Alexander realized this, and if he did not satisfy the people with territorial acquisitions, as well as glory and prestige, he could eventually meet with his father's fate.

From the first day of the Congress, the Polish question was the key issue. Russia claimed, at the least, all the territories of the Duchy of Warsaw, the nominal ruler of which was King of Saxony. This meant that Prussia would lose the greater part of the provinces which she had annexed after the Third Partition. As compensation, Prussia would receive the whole of the realm of Saxony, whose King, Frederick August, also Duke of Warsaw, had been too long faithful to Napoleon and was now a prisoner in Berlin. As for Austria, to indemnify her for the territories that she gave up in Galicia, she would be granted Lombardy, Venice, and the Dalmation coast.

To emphasize the importance which he attached to his plan, Alexander declared, "I have 200,000 men between the Oder and the Vistula. Drive them out if you can! I will keep what I hold. I will go to war rather than renounce the territory I occupy! If the King of Saxony refuses to abdicate, he will be conducted to Russia and he will die there. One king of Poland has already ended his days in Russia. Frederick August would do well to remember the fate of King Poniatowski who after the Third Partition of Poland died in St. Petersburg as a hostage of my grandmother."

Since Prussia, compensated for the loss of her Polish provinces by gaining Saxony, would most probably remain allied with Russia, such a partnership would effectively mean the end of Austria's leading role in the area, especially in Germany. Consequently, Metternich vigorously opposed this arrangement by which Austria's two northern neighbors, Russia augmented by Poland and

Prussia by Saxony, would thus have a hegemonial position in Central Europe at the expense of the Habsburgs. "To have the Russians in Warsaw and along the frontiers of the Carpathians and the Prussians in Leipzig and Dresden, along the frontiers of Bohemia—no, we shall never agree to that. We would rather go to war."

Metternich soon found an adroit ally in the person of Talleyrand, who supported Metternich by taking advantage of Alexander's boastfulness, and by coining a few polished aphorisms which he developed with his usual skill. Talleyrand argued: "The first need of Europe is to banish forever the idea that rights can be obtained by force of arms. The balance of power and the sacred principle of legitimacy cannot admit the total subjection of Poland to Russia, any more than it can admit the overwhelming predominance of Prussia in Germany and of Austria in Italy. Do the Russians really need territorial gains? Far from having lost anything during the last twenty years, Russia has acquired Finland and Bessarabia, with Napoleon's backing. She has been invaded by Bonaparte and frightfully devastated. What she needs is internal reconstruction and not further territorial expansion."

The British representative, Lord Castlereagh, thoroughly backed Metternich and Talleyrand. "We didn't do battle with Napoleon for twenty years to see Europe dominated by Russia." So, in the official sessions of the Congress, and even more acrimoniously behind the scenes, the squabbling went on for weeks. While the proceedings were mainly centered on Poland and Saxony, the fate of Naples, Tuscany, the Papal States, Modena, Lucca, Parma, Hanover, Switzerland, Belgium, the Rhineland and the German principalities would also be decided. A monumental task faced the peacemakers of Vienna. It didn't prevent them, however, from enjoying themselves.

Aside from being a momentous political event, the Congress was a gigantic carnival. After twenty years, during which Europe was ravaged by bloody revolutions and horrible wars, prospects for establishing a lasting peace had come at last. The vulgar wench Revolution had been vanquished. The old feudal order reasserted itself. This sense of boundless triumph was reflected in an orgiastic sensualism that ran through the delegates and set them on fire. Scores of women, enjoying a new freedom, pursued men through the balls, receptions, and dinners, while pretending to be pursued themselves. The princes, kings, and emperors abandoned themselves to the intoxicating gaiety and pleasures of a Vienna gone mad—it was a Saturnalia of the old world.

Vienna in 1814 was a city of medium size in comparison to London and Paris; it had fewer than 200,000 inhabitants. The most important royalties, like the Tsar of Russia and the King of Prussia, could be accommodated in the immense complex of Imperial palaces, the Hofburg. Around the Hofburg spread the residences of the aristocracy, the homes of the middle class and the hovels of the poor, crowded in a maze of medieval narrow streets. While shops, cafes, restaurants, and theaters abounded, inns and hotels were too few to care for the needs of the people who came to attend the Congress.

The host of the Congress, Emperor Francis I, and Metternich quickly regretted their invitation to such a giant and costly gathering of celebrities. Inflation was rampant by early autumn, and the expenses of the royal tables at the Hofburg were never less than 50,000 florins a day, roughly the budget for the daily expenses of the entire Ministry of Foreign Affairs.

The unexpectedly large influx of visitors also alarmed those authorities responsible for security—but it delighted the residents of Vienna. For them this meant new business and public pageantry, so much desired after the years of wartime austerity. The Viennese were proud to see their Emperor playing host to the most important people of Europe. After the humiliation of recent defeats, these were much more pleasant times. The people did not anticipate that the strain on the State budget would soon result in new taxes and excise duties that would affect them for years; initially, the enthusiasm for the Congress was remarkably widespread. Many volunteers rushed to offer services to the authorities. Scions of noble families applied to become pages and equerries, while the sons of the poor lined up for jobs as coachmen, valets or footmen; those wishing to be employed as secret agents besieged Baron Franz Hager, Chief of the Constabulary.

From the beginning it was obvious that surveillance of the distinguished foreigners would be far beyond the capacity of the regular police so volunteers were welcome. They were to infiltrate the embassies as servants to report their master's activities. Much time was wasted in Hager's intelligence network. One especially hardworking team spent days pasting together scraps of paper rescued from diplomatic wastebaskets. Another department steamed open all letters which they intercepted entering or leaving Vienna. The most scandalous of these were submitted to Metternich and to the emperor himself. Francis had a passion for reading secret reports and derived much amusement from some of them, especially those describing amorous adventures of his distinguished guests.

While Baron Hager toiled unremittingly to prepare for the Congress, no one worked harder than Prince Trauttmansdorff, Marshal of the Court and Master of the Horse. He was in charge of installing the visiting sovereigns and their suites at the Hofburg and of arranging official receptions. It was calculated that about forty tables must be set up every night for dinner. Another of the Marshal's responsibilities was supplying carriages to the distinguished guests. The two decades of war had resulted in gross neglect of the court stables. The old barouches and coaches had to be repainted dark green and imperial eagles emblazoned on their doors. Fourteen hundred horses and the requisite number of coachmen and grooms in yellow and black Habsburg liveries had to be outfitted and trained.

But, the liveries and stables were a lesser detail compared to the problems of protocol facing Trauttmansdorff. The guest list was enormous and there was no precedent to guide him, for no international conference of this scale had ever taken place. The complex and touchy problem of precedence was solved by seating sovereigns according to age. To assist him he had the eager and enthusiastic hostess Empress Maria Ludovica. This charming, delicate Italian princess, the third wife of the twice-widowed Emperor Francis, was ready to make any sacrifice to assist her husband and ensure the success of the Congress. Although racked with tuberculosis, the twenty-seven-year-old, frail, blue-eyed, blond Empress threw herself into the task of aiding the Marshal of the Court and hastily organized the Festivals Committee to plan the entertainment for the foreign guests. Naturally artistic, patron of art, music and the theater, the Empress coordinated the talents of several artists to redecorate the somewhat dilapidated Hofburg Palace and the adjacent Spanish Riding School. Under her skillful direction the palace was refurbished, sparkling with fresh paint and plaster.

★ ★ ★

Alexander, as the "Agamemnon of the Kings," at thirty-seven and full of zest, was the dominant figure of the Congress. The excitement of the Congress affected Alexander as well as his rivals Metternich and Talleyrand, the latter always in search of new love affairs, despite his sixty years. Although there was little prudery in the high international circles of those days, they both scandalized even the prurient by their casual and cynical displays of sensual indulgence on a grand scale. Alexander bested all his rivals in gallant affairs. He was accompanied by a harem of ladies. He forced his wife, Elizabeth, to come to Vienna against her will, and for the sake of protocol he demanded that she appear at most official functions. Maria Naryshkin he brought as his chief mistress. There was also his sister, Catherine. She disappointed her brother, however. Soon after her arrival in Vienna she decided to drop him from her life. After the death of her first husband, George, she sought a mate more worthy of her standing as a Grand Duchess. "I've had enough of stewing idly in a provincial city like Tver," she bluntly declared to her brother. "I want to be a Queen." She pretended to fall in love with the young Crown Prince William, heir to the throne of Württemburg. Like a huntress on a safari, she pursued him with her usual energy, determined to marry him, and succeeded in doing so.

As in the past Elizabeth was a liberal and complacent wife. She was delighted that the scandalous romance of her husband with Catherine was over, and closed her eyes to his other amorous adventures. Moreover, during the Congress, Elizabeth's love for Czartoryski suddenly revived, and he reciprocated. The Prince was with her during all moments free from official duties. They even went so far as to ask Alexander to agree to a divorce in order to allow them to marry. The episode resulted in an estrangement of Alexander from his friend and advisor. "What an arrogant person Prince Adam has become! My tolerance has turned his head. It is the privilege of a Russian Emperor to divorce his wife, but not vice-versa."

At the Congress Alexander's routine was unbroken. He would rise early and rub his face with a block of ice to tighten his skin. He was proud of his rosy, youthful complexion and wanted to keep it forever. After breakfast he conferred with secretaries and aides. Around noon he lunched, often with co-workers, and then plunged into social activities. He was at most major receptions and went to great lengths to be charming to pretty women. One of his numerous advantages was his dancing skill. Tightly buttoned into his military tunic with a stiff, high collar, his legs encased in tight white kid breeches, it was his custom to leap up at the first sound of dance music. He was also a charming conversationalist, full of interesting anecdotes and titillating compliments. A flirtation with such a glamorous and prestigious man brought increased social standing. It was no wonder that ladies of high rank competed for his favors. Among them was Princess Catherine Bagration, widow of the brave general who was mortally wounded at the battle of Borodino. She was, on her mother's side, a great-niece of Catherine II and, consequently, a second cousin of Alexander. She parted from her rather crude and martial husband soon after their marriage and lived mostly in Dresden and Vienna where she was, at one time, a mistress of Metternich, by whom she had a daughter. She was a fierce Russian patriot and supported, as well as she could, Alexander's Polish plan.

The chief rival of Catherine Bagration was Wilhelmine of Sagan, heiress to a great fortune. Wilhelmine was the eldest of the four daughters of the late Duke of Curland. She had inherited vast estates in Livonia, as well as in Silesia and Bohemia. She also had been Metternich's mistress. Despite numerous stormy quarrels between the former lovers, the Austrian charmer retained considerable dominance over her through flattery, blackmail and generous gifts. He influenced her belief that fulfillment of Alexander's Polish scheme would mean an Austrian war against Russia and Prussia. As a consequence, as a legal subject of the Tsar, she risked losing her extensive properties in Austrian Bohemia and, perhaps, also in Prussian Silesia should the Austrians reconquer this province taken from them only two generations ago by Frederick II. Hence it was in her vital interest to persuade the Tsar to seek a compromise and give up his Polish plan to protect her personal fortune. Success in such an intrigue, implied Metternich, would be richly rewarded by a Habsburg grant of new large estates in Bohemia.

Wilhelmine needed little encouragement. Her feminine pride, as well as her greed, made her fling her net around Alexander. Thus, both Wilhelmine Sagan and Catherine Bagration tried to influence important matters at the Congress by manipulating the Tsar. They were both ambitious, beautiful, experienced women, eager to dominate men by pleasing them. They were both subjects of the Tsar, living abroad and belonging to the adventurous cosmopolitan set that owned properties in other countries, and hence were persons of divided loyalties. The duel between them for Alexander's favor was avidly watched by Viennese society. Initially Wilhelmina was ahead in the race. But soon her aggressiveness and excessive flattery, as well as her lingering connection with Metternich, put Alexander on guard. He dropped her soon after the formal opening of the Congress.

★ ★ ★

Each sovereign attempted to outdo others of the princely throng by hosting splendid balls, receptions and other festivities. The Habsburg Imperial tournament and carousel was the most sumptuous event of all. It was presented on November 23 at the Spanish Riding School built by Charles V. The cream of European aristocracy was invited by the host to attend the spectacle. At each end of the vast arena were constructed large galleries that ran the entire width of the huge building, seating twelve hundred spectators on benches arranged in tiers. Above the galleries were three balconies for the two orchestras and a choir of young boys who sang at the opening and closing of the festivities, as well as during intermissions. The boys appeared, dressed in Renaissance costumes of the yellow and black Habsburg colors with black berets with white ostrich feathers. The floor of the arena was covered with sand and sawdust. Hanging from the ceiling, a dozen gigantic chandeliers, sparkling with wax candles, made the interior as bright as day.

At eight o'clock a flourish of trumpets announced the opening of the tournament. Twenty-four ladies of Vienna society with their escorts entered the arena, separated into four groups, each costumed in green, crimson, blue or black, and crossed the arena under the intent gaze of thousands of eyes. Then the herald announced the entry of the sovereign monarchs. The Habsburg anthem "God Protect Our Emperor" was played by both bands, and sung by the boys in the choir. Everyone stood and thunderous applause followed. The Austrian Emperor and the Empress took their places in the center of the gallery. Other sovereigns and princes arranged themselves in order of precedence and age.

After the Emperor Francis rose to announce the opening of the tournament, the hall resounded to stirring martial music. Twenty-four knights, the flower of the Empire's nobility, rode into the arena on richly caparisoned Spanish horses. The knights wore close-fitting velvet doublets with puffed sleeves and satin lapels, the fronts ornamented with gold buttons; tight breeches; yellow half-boots with gilded spurs; and large hats turned up in front, where a white ostrich plume curled to the left side was fastened with a diamond clasp. Their swords, held by a belt, were encrusted with diamonds. The knights also divided into four teams, each team wearing the color of the group of ladies for whom they were to do battle. Twenty-four pages in Habsburg liveries, holding banners aloft, preceded them. They were followed by the same number of armsbearers dressed in Spanish fashion. Each lady gave her knight a scarf matching the color of the knight's costume.

After saluting the sovereigns and their ladies with lowered lances, the knights began their tournament to musical accompaniment. At a gallop they caught rings suspended in front of the Imperial tribunal. They threw javelins at simulated Turks' heads in colorful turbans. They picked them off the ground at full gallop and threw them again. Then, at full speed they cut apples in two with their swords. They performed maneuvers and jumps of all kinds that were as graceful as they were swiftly executed. Thunderous applause greeted the prowess of the knights. They next divided into two groups, put on protective helmets and breast plates to face each other in combat. At the sound of a trumpet they charged in an attempt to unhorse their opponents.

After this simulated medieval tournament guests were entertained at a banquet at the Hofburg Palace. At the principal table, for the royal guests, the meal was set up on one of the higher tiers and laid out on gold plates. At the left was a table for the victorious knights and their ladies. At the right were seated the diplomatic corps and the chief military personages of all the delegations. Around the hall and in the adjoining rooms were many smaller tables for other guests of distinction. Never before was there seen in Vienna such a spectacle as the Imperial grand fest at the Spanish Riding School. Europe was hungry, plagued by an epidemic of cholera, ruined, raving, fearful of the future. No matter, the Old Regime had resolved to celebrate what it believed to be its resurrection.

★ ★ ★

The two leading patrons of the Congress were accompanied by their spouses, but the ladies remained in the shadows, appearing rarely, only at official functions of crucial importance. Count Clemens Metternich, then a promising young diplomat, had married Eleanore, born Princess von Kaunitz, for her wealth and social position. She was not attractive, but a shrewd and understanding partner. Theirs was a classic marriage of convenience. The granddaughter of Marie-Therese's powerful chancellor, she was quite satisfied to be the consort of her father's good looking and brilliant successor. In Dresden, his first post, she had been obliged to look on as Clemens enjoyed a love affair with Princess Catherine Bagration. Now she was humiliated again by his liaisons with numerous women, but her love for their children, for whom she cared more than anything else, took precedence over her feminine pride.

Because of Czartoryski's presence, Alexander's wife, Empress Elizabeth, didn't mind her husband's new love affairs. Both spouses accompanied their husbands to official functions and were treated with all attention due their respective ranks. Yet, after these formal ceremonies were over, they discreetly retired to their residences while their husbands, under the pretext of "important private conferences" or "interviews," indulged in all sorts of wild adventures. The aphrodisiac aura of Vienna caused Alexander to forget the religious experience which had so heavily influenced him during the crucial moments of the 1812 campaign. He left his Bible in a drawer and threw himself into the enjoyment of carnal pleasures. Alexander's behavior was closely watched by Baron Hager's agents, and their spicy reports were often read with glee by Metternich after his morning coffee. One of the reports stated: "The kind of life the Emperor of Russia has led in Paris, in France, in London and now in Vienna, has ruined his reputation everywhere, and rumors of his notoriety have even reached Russia. Some persons close to the Emperor of Russia, who have had the opportunity of studying his character, insist that Alexander, too, is slightly deranged and will end like his father."

Much of Alexander's amorous activity was focused on the Schenkenstrasse, a small lane only a few hundred yards from the Hofburg. Coincidentally, Duchess Wilhelmine of Sagan and Princess Catherine Bagration had leased opposite wings of the same mansion in Schenkenstrasse. After a passing flirtation with Wilhelmine, Alexander chose Catherine as his steady companion, meanwhile neglecting Maria Naryshkin. The affair with Catherine seemed to develop delightfully. After the first night with Alexander, Catherine noted in her diary, "During the most climactic moments with my lover I prayed to God, 'My Lord forgive me for the excess of my pleasure' " *("Pendant les moments les plus decisives avec mon amant je priais a Dieu—mon Dieu je demand pardon de l'excès de mon bonheur.")* But nothing that exciting could last forever.

On November 30, Catherine had retired early to bed with a headache, having sent her servants out of the house for the evening. She was soon disturbed by the porter ringing her bell. Dressed only in her negligée, she came down the staircase and saw Alexander. With a show of surprise and proper modest confusion she ushered him upstairs to her room. There Alexander was surprised to see a man's hat, lying on a chair. "What is this?" he asked indignantly. "It belongs to my decorator, Monsieur Jean Moreau," explained the Princess. "He has come to prepare the house for my ball tomorrow." The fanciful tale did not satisfy the Tsar. "Your decorator must be a very rich man," he remarked sarcastically. "How is it that he wears such an expensive hat, with an ostrich feather?" The Princess, confused, was at loss to explain the incident. Throwing the hat on the floor, the furious Alexander left the house, never to return to it again.

The mortified Catherine bombarded him with apologetic letters, all in vain. In desperation she arranged one expensive reception after another and flung herself into the arms of various incidental lovers. Eventually her parties often degenerated into wild orgies and she became one of the most talked-about ladies of the Congress. A police report submitted to Metternich thus described the atmosphere of her house: "A daughter of Prince Starhemberg, with her parents, attended the New Year's party given by Princess Bagration. Childish games were played—forfeits, round games, and the like. While these were going on, the daughter retired to the most distant room with a Russian officer, who locked the door. Prince Starhemberg observed this, and, furious at the girl's refusal to open the door, had the lock broken and found the girl in a state of undress. Once again it was said that the Bagration house was a brothel, and that it was surprising to see a mother bring her daughter there."

* * *

The end of the affair with Catherine Bagration marked a major turning point in Alexander's behavior. It was caused by the rapidly deteriorating position of Russia. He became aware of the fact that Austria, supported by Britain and France, was mobilizing and getting ready to fight Russia and Prussia over the division of Poland. By December his associates observed in him a deep change of mood. His growing nervousness was so striking that it was remarked upon even by strangers. It was reflected in his search for solitude, and his diminished interest in social affairs. He began to devote more and more time to serious political discussion and diplomatic negotiations while by-passing many balls and receptions. There was much speculation as to this sudden change. Metternich at first hoped that Alexander had abandoned the struggle for Poland because of the growing influence of the anti-Turkish Greek associates Prince Ypsilani and Sturdza, who wished him to champion the cause of Greek independence and in general raise the problems of the Eastern question at the Congress. Others said Alexander had lost his enthusiasm for the Poles because Czartoryski and the Empress Elizabeth had rekindled their old love affair and were insisting on divorce. Soon one of the causes of Alexander's baffling mood change was discovered by Hager's agents, who regularly intercepted the Tsar's correspondence. There had been increasingly intense exchanges of messages between a mysterious lady, Baroness Julie von Krüdener, and an intimate friend of Alexander, Roxandre Sturdza, lady-in-waiting of Elizabeth and sister of his secretary.

In November of 1814, Roxandre received a letter from Julie in which the Baroness had written, "Please warn the all-beloved Man of Destiny that a new storm is approaching. It will mean that the Bourbon lilies will disappear momentarily. Napoleon is presently preparing his return to France. Beware!" Alexander was puzzled by the message and discussed it with Roxandre. How could a man, isolated from the world and closely guarded by the commissioners of the allied powers, escape his internment? Yet, he was flattered by the reference to himself as "the all-beloved Man of Destiny." The mysterious message haunted him. He awoke several times during the night, frightened by the nightmares of a man on a white horse in a black hat and gray coat, galloping over a mass of dead bodies.

In January and February 1815, the Baroness sent through Roxandre a new warning to "him whom we all love and respect." The message ended with the words: "The man whom he fears is about to return to menace all of us." This time, Alexander expressed to Roxandre a desire to meet the authoress of these cryptic warnings. "If she is a clairvoyant as she claims, she may be able to tell me something about my future and direct me in breaking the coalition shaping against me," he said. Roxandre, always eager to please her master, forwarded the message to the Baroness. The answer did not, however, arrive in time.

★ ★ ★

Metternich was conscious of his historical role and that of the Congress which he had initiated and over which he presided. To immortalize the unique gathering of the most distinguished diplomats of the era, he had asked the French artist Jean-Baptiste Isabey to paint a collective portrait of the chief delegates to the Congress. Isabey was chosen because he had been, as a young man, a court painter for Louis XVI. The fact that he occupied a similar position under Napoleon was overlooked because of his artistic prestige and his social graces. The work of painting a huge canvas was painstaking and protracted. It required well over twenty sessions of one to two hours each. At the beginning of March 1815, the huge painting was about to be completed. Only two or three sittings were required to finish it. On March 4, at 5:30 P.M., an unusually long sitting made the distinguished models anxious to leave the big hall and join various social functions.

Isabey's sharp eyes focused alternately on the canvas and the table at which the leading diplomats were seated and he noticed their growing restlessness. "Gentlemen, shortly you shall be free to leave, to change and go to your social engagements. The sitting will end in a few minutes. The light has become dim, hence the delay," said Isabey, while standing with brush in hand near the easel. "Two or three minutes more, gentlemen. I know how valuable your time is. I know it very well. But if punctuality is the courtesy of kings, precision is the courtesy of an artist. Remember that I painted the unfortunate Queen Marie Antoinette. She was patient, as well as beautiful. The saying that beauty is the only duty of a queen is not entirely correct. Patience is another. Please be patient. After all, Napoleon is safely interned on the Island of Elba. There is no hurry." The delegates laughed; they knew that Isabey liked to joke.

Isabey had hardly finished these words when a lackey flung open the doors of the hall and an Austrian colonel rushed to Metternich, stood at attention and reported, "Your Highness, I am extremely sorry to interrupt this sitting, but we have just received the most alarming news from the British consul in Genoa. Bonaparte has left the island of Elba aboard a ship. Its destination is unknown!"

If a thunderbolt struck the hall, it would not have made a more powerful impression on those present. They sat as if paralyzed. Metternich was the first to regain his composure. He jumped to his feet and, controlling his excitement, said, "Gentlemen, this is no time for patience. This is the hour of grave decision. This is the time for resolute action."

By ten o'clock that evening, the leading allied statesmen were gathered in his study at the Ministry of Foreign Affairs to decide on a course of action. Various scenarios were debated. The news placed Alexander in an embarrassing position. He was acutely conscious that it was on his initiative that Napoleon had been assigned to the island of Elba and not exiled to the much safer Azores. He was also aware that Austria, Britain and France were plotting against him. Yet, again, all of them now faced a rabid Napoleon. There was some question as to whether he would sail for France or for Italy. But as a precaution special couriers were sent out from Vienna at once to alert the commanders of all allied armies.

Meanwhile, on March 1, 1815, Napoleon had safely landed at the Gulf of Juan near Nice with no opposition from the French armed forces or local civilian authorities. Quite the contrary. Everywhere he appeared he was greeted enthusiastically. His triumphant march from the South of France to Paris was a unique phenomenon. One French unit after another surrendered to him. The rapidly changing mood of the French people was reflected in the headlines of the Parisian newspaper *Le Moniteur.* On March 5, it informed the public that "the Corsican Monster has landed in the Gulf of Juan." Two days later the headline was "The Cannibal is marching toward Grasse." One March 12, the Parisians were informed that "The Usurper has entered Grenoble." On March 16, the paper calmly stated that "Napoleon is marching toward Fontainebleau." On March 20, French readers learned that "His Imperial Majesty is expected tomorrow in Paris." Meanwhile, Louis XVIII hurriedly fled Paris and returned to England. As Victor Hugo put it, this was the most successful invasion in history; it was carried out by one unarmed man firing not a single shot.

The unexpected and unparalleled triumph of Napoleon made a profound impression on Alexander. After a moment of reflection on the neglected warnings of the Sybillian Baroness, he declared, "No peace with Napoleon! The first thing is to crush him! We can decide afterward on the political future of France." The words betrayed his doubts about the wisdom of his previous support of the Bourbons, whom he despised, especially the ridiculously fat and aggressively arrogant Louis XVIII. To one of the British delegates to the Congress, Lord Clancarty, who reminded him of the principle of "legitimacy," which had been declared one of the main cornerstones of the allied policy, he declared, "The French nation does not want the Bourbons. See how calmly they have let them go. Do you want to impose on the French people by force a government which they have just abandoned?"

Though speaking of force, Alexander was momentarily forceless. At that instant the bulk of the Russian army was either in Poland or had been withdrawn to Russia. It was clear that Russian forces would not be in a position to fight Napoleon for several months. Yet, orders had to be dispatched to Barclay de Tolly to prepare his troops for a march westward as soon as it was feasible to do so. Since the Austrians were engaged in pacifying Italy at the time, it was agreed that the task of defending the threatened frontiers of the Netherlands should be left primarily to the British and the Prussians. Meanwhile, Schwarzenberg, as supreme allied commander, would concentrate an Austrian army on the right bank of the Rhine ready to invade France in conjunction with the Prussians under Blücher. The British entrusted Wellington with the command of the Anglo-Dutch mixed contingent that was to gather in Belgium.

While the military leaders were hastily preparing for hostilities, the diplomats drew up, at top speed, the final draft of the resolutions of the Congress. In facing the peril created by Napoleon's return, harmony was reestablished among the powers. As a gesture of his solidarity with his allies, Alexander accepted territorial sacrifices in Poland. The bulk of the Duchy of Warsaw was to be annexed to Russia, but Prussia was to keep Posen, Bromberg and Thorn; she was also to receive the Rhine provinces as consolation for the loss of Saxony, whose integrity was to be essentially maintained. Austria was given the province of Tarnopol in eastern Galicia, ceded to Russia in 1809 after Wargram, and she was also to regain the rest of Galicia except Cracow, and to pocket Lombardy, Venice, Trieste, Dalmatia and Illyria as well.

As soon as he installed himself in Paris, Napoleon tried to split the new coalition. He ordered a search of the studio of Louis XVIII at the Tuileries Palace. In a drawer of the King's desk was found the text of the treaty of January 3, 1815. In it Austria, France and Britain had pledged themselves to curb the ambitions of Russia in Poland by threatening war. As soon as this came to his knowledge, Napoleon communicated it to the Russian Chargé d'Affaires, who at once left for Vienna. Seeing the document, Alexander exploded.

His aide-de-camp, Capo d'Istria, who was present, described how the Tsar stamped up and down the room, his face purple, his eyes darting fire, and shouted, "This is the work of those two poisonous snakes, Metternich and Talleyrand."

The confrontation which he immediately staged with Metternich was short and dramatic. With his most haughty air he showed the treaty and asked, "Do you know this document?"

Then, scarcely troubling to listen to the stammering excuses of his rival, he said in a calm voice, "While we live there must be no mention of this . . . ever! There are more urgent things for us to do. We must think of nothing but our common struggle against Napoleon."

CHAPTER 14

The Baltic Baroness

Alexander did not attend the last sessions of the Congress of Vienna and the signing of the treaty on June 9, 1815. He feared that in their strategic calculations, Wellington, Blücher and Schwarzenberg would be able to break Bonaparte's back and enter Paris before the Russians fired a single shot. On May 25, Alexander left Vienna for Heilbronn on the Neckar, where he established his headquarters on June 4. The allied council of war, over which Alexander presided, was devoted to outlining the military campaign against Napoleon. The allied forces were to concentrate on the Rhine between Basel and Coblenz. The Anglo-Prussian army would form the right wing and attack in the direction of Langres; the Russian contingent, which could not reach the Rhine before July, would form the reserve force and remain concentrated around Mainz, ready to intervene according to the turn of the battle. The die was cast.

Alexander stayed at Heilbronn in Germany impatiently awaiting the arrival of the first Russian troops. One June morning, Peter Volkonsky knocked at his door and announced that a lady who called herself Julie, Baroness von Krüdener, insisted on being received immediately. By a curious coincidence, Alexander had, at that moment, been thinking of her prophecy concerning Napoleon's return, and felt a keen desire to meet her. When told of her sudden appearance, he said to Volkonsky, "To have divined my thoughts like this she must have read my very soul. The hand of Providence is evident here again."

The Baroness was a fascinating cosmopolitan personality. She was born at Riga in 1764, the daughter of a Baltic German landowner, Baron Otto von Vietinghoff. She had married a Russian diplomat, Alexis von Krüdener, at the age of eighteen, and accompanied him to his posts in Venice, Copenhagen and Berlin. They had two children, Paul and Juliette. Alexis and Julie separated in 1792, and he died ten years later. Julie soon became famous for her numerous, bizarre amorous adventures. When her semi-autobiographical, sentimental, sensuous novel *Valerie* was published it was an instant success and she became a celebrity overnight. She surprised her friends by suddenly abandoning her worldly life as a result of a sudden religious conversion. She published several essays and pamphlets inspired by a mystical spirit, and theological reflections on the Bible. The versatile literary and religious activities of the Baroness had been brought to Alexander's attention by Roxandre Stourdza. While her brother acted as the Tsar's private secretary, she herself was, at one time, Alexander's intimate companion and, jealous of Catherine Bagration's initial ascendance, had acted from the background to retain her influence on her powerful friend by being useful to him.

Admitted to his room at once, the Baroness surprised Alexander by her youth and vigor. She wore a simple but elegant black dress, with no jewelry except a diamond cross on a silver chain around her neck. At forty-eight, the strange visitor appeared to be an attractive woman in her thirties. Despite her too generous bosom, her figure was slender, her complexion fresh, her mouth sensuous, her eyes large and expressive. Her voice was melodious and gentle, seductive and persuasive. The German poet, E. M. Arndt, who met the Baroness at about this time commented, "This woman, although aging, exhibited strong evidences of beauty. She was suffused with the magical radiance of a penitent but yearning Magdalene." She was perhaps not a ravishing beauty but she embodied a combination of good looks and sparkling intelligence, qualities that appealed to Alexander, then a lonely warrior starved for such companionship.

At their first meeting the Baroness gently admonished the Tsar for not having listened to her prophecies and for having led a scandalous life, "unworthy of a Christian prince." She wanted him to confess his sins to her, and he was delighted to do so. He was able to tell her "all the griefs and the passions which had troubled his life from childhood on." She urged him to repent and to redeem himself through venturing on "a sacred mission to save the world." By the end of their first meeting Alexander had fallen under her spell. To Volkonsky he admitted, "How fortunate am I to be granted this supernatural inspiration at such a critical time. Providence is again merciful to me. The appearance of this fascinating creature is surely a sign from Heaven. I must speak with the Baroness more often. Please, provide her with everything that she needs to stay with us for as long as she wishes. But first, find my Bible! It is somewhere among my shirts or in the pocket of my winter coat, the one I wore in Moscow. Thus far I have had no time to study the Holy Scriptures because I have been living with one foot in the stirrup. But from now on, I will make it my daily reading. The Baroness will guide me."

From Heilbronn, Alexander moved some days later to Heidelberg, where the Emperor of Austria and the King of Prussia had just installed themselves. The Baroness accompanied him and took lodgings near Alexander's. Ensconced in the little cottage on the Neckar during the Hundred Days, Julie urged Alexander to persevere in the war against Bonaparte, quoting Psalms 35 and 37: "Yet a little while, and the wicked will be no more." Their interviews, which usually began at six o'clock in the evening and ended about two o'clock the next morning, were shrouded in secrecy, and we know of them mostly from the Baroness's indiscretions and from Alexander's casual remarks and his letters to his mother. He would listen to her for hours, almost hypnotized, tears streaming down his face.

The Baroness's views on Christianity were chaotic and eclectic.

According to her, the Almighty endowed all His creatures with a full perception of right and wrong, and with a complete freedom of choice. Yet, in most cases, understanding of right and wrong does not follow inner convictions, but is prejudiced by environment and social position. The wisdom of the world is stupidity. The era of the enlightenment, which tried to reduce everything to scientific formulas, rejected the intuitive grasp of religious mysteries, made us myopic and narrowminded. By prayer and meditation we must seek the Divine Grace to achieve mystical illumination. "Touched by cosmic flashes, we can experience Divine enlightenment," she convinced Alexander. "The scales can fall from our eyes and love can penetrate our soul and allow us to act in harmony with God's will."

Although a Lutheran, the Baroness scorned all denominations with equal disdain. "The sensual Catholics are too absorbed by ceremony and still see shadows rather than realities," she preached. Moreover, Catholics remain the slaves of tradition. On the other hand, the cold, narrowminded Protestants bypass the deep mysteries of Christianity and are seduced by reason, which they worship because it gratifies their pride. "Rigid confessional ties are like shackles and should be rejected," she insisted. Those who turn to the invisible mystical Church in order to find the Lord's "children everywhere, in every Christian denomination, are the true seekers of the revealed Truth. We ought to unite our efforts, mutually correct our respective errors, and return to the glorious days when Europe was still the home of one, undivided Christian religion."

The Baroness was against institutionalized priesthood and was convinced that any faithful believer, including women, could preach and administer the sacraments. "A woman who knows the secret of spiritual tribulations and who is spiritually beatified and sanctified by the love of Jesus Christ, a woman who breathes only the truth, is worthy of priesthood." She often mentioned to her friends that "the way to spiritual elevation leads often through the physical union of two equally inspired persons." "Body and soul, both God's creation," she argued, "are equally holy." Sex is necessary to salvation. Without sex it is impossible to approach God spontaneously, directly and to fully carry out his mission on earth. The union of the sexes is the first step towards union of humankind with God in the ultimate mystic marriage." According to her, the love of people who shared the same spiritual link as she and the Emperor had spontaneously formed, constituted a mystic marriage. Such a union of souls and hearts represents what the Greeks called *agape* and not merely satisfaction of physical *libido* or *eros*.

"The more I listen to you, the more I feel that I am an instrument of God's will," Alexander acknowledged, and he tried to absorb every word the Baroness uttered. She encouraged this conviction by saying, "You are God's Elect, his well-beloved, the hope of the people!" On several occasions, the Baroness described her relation to Alexander as "like a mother who watches anxiously over her son." And indeed, he often admitted to Volkonsky that he followed her advice "like a meek, obedient child."

★ ★ ★

After the news of the allied victory at Waterloo, Alexander decided to proceed to Paris on June 24. Julie Krüdener determined to accompany Alexander in order to give him spiritual consolation. Traveling with a Russian passport, in the wake of the allied armies which converged on the French capital, Alexander and Julie reached Paris by July 14. Their journey was described by the Baroness: "We passed through a country torn by political passions and infested with common crime, often arriving on the morrow of some pillage or revolt. Almost everywhere in the villages crowds there abandoned weapons and surrounded our carriages. Both the Emperor and I preached the Gospel and just retribution, but also the mercy of the Savior who in his boundless love wishes only to save us from the sin of blind revenge."

And indeed, during the second French campaign, Alexander again instructed Russian soldiers entering France to come in friendship, not hatred, and to forget the sufferings Napoleon had inflicted on their country and not blame them on the French people. He still insisted on distinguishing between Bonaparte and the masses of the French. "The Great Powers cannot exercise the right of conquest here because the essential thing is, by treating France with justice, to establish the authority of the King, to avoid revolution, to assure peace and the happiness of the French people. The second restoration and the legitimate monarchy must be given another chance to reestablish France as a vital element in European equilibrium."

Julie's first residence in Paris was the Hôtel de Mayence on the south bank, but after a few days she moved to new quarters in the rue Saint-Honoré, where her garden adjoined the palace where Alexander was installed. Thus he could visit her frequently. The Baroness's daughter, Juliette, reported nightly visits from 9 P.M. to 1 A.M. "Mama and Alexander are alone very often. His visits are always shrouded in secrecy."

As the final showdown with Napoleon was approaching, Alexander came to rely more and more on the Baroness's advice. She followed him throughout the second French campaign of 1815. She gave moral support during his frequent moments of depression and discouragement when the outcome of the war seemed to hang in the balance.

The Baroness was extremely busy. She arranged frequent communal prayer sessions for people of high rank and social standing to beg God for guidance. Chateaubriand, in his *Memoires d'outretombe (Memoirs from Beyond the Grave)* devoted a passage to the Livonian sorceress: "The Baroness von Krudener had shifted from romanticism to mysticism. She was living in a mansion in the Faubourg Saint-Honoré. The Emperor Alexander visited her incognito by way of a door in the garden, and their politico-religious conversations were concluded with fervent prayer. The Baroness invited me to one of her celestial witches' sabbaths. Though I am a man of chimeras, I hate unreason, I abominate the nebulous, and I despise charlatanism. The scene bored me; the more I tried to pray, the more I felt my heart drying up. I could find nothing to say to God, and the devil tempted me to laugh."

After the second defeat of Napoleon, Alexander could relax and enjoy Paris. He tried to visit some of the masterpieces of the French capital. This included the Hôtel des Invalides. He found the veterans who lived there to be deeply afflicted. The trophies of their glory, the cannon taken at Jena, Austerlitz, and Wagram had just been carried away. "Be consoled, my brave fellows," he said. "I will intercede with the sovereigns, my allies, that they may leave you some of your glorious souvenirs." He ordered that twelve Russian cannons, captured by Napoleon at Austerlitz, should be left at the Invalides. When the obsequious French offered to change the name of the bridge of Austerlitz, the Tsar said, "No, it is enough that it is known that the Emperor of Russia has passed over it with his armies."

He visited the Louvre and admired a series of paintings that Napoleon had commissioned by the artists Jacques Louis David, Jean-Baptiste Ingres and Louis Gros, all of which attempted to transform history into legend and to solidify in the collective imagination his own heroic exploits. Alexander for a long time contemplated the painting of Louis Gros entitled "Bonaparte and the Lepers of Jaffa." Napoleon had persuaded the artist to present him touching the lepers with a Christ-like gesture, as if healing them miraculously. "This clever man," said Alexander to the Baroness, "consciously presided over the fabrication of his own myth. I wonder how future historians will accept all of this."

★ ★ ★

While Napoleon was sailing to his exile at St. Helena, Alexander ordered a great military pageant on September 19, on a hillside at Vertus near Epernay, in Champagne, some seventy-five miles east of Paris. The parade was intended as a show of the Russian military might that played no role at Waterloo. In radiant late summer sunshine, the village of Vertus was transformed beyond recognition by colorful stalls set up to accommodate the spectators. Large tents, gaily festooned, graced artificial gardens. Splendid officers mingled with hawkers and society ladies. Before the assembled sovereigns, princes, generals and a great crowd, Alexander's troops were deployed in perfect order like toys arranged by a pedantic choreographer in front of the distinguished guests. These included, along with Emperor Francis and King Frederick William, an international array of princes, field-marshals, generals, and diplomats.

A twenty-one-gun salute greeted the sovereigns and signaled the start of the parade. Never before had there been such a grand display of military showmanship; some 100,000 men with nearly 500 cannons marched past the allied leaders. Since voiced commands could not carry over such a mass of humanity, various stages of the parade were regulated by a sequence of rockets, in all the colors of the rainbow. Only after each rocket shot did the commanders of battalions, batteries and other units snap orders to their soldiers. As the first roared up, onlookers witnessed the vast multitude of men react as one and come to attention. Thunderous applause followed. At the second shot, soldiers presented arms. On the third, the soldiers shouldered their arms. Then they fell into battalion columns, and prepared to march. At the sixth shot the columns commenced to march past the distinguished guests. The heart of the lover of grandiose parades rejoiced at the sight of the robot-like ranks obeying his commands in perfect order. "This magnificent parade makes me as happy as any victory on the battlefield," said Alexander to the Baroness, who stood just behind him, whispering remarks of admiration. After the parade the delighted Tsar descended from the viewing hill, mounted his dark horse the Eclipse, and rode to thank the troops for their splendid performance. Then he chatted with the officers and soldiers, as he had seen Napoleon do.

The following day, September 21, 1815, was the feast in honor of the warrior-saint Alexander Nevsky, and the Tsar's nameday. To honor his patron, seven altars were set up on the field and at each an Orthodox priest celebrated Mass. The main service was held on the Place de la Concorde on the very spot where Louis XVI had been beheaded. This time all the soldiers were unarmed and the cavalrymen dismounted. When the priests initiated their chants, thousands of Russian voices rose to the skies in the ancient Slavonic hymns. The crowd of curious foreigners who had ventured to attend to two-hour-long services, was delighted. After the Mass, the Tsar walked in stately procession, worshiping for a time at each of the seven altars in turn.

That night he told Madame Krüdener, "This day has been the most beautiful of my life. My heart was filled with gratitude for my brave soldiers and for the Christian charity with which my men treated their former enemies. I wept at the foot of the Cross as I asked for the safety of France and the welfare of mankind."

Then he asked the Baroness, "But how is this welfare to be achieved?" She opened the Bible and read Psalm 23: "Thou shalt guide me with Thy counsel and afterward receive me into glory." "This verse," she said, "assures you that God is thinking with you. It brings to bear upon your problems and thus gives you, as His anointed, that keen perception of wisdom called insight. You must meditate more, put every problem in God's hands and submit to His voice." Then she added, once again, "Pray! Pray like a child! If you are hesitant and are in doubt, pray! Seek this divine grace which God always accords through the love of His Son! You will realize that man cannot be happy, either in this world or the next, without Jesus Christ, without the conviction that salvation comes only through Him, from His inspiration. You should have more courage. You should have more sense of direction. No wind favors him who has no destined port."

"What do you mean? I fail to follow your thought." She replied with confidence, "It is your duty as the most powerful monarch of all to realize the Kingdom of God on earth, whose King is the God-Man, Jesus Christ. I believe that He will reign on this earth in a visible, tangible human form. It is your duty to hasten the coming of His reign by creating institutions through which the Kingdom would be brought about more quickly. Did you ever think of establishing a royal league, a fraternity of monarchs with views similar to yours? Individuals are mortal, but institutions survive them. You should have more vision and act accordingly. The reign of the Savior will come if you form an alliance of all those rulers who are loyal to the faith. Let them swear to fight with a common accord against all those who wish to tear down religion. Wish it to be the foundation of our society, and you will triumph. Put your ideals on paper. Draft a formal document, a spiritual union as well as political alliance, and submit it to your fellow monarchs."

While Alexander took a pen and piece of paper the Baroness continued, "The old order of international relations, based on force and diplomatic subterfuge, ought to be absolutely rejected," she reasoned. "It must be replaced by one founded on the sublime truths which the eternal religion of God the Savior teaches us. War is a beastly madness. Peace and brotherhood should be your aim. Sovereigns should treat each other not as rivals constantly struggling for territory, but as brothers, and their subjects as they would treat their own children. The other-worldly Kingdom of God on earth must become the basis of the law of nations."

During the following sleepless night Alexander drafted in his own hand the most dramatic documents of his life, which he entitled The Treaty of Holy Alliance. The Treaty's preamble affirmed his intention to base his conduct "on the sublime truths contained in the eternal religion of Christ our Savior." The essence of the three articles that followed concerned a few basic principles. Firstly, monarchs who subscribed to the Treaty would remain united by the bonds of a spiritual, indissolvable brotherhood; they would agree to treat their subjects as a good father treats his children, and would direct them in a similar spirit for their protection, for justice and for peace. Secondly, the only principle in operation, either between the signatory governments, or between their subjects, would be that of rendering reciprocal help and assistance in case of need. Thirdly, all the Powers that wished solemnly to avow these two fundamental principles by which the Holy Alliance had been inspired, would be received with much ardor and affection into its bosom. The monarchs subscribing to the Treaty would consider themselves designated by Providence to govern their subjects with justice, compassion and maternal care.

The Treaty of the Holy Alliance was signed in Paris on September 15, 1815, by the Emperor of Austria, Francis I, the King of Prussia, Frederick William III, and, of course, Alexander. Other rulers of European states hesitated. Most heads of smaller German states eventually adhered to the Alliance in principle to please the powerful Tsar who had helped to liberate them from Napoleon's domination. The Prince-Regent of Britain, the future George IV, acknowledged the exalted spirit of the pact but refused his assent to it "since it has been concluded directly by the sovereigns concerned, while the British constitution provides that treaties must be drawn up by the responsible ministers." In private, both Castlereagh and Wellington frankly declared that they could see nothing in the Holy Alliance but hollow verbiage, "where the sublime is at odds with the ridiculous." Castlereagh privately called it "a bit of mysticism and nonsense."

The United States was also invited to join. At first American public opinion was favorable, but later, the U.S. was alienated by Alexander's support for the reestablishment of Spanish colonies in the New World, and denied ever endorsing the idea. Pope Pius VII refused to adhere, saying that "the Church had provided a Christian framework for international relations since time immemorial." The Sultan of Turkey also refused to subscribe to the Alliance because he suspected that the arrangement among the Christian rulers could be turned into another crusade against his shaky domain.

★ ★ ★

The drafting of the Holy Alliance treaty was the watershed of the Baroness's ascendancy over Alexander. By August, the awkward disparities of their positions and habits began to surface and make their symbiosis increasingly difficult. Moreover, Julie's restless and domineering character put a strain on the strange friendship with her powerful friend. She insisted on extending her moral guidance to a supervision of his correspondence and his social contacts and began to open those of his private letters that seemed to be from ladies. She would then make fiercely jealous scenes and accused Alexander of "relapsing into his old, sinful habits."

She began also to make increasing demands on Alexander's generosity and to ask for large sums of money for various "good causes." Moreover, some of her eccentric friends appeared, asking Alexander for land in Russia to establish new churches and schools of evangelical teaching. All of this upset Alexander. Increasingly; he insisted on freedom from her "insufferable tutelage." Tension mounted, and by the end of August 1815, the crisis was recorded in her daughter's diary. Juliette noted: "Mama cries, suffers. Alexander is annoyed, gives in momentarily, but then insists on her departure."

Soon after the proclamation of the Holy Alliance, the accumulated tensions between Alexander and Julie exploded with a vengeance and the mystical-sentimental union collapsed. On September 28, just two weeks after the signing of the Holy Alliance document, Alexander left Paris, remarking in a letter to his sister Catherine, "I was glad to be out of this accursed Paris, where I was followed by a jealous, domineering and obsessive woman. While urging me to be an instrument of God, she tried to make me into her own instrument."

This was the end of the idyll, the "mystical union of two kindred souls." Disillusioned and penniless, Julie was compelled to return to her Latvian home. She felt betrayed and abandoned by "the one she had worshiped and who now had not even a single flower for me." She died on Christmas Eve, 1824. Dying, she complained, "One meets gratitude as rarely as a white crow."

CHAPTER 15

In Search of Salvation

*F*rom the end of 1812 to the close of 1815, Alexander was away from Russia. Preoccupied as he was with the liberation of Europe, he came close to forgetting his own people. For a decade the Russians had fought virtually without respite against the French and their satellites and against the Swedes and the Turks. Meanwhile the internal administration was in a shambles. The western provinces of the Empire were largely in ruin and misery was widespread. Disorder, violence, embezzlement and all sorts of abuses of power were evident. The monetary costs of the war, the devastation of the Napoleonic invasion, and the restrictions of the continental blockade, plus a series of epidemics and famines, exhausted the Imperial treasury and devastated the country's economy; inflation was rampant. When on December 15, 1815, Alexander returned to St. Petersburg, he was almost a stranger in his own land. Even high Court officials whispered among themselves, "Our Tsar is a foreigner. He absents himself from Russia. He appoints foreigners to high office and gives preference to Austrian interests. He is slavishly subservient to Prince Metternich." More outspoken people voiced their shock at Alexander's refusal to help the Orthodox Greeks, who had revolted against their Turkish oppressor and had implored Russia's aid in vain. To those urging him to assist the Greek patriots in their fight for freedom he barked, "As for the Greeks, I call them rebels against their legitimate sovereign."

In the spring of 1816, veterans of the Russian expeditionary corps in Europe began returning from France by sea; the first contingent landed at Oranienbaum near St. Petersburg. The day after their debarkation they attended a religious service and then marched in parade past their Tsar. Alexander appeared on the same fine black horse on which he had entered Paris. He watched his troops greet him. The soldiers observed him with delight. Their heavy tread reverberated like distant thunder as they marched past him proudly and confidently as they had done many times before. That day many wore campaign medals purchased with blood. They shouted, "Long live the Tsar!" Alexander smiled and waved his plumed hat to acknowledge their greetings. Yet already during this triumphant parade the heroes of Borodino and Leipzig could not help but notice guards mercilessly beating people who attempted to draw too near the Emperor. Almost under his horse, a peasant crossing the street was beaten with clubs.

During the campaigns through Germany and France these young soldiers had become acquainted with European ways of dealing with the populace. Many of them had read and admired the French Declaration of the Rights of Man and the Citizen. Now they compared it and all that they had seen abroad with what confronted them at home: enslavement of the great majority of peasants, cruel treatment of subordinates by superiors, and contempt for the rights of citizens by brutal bureaucrats.

While Alexander was warring against Napoleon, hobnobbing with foreign statesmen and rearranging the affairs of Europe, Russia had been administered by Arakcheyev. Since the Gatchina days, there had grown between these two individuals a strange relationship. In a way they were like an older and a younger brother, or perhaps father and son. By a mixture of cajolery and brutal candor, dog-like devotion and cunning intrigue, Arakcheyev had gained Alexander's absolute trust. In Alexander's eyes he joined incorruptibility with a deep personal devotion that was akin to servility. During the Tsar's long absences, Arakcheyev acted as the Vice-Emperor. Known by his enemies either as "the Watchdog," or "the Bulldog," he was the sole repository of executive power. He was the Tsar's right hand, his Grand Vizier.

Arakcheyev's paramount position was bolstered by the implementation of one of the Tsar's pet ideas. In 1816, while in France, Alexander read a book written by the French General Servan entitled *Sur les forces frontières des etats,* which had a profound impact on him. He found in it the theoretical formulation of the concept that had haunted him since the spring of 1813. Servan advocated the creation of military colonies along the frontiers of the Napoleonic Empire. It was a way of rewarding the veterans, by granting them farmland which would provide them with a livelihood in peacetime. The troops would live at home and cultivate the soil, while being easily available for mobilization when needed. Napoleon liked the idea but, absorbed by unending wars, had not found time for practical implementation of the plan. After his return from the campaign of 1815, Alexander was determined to give the scheme a thorough test. He ordered Volkonsky to translate this work into Russian to make it accessible to Arakcheyev, who was not versed in French. When the translation was completed, Alexander sent it to his faithful friend, supplemented by his own comments: "The Army drains our resources. We must cut our military budget. To achieve an independent and self-supporting militia, we have to create military settlements along our frontiers. I want you to organize and administer them."

As a man anxious to consolidate his own power base, Arakcheyev greeted this plan enthusiastically. He found in the military colonies the fulfillment of his desire for autonomous, unlimited power. After several years, however, the military colonists, serfs and career soldiers became victims of his sadistic impulses. The settlers/soldiers lived and worked according to strict regulations and were completely dominated by non-commissioned officers and commanders appointed by Arakcheyev. Every failure to carry out orders, on often capricious whims, was punished with utmost severity. Since torture and the death penalty had been abolished, Arakcheyev resorted to flogging, a standard discipline in the Russian armed forces. However, two or three hundred blows were enough to finish off even a strong man. When he was chided by some civilian administrators for using this sort of deadly punishment, and thus breaking the law, he would reply, "My settlers are soldiers, first of all. As such, they are subject to military discipline. As for the number of blows, it is up to the commanding officer of the settlement to decide the matter. I can't be bothered by such petty details." Although informed of such acts of cruelty, Alexander remained silent and excused himself, "I trust Count Arakcheyev and will not interfere with his decisions within his exclusive domain."

⋆ ⋆ ⋆

A second man on whom the absentee ruler came to rely was another companion of the Gatchina days, Prince Alexander Golitsyn. During his youth, the Prince had been a worldly and dissolute man known for his orgies at the Red Tavern and other similar establishments. Then like Alexander, Golitsyn experienced a religious conversion. During the reign of Tsar Paul he had been banished from the capital for his wild adventures and military insubordination and had to reside in Moscow. There he tried to make up for his rather haphazard education by extensive reading of learned books and religious works. Under their impact and the influence of a few saintly monks, he had abandoned his frivolous life to concentrate on the study of the Bible and of Orthodox and Protestant as well as Catholic, writers. His credo was that perfection consisted of the triumph of the spiritual over the body, which should be constantly disciplined and mortified. The old roué became a fervent mystic.

On Alexander's return to St. Petersburg from his foreign travels, Golitsyn again became his close companion, sharing with him his investigations into "the sacred mysteries of our Orthodox faith." United this time by a common interest in the religious renewal of Russia, Golitsyn often dined with the Emperor during the following ten years, and took these opportunities to deepen the Tsar's growing interest in religious mysticism. Golitsyn encouraged Alexander's mystical tendencies by arguing, "At its beginning, Christianity was nothing but a mystic sect. No one who had failed to pass certain tests and was not purified could enter the community. Secular rulers have made possible the transforming of Christ's mystic teachings into a hierarchical and ritualistic religious form. But having created the ritual, all their invention could not bring to light its mystery. Yet, there is no religion without mystery. . . ."

Eventually, Golitsyn was appointed Procurator of the Holy Synod, an office which required that he preside over the Supreme Council of Bishops of the Russian Orthodox Church. A few years later Alexander added to his duties those of the State office for non-Orthodox religions. Contrary to all expectations and dire predictions, Golitsyn proved an efficient administrator. The latter job was especially difficult. In that capacity he had to deal with a variety of religious denominations outside the Russian Orthodox Church, the largest of them being the so-called Old Believers or Old Ritualists. They represented that branch of the Orthodox Church that had separated itself from the main body in the seventeenth century church when they refused to accept the revised ritual and service book imposed on the Church by Patriarch Nikon. Later, the Old Believers split into numerous subsects, with varying dogmas and liturgical practices. The most radical of them rejected not only the old service books and the traditional liturgy, but also the hierarchical priesthood and all sacraments except baptism and confession. They regarded all other Christians as being in the grip of the Anti-Christ, represented by the person of the Tsar, who, according to them, was a heretic and an imposter. This was, of course, viewed by the State as high treason, and the Old Believers were persecuted, often cruelly.

Another large sect was the Flagellants, popularly called the Khlysts. Their name derived from their practice of lashing themselves with whips and sticks (in Russian *khlestat*), punishing themselves for their sins and, thus, supposedly attaining a higher state of spiritual awareness. The Flagellants interpreted spiritually the biblical prophecy of Christ's second coming. They believed that he would return in the souls of each of them in their life times. Their mortification of the flesh was regarded as preparation for the reception of this Holy Spirit. They combined flagellation with ecstatic dancing and singing; they tended to abstain not only from alcoholic beverages, but from frequent sexual relations. Those who adhered strictly to the rules of complete abstention were venerated as holy men and were regarded as spiritual leaders of the sect.

In addition, there existed cults, some of them a threat to society. The foremost among these were the Castrators. Members of this sect took literally Christ's admonition, "If your hand is an occasion of falling to you, cut it off. It is better for you to enter eternal life maimed than to have two hands and be cast into hell, into unquenchable fire. And if your foot is an occasion of sin to you, cut it off. It is better for you to enter into eternal life lame than to have both feet and be cast into hell. And if your eye offends you, pluck it out. It is better for you to enter the kingdom of God with one eye than to have two eyes and be cast into hell."

The Castrators indulged in orgiastic initiation feasts that some observers called satanic. After participating in a drunken orgy, the male candidates, dressed in long white robes, were enticed to undergo castration. In the ritual language the ceremony was called "baptism by fire" because the castration rites were originally carried out with a red-hot iron and only later amended to allow a sharp knife to be employed. Men are conceived in the loathsome animal like lust, degrading to creatures that should strive for spirituality above all. The early Christian males, argued the leader of the sect, all practiced this operation to rid themselves of carnal desires and thus make certain that they reached the other world free of sin. Women sought to make themselves infertile by a variety of dangerous operations and some cut off their breasts. The sect's practices caused members to be considered insane and even criminal. They were obliged to swear to keep the secrets of the sect from their family and friends.

In general St. Petersburg society was highly interested in otherworldly speculations and Oriental cults. Side by side with those with a sincere interest in the Bible were others primarily concerned with a fantastic interpretation of the Apocalypse. Society people toyed with the occult and not infrequently joined Oriental experiments. In the streets and alley ways wandering monks and lay pilgrims told stories of recent miracles, and asserted that they alone knew God's will.

The number of sects and cults was difficult to ascertain, but Golitsyn estimated that in one form or another, they touched nearly half of the Christian community of Russia. Golitsyn considered it his mission to reunite them under the leadership of the official Orthodox hierarchy. The means to accomplish this was a problem, however. He argued that persecution, torture and even the death penalty, widely used against the sectarians by previous governments, were counterproductive, and only created martyrs. He advised education and persuasion in dealing with the sectarians, and organized Orthodox missions that aimed to enlighten and convert to official Orthodoxy.

The sectarians were, however, not the only problem Golitsyn faced. He was aware of the existence of numerous secret societies and tried to infiltrate them with his agents. To this end he even used his young nephews, Guards officers who had joined the Free Mason lodges and other secret fraternities. Through them he kept watch on underground activities. However, the reports of his various secret agents convinced him that the secret societies were too scattered and immature to be treated seriously and he then concentrated on the religious sects.

The special position of Arakcheyev, irked Prince Alexander, who, as a man with an essentially Western upbringing, resented his influence over Alexander. The well-mannered and educated aristocrat could not even bear to have the boorish martinet in his presence. To the objections of the friend of his youth, Alexander would answer, "I know that Arakcheyev is gross, ignorant, uncultivated. He has, however, a great deal of practical sense, courage and initiative and is endowed with an enormous capacity for work. He has also a scrupulous application to detail. He combines a rare probity with a scorn for honors and material gain. And he has an inflexible willpower and a fanatical passion for commanding men. I couldn't do without him."

* * *

Despite Arakcheyev's influence, Alexander took an ecumenical view and showed great tolerance in the matter of religious opinion. "I think," he would say, "that it is indifferent to God whether one invokes Him in Church Slavonic, Greek, or in Latin. The essential is to do it from a sincere heart!" In 1818, while in Berlin on his way to the international Congress at Aachen, Alexander listened attentively to a sermon delivered by a Lutheran bishop. He invited the bishop to talk with him at length on spiritual matters, and asked him to visit Russia.

It was this search for the spiritual values of any Christian denomination that prompted Alexander to receive in St. Petersburg, in 1819, two representatives of the Society of Friends. They were allowed to establish a printing press in St. Petersburg and to run the Bible Society.

This tolerance provoked a sharp reaction on the part of the Russian Orthodox hierarchy. The Holy Synod declared that the doctrines and beliefs of the Quakers were heretical, and that the Orthodox Church alone could interpret the true meaning of the Divine Word. Yet, in 1822, Alexander, while on his way to the Congress of Verona, stopped in Vienna specifically to discuss monastic life with Prince Alexander von Hohenlohe, a Roman Catholic abbot. This ecumenical stand was the cause of great consternation in the Orthodox establishment. Before the trip Alexander had to give his mother a solemn promise not to visit the Pope. The Dowager Empress had fallen under the influence of fanatical preachers and feared that the Pope, whom she called "an anti-Christ in a white sheepskin," might induce her son to embrace Roman Catholicism.

One of the most radical of the Orthodox clergymen was the impetuous and frenzied monk, Archimandrite Photious. Born in

1792, the son of a village sexton, Photious spent a sad childhood during which his father, a sadistic drunkard, often beat him so severely that Photious fell unconscious. Later, when the boy entered a seminary in preparation for the priesthood, the beatings were resumed by the clerical educators who considered their pupil to be overly independent and cantankerous. This early training in mortification made him an introverted man, dedicated to meditation, prayer, fasting and flagellation. Very early in his ecclesiastic career, Photious revealed gifts of hypnotism, clairvoyance and charismatic healing with the laying on of hands. Photious was subject to hallucinations. He was convinced that fate had cast him in the role of prophet in the tradition of the Old Testament. In his autobiography he related how, in his own cell, he confronted the devil Beelzebub with a crucifix. Not content with observing the standard monastic rule, he mortified his flesh by wearing chains, which wounded his body, as well as a hair shirt, which prevented the healing of the wounds. He slept in an old coffin, explaining, "This is my bed. And not only my bed, but the bed where all of us shall lie while awaiting the Last Judgment."

Photious applied all his talents to the fight against heresy and moral corruption in the capital. In 1820, he converted the well-to-do Countess Anna Orlov-Chesmensky, a rich spinster and malicious Satanist and transformed her into a bigoted Orthodox fanatic. She offered her immense wealth and powerful influence to his service, and introduced Photious to the Dowager Empress, whose idol he soon became. The star of Photious shone brighter with every day. Many people holding high positions at the Court were attracted by the ascetic appearance and the fiery speech of this archimandrite and by his repeated miraculous acts of healing.

In due time, Photious became an intimate friend of Arakcheyev, who shared the monk's intolerant views. While Golitsyn was no friend of the self-styled prophet, Arakcheyev and Photious did become closer allies. Favors were conferred on Photious: the Dowager Empress persuaded Alexander to offer him the abbotship of the wealthy Yuriev monastery in Novgorod and Arakcheyev often visited him there.

All the honors and riches showered on Photious did not modify his ascetic ways and his dedication to the self-prescribed task of seeing the Russian Orthodox Church triumph over all dissent. In close cooperation with Arakcheyev, Photious planned the defense of the Russian Orthodox Church from its real or imaginary enemies. Together they plotted how to win the Tsar over to their methods of extirpating dissent and heresy, root and branch, by force if necessary. "For this," Photious repeated, "I am ready to give my life. I welcome martyrdom!"

Sensing his popularity, he did not shrink from openly accusing the Tsar of professing not traditional Orthodoxy, but a false, eclectic, tepid Christianity, a mixture of Protestantism, Catholicism, and vague non-descript mysticism. Photious did not hesitate to condemn Maria Naryshkin for "luring the Tsar into yielding to diabolical ecstasies of the flesh" as well as into the "Papist heresy," embodied mainly by the Jesuit Order.

⋆ ⋆ ⋆

Isolated by the autocracy and by his own suspicious character, Alexander suffered greatly from loneliness. His troubled soul prompted him to seek refuge in constant travel. The justification for these journeys was the need to inspect his vast Empire after his protracted absences. But the real reason was to be found in his troubled conscience. During the years from 1816 to 1825, he made fourteen trips through Russia, in addition to four visits to attend the congresses at Aix-la-Chapelle (Aachen), Troppau (Opava), Lajbach (Ljubljana), and Verona. In fact, he spent two-thirds of these years outside his own capital. During the years 1816 and 1817, couriers sped after him in a wild rush from St. Petersburg to Moscow, Warsaw, Tula, Kursk, Kiev, Mogilev, Smolensk, Vitebsk and Novgorod. Alexander refused to stay more than a few days in one place. If under one roof for more than a week, he became restless. He ordered his carriage to be ready for travel at any time. When he did reside in St. Petersburg, he passed most of his time in seclusion, plunging deeper and deeper into religious mysticism. He seemed unable to stay in one place, and moved incessantly, at a pace which gave him little time to absorb what he saw. He was often away from his capital for months, and this brought the whole course of public affairs to a standstill. As Golitsyn complained, "Russia is governed from the seat of a carriage." His office as ruler of one-sixth of the earth seemed no longer to interest him. Apart from spiritual readings and religious discussion, all seemed to him tedious and wearisome. Important State papers requiring his decision and signature accumulated on his desk. Only Arakcheyev's and Golitsyn's occasional intervention could move him from his somnolence.

Many of his trips were appallingly uncomfortable. Most Russian roads were no more than tracks, all dust in summer and mud in the autumn or spring. Only when he traveled officially, staying with local, provincial governors or rich landowners, did he experience the comfort to which he had been accustomed. Yet, some inner compulsion drove him on and on.

The people the Tsar encountered were impoverished, frightened and intimidated by petty tyrants, the local bureaucrats. The villages, no matter where situated, near a great city or in a virgin forest, north of Vologda or on the shores of the Black Sea, were customarily nests of miserable hamlets stretched along the one road, muddy or dusty according to the season. The one prominent feature among these dilapidated thatched-roofed, rough-walled cottages was an Orthodox church or chapel. Sometimes, in a nearby deserted cottage, there was a village school, intermittently attended by children of the reluctant and apathetic peasants. While inspecting the schools, Alexander often found that both the priest and the school teacher were drunk. Village crimes, theft, drunkenness, unpunished murder, and family ruin formed a foul quagmire. What depressed him most was the human cruelty and greed. He had decreed that individual sales of serfs were illegal and that they must not be sold separately from their families. Despite this, during his first inspection trips he learned that currently, twenty years after this decree, thousands of human beings were being put up for sale with full permission of the authorities, and children were often wrenched from their parents and husbands from wives.

At an auction, an old peasant woman was sold for two rubles fifty kopecks, almost on the doorstep of the Winter Palace. He was not above exclaiming aloud, "The swines! Oh, the scoundrels! We unhappy rulers are surrounded by them!"

He once inspected the Tula arms factory, unannounced. A cursory look at the operation, which produced infantry rifles, convinced him of its inefficiency. The machinery was poorly constructed, ill-maintained, and indifferently utilized by lazy, passive workers, who stood in front of their machines, staring at each other or quarreling about what was to be done next. Some superintendents were asleep and even drunk. Alexander summoned the director of the factory, berated him for not supervising his personnel, and ordered the drunken engineers dismissed.

"At your order, Sire. But where do I find replacements? They are the only people available for the job."

Alexander left Tula deeply saddened and in a depressed state of mind. Back at the Winter Palace his mind was captivated by the idea of abdicating, of breaking away from the ridiculous pretense that he was the autocratic ruler of his realm. To abandon the harlequinade of the Court and wander freely where the roads would lead him; to rush straight ahead over the limitless plains of Russia, through the purging gale of snowstorms and blizzards and not to be bothered by the hopeless state of his ungovernable Empire. . . . The promptness of his decision to travel, travel and travel, the rapidity of his journeys, their zig-zag courses, seemed a classical symptom of depressive mania.

"How can people be made over?" he asked himself. His experience of life told him that in Russia it was almost impossible to have change without compulsion. And yet his nature, his temperament, was instinctively repelled by naked force. He left this to Arakcheyev and soothed his conscience by pretended ignorance. Was Golitsyn's prescription, patient work of persuasion and education over time, the only solution, he asked himself, and found no definite answer.

After one trip he complained to Golitsyn, "Wherever I go, everywhere I see sloth, theft, bribery or at the least incompetence. Most people are driven by greed. When I appear, they play act and mostly do it badly. Do you wonder I am tired and discouraged?"

"Do you know what I discovered during my last visit to the Nizhni Novgorod region?"

"What?"

"The influence of sorcery on our peasantry is still overwhelming. If something goes wrong in a family, be it crop failure, drought, family discord, infertility, epidemics, or illness, it is attributed to sorcerers and witches. Sorcery is feared not only by the peasants, but also by upper classes, squires and merchants and even by some clergymen. Not Jesus Christ, not the Holy Trinity is worshiped by our peasants, but the old pagan deities: Perun, Volos and Mokosh. Many enlightened clergymen fight against these idols by declaring them to be evil spirits, thus rendering them satanic. All to no avail. In secrecy, at night, the peasants congregate in the forest and worship, offering food, drinks and bizarre emblems of pagan creeds. It is safer, one old peasant told me, to be on good terms with both the good and evil spirits. The Devil is a powerful spirit. The evil ones may spoil one's crops. . . Despite their formal piety, and their outward submission to the precepts of our official Church, the majority of Russian clergymen possess only a very superficial knowledge of our prescribed doctrine. They themselves received inadequate instruction at our seminaries. Their own faith is naive and superstitious and passes through them to the people."

"But what is to be done?"

"I believe we need more education, more enlightenment, starting with the educators, the clergy, who operate our parish schools. This means reform of the seminaries. We need more money to be assigned to them and to improve their wretched condition."

Golitsyn explained, "As you know, Sire, if a parish priest visits a manor house, a squire almost never invites him to his dinner table. The priest eats with the servants, in the kitchen, and if he gets a couple of rubles as a donation, he kisses the squire's hand or even genuflects before him. This must change! We must better the economic status of the parish clergy and bolster their social status."

★ ★ ★

While the idea of ecclesiastic reform was good, its implementation was most difficult, both because of shortage of funds and because of the intricate nature of the problem. During the inspections that followed the talk with Golitsyn, Alexander began to pay special attention to the village clergy, only to discover that indeed they lived in a wretched state of poverty and ignorance. Without a salary, they were entirely at the mercy of the peasants whom they needed to please and from this they often fell into an embarrassing dependence on their parishioners. Unlike the celibate clergy of the Roman Catholic Church, the parish clergy of the Orthodox Church was married, and therefore preoccupied with providing for the needs of their often very large families. The clergy formed a separate estate, almost a caste, and its demands and group interests determined the disposition of property, marriages, and appointment to clerical positions. Typically, a cleric's son attended a church school and seminary, married the daughter of another cleric, and assumed the position of his father or father-in-law. The families thus steeled the walls around this entire social class. It rarely admitted outsiders to its fold, and it reluctantly released its progeny to lay careers.

Alexander once visited the seminary of Vladimir, considered a model for other institutions of this type. What he learned frightened him. With a student body of over one thousand, the seminary received from the government the puny sum of 9,000 rubles for all of its expenses. The physical facilities of the schools were deplorable. The buildings were dirty and in disrepair. They remained poorly heated throughout the long and harsh Russian winter months. Students huddled around embering stoves, wrapped in all their warm clothes, attempting to keep each other warm. The food was poor and insufficient. Consequently, a gnawing state of half-hunger was the ever-present companion of the young seminarians. The Tsar was told by the rector of the seminary that, returning from the summer vacations spent in their home villages, many pupils brought some provisions with them. In addition, wealthier ones received a few food parcels, but even this outside help was not enough. The teachers were paid so poorly that the better ones often chose to go into private tutoring or government service, as Speransky had done.

The seminary teachers often exploited the pupils to their own selfish ends, sending them on private errands and using them as domestic servants, etc., instead of imparting to them whatever knowledge they might possess. Under the circumstances, the academic accomplishments at the schools left much to be desired.

"How sad is my Russia, how sad it is," Alexander complained to Golitsyn after one of these inspection journeys. Yet an inner voice whispered that he had some responsibility for this backwardness, for this sloth and decay because he had allowed most of the State budget to go to the Court and the army. Was he a careful steward of the patrimony entrusted to him by Providence? Where were his youthful dreams of radical reform, of improving the lot of the people, of educating them? What had he been doing for the two long decades of his rule—dining, dancing, running after a most bizarre variety of ladies, hobnobbing with foreign statesmen, getting involved in ambitious international schemes, waging wars far away from his native land, wars that flattered his ego but brought little profit to the Russian people. He felt desperate, helpless. Deeply rooted reproaches fastened in his mind, like barnacles on a whale. In his despair prayer was his only solace as he faced the creeping rot of his self-doubt. He pleaded, "Help me, dear Lord, oh, please help me. I am powerless. I can do nothing on my own. Only you can enlighten me and heal my wretchedness."

Days and nights of fervent prayer and desire for contrition for past sins alternated with protracted periods of spiritual lethargy. One day he regretted the past, another he embraced it, then again he was repelled by the carnival quality of Court life. This endless sequence of balls, masquerades and official dinners appeared disgusting, sickening and obscene. Weren't those extravagant Court receptions mere exhibitions of human vanity? All these took place at the expense of millions of wretched human beings who were rotting in the morass of poverty. This psychological roller coaster kept Alexander constantly on edge.

Alexander was torn between the desire for expiation for his sins and the unceasing nostalgia for his lost youth. While reproaching himself for his vain, glorious, empty, selfish past, while regretting the missed opportunities for improving the lot of his people, he could not help but regret some of the passionately exciting moments of his life, the intoxicating recollection of his numberless affairs of the heart and the idolatry in which he was held by many of the most exquisite and exciting women of Europe. He desired virtue and yet also longed to relive his past follies. Where were those incomparable romantic follies he had so deeply savored? Where was that spirit of Bacchanalian abandon of his youth? Where were those orgiastic revels, those titillating visits to the Red Tavern, where were they? His amorous adventure had made his private life a mess. He had neglected his best and truest friend his wife Elizabeth. He quarreled constantly with his mistress, Maria Naryshkin, whom he suspected of infidelity. He had placed himself in an emotional limbo and had not the strength to extricate himself from this trap. He wished to fall to his knees and beg forgiveness from Elizabeth, but had no courage to do so. He wanted to alter his life and yet was fearful of change. Was he no more than an aging playboy, retired from business, or a hypocritical and sanctimonious man who was to make virtue out of necessity? Then he returned to meditations that helped him to transcend earthly reality and opened the way to his quest for self-discovery. Deliverance from sorrow through surrender to the infinite filled the innermost recesses of his heart. More and more he realized how quickly life was flowing through his fingers while he performed boring, often meaningless, acts of bureaucratic and military routine. His determination to search for a total, all-embracing, idealistic love through penance and sacrifice captured his imagination. "My life has been nothing but a huge masquerade. For some quarter of a century I have been tying myself in knots to prove to the outside world how powerful, successful and satisfied I was. Actually my life has been as repetitive as the seasons, while the monotony and artificiality of the Court and military routine exhausted my mental and spiritual powers." Deep down he felt a frightening emptiness and alienation from reality.

He was so drained by internal turmoil that he had insufficient energy for even the most fundamental domestic problems of his realm. He felt that Russia was out of control, drifting in a direction he was unable to anticipate, yet he felt powerless to stop this drift.

⋆ ⋆ ⋆

Meanwhile, many restless young people, disillusioned in their hopes for reform and progress, were groping for a purpose in their lives. Some found it in drinking and debauchery, some in strange cults, and some in the activities of secret societies. A variety of these mushroomed in Russia after the return home of thousands of officers from the Western campaigns. Many Free Masonic and Carbonary lodges were formed by these mostly young, impatient men, intoxicated with liberal ideas. Some lodges were camouflaged as fraternal societies, some as social or cultural clubs. One of the first to be founded was the lodge of The United Friends, followed by that of The Three Virtues. The most fashionable of the literary fraternities was called The Green Lamp which served as a cover for a Masonic lodge. At the Green Lamp, hearty eating, heavy, riotous drinking and card playing were mixed with hefty political debates. The most controversial topics concerned constitutional monarchies vs. republics, emancipation of peasants, with or without land, and instant transformation of the obsolete autocratic system vs. a gradual transformation under a duly elected legislative assembly.

Both Golitsyn and Arakcheyev observed these phenomena with anxiety. Golitsyn advised tighter administrative measures to control the flow of insidious books and revolutionary ideas. Preliminary investigation discovered that, besides the army, the universities were a hotbed of ferment. Golitsyn enacted a series of reprisals. At the University of St. Petersburg, a number of liberal professors, among them outstanding men in their respective fields, were dismissed. The chief accusation against them was their alleged sympathy with the constitutional form of government and their support of atheistic ideas.

Arakcheyev, however, considered these measures insufficient. He urged instant arrest and deportation of the rebellious students and professors to Siberia. By that time he was entirely under the thumb of Photious, who had persuaded Arakcheyev that "Satan senses the approach of the end of his reign on earth and therefore uses his last and most cunning efforts to pervert men." An all-out, ruthless campaign should be undertaken against every appearance of what he thought was "the plotting of Satan." Even Golitsyn was to him too tolerant, too lukewarm. On Photious's insistence, Arakcheyev gathered his agents' reports of the secret societies to submit to the Tsar, who had hitherto supported Golitsyn's policies of limited and selective reprisals. One January morning in 1820, Arakcheyev appeared at the Tsar's studio with a thick folder under his arm. "Sire, I have just received numerous important reports. May I convey these papers to Your Imperial Majesty?"

"By all means do so, but be brief as I must review the changing of the guards at noon."

"According to my informers," began Arakcheyev, "on January 9, 1820, six young people gathered at the apartment of the two brothers Sergei and Matvei Muravyov-Apostol. Present also were their cousins Nikita and Alexander Muravyov, Prince Sergei Trubetskoy, Count Alexander Bestuzhev and well known poet Kondraty Ryleyev. All are members of a military conspiracy that I have been watching for several months."

"What was the purpose of the meeting? What did the six talk about?"

"The purpose of the meeting was to welcome and hear a speaker, the leader of the southern branch of the plot, Colonel Paul Pestel. In his speech, Pestel outlined the gist of his recently written pamphlet entitled "The Russian Truth." The pamphlet urges the elimination of serfdom, division of the land among peasants, abolition of our monarchical system and establishment of a republic. Pestel is a strange person, who comes from a respectable family. His father for many years occupied major positions of state, at one time as director of the Postal Services and then as governor of Siberia. With an influential father and much ability, Colonel Pestel, now twenty-eight years old, could expect to be raised to the rank of general before he reaches forty. But his ambition goes far beyond this. Some of his friends note that physically he bears a strong resemblance to Napoleon. And, indeed, he has Bonaparte's ambitions."

"How is he regarded by his friends?" asked Alexander.

"His prestige is enormous. His co-conspirators fear him. He could become supreme dictator should the revolution be victorious. He resents the comparison with Napoleon and thinks of himself more as the future George Washington of Russia, her first elected president. Pestel is fascinated by the United States of America and its form of government."

While the Tsar was looking over the report, Arakcheyev interjected, "Pestel actually is a Russian Jacobin."

"Are you sure he is Jacobin? After all, the Jacobins were bloodthirsty regicides."

"Pestel speaks openly of the necessity of executing the entire Imperial family. This, he insists, is a must. It would be a symbol of the triumph of the new republican order over the old autocracy. He also wants the Winter Palace burned; also as a symbol, the Russian Bastille. Brutus and Robespierre are his heroes. In the speech I have just mentioned to you, Sire, he was so arrogant as to criticize your foreign policy. For instance, he said that your Holy Alliance is an instrument of black reaction that is being turned into a Holy Inquisition, that you are a puppet of Prince Metternich!"

"That is incredibly arrogant," murmured Alexander.

"Pestel also says that you learned nothing from the lesson of the Napoleonic invasion, that you refuse to admit the role of the people in the defense of our country, and glorify only yourself. That you watch the day's landscape through glasses so tinted by Metternich's obscurantist ideas that they make you blind to political matters. What is worse, Pestel is also a militant atheist. This, of course, goes hand in hand with his republicanism. The trouble is, when people stop believing in God they believe in nothing. No God, no monarch."

Then Arakcheyev glanced at another confidential police report and continued. "The best proof of Pestel's evil intentions is his fondness for close contacts with the common people. Despite his military rank he is willing to degrade himself by mixing with the peasants. My agents saw Pestel perched on the edge of a peasant cart piled up with sacks of corn, having a lively chat with serfs crowded round him. Another day my agents saw him having breakfast with peasants, just a crust of black bread and cabbage soup. Pestel is also eager to fraternize with the rank and file, with non-commissioned officers and even with the common soldiers. He teaches them to read and write, even eats and drinks with them in the barracks. He appears to be recruiting them for his planned rebellion. This is also the idea of a young poet of the name of Ryleyev. As an executive secretary of the Russo-American Trading Company he is in constant contact with foreigners, especially Americans, of course. It was he who persuaded Pestel that grass roots agitation among the masses is a precondition for any successful military mutiny. They both propagate the nefarious idea that all people are equal. Isn't that revolting?"

"Alas, as a young man, I also shared these delusions," whispered Alexander.

"But, Sire, these people are not only rebellious. They are morally degraded. For instance, these secret gatherings involve not only subversive speeches but end in drunken orgies, singing of dirty songs and even going to the Gypsies. Debauchery is now a norm among those cynical young men. Bestuzhev once invited Ryleyev to visit a brothel with him. 'I am married,' replied Ryleyev. 'So what,' retorted Bestuzhev, 'does that mean you can't have lunch in a restaurant just because you have a kitchen at home?' "

"This is nothing out of the ordinary. In my Gatchina days, going to the Gypsies and hearty drinking were regarded as the norm of officers' off-duty time. Where everyday existence is stifled by the supervision of constant drill and other boring and routine activities, relaxation takes the form of womanizing, drinking and gambling."

"What am I to do with these rascals, Sire?" asked the astonished Arakcheyev.

"Alas, as a young man I shared so many of their illusions. It is not up to me to be severe toward these restless youngsters. Watch them all, but especially Pestel. He is the only really dangerous one. The others seem to me only a bunch of drunkards, whoremasters and windbags."

"What, no arrests, Sire?"

"No arrests."

"Are you quite sure, Sire?"

"Yes, I am quite sure. At least for the moment."

★ ★ ★

Arakcheyev was shocked by his master's lenient attitude toward the conspirators as well as the religious dissenters and the Bible Society. After his visit, and Alexander's unexpected tolerance, he began to plot the removal of his most hated rival, Golitsyn, to whom he also ascribed tolerant attitudes. Arakcheyev's scheme relied on Photious's charismatic personality and his power of persuasion. It was not difficult for Arakcheyev to win Photious's support, to convince him that the true enemy of the Orthodox Church was Golitsyn, the effete, weak and hypocritical sponsor of the Quakers' Bible Society, while the Tsar was his shield, his protector. Arakcheyev needed only a quarter of an hour to convince Photious that Golitsyn was at heart a wolf in sheep's clothing.

It was enough to inflame the imagination of the fanatic monk. In several public sermons he denounced Golitsyn and his tolerance toward political and religious dissent. And in a critique obviously aimed at his protector, the Tsar. Photious's references to "open adultery displayed at the highest places" obviously referred to the Tsar himself. When Alexander heard of these remarks, he summoned Photious to the Winter Palace. He was determined to administer a sharp personal reprimand to the outspoken monk.

The interview took place in February 1820. To bolster his courage Photious was accompanied by Arakcheyev. Ascending the white marble stairs that connected the large downstairs waiting hall with Alexander's studio, Photious crossed himself repeatedly as if to exorcise the evil spirits that had haunted these quarters for generations. When he entered the Tsar's studio, Alexander lifted himself from his chair and said, "I summoned you because your sermons are subversive and inadmissibly arrogant. You dared to criticize me, your Tsar and Master, openly, in public."

Photious ignored his host. Noting an old Byzantine icon of Christ, brought by Zoe Paleologue from Constantinople, he fell to his knees and prayed silently for several minutes. Only when he arose from his knees did he turn to the Tsar, and with the words, "Sire, our first and most imperative duty is to worship God Almighty and only then his servants, even if they are all powerful monarchs, like you, Your Majesty.

Photious's behavior and his words irritated Alexander. "You are bad mannered and as arrogant as you have been described to me. Even more so. Don't you know how to behave in front of your Emperor?" He halted, and then, raising his voice, almost shouted at Photious, "Do you realize that your behavior is subversive and most offensive to me? Do you know that I may have you whipped and sent to Siberia?"

"You may ban me to Siberia, Sire. You can whip me. You may break me on the wheel or even impale me. But even in dying, I will still shout that you are an incorrigible sinner and, therefore, condemned to eternal damnation, condemned to fires of hell."

Alexander was astounded. During his lifetime, no one, not even his father, had spoken to him in such a way. Photious continued his harangue. "You not only tolerate heresy, Sire, you openly live in sin, a public scandal. You have abandoned your legally, nay sacramentally, wedded spouse. You have consorted for a long time with a concubine who is a married woman, and, what is worse, a Papist. The death of two children you had with her was a visible sign of God's wrath, of God's punishment for your open, scandalizing adultery."

Photious stopped here to catch his breath. He dipped into his pocket and produced a handkerchief with which he began to wipe his foaming mouth. Then he continued, "Repent! Make a confession of your sins. But true confession is valid only if you not only renounce your sins, but also carry out immediate and sincere acts of contrition, penitence and reparation. You must return to your legally wedded wife. You must beg her forgiveness and make her an intimate companion of your body and soul."

Listening to the abusive harangue of Photious, Alexander was transfixed. As he struggled with the desire to have Photious arrested, publicly whipped, and then condemned to hard labor, the voice of his conscience whispered to him: "This is only what I have been thinking in my solitary hours, during my journeys and meditations. Photious's admonitions are echoes of my own thoughts." Yet he had an irresistible desire to defend himself. When Photious stopped to wipe the sweat from his brow. Alexander grasped the moment to present his case.

"I am guilty, I admit, but not so guilty as you think. It is true that, when certain unfortunate events ruined my domestic life, I sought the society of other women. I imagined, no doubt wrongly as I now clearly perceive, that since convention had united my wife and myself without our own genuine consent, we were free in the eyes of God. My rank obliged me to respect convention, and I did. I believed I was at will to give my heart where I wished. Circumstances pushed me into the arms, alas, of a married woman. My beloved also, finding herself in a similar awkward position, fell into the same regrettable error. Her husband consented. We assumed there was nothing for which we should reproach ourselves since her husband willingly agreed to our relationship."

"What you say is nothing but hypocrisy, a miserable cover for open, shameful adultery. The consent of your concubine's husband is here quite irrelevant. Although you are our anointed ruler, Sire, you are also an ordinary mortal, a creature as we all are. Aside from your duties as ruler, you have more fundamental obligations which nothing can alter: the moral obligations of a man towards his God, obligations toward your own immortal soul."

"But, as I have already said, only the unfortunate circumstances of my life lured me into sinful relations. Now I want to change and repent."

"This is good. But, if you are sincerely devoted to the salvation of your soul and those of your subjects, why do you tolerate the heretical activities of the Jesuits, the works of Anti-Christ? Foreign universities are the forum for all sorts of devilish practices and dangerous plots. Young people acquire from them notions that are opposed to religion and morality. Russia is full of secret societies advocating free thinking, even open atheism. Your bosom friend, Prince Golitsyn, is too soft, too permissive toward religious dissent. Dismiss him. He only pretends to be firm with agnostic professors and students, with atheists and Freemasons. He tolerates Quakers, and their Bible Society that is only a smoke-screen for the infiltration of the liberal poison into our country."

"What am I to do?"

"Forbid Russian students to attend foreign universities. Control more tightly the flow of books from abroad. Banish those black devils, the Jesuits. Dissolve the Bible Society. Be ruthless, if necessary. God made you father of your subjects. A good father must be a strict master! Arrest and punish your officers that plot against you. If you don't act now, you will have soon a Carbonari revolt in Russia."

Alexander was overwhelmed yet he tried to continue his defense. "I know that Golitsyn was once a member of a Masonic lodge. As a matter of fact, I also belonged to the same lodge as a young man. But he resigned from it, as I did, a long long time ago. Since his reconversion he has been a most devoted Christian."

"What kind of Christian? Certainly not a true loyal follower of our Russian Orthodox Church. His activities, his wishy-washy policies, belie your words, Sire. He is still a crypto-atheist. Once a Freemason, always a Freemason. His tolerance is a cover for indifference and a lukewarm attitude. Remember what Jesus Christ said about lukewarm people: they will go to hell before harlots and tax collectors. Golitsyn's alleged friendship is only designed to mislead you, Sire. You have only one loyal man who never lies to you. He is Count Arakcheyev."

When the exhausted Photious interrupted this torrent of words and once more kneeled before the icon of the Holy Virgin to pray, the Tsar was a broken man, overwhelmed by the monk's aggressive eloquence. After a quarter of an hour, when Photious stood up and was ready to leave the room, Alexander stopped him and whispered, "Please don't leave me yet. Stay with me for a while. I need your spiritual counsel, your support. I will dissolve the Society. I will return to my wife. I promise you. You can trust me. But, first of all, I beg you to hear my confession."

Following these words the autocratic Tsar of all the Russias fell to his knees before the foaming monk, and made his long-delayed confession of the sins of his life. At the end of it, with a slow, deliberate gesture, Photious made a large sign of the cross over Alexander's head while whispering, "I absolve you from the heavy burden that has poisoned your conscience for so long, and I bless you in the name of the Father, the Son, and the Holy Spirit. Amen. Go in peace and carry out your solemn promises of contrition and reparation."

After the absolution the Tsar kissed the sweating, emaciated hand of Photious. When Photious turned toward the door, Alexander ran for it, opened it and once more kissed the monk's hand. On the other side of the door stood Arakcheyev.

Three days later Prince Golitsyn was relieved of his duties as Procurator of the Holy Synod and Minister of Spiritual Affairs. The Ministry itself was abolished and its work was entrusted to a newly created section of the Holy Synod. In the universities of Dorpat and Vilna, professors were expelled for teaching rationalistic philosophy and recommending "subversive" works to their students. At the least sign of protest, students were immediately regarded as rebels and threatened with, and on some occasions actually punished by, exile, conscription, or imprisonment. Students were forbidden to attend most foreign universities on the grounds that these were seats of anti-religious and immoral ideas.

The Russian universities were prohibited from enrolling students who had formerly attended foreign universities because those students "brought with them atheism and propagated customs of disobedience from the universities abroad." The Jesuits were banished from Russia. The Biblical Society was dissolved and its library publicly burned. The ceremony was attended by Photious and Arakcheyev. Before igniting the piles of forbidden books, the monk gave a vitriolic sermon, denouncing all religious heterodoxy. "To be a true Russian, one must be an Orthodox Christian, a Christian loyal to our Mother Church." He ended by proclaiming the book burning a symbol of the victory of native orthodoxy over foreign heresy. The triumph of the Russian Savonarola was complete.

CHAPTER 16

Why Taganrog?

Photious's visit to the Winter Palace shook Alexander to the core. He asked himself repeatedly: "Am I adequate to fulfill the pledge that I, myself, enunciated in the treaty of the Holy Alliance? Am I worthy to be ruler of a vast Empire? Yes." His energy was at a low ebb and his routine duties were burdensome to him. Even military parades were a drain on his sinking energy.

After more than two decades on the throne, he was increasingly frightened by the scope of his responsibilities. Hitherto he had treated them perfunctorily, taking for granted his role as ultimate arbiter of all major state matters. Photious's harangue, however, made him rethink the magnitude of his duties. He was not only the visible symbol of the Empire, of its sovereignty and unity, but also the sole, absolute, master of his subjects. In this role he had no competent, reliable aides, no cabinet of ministers, as a British king had. At his side was only a group of, in general, poorly educated, corrupt sycophants. In practice, he was not only head of state but also his own Prime Minister and Commander-in-Chief of the army and navy. Moreover he was the Supreme Judge of the Empire; all of the Court verdicts were pronounced in his name. The Senate was intended to assist him in crafting laws, but did the Senators really help? They were a timid crowd of dispirited, servile non-entities. Only a few of them had any legal training. To top this accumulation of endless responsibility, he was the secular head of Russia's Orthodox Church. Was he capable of discharging this enormous duty?

Distressed and bewildered, Alexander returned to the thought that had haunted him for years: to rid himself of the awesome burden of the Crown. However, the obstacles were monumental. His younger brother Constantine did not fit the position, neither physically nor mentally. His exterior was unprincely—repulsive and ridiculous. His ugly, flat-nosed face carried an expression that to many people seemed inhuman. As a malicious French traveler in Russia put it: "A creature like that must be a product of an old Tartar woman raped by a young gorilla." He wore spectacles, and when he needed to focus closely, he contracted his eyes in a disagreeable grimace. His voice was harsh and tended to bluster, even in private conversation. He moved awkwardly and his manner was brusque and even rude, his speech vulgar and offensive.

Fortunately, Constantine, conscious of his limitations and frightened by the fate of his father, had no wish to rule. He resided in Warsaw as Commander-in-Chief of both the new Polish army and the Russian garrisons stationed there to watch the restless Poles. He led a life of dissipation and distinguished himself by his brutality. Already in 1819, his marriage to Princess Julie of Coburg had been annulled because of his perverted and exhibitionist behavior and her eventual desertion. After a long and difficult courtship he finally took as his second wife a Polish woman, Joanna Grudzinska. Although he still bore the title *Tsarevich,* assigned to him by his father, it was unthinkable that Constantine, married to a Roman Catholic and a commoner, could ever ascend the throne of the Romanovs.

Next in line was Nicholas, eleven years younger than Alexander. Unlike Constantine, Nicholas was remarkably good looking, efficient, and hard working. He was, however, no more than a soldier: stern, determined and disciplined, a man of steel but of empty head. His general education was limited and his inflexibility and narrowmindedness were serious drawbacks. Alexander was perplexed, but he had little choice. As early as the summer of 1818, he warned Nicholas that he looked upon him as the person who would one day replace him. "You seem astonished to hear this, but let me tell you confidentially that our brother, Constantine, has never cared about the throne. Brace yourself for the task ahead of you."

While saying this in private, Alexander refused to state publicly that Nicholas, not Constantine, would succeed him. Both younger brothers found the situation embarrassing. Finally, Constantine prevailed on Alexander to at least set down his intention in writing. After consulting with Prince Golitsyn, Alexander drew up a document in which Constantine formally renounced the throne. Golitsyn made four copies in his own hand. Absolute secrecy was observed: no clerk was allowed to handle the declaration. The Synod, the Senate and the Council of the Empire each received one copy in a sealed envelope, while the fourth copy was deposited at the Church of the Assumption in Moscow. Each envelope bore the inscription: "To be opened only after the demise of His Imperial Majesty Tsar Alexander I." The general public, however, was never informed of the arrangements.

★ ★ ★

While coping with the problem of succession to the throne, Alexander had to face delicate problems in his private life. He had sworn to Photious that he would return to Elizabeth. Yet, to fulfill the promise required tact and time. He had been separated from Elizabeth by two decades of numerous scandalous infidelities. Even before Photious's diatribe, during his long journeys Alexander devoted much time to consideration of the possibility of reconciliation with his wife. The harsh admonition of Photious finally pushed him to action. Yet, the reconciliation seemed to him not an easy matter. His links to his three children, the two daughters and one son of Maria Naryshkin, presented a strong obstacle. His love for one of the girls, Sophie, was as deep as any attachment of his life.

For several months before approaching Elizabeth, Alexander

suffered from a depressive melancholy that deepened his chronic neurasthenia. Remarks were made about his bowed head, his slow walk, his suspicious and mournful glance, his sudden alternations between torpor and agitation. Again, he sought solace in prayer, often throughout an entire night. According to one of his physicians, Tarassov, "He remained kneeling in prayer so long that large callosities formed on his knees."

One night, as he was meditating on the crucial decision and searching for consolation in the Bible, he came across a passage from one of St. Paul's letters: "If I speak with all the eloquence of men or of angels, and have no love, I become as sounding brass or a tingling cymbal. Love alone forbears all things and is patient. Love alone can bear the burden of the living for there is nothing love cannot face." As he had often done, Alexander treated these words as particularly applicable to his private life. "How was it possible that, having read this passage many, many times, I missed its true meaning?" he scolded himself. Now, the sentence was experienced like a flash of illumination. Hitherto the tide of circumstances carried his emotions in most unpredictable directions. Now, suddenly, all his past erotic adventures appeared to him as hopeless attempts to chase after something that was close to him, yet ignored and even scorned for years. All doubts about the reconciliation vanished. He resolved to be his own master, and to turn his life around, once and for all. The feeling of inner liberation filled him with a happiness that he had not experienced for a long time. Everything now depended on his wife's attitude. Would she agree? Would she forgive him for all the sufferings and humiliations he had inflicted on her?

The next morning he visited Elizabeth, fell on his knees, and begged her for forgiveness for his follies. He imagined that the reconciliation would be a long, complex, painful process. Yet everything was wonderfully simple. Since the final break with Czartoryski, at the close of the Congress of Vienna, Elizabeth had suffered from isolation, and was starved for genuine affection. While Alexander wept, she welcomed his humble apologies and declared the past to be the past. Alexander was enraptured. The ease with which they resumed their life together was a pleasant surprise to him. He felt like a reborn individual. From the hopelessness of a deep personal crisis, a new being emerged, like a butterfly leaving its cocoon.

Alexander's return to Elizabeth was long delayed, almost too late to make up for more than a quarter of a century of alienation. It wasn't, however, difficult for Alexander to rediscover the value of her tender heart and to appreciate her instinctive understanding of his needs. On the other hand, to Elizabeth he brought what she then needed most—a reciprocal close companionship. She treasured each moment, meals with him and shared conversation.

Alexander tried his utmost to make up for the years of neglect and estrangement. There developed between husband and wife so long alienated from each other, a renewal of intimacy and trust. Alexander curtailed his compulsive travels. They were often together, walking and discussing common interests, reading the same novels and poems, especially those of Byron and Goethe. Alexander ordered rooms furnished to her taste for Elizabeth to be located next to his own apartments. All of her foibles were allowed for, even if they clashed with his wishes. She was fond of little Pekingese dogs; he hated them. Yet he allowed her pets to sit on the sofas and chairs, anywhere. Alexander and Elizabeth dined and supped tête-a-tête, without the attendance of servants. They insisted on being left alone. They went for drives together and Alexander planned little trips with meticulous care. Reinvigorated by domestic bliss, Alexander resumed routine work on both civilian and military matters with gusto.

⋆ ⋆ ⋆

Actually, circumstances conspired to bring the couple closer together. In September 1823, at military maneuvers, Alexander had been kicked in the leg by a horse with a blow which left a deep wound. Badly attended to by a military doctor, the injury proved serious, and the wound constantly festered. The accident was compounded by another illness. On January 6, 1824, the feast of the epiphany, as was customary the Metropolitan of St. Petersburg, in solemn procession, blessed the waters of the Neva. Despite the recent injury, a bare-headed Alexander took part in the long service, celebrated in front of the wing of the Winter Palace facing the river in an icy wind. He was deeply moved by the solemn services commemorating the baptism of Christ by St. John in the waters of the Jordan.

Alexander returned from the ceremony shivering with cold. The next day he suffered from high fever. Pneumonia was diagnosed by his physician, Dr. Tomassov. Then bleeding and festering reappeared on his injured leg. The infection spread so rapidly that the doctors feared that gangrene was imminent and contemplated amputation. Fortunately, a turn for the better manifested itself a few days later, but complete recovery was not assured until the middle of March.

In the distress of the long convalescence, Elizabeth acted as nurse. Alexander wanted to have her always by his bedside. Sometimes they would read for hours, stopping now and then to rest and then chatting and exchanging views on the passages they had just shared. One day Elizabeth was delighted to hear from his lips the words: "I owe my recovery to you. I can't live again separated from you. You are more than my wife. You are my darling mistress as well as my best friend."

"But our happy time together is fast running out," acknowledged Elizabeth. "My tuberculosis is progressing. I know that Dr. Wylie does not want to tell me this directly, but I overheard him saying to Dr. Tomassov: 'The poor Empress may have, at best, only a few months to live.'"

"But darling, we must do all we can to help you, to cure your lungs. Perhaps we could find some milder, warmer spot in Russia to recover your health. What about the Crimea?"

"I will go anywhere with you. But both doctors Tomassov and Wylie believe that Italy or Egypt would be better."

As the preparations to spend the winter of 1824–25 in Italy were underway, Elizabeth fell more seriously ill. She suffered from fever, persistent cough, poor circulation, heart palpitations, and extreme anemia. The doctors were alarmed by the sudden worsening of her condition and diagnosed not only the advanced tuberculosis, but also a cardiac condition.

Alexander's distress over Elizabeth's health was suddenly augmented by a natural disaster. In November 1824, St. Petersburg was inundated by the rising waters of the Neva. Never before had the river risen above its granite quays and overflowed with such violence. Within a few hours, tidal waves submerged the lower half of the city. Alexander flung himself into work supervising the emergency, in which most of the city's garrison was involved. While trying to rescue an old woman who could not swim, he heard an aged blind beggar shout to the crowd: "The flood is a punishment from God for our sins! It is only the first of the plagues to come!" Alexander could not prevent the thought: "Alas, it's also a punishment for my sins."

As the months passed, Elizabeth's condition plunged him into still deeper despondency. She had spells of faintness and hallucinations, and coughed constantly, spitting blood. Her strength was failing. The doctors advised that she must spend the approaching autumn and winter in a warm, dry climate away from the cold and damp capital. Alexander reached a strange decision announced by an August 1825 court communique: The Tsar would accompany his spouse during her convalescence at Taganrog, in the south of Russia, and they were to remain there for the coming winter. Astonishment was shown at the strange choice of Taganrog. It was an unlikely place to restore the Empress to health. It was a citadel town, built by Peter the Great in 1689 at the northern extremity of the Sea of Azov near the mouth of the Don, to protect Russia's shaky position on the Black Sea. The puny miserable town, adjacent to the naval harbor of the shallow putrid sea, in wild and swampy country over a thousand miles from St. Petersburg, was a bizarre choice.

If Elizabeth could not endure the harsh winter of St. Petersburg, why did she not go to Italy or Egypt as repeatedly advised by the Court doctors? Why did she not go for the winter to the southern coast of the Crimea, to sunny Yalta, where there was an old villa and a fine garden? But perhaps she did not want to leave her husband. Rumors and speculation circulated in Court circles. Perhaps the Tsar had decided that he needed to inspect the Black Sea fleet. Perhaps Alexander finally decided to fight for the Greek insurgents who had risen against Turkish oppression and were in dire need of help from the Orthodox Tsar. The Catholic French and the Protestant British had extended some help to the valiant Hellenic freedom fighters. Had they perhaps finally shamed Alexander into belated action? Many volunteers from all over the world had flocked to the ranks of the Greek insurgents, including the Tsar's former adjutant, Capodistrias, and Elizabeth's favorite poet, Lord Byron. Such speculations were whispered in the Court and in military circles. Nevertheless, the bizarre choice of Taganrog as a winter resort for an ailing Empress could not be rationally explained. But who could argue with the Tsar's firmly expressed will?

★ ★ ★

As soon as the announcement was made, the Grand Marshal of the Court staff sent an architect and artisans to Taganrog to put the simple house of the local governor in a proper condition to lodge its unexpected and distinguished guests. Alexander had fixed September 13 for his departure. Early on the morning on September 13, as the Tsar's carriage was prepared to leave the capital, the city was plunged in darkness and fog. At the old monastery of his patron, Saint Alexander Nevsky, the Tsar halted and ordered all the doors to be closed and a solemn funeral service celebrated. Kneeling for nearly two hours, he prayed, and at the end of the service, prostrated himself on the marble floor of the church. Before departing, he left ten thousand rubles and requested that the abbot "pray for my health and the salvation of my soul."

When Alexander stepped back into his carriage, his eyes were filled with tears. On his way out of the capital, before reaching its southern gate, he turned back, bowed and crossed himself, looking at the spires of the cathedral emerging from the morning fog. When he reached the gate he ordered his coachman Ilia to stop. Standing in the open carriage, he contemplated the panorama of the capital for a long time, as if bidding it goodbye. He began his journey, as usual, posthaste, and arrived at Taganrog of September 25, bringing with him only two adjutants and two valets.

Too weak to tolerate such a long journey, and forced to rest for days at a time, Elizabeth left St. Petersburg on September 15. She took with her a very small suite: two ladies-in-waiting, two doctors, three subaltern officers and the domestic staff of five servants and cooks. In preparing for her comfort, at each halting station, the Tsar had personally inspected every house in which Elizabeth would stop on her way, as if to assure himself that everything was done for her convenience, that the smallest detail was in order. Arriving safely at Taganrog on October 5, she was delightfully surprised by the comfort which he had managed to improvise for her. The house was small and simple, a one-story modest structure. It faced the street, while in the rear was an orchard which stretched to the harbor. Elizabeth's quarters consisted of a bedroom, a dressing room and a boudoir, that Alexander had embellished with fine furniture to make her feel at home as much as possible—carpets, draperies, pictures, mirrors and chandeliers—all from her apartment in the Winter Palace.

For himself Alexander reserved only two chambers, the large one of which served as a study, the other as a dressing room. The spacious entrance hall was used both as drawing room and dining room. One of the windows presented a panoramic view of the Sea of Azov and the naval harbor. Another window opened on the courtyard, planted with plum, fig and cherry trees as well as flowers. The whole gave the impression of a fairly prosperous merchant's house, but not of an Imperial residence. Why the powerful Russian Tsar took a fancy to such a parochial abode was a question to which no adequate answer could be obtained. Alexander's closest friend and adjutant, Prince Volkonsky, pointedly refused comment.

For about four weeks the Imperial couple rested in seclusion—walking, reading and relaxing. Towards the end of October, enjoying the unexpectedly long and hot Indian summer, they made several excursions and visits to the countryside. Only at the beginning of November did Alexander return to his routine duties and deal with the accumulated pile of documents on his desk. Rested and in good spirits, he managed to take care of them with remarkable efficiency. Elizabeth's health seemed to be stabilizing. The stay at Taganrog appeared to be a success.

★ ★ ★

With the advance of autumn, Taganrog was sunk in provincial apathy and somnolence. Only a few people noticed that on November 13, a large, elegant British yacht cast its anchor in that part of the harbor reserved for Russian naval units. No one except its captain went ashore for the necessary formalities with the Russian authorities. Rumors about the yacht's presence began to circulate among the local Greek and Armenian merchants and the local tavern girls. Especially disturbed were the girls, who asked themselves why no British sailors, usually excellent customers, were allowed to go ashore on leave. Why the strange quarantine? What was this luxurious yacht doing in such a desolate place?

Meanwhile, Alexander continued his activities. The day of November 14 was spent inspecting the military barracks and the harbor's facilities as well as the naval hospital. He paid a great deal of attention to a few gravely ill sailors, especially a lieutenant commander suffering from a strange tropical illness the doctors could not diagnose; he ordered the chief surgeon to keep him personally informed of the state of health of the naval officer. There were some who suspected the sailors were suffering from cholera.

On November 15, the Tsar received a courier, Captain Ivan Maskov, who brought important papers from St. Petersburg for signature. Glancing at the huge volume of the papers, Alexander decided to deal with them later on, following a second visit to the naval hospital. Afterwards, Alexander ordered the captain to follow him home in his carriage. Along the way an accident took place. Maskov's tipsy coachman ran his horses too fast, and at a sharp turn in the road the rear wheel hit a boulder. The carriage was overturned. The captain, thrown to the ground, suffered a concussion and his spine was badly damaged. Alexander ordered

Dr. Tarassov to take care of Maskov and to keep him informed of his condition. Unable to deal with the case, Tarassov transported Maskov to the naval hospital where, he hoped, the captain would have the proper care.

Shortly thereafter, Alexander began to experience a variety of physical complaints. He told his doctors about having headaches, cramps and spasms. The next day he took to his bed. Doctors Wylie and Tarassov, after examining the patient, concluded that there was no abnormal temperature and that the Emperor revealed no symptoms of a serious illness. Since the patient also complained of constipation, he was given a laxative as well as a sedative and left alone to rest. The following day Alexander again stayed in bed, voicing additional complaints. Those closest to him differed as to his condition and the nature of his illness. Dr. Tarassov ascribed the complaints to his neurotic disposition, familiar to him for years. The reports about the Emperor's health were contradictory. On November 18, Peter Volkonsky noted that the Tsar had spent a good night. Dr. Wylie, on the other hand, noted in his diary: "The night from November the seventeenth to the eighteenth was bad. I am afraid that it may turn for the worse. Spells of vertigo, vomiting, attacks of fever and fainting fits repeat themselves too often." In Doctor Tarassov's diary, is the entry: "I am at a loss at diagnosing his mysterious illness. I have noticed that, strangely enough, the Emperor is preoccupied with something other than his health. These unexpressed thoughts seem to dominate him completely." In his description of the day of November 18, Volkonsky stated that he had to interrupt Wylie and Tarassov's dinner because the Emperor allegedly felt feverish and vomited again. Elizabeth's diary, on the other hand, does not reveal much anxiety about her husband's condition. A letter to her mother in Germany indicated that, despite an occasional headache, Alexander's health was satisfactory and that the couple continued their quiet and rather monotonous existence, not unlike that of an upper class bourgeois family.

* * *

On November 29, the Tsar was informed that Captain Maskov had died in the local military hospital. The news electrified Alexander. He seemed to forget his complaints, and became very alert and active. When Dr. Wylie wished to give him a sedative, Alexander refused. He jumped up from his bed, saying, "I have important matters to discuss with the Empress." He cloistered himself with her, and dismissed both his servants, ordering them, "Don't bother us. Leave us alone."

All of this excitement and the rapidly changed mood of his master deeply intrigued Alexander's old personal valet, Ivan Melnikov. Ivan believed that to best serve his master, it was necessary to know everything about him. He had a longstanding and deeply rooted habit of eavesdropping on conversations of the Tsar with his wife and friends. Through the keyhole Melnikov tried to listen and watch the conversation with the Empress. He was puzzled by what he saw. Being hard of hearing, he caught only a few disjointed phrases. The astonished old valet saw his master kneeling in front of the Empress, kissing her hands and saying, with tears flowing profusely from his eyes, "Darling, forgive me, forgive me." The empress, equally tearful, whispered in a barely audible voice, "My illness is fatal. I am going to die soon. My illness is terminal. God bless you. God bless you." Irritated by his inability to understand the meaning of the conversation, Melnikov decided on a cunning stratagem. He knocked and without waiting for a response, promptly entered the room, holding a lighted candle. "Did not Your Majesty ring for me?" he inquired.

"I did not ring for you! Why did you come with this candle?"

"Because two candles burning on Your Majesty's table in the bright daylight foretell death, while three candles symbolize the Holy Trinity, enlightenment and blessing."

"Go away, you superstitious old man," snapped his master. "Go away and don't bother us!"

Elizabeth left the room while the Tsar summoned both his doctors. When they entered, he personally locked the door. After a confidential talk lasting some forty minutes, Dr. Tarassov left and drove to the naval hospital with a large sealed envelope in his hand. Prince Volkonsky was at his side.

The chief surgeon was astonished when Dr. Tarassov produced the personal order of the Tsar to hand over Maskov's body at once. "This is His Imperial Majesty's order," insisted Prince Volkonsky.

The evening of November 30, Doctor Tarassov returned to Alexander's room with Prince Volkonsky and reported on their visit to the hospital. In the dark of night, the Prince cautiously opened the door leading into the courtyard. There he met four sailors carrying a long wooden box. The four deposited their burden in the Emperor's dressing room and went away. Volkonsky followed them to the door and told them to return in the morning. Wylie, together with Tarassov, made preparations for embalming the body. In the morning, the four sailors returned and carried away the wooden box. At dawn the following day Maskov's official burial took place at the local cemetery with all due military honors, but without the casket ever being opened.

The morning of December 1 was misty and chilly. People who had attended an early religious service offered for the recovery of the Tsar went directly from the church to his home in order to get the latest news of the Tsar's health. They were shocked to learn that he had died of cholera the previous night.

On November 30 and December 1, no one but the empress was permitted to enter his bedroom. The same strict precautions were taken the following day. People were shocked but did not dare to protest openly. Preoccupied with mourning for their monarch, they failed to notice that the British yacht had left the harbor sailing toward the Black Sea Straits and beyond. Only an old Armenian carpet merchant, Aram Gybian, remarked acidly, "My father used to say: 'The English are strange, haughty, arrogant people. They never shake your hand when greeting you and they leave without saying goodbye. They didn't even lower their flag to half-mast to honor our deceased Tsar!"

In the evening of December 2, the embalmed body, dressed in a field marshal's uniform, was placed in the Tsar's dressing room. Only very few people were allowed to see the corps. On the following day, the body was deposited in a wooden coffin which, in turn, was encased in a brass casket that was closed after a brief visit and prayer by the Empress. There was no viewing by the awe-struck people who came to pay their last respects to the monarch. The explanation for this was that cholera was a highly contagious disease and that its spread was greatly feared.

Dr. Tarassov, when asked later by courtiers in St. Petersburg why he had allowed this procedure, so contrary to the ritual and traditional practices of his Church, answered, "We feared an outbreak of cholera in the south of Russia, where there was an epidemic only a few years ago." Servants who caught a glimpse of the body before the coffin was closed reported that, by that time, the Tsar's face was already so disfigured as to be unrecognizable: yellow, swollen and covered by red spots. All sorts of rumors began to circulate.

The news of the Tsar's death from cholera reached Moscow and St. Petersburg and produced a crisis. For several days it was not certain who was the rightful heir to the throne, Grand Duke Constantine or Nicholas. Finally, after protracted negotiation Nicholas announced that he would ascend the throne; this precipitated a military mutiny in St. Petersburg on December 14. Nicholas instantly suppressed the hastily improvised rebellion by a few well-placed artillery salvos that left a heap of corpses on the Senate Square. Hundreds of conspirators were arrested and tried. Five of the ring leaders, including Pestel, were hanged, while many more were banished to Siberia for life.

Elizabeth did not live long. She died just before the military conspirators staged their mutiny against the new Tsar. Meanwhile, the funeral cortege slowly proceeded from Taganrog to Moscow and St. Petersburg, stopping at various provincial capitals. The casket remained closed. It was opened only briefly on March 18 to allow the members of the Imperial family to view the body, just before the traditional solemn Requiem Mass at the Cathedral of Our Lady of Kazan. On March 25, the casket was taken to the church in the fortress of SS. Peter and Paul for burial.

It was a gray, cloudy morning, and the procession, led by the bareheaded young Tsar Nicholas, moved slowly on foot along the capital's streets, lined with soldiers and huge crowds of people. Many of them, especially women, sobbed. The mournful journey through the slush of the half-melted snow took two hours. Finally the casket was lowered into the newly built vault. Thunder of a hundred cannons announced to the people of Russia that their former ruler, Tsar Alexander the Blessed, was laid to eternal rest.

CHAPTER 17

In the Siberian Wilderness

Siberia—the very word sends shudders down one's spine. The huge Siberian subcontinent is a world unto itself; most of it is covered by forest and swamp, frozen under the snow for half the year, water-drenched and mosquito-ridden in late spring and summer. It was first penetrated by the Muscovites in the sixteenth and seventeenth centuries. The scattered Siberian tribes of that era offered little resistance to the Russian conquerors, though the daring raids of Cossack adventurers and other pioneers could easily have been repulsed, since the Siberian tribes were able fighters. This did not happen because the local population did not at first regard the explorers as invaders, but showed them hospitality, supplying them with guides and advice. The tribes wished to trade with the Russians for the basic commodities which the natives lacked: iron tools, firearms, fabrics, beads, etc. This circumstance allowed the Russian pioneers to proceed speedily into Siberia and to reach the shores of the Pacific early in the seventeenth century.

Indigenous tribes of Siberia had subsisted by hunting, fishing and the breeding of reindeer, but with the influx of Russian settlers during the eighteenth century farming became increasingly widespread. Soon the Tsars put the vast and frozen Siberian wilderness to another use. Already in the seventeenth century, Siberia was to Russia what Australia was to become a century later to the British Empire, namely, a place to unload those whom the Tsars regarded as undesirable: criminals, political prisoners and religious dissenters. By the beginning of the nineteenth century, Siberia had become a huge, frozen dungeon.

Ironically, it was the political exiles such as the officers who had revolted against Tsar Nicholas I in December of 1825, who gradually discovered some positive aspects of their Siberian exile—its rudimentary freedoms and its abundant economic opportunities. For these outcasts, who did not break down under the harsh regimen, the Siberian wilderness represented an opportunity to set up alternative models of social and political organization, settlements free of serfdom and factories operated with voluntary labor. Both attracted refugees from the rest of the Empire and bold individuals in search of adventure and fortune. The region was Russia's new frontier, her "Wild East." The exiles and their descendants were frequently the pioneers of educational and economic development of the region.

Economic opportunities were present in the enormous potential wealth of the hitherto neglected subcontinent. Along with abundant gold, silver, platinum and diamonds were the precious furs, especially silver fox, ermine and sable, often called "soft gold." Great fortunes were quickly made exporting the furs to Europe, China and eventually to America. Along with mining and hunting, the processing of furs also became a big business in Siberia and the highly profitable trade gave birth to a characteristic form of social organization, the net of fraternities in Russian called *yamshchina*. Its members, or *yamshchiki,* engaged mainly in hunting, transporting and selling pelts of the valuable animals, either to the rest of the Empire or abroad. In addition, the *yamshchiki* engaged in transporting other valuable wares such as silk, tea and spices through the Siberian wilderness. During the winter, *yamshchina* gangs formed huge caravans of sleighs drawn by reindeer or horses which traveled from Mongolia to the great Russian fairs at Kazan, Nizhny, Novgorod and Moscow. The *yamshchina* was a dynamic organization with its own rigorous traditions and unwritten law. Only the most robust and resolute men were capable of carrying the heavy load of precious wares from Siberia to central Russia. The *yamshchiki* were exposed not only to frost, blizzards, but also attacks by bands of highway robbers, some of whom had escaped from Siberian prisons and lay in wait for the passing caravans. Aside from trading in their precious cargoes, the *yamshchiki* were themselves not above engaging in banditry. They robbed rich travelers, attacked the mails, wiped out official convoys transporting government money, and plundered villages and towns, leaving behind a trail of blood.

In order to be a member of a *yamshchina,* one had to swear allegiance and become a blood brother to its boss, usually a powerful and domineering godfather-type. Initiation into a *yamshchina* was an elaborate ritual that involved exchanging toasts of blood between the chief and the newcomer, and swearing an oath of allegiance to him. Loyalty to the leader was brutally enforced, any disobedience being cruelly punished, often by hanging or stabbing. Personal quarrels between members of the gangs were settled by the chief, acting as supreme judge. Marriage was not permitted. If a *yamshchik* married, he had to leave the fraternity, swearing never to betray its secrets. Betrayal of a *yamshchina* secret was punishable by death.

★ ★ ★

One of the most famous *yamschchik* chieftains at the beginning of the nineteenth century was Gregory Khromov. He was the only son of a Siberian bandit who had been hanged in the market square of Tomsk for having strangled a local policeman who tried to apprehend him. Gregory's mother died of cholera soon after the execution of her husband. Left to himself at the age of eleven, Gregory lived for several years by his wits, wandering from village to village doing menial jobs, mainly skinning fur-bearing animals for various *yamshchina* bands. At the age of fifteen he joined one of them. Initially he was treated as an apprentice and continued to skin and tan the pelts brought in by senior comrades. However, he soon began a rapid rise because he possessed a talent invaluable to any *yamshchik:* he could invariably find the way through the thick underbrush of the great forests to the breeding grounds of the valuable animals. He was in love with nature, and knew her as one knows a well-read book. He was familiar with the habits and voice of every beast and every bird. He could imitate the strains of the nightingale and the bullfinch, the bellowing of the deer, the roar of the enraged bear, and the howl of a wolf. He believed in close ritual ties binding wildlife with humans. He was convinced that they had transferable souls, and were actually symbols of ancestors incarnate. He was, moreover, an enterprising lad endowed with an inborn ability to lead. Thus, within a few years the young man became an assistant to his gang's leader and when his chief was killed at the Manchurian border in a skirmish with Chinese brigands, Gregory Khromov was selected undisputed leader of the band. Khromov was an impressive individual. His appearance was striking. He was of medium height, lean and broad-shouldered. Gray was beginning to show in his mustache and beard. His sparkling, crafty, penetrating eyes were never still. Khromov spoke slowly, using a sort of jargon, often vulgar, but always colorful.

The adventurous life developed in Khromov a kind of savage romanticism. When drunk, he liked to tell wild stories of his violent and sordid adventures to his friends. These tales were mostly gloomy, bloody and savage and centered around fierce fights with competing gangs or the police. The police, however, were not beyond making deals with the local band leaders, and often tried to collect a tribute for ignoring criminal acts perpetrated by the *yamshchiki*. His favorite reminiscences were those related to the fierce competition.

"One night my comrades and I killed twenty-three brigands who tried to intercept our caravan. We caught and hanged them on the pine trees by the road. On the trails we reached the village of

Mokroye. We had a real good time there. The peasants of that thievish village paid dearly for the shelter they had given to the brigands who dared to attack us. We hanged every tenth male. We spent three wild days there, with plenty of young and pretty girls. That village will remember us!"

During one of his wanderings Khromov met, in a Tomsk tavern, the innkeeper's concubine and fell madly in love with her. By that time he had more than enough money to buy the woman from her master. She was a true Russian beauty: stout but shapely, with dark hair and black shining eyes. Khromov loved her in a savage way. He dressed her in gowns imported from Paris, surrounded her with fabulous luxury and pampered her with expensive gifts. When drunk or jealous, he thrashed her with pitiless cruelty and then groveled at her feet imploring forgiveness.

Once married, he decided to leave his band, settle down, and lead the life of a respectable citizen. He bought a large tract of land near Tomsk on the bank of the river Ob. In an extensive wooded area he built a house resembling those of the gentry, like one of the imposing residences he had seen while traveling through central Russia with his cargoes. It was a long, one-story, whitewashed wood dwelling with six columns in front, surrounded by a large garden. There was a stable behind the main house where he kept several horses and dogs for hunting. He was a hospitable, generous and congenial host. Occasionally, when hit by nostalgic longing for his adventurous youth, Khromov arranged wild parties that usually ended in an orgy of mad drinking and smashing of glasses, bottles, and mirrors. "My broad coarse Russian nature needs an occasional outlet. I am suffocated by this dull bourgeois existence," he would explain.

Khromov was helpful to many people of the town. That is why his occasional outbursts of destructiveness were easily forgiven. Heavy drinking was a deeply rooted Russian custom and Khromov was not much different from his contemporaries. After several years his past was forgotten, and he began to gain popularity, not only with the local officials, to whom he often paid handsome bribes, but even with the local Orthodox bishop, to whom he once presented a splendid sable fur coat. Thus, Khromov lived the life of a rich, respectable, retired merchant, comfortable, bored and restless.

★ ★ ★

The month of September 1836 was unusually mild by Siberian standards. Only gusty Arctic wind, night frosts, and occasional light snow foreshadowed the coming of the long and severe winter. During the day, the warm air was filled with the fragrance of pine trees. On the evening of September 16, as a spectacular sunset faded from the skies west of Tomsk, a stranger entered the inn owned by Arkady Morozov. The stranger made the signs customary there of the cross before the icon hanging in the corner and then greeted the owner, asking if he could spend the night at the place for a modest fee. Morozov agreed, and said that twenty kopeks would be the price. The stranger paid Morozov, took off his long woolen coat and sat at the table. He asked for a cup of hot tea, and, from his bag, took a large chunk of black bread.

Morozov, a former convict released from laboring in a gold mine for good behavior, watched the stranger closely. The visitor was a tall man of about sixty years of age, of military bearing. His gray beard, his high forehead and mane of long hair, gave him a distinguished look. He was obviously not a peasant or merchant as were most of the customers of Morozov's inn. Who was he? The visitor remained silent as if deep in thought. When asked his identity and his itinerary, he made short and enigmatic replies. The innkeeper became suspicious and reported the presence of "a strange tramp" to the local police chief, with whom he wanted to be on good terms.

The next morning, when a police sergeant arrived at the inn to interrogate the visitor, he replied, "I am Fyodor Pavlovich Kuzmich."

"Where is your passport?"

"I have none. I lost it in Odessa, while returning from a pilgrimage to the Holy Land. The passport was probably stolen from me by a harbor thief."

"Fancy not having a passport. Don't you know that a Russian subject is composed of three parts: body, soul and passport? I have to arrest you. Come with me and tell your story to Captain Serdiuk, the Chief of Police."

Captain Serdiuk, seeing Kuzmich's fine features and genteel manners, at once grasped that this was no ordinary tramp. When asked his business, he replied, "I am an itinerant pilgrim in search of a place to stop for rest and meditation."

"What did you do previously?"

"I was an army officer. But recently I was on a pilgrimage to the Holy Land."

"For long?"

"About ten years. I was engaged by our Orthodox monks in guarding the Church of the Holy Sepulchre."

"Fancy spending ten years abroad in the Holy Land. Usually people go there only for a few weeks, or months at best. You must be one of those English or Turkish spies who roam our country under the pretext of returning from their 'holy' pilgrimages. Tell me frankly who you are or I will *make* you speak."

"I told you I am Fyodor Pavlovich Kuzmich, a retired army officer, returning from a pilgrimage to the Holy Land. I lost my passport."

"This is a flagrant lie!" snarled the police chief. "I am too busy with other things to talk to you at length. Maybe twenty lashes would open your mouth and save me time investigating you."

Turning to the sergeant who brought Kuzmich to the station he ordered, "Direct Slivov to administer to him our preliminary treatment—twenty lashes to open his mouth. When he recovers, I will speak with him again."

"Yes, Sir," barked the sergeant, saluted his boss, and led Kuzmich to the adjoining room, where the executioner, Gregory Slivov, was dozing. He also had been a convict banished for life and sentenced to hard labor for having killed his master locksmith in a drunken brawl. Slivov received his freedom early in exchange for taking on the task of flogging. After a dozen years of whipping, he became extremely skillful at his job, a real artist. He could manipulate his whip so precisely that he could snip off the head of a flower in a vase without breaking the glass. Since he had no regular salary and was paid by the number of lashes he dealt, ten kopecks each, he was more than eager to be called upon. Awakened by the sergeant, Slivov was delighted that a new victim had appeared after he had been idle for several days. He grasped his whip of twisted hide attached to a long handle. The tip was divided into three smaller lashes, each weighted at the end with a ball of lead.

Kuzmich was bound to a thick board called a "mare," wide at the top and narrowed towards the bottom. By means of an iron leg, the mare was made to incline at an angle of about thirty degrees. At the upper end of the board were three hollowed-out areas, the center one to accomodate the face and head, and those on either side to hold the hands, that were bound down with leather thongs, while the feet were secured at the bottom. The executioner took up his position a few yards away and began his work. He moved silently and smoothly. Unlike others of his profession, he did not scold his victims or express strong doubts as to their mother's morals; a most popular swearing. Slivov advanced quickly to gain momentum, and brought down the lash with full force on Kuzmich's back. This he repeated two or three times, letting the lash fall in the same place. Then he came from the other side, bringing it down from a different direction. Then he waited for the prisoner's reaction.

The official pay was meager; Slivov made most of his money from those he flogged. The law stipulated a certain number of stripes, but did not specify how the recipient should suffer. When bribed by the culprit or his friends, Slivov brought down the first blow with relative severity, causing the victim to scream and leaving visible marks. Then he diminished the force of the remaining blows. If he were not bribed, however, he would begin gently and gradually increase in severity. By ceasing his flogging, Slivov wanted to give his victim a chance to whisper how many rubles he would offer for leniency. He was greatly surprised that no such offer came forth.

Kuzmich had neither money nor local friends who could bribe Slivov. As a matter of fact the poor pilgrim was not even aware of the practice of bribing the executioner. So, for Kuzmich the twenty lashes were as severe as the experienced executioner could administer. After the last lash, Slivov unbound his bleeding victim and, wiping his forehead, reported to the police chief, "Sir, it is all over. I did my best but he did not say anything except: 'I am Fyodor Kuzmich. I am returning from my pilgrimage. I am innocent.' This villain must be a tough well trained spy to suffer twenty honest lashes of mine and not betray who he is. What about twenty lashes more?"

"All right, twenty more," snapped the captain.

Yet, despite forty lashes, the groaning, bleeding and half-conscious prisoner persisted in his original story. Wondering at the distinguished looks of Kuzmich as well as by his inflexibility, Captain Serdiuk informed the governor of western Siberia of the mysterious stranger with a military manner but no passport and a bizarre story of living no less than ten years in the Holy Land.

* * *

The governor, Count von Osten-Sacken, was so intrigued by the report that he came in person to scrutinize the prisoner. The Count, in turn, was astonished at the fine features and aristocratic manners of the alleged spy. He attempted to gain more information, but Kuzmich stuck to his story. "We will check your tale with the abbot of our monastery in Jerusalem. A saintly man, I used to know him when we both lived in Moscow. . . . We will also get in touch with the authorities in Petersburg. They may have your criminal file at the Police Ministry. If you lie, if you are an English or Turkish spy, or, God forbid, a deserter, we will hang you publicly on the market square here in Tomsk. People are bored and need occasional entertainment."

And indeed, the Governor at once sent an urgent report of the strange case of "an alleged Fyodor Kuzmich, suspected of spying and/or desertion" to the chief of gendarmes, Count Berkendorff. Weeks and months passed without an answer. Kuzmich, meanwhile, was kept under lock and key in the local prison, together with common criminals, primarily thieves and murderers.

After more than six months of waiting, the Governor received a surprising instruction from the capital: "Fyodor Kuzmich is to be freed at once, issued a regular passport, but forbidden to leave Tomsk. His doings are to be watched closely and reports of anything out of the ordinary are to be submitted to me personally." The letter was signed, "Alexander Count von Benkendorff, Chief of the Third Section of His Imperial Majesty's Chancellery."

The order puzzled the Governor, but, being a good bureaucrat, he had to carry it out. Anxious for his career, he again visited Kuzmich, this time to apologize for the "accidental and involuntary inconvenience." The Count ordered his immediate release and gave him ten silver rubles, a set of fine undergarments, as well as a warm fur coat and a pair of deerskin gloves. Kuzmich was a free man. Confused and unable to decide what to do, he returned to the inn from which he had been dragged to prison. He wanted a bath and at least a few days to recover from some six months of incarceration.

Meanwhile, the Kuzmich story became the talk of the town. One of the men who had been from the very beginning intrigued by the story of the distinguished pilgrim suspected of espionage was Gregory Khromov. He was bored with his existence as a retired *yamshchik* and often patronized the local taverns. He liked to meet the rare visitors to sleepy, provincial Tomsk. A good place to look for such people was at Morozov's tavern and inn where, to his wife's chagrin, he visited all too often. When Khromov observed Kuzmich drinking his tea in the corner of the inn he immediately grasped that this was the unusual visitor. He approached Kuzmich with the offer of a glass of vodka and was surprised to be met with a firm refusal, "While visiting the Holy Land I made a pledge to never again touch hard liquor."

"There is no life without drinking. Is it true that you were a pilgrim in Palestine? Where do you plan to stay?"

"I intended to stay here for several nights and then find some quiet place to continue my life of prayer and meditation."

"Stay with me," said Khromov. I have a large house. My wife, Matryona Alexandrovna, would love to hear your stories of the Holy Land. She wants to go on a pilgrimage next year."

With an imperial gesture he ordered Morozov to summon the driver of his sleigh waiting outside the inn. Then he put on his fur coat and requested that Kuzmich do the same. They mounted the large, comfortable sleigh, and, after a quarter hour's ride, they reached Khromov's mansion. His wife anxiously awaited him. Kuzmich was struck by her majestic beauty and the elegance of her traditional dress. She wore a long flowing, pyramid-shaped overskirt, called a sarafan, with a row of small silver buttons down the front of a billowy sleeved blouse of colorfully embroidered batiste.

"Where have you been so late? I thought you were drunk again," she snapped. "I'm surprised to see you sober. Who is your companion?"

"This is Fyodor Kuzmich, our guest. He spent some ten years in the Holy Land and can tell you all about it. Bring us some hot tea."

The hostess bowed to the guest and said, "Welcome! God be with you!"

She shortly returned with a samovar, the tall brass vessel used by the Russian people for making tea. On a tray were two glasses, a loaf of bread and a saucer of salt, the traditional Slavic symbols of welcome.

"I am deeply grateful," Kuzmich said. "Your truly Slavic warm welcome is more precious to me than refreshments. I will pray and ask God to reward you for the Christlike hospitality that you have shown to a stranger."

"I am very happy that God so unexpectedly arranged for me to meet you. I hope that you will tell me about your stay in the Holy Land."

"I will, in due time, but tonight I am too exhausted."

"Of course, of course. Drink your tea and meanwhile, I shall order my maid to prepare your room."

Then she added, "The day after tomorrow is Easter Saturday, so you can attend the holy liturgy with us and share in God's blessing to us. We usually have guests for Easter breakfast on Sunday.

As Matryona was talking with Kuzmich, Khromov noticed a book protruding from the guest's bag and inquired, "And what kind of book is that?"

"This is my Holy Bible," answered Kuzmich.

"May I have a look at it?" He took the Bible, opened it, and glanced at a few pages without being able to read them.

"Is it true that from too much reading one can lose one's wits?"

"Oh no. This is a wise book. I am continuously learning something from it."

Khromov put the book on the table and continued the chat, but his wife said impatiently, "Let us all go to bed. Our guest deserves a good rest. Tomorrow is Holy Friday and we will all go to the local bath. He fast the whole day. But now all go to bed! Good night, good night."

* * *

On Saturday evening, Kuzmich's host prepared to attend the Easter service at the local cathedral. The driver brought round to the front door a large and comfortable sleigh with a bearskin rug to protect the occupants. The horses were shielded from the slivers of ice thrown up by their hooves by a coarse mesh. At the crack of the whip, the ponies trotted gaily through the snow covered streets, across the town to the marketplace. Primitive shops lined the modest square, and peasant carts and sleighs parked along the wooden sidewalks still largely covered with snow. Tomsk's dwellings were mostly low, square log houses with ornamented window casings and flatly pyramidal roofs, with high board fences separating the scattered households. In the middle of the market square stood the large red Orthodox cathedral with green onion dome.

In the dim light of the sanctuary, Kuzmich's gaze was arrested by the glowing, golden altar screen closing off the chancel. Encrusted with icons, it was decorated with fir garlands for the Easter holiday. The church was filled to capacity, and everyone, except a few very old ladies, was standing. In front was an area reserved for officials and military personnel. The rest of the cathedral was crammed with row upon row of ordinary people—merchants, artisans and peasants—pressed together, each person with a lighted candle in hand.

Slowly the solemn service progressed. The priest and the deacons presided behind the screen in magnificent blue and silver brocade robes ornamented with embroidered gold crosses. In his right hand the priest held a large cross and in his left, three candles. A deacon, swinging a censer before the icons, sent whiffs of perfumed air rising over the crowd. When the cathedral bells boomed, men posted under the chandeliers lit fuses connecting the wicks of hundreds of candles. The flame ran quickly from one candle to another until the entire constellation of chandeliers was ablaze with light. Priest and deacons continued their haunting chant, and then recessed down the nave—clergy bearing icons, crosses and banners—followed by local dignitaries, officers, soldiers, and finally the rest of the faithful. The procession, symbolizing the journey of the women of Jerusalem to the Holy Sepulchre, circled the outside of the cathedral, and reentered the church, where chanting and the traditional greeting of the priest: "Christ is risen," echoed, as did the congregation's response: "He is risen indeed." Jubilant parishioners hugged and kissed each other. Then the priest and the deacons stepped forward as people moved towards them to kiss the Cross. After the two-hour service everyone dispersed hurriedly, chatting in hushed voices, gossiping and joking.

The next morning Morozov invited Kuzmich to the family Easter breakfast. As some thirty guests soon arrived, the drawing room filled to capacity with people, many of whom were local merchants. In the center of the breakfast table was a large lamb, carved of butter and holding a flag with a cross on it, surrounded by a staggering array of brightly colored Easter eggs. The breakfast began with *zakuski,* pickled mushrooms, a variety of salads and caviar. Then came all sorts of sausages and meat delicacies—lamb, veal and a whole roasted piglet. Three huge sugar-coated

Easter cakes, called *baby,* were served for dessert and there was a profusion of vodka and wine. It was all too much for Kuzmich.

Half-way through the feast, when most guests were already tipsy, he quietly slipped out of the room to meditate. He was disturbed only slightly by the drunken singing of the crowd.

★ ★ ★

Kuzmich's evening meditation was interrupted, however, by his hostess who insisted that he join the guests and tell his story to the assembled group. He was overwhelmed by an avalanche of questions about his years spent in Palestine. "What holy places did you visit? Where did you stay" and so on and on. Kuzmich tried to deal with the situation. He felt obliged to do so, if only to repay Khromov's hospitality. Most curious was the hostess. "How did you go to the Holy Land?" she inquired.

"I arrived in Jaffa by ship from Constantinople. After a few days of individual sightseeing, I joined a group of pilgrims led by Father Oleg Korolanko from Kiev, well-known for his biblical learning and his many journeys to Palestine. Most of the pilgrims were in rags, barefooted and carrying their shoes in their hands. Many of them were Old Believers who had abjured tobacco and alcohol and had spent most of their life savings on such a pilgrimage. Many of these beggars had set off with their bags on their back and their rosaries in their hands to seek Heaven's pardon for their sins. To reach Jerusalem we had to travel a great distance mounted on donkeys and camels. Then we walked for three or four miles past cultivated fields to a deep valley, where we first caught a glimpse of the Holy City. In the distance were mounds of ruins, and beyond that saw-toothed ramparts and towers. The object of our pilgrimage—Jerusalem. What a sight! We fell to our knees, kissed the rocky soil and sang several of our beautiful Russian hymns. Then we prostrated ourselves in silent meditation, thanking God for the privilege of seeing this sacred place."

"Oh, how I wish I had been with you," exclaimed Mrs. Khromov.

"After a walk of a mile or so, we reached the gate of David and entered the heart of the city. We were lodged at the hospice run by our monks for the Orthodox pilgrims. On the following day we visited the wonderful places where Jeremiah and Isaiah prophesied and where, centuries later, Jesus taught, healed and was crucified. Now the city is a teeming expanse of shops and bazaars operated mainly by Turks, Arabs and Persian merchants and craftsmen."

"How many Orthodox Christians still live there?" asked Khromov. "What kind of life do they lead?"

"The lot of the very small group of Christians is deplorable. Alas, the Moslems regard us as infidel intruders. Subject to unceasing persecution, these poor creatures try to forget, at the foot of the altar, their sacrifices, and their profound misery. They live in constant danger of Turkish wrath, persecution and even martyrdom. Only the fear of military intervention by our good father, the Tsar, protector of these Orthodox people by treaty, prevents them from being expelled or even slaughtered."

"Oh, how sad, how sad," whispered Matryona. "Did you stay long in the Holy Land?"

"As a matter of fact, for several years I worked with the monks who guarded and served the Church of the Holy Sepulchre. As a lay brother I was initially employed as a gardener. After three or four years my health deteriorated, and I then served as gatekeeper. We lived in constant danger from the Turkish and Arab urchins attacking our monastery and trying to break the windows of our church, or even to set it on fire."

"How awful! This is a sacrilege," shouted the hostess. "Thank God for our little father, Tsar Nicholas. Thank God for his protection of our people there."

"Actually, the Moslems are not the only danger to our guardianship of the holy places. Jealous Catholic monks are another. The Franciscan friars constantly demand their share in taking care of the sacred places. Numerous attempts were made by them to seize the Basilica of the Holy Sepulchre. At times pitched battles were fought at its entrance between them and our brave friars. Even the staffs from which the church banners hung were used as weapons. The Turkish local governor was delighted to see such incidents, of course. The police intervened and casualties of these brawls had to be taken to the hospital. Some of them died. These episodes were most distressing to me. The constant quarreling among the Orthodox and Catholic guardians of the holy places is a scandal. It is an abomination of abominations. It provides the Turkish authorities with a pretext to intervene."

"How do you explain the shocking behavior of those monks, who are supposed to set a good example for the pilgrims?"

"I have no explanation. Perhaps the devil, who tempted Jesus in the desert three times and failed, still roams the Holy Land and tries to avenge his failures, filling Christ's followers with pride, pettiness and hate."

"How do the Turks treat our people," asked one of the old merchants.

"Turkish rule is very, very harsh, indeed. Christians are not permitted to build new churches. They may not sing their hymns aloud and must pray either silently or in a low voice. They are compelled to show respect to the Moslems. When a Turk enters a room, all infidels must stand and bow to him. If a Christian kills a Moslem, his penalty is death. If a Moslem kills an infidel, he pays only a small fine."

"What impressed you most, my dear Fyodor Pavlovich?" asked Khromov.

"One of the deepest impressions of my stay in Palestine was my walk along the Way of the Cross, or *Via Dolorosa,* as the Catholics and Protestants call it. Today the Way of the Cross is a narrow, congested noisy street. The bargainers, buyers and beggars are oblivious to the pious pilgrims who often follow the Way of the Cross on their knees. Yet Jesus Christ carried his cross here and trod these very cobblestones. His road ended on the hill called Golgotha, or the Hill of the Skull. Now the place of his crucifixion is enclosed by the Basilica of the Holy Sepulchre that is cared for mainly by our Orthodox friars."

"Thank God for these pious and brave friars!" murmured the hostess, as she served another glass of tea to the exhausted Kuzmich.

"The cupola of the basilica is built of stone blocks cemented with stucco. Six pilasters support the vault and are separated by an arcade, which forms a circular gallery. The actual Holy Sepulchre is a low marble altar enclosed in a square chapel, also of marble, and lighted by numerous oil lamps. Hangings of embroidered velvet entirely cover the interior walls. A painting within, above the sacred stone, represents the Resurrection, the triumph of Our Lord over death. It is impossible not to feel profound emotion and awe on viewing this humble tomb. When we entered on the marble floor of the basilica, Christians of Cyprus and Abyssinia were peacefully prostrated beside pilgrims from our Kiev, Tobolsk, Novgorod and Tbilisi. In quitting this sacred place, I said to myself: How am I to speak of Jerusalem? I, whose noblest emotions were so often stifled among the crimes, prejudices and the incongruities of a corrupt world?"

Kuzmich stopped, and tears flowed from his eyes.

"Are there any Jews still living in Palestine?" asked Khromov.

"Eight or nine thousand of them still inhabit their Promised Land. We visited their ghetto. A narrow, craggy space, covered with filth, which can scarcely be called a street, divides the houses of the Jewish quarter from the rest of the city. Pale and sickly creatures, they engage in petty trade, handicrafts and frenzied Islamic disputes. Descending by a flight of broken steps into a cellar, we learned with surprise that it was a synagogue. Children in tatters were taught by an old blind rabbi of the history of the city, where their ancestors worshiped the God of Israel in a splendid temple of Soloman beneath marble porticos and a roof supported by cedars of Lebanon. On the day of our arrival, we saw the whole male Jewish population of the Holy City gathered in the valley of Kedron. For a fee, the Turkish governor of Palestine had given the Jews permission to celebrate there the festival of the tombs. Such are the remains of this great nation.

"And what is the attitude of our people, our pilgrims, toward the Jews?"

"Our peasants are often harsh and scornful toward them. One day one of our pilgrims stopped and cursed a Jew. He claimed that when he passed through Via Dolorosa he was abused by him. He felt so embittered towards the Jews that he cursed the whole race. He regarded them unworthy of living on this sacred earth. Later-on, he acknowledged to me that he had a strong aversion toward them. Hearing this, I tried to bring this man to a better understanding and said to him: 'My friend, there is no charity in your cursing the Jews. They are also creatures of God, as we are, and you should be compassionate toward them and pray for their conversion. Believe that your hatred is the result of your not being firmly grounded in the love of God and not being at peace with yourself.' "

"What did your peasant answer to that?" asked Khromov.

"He didn't want to listen to me and went away with another curse on his lips."

After a moment of rest and another cup of tea, Kuzmich continued his narrative. "In quitting the basilica of the Holy Sepulchre, we followed the route to Mount Cavalry, while the pilgrims walked to what is called the castle of Antonia or the former palace of Pilate. This is a large structure, surmounted by a tower. We were permitted to ascend to a terrace, where we saw the large space formerly occupied by the temple of Solomon. Alas, on its site are now two large mosques. The Moslems are persuaded that the prophet Mohammed ascended to heaven mounted on a white-winged mare with the face of a woman. They also believe that Mohammed is to return to Jerusalem at the Last Judgment, accompanied by Jesus Christ and Abraham. In the valley of Jehoshophat, Mohammed will judge all the souls of the world resurrected and gathered there."

"Oh, how wonderful to listen to the words of a saintly man like you, Fyodor Pavlovich. I have never heard such an enchanting account," murmured the hostess. "Please continue. Please continue."

"I blush at the feebleness of my humble inadequate account when I recall the wondrous effect the Holy City produced in me. Please allow me to rest for a while before I continue. . . ."

★ ★ ★

It was already dawning when the intense discussion of Kuzmich's journeys in the Holy Land ended. The sleepy guests gradually left Khromov's mansion. Left alone, the host asked Kuzmich, "Why did you return to Russia?"

"Nostalgia, my dear friend, nostalgia. Palestine is a beautiful and sacred land, but so is our Russia. After a few years spent in a small, dry, arid land, my impetuous Russian soul began to long for our endless plains, our snows and rains and our huge, green forests. . . ."

"But why did you decide to settle in Siberia, of all places?"

"Siberia is also a part of our dear motherland. Here I hoped to find a quiet place to continue my prayer and meditation. Could you help me find such a place?"

"Let me think about it. Let me sleep it over. . . It is already late. We shall talk about it tomorrow. Good night, Fyodor Pavlovich. Good night. Many, many thanks for your wonderful stories. Many cordial thanks. Sleep well."

The next day Kuzmich was surprised at his host's request to repeat his story to a group of some fifty additional guests who had not attended the first Easter-day festivities. Then came the third day of the celebration, equally drunken and noisy. He could not refuse. But as the group became more inebriated and clamorous, he was convinced that he could not live among such a society. He had come to Siberia to find solitude and peace, and here he was besieged by a swarm of people, bombarding him with questions and demanding every petty detail of his wanderings.

After the third evening Kuzmich was thoroughly exhausted and repeated to Khromov his humble request for help in finding a solitary place for prayer, meditation and study of the Holy Scriptures.

"And now tell me why you want to live in solitude. Solitude means laziness, idleness. I was taught by my mother that laziness is sinful."

"The person who lives in solitude is not idle. The hermit's

activity is of a higher order. He contemplates the vanity of earthly existence. Contemplation is the true goal of silence! Solitude and silence are vital to prayer, while mortification prepares our spirit for atonement for our sins."

"Well, if you insist, I will show you a place where you could be your own master."

Silently, Khromov led his guest half a mile or so into the forest surrounding his mansion, and showed him a wooden cottage with a thatched roof.

"You are welcome to live here," he said. "It is an old hut that belonged to a former woodsman. Although it is in disrepair, it is possible to live in it. You can stay here as long as you wish. We have enough food to share with you. Close by you have a brook full of fish, if you are fond of fishing."

"How am I to thank you, my dear friend. I can reciprocate only by praying for you and your family."

"That is enough for me. I am a miserable sinner and I do need your prayers more than anything else. Stay here with God and stop thanking me. I am indebted to you for your stories and for your prayers."

That very morning Kuzmich brought his modest belongings, a bag with a few pieces of clothing and some books into the cottage. A new phase of his existence began for him.

* * *

In his cottage, Kuzmich led the simple life of a hermit. Everything in his life was pared to a minimum: food, dress and behavior. The one room held a table and a chair. On the table there was his Bible, a pencil and some paper. In one corner were a large clay basin and an earthen water pitcher for washing. The bed had wooden slats instead of a mattress, heavy quilted blankets and a straw pillow. Like other peasants of Siberia, in winter Kuzmich wore a high fur cap and a heavy fur coat as well as thick felt knee-high boots. Summer garb was a handwoven peasant smock of coarse linen that came down to his knees. It was tied at the waist with a common cord. A pair of linen trousers and bast shoes completed his attire. A loaf of bread, divided into three parts—one for breakfast, one for lunch and one for dinner—sustained him, supplemented by occasional gifts from Khromov's wife: milk, cheese, mushrooms, eggs or fish, since the hermit refused to eat meat. He left his cottage only to walk to Sunday services.

After a few months of solitary existence the story of the strange hermit spread through the town and Kuzmich began to receive visitors. They were mainly poor, sick people and wanderers, attracted by the fame that followed his colorful narratives of the Holy Land. When asked by Khromov why he had broken his pledge to lead the life of a hermit, Kuzmich replied, "Hospitality is a form of charity. Saint Benedict wrote in his rule that monks of his order should receive strangers as Christ himself. Hospitality must be complete. It is not enough to share one's bread with whomever comes to visit, though when a person comes in, the first thing you offer is food. God comes to us as food. One ought to share also God's teaching. . ."

Since Kuzmich shared everything with his visitors, asking nothing in return, in a few years he became a well known personage in Western Siberia. He was usually referred to as "the saintly old man of Tomsk," who never failed to help people with food and advice. One particular incident gave him a reputation as a healer. A local merchant knocked on his door late one night, begging him, "Please help me! My wife is in serious trouble."

"What is the problem?"

"By mistake, our cook fried the Friday fish in cod liver oil which my wife can't tolerate. She choked on the fish and a fishbone caught in her throat."

"I am not a medical doctor."

"But you are a saintly man. Help my poor wife by praying for her. You are a man of God, always concerned about your neighbors and the Almighty will listen to you."

After a moment of concentration and fervent prayer, Kuzmich said, "You said that she has such an aversion to cod liver oil that she cannot tolerate even the smell of it. Therefore, make her drink a spoonful of oil. This will cause her to vomit and bring up the bone.. The oil will also soothe the wound in the throat caused by the bone and she will recover."

"But how can I give her the oil. She won't take it. She is delirious, her throat is swollen, and she is already choking!"

"Use force, if necessary. Hold her while you pour it down her throat, and make her swallow the oil."

The merchant obeyed. He poured oil into a glass and somehow caused his groaning wife to swallow it. And indeed, she immediately began to vomit violently and brought up the bone. After half an hour she felt better. The news of this spread throughout the district and people began to regard Kuzmich as a saintly miracle worker. The peasants streamed to him with their problems even from distant villages. They brought him gifts and money, and showed him deep respect. He accepted these signs of deference for a year or so until his conscience began to trouble him and he divided the money among the local beggars. Yet, he became afraid that vainglory would ruin not only his peace of mind but his spiritual life. His only consolation was the thought that along the road of his moral development he was helping fellow human beings.

* * *

One January evening, as Kuzmich was drifting off to sleep, he seemed to hear a knocking at the door. For a moment he was not sure whether he was asleep or awake. But his slumber was broken by another strong knock. And the knock was repeated. A fearful female voice implored, "Let me in, please let me in, in the name of Christ. I have been stranded. I am frozen." Kuzmich got up and looked through the window. In the snow and darkness, he saw a woman in a heavy fur coat and a cap, under which he could make out a frightened face.

"Open the door," she shouted. "Please help me. Please. I am frozen."

He put on his fur coat and opened the door. The blizzard swept the swirling snow across the path into his cottage. A young woman entered the room stamping snow from her boots and flailing her frozen hands. "Who are you? What do you want?"

"I've lost my way," she said.

She stood for a while in the center of the room, melting snow dripping from her fur coat. Then she slipped off her long beaver coat and took off her cap, which had caught in her hair, and long woolen scarf which she wore beneath the cap. Kuzmich saw a tall attractive woman of about thirty, dressed in a rich silk oriental dress. At once, she appeared to him most alluring. When their eyes met he felt a strange fascination with her radiant personality. She noticed this and smiled.

"Please forgive me for disturbing your sleep, but you see the situation I am in. My sledge strayed from the road and I stumbled upon your cottage." She observed carefully, noting the curling gray hair around his balding head and white beard, the fine and well-chiseled nose and the blue eyes. All this she found rather puzzling. Such a distinguished looking man in this solitary cottage. How strange to find such an aristocratic creature in the Siberian backwoods.

"Won't you sit down," said the embarrassed Kuzmich, pushing toward her the only chair he had. He heard the rustling of her silken dress and caught the potent aroma of an exotic perfume. Again he sensed a strange attraction to the young woman. He felt slightly dizzy.

"Oh, merciful Lord, help me," he prayed in his heart. "I am sweating all over. I am confused. I don't know what is the matter with me."

He promptly recovered from his momentary lapse, but his face became pale and his hands trembled. Gazing at the young woman, he murmured, "What do you want from me at this late hour?"

"I am Tamara Simich. I came here from Moscow to find my husband, Ilarion Petrovich. We owned a tavern in Moscow and for over six years we lived happily together with our three children. One evening a Gypsy girl appeared at our tavern and offered to tell fortunes to our customers for a silver ruble each. My husband was one of those naive enough to trust her. When she saw his palm she shouted, 'Your future is far, far to the East buried deep in the ground. You should prospect for gold in Siberia!' They began to chat and drink and whisper. She must have bewitched my poor man because a few days later he ran away from me. This happened last June. At Christmas he wrote to his brother from Tomsk. That is why I think he must be somewhere near here. I left my children with my mother and went to Orenburg by postal coach. From there I came here by sleigh, but by night we ran into a snowstorm and my driver lost his way. He is waiting outside, frozen and frightened like myself. Could you let him in also? He, too, needs some rest and warmth."

"How can I help you both? I have only this room of mine and a small, narrow hall. Perhaps I can accommodate your driver in the hall and I can sleep next to him, while you rest on my bed. But I am afraid it is so hard that you won't be comfortable on it. In the morning you must leave."

"I am so exhausted I could fall asleep anywhere . . . I am most grateful for your hospitality."

"But promise me that tomorrow at dawn you will depart."

"I will. I will. But you must help me locate my husband. You seem to have lived here for a long time and must know many people. Perhaps one of your friends may know of a merchant from Moscow, about six feet tall, with a short reddish beard. He is prospecting for gold with a young Gypsy girl about twenty years of age."

"This we can discuss tomorrow. I will make you some tea and give you the only food I have, some black bread. Alas, I have no sugar. Then go to sleep and rest."

While Kuzmich was boiling the water and cutting the bread, Tamara rested on the chair and examined him closely. His fine looks and courtly manners intrigued her more and more. The warmth of the room had a relaxing effect on her. After sipping on two cups of hot tea, her curiosity won the upper hand and she began to ask him questions.

"What are you doing here in this wilderness? Are you perhaps one of those officers who rebelled against our good Tsar Nicholas and were then exiled to Siberia?"

"Madame, I am too tired and sleepy to discuss with you my past and your plans for searching for your husband. I have tried to live a life of a hermit, a life of prayer. May I give you some more tea and bread?"

But Tamara would not give up. Her fascination with her mysterious, distinguished host grew. From the chair she moved to the bed and sat beside Kuzmich. "You don't seem to be interested in my fate, in searching for my husband. You don't want to understand my situation. My heart is so lonely and frightened. You can feel how it beats."

Kuzmich remained silent and was still more embarrassed. The silence was broken only by the snoring of the driver, who slept in the hall covered by his fur coat. Tamara pressed her body closer to Kuzmich's, whispering, "I am so lonely. I am so lonely." She grabbed his right hand and put it to her left bosom. "You feel how my heart beats, thirsting for compassion."

Kuzmich was shaken and felt that his suppressed passion had gone beyond control. Tamara pressed her body closer to him. She then put his left arm around her waist and pressed her lips to his. "My God," Kuzmich muttered, "grant me strength against my lust."

"Don't be so shy," Tamara whispered. "Have mercy on my loneliness. My parish priest, Father Ilarlion, told me that the embrace of a saintly man is good not only for one's body but also for one's soul. Kiss me. Kiss me. . . ."

* * *

After Tamara's visit, Kuzmich increased the severity of his regimen. He declined anything superfluous and finally reached a stage where he accepted nothing for himself except some black bread, tea, fish and vegetable soup. Everything else that was brought to him: honey, tea, sugar, milk and eggs, he distributed among the local poor and the itinerant beggars. He passed more time in prayer and meditation.

Years went by, monotonous and uneventful, marked by blizzards and mountains of snow in winter, and wolves prowling in the outer suburbs of Tomsk, clouds in summer, and deep mud in the spring and autumn. Except for a small group of officials and rich merchants, most inhabitants of Tomsk continued to exist in squalid poverty and boredom, broken only by religious festivities and bouts of wild drinking on holidays. Meanwhile, Kuzmich's renown as a faith healer and miracle worker spread throughout the region, especially after he cured a twelve-year-old boy whose left hand had been paralyzed by a fall. He was brought by his mother from Omsk and shown to the embarrassed Kuzmich. First he refused to do anything, claiming incompetence. When she knelt before him, begging for help, he agreed to lay his hands on the boy's head and pronounced a benediction prescribed for such cases by a monk from the Mount Athos monastery, whom he had encountered on his way back from the Holy Land. As this did not produce any visible result, he instructed the mother to massage the boy's hand three times a day while feeding him fresh berry juice with each meal. Months later Kuzmich received a letter thanking him in effusive words for "the miraculous cure." He was again surprised and embarrassed. "I only pray. It is God Almighty who heals," he kept repeating to the grateful families who showered him with gifts and praises.

Kuzmich was so busy with his charity work that he was indifferent to political events and the profound changes occurring around him. When, in 1861, the news reached Tomsk that the son and successor of Tsar Nicholas I, Alexander II had freed the serfs, it caused a great deal of discussion among the people. There were very few serfs in Siberia, mostly servants of the high bureaucrats and rich merchants. Actually the only real serfs were fugitives who had run away from cruel landlords. Kuzmich, however, refrained from discussing the subject. His only comment was, "I have always believed that it is immoral for a man to hold another human being in bondage. God created us all as his children and we are all equally loved by our Heavenly Father."

After the incident with the boy from Omsk, the number of

peasants seeking his help became an avalanche, leaving him less and less time for meditation and prayer. Doubts about the value of his various activities began to creep into his soul. At times he likened himself to a living spring that had once bubbled forth, but now was reduced to a trickle. Did he turn from prayer to healing because this flattered his ego? "I was a happy hermit and now I pretend to be a fake faith healer. I am a charlatan, he thought. Lord, help me in my predicament." On other occasions, when he felt inner satisfaction from his good works, he was inclined to believe the contrary. "Perhaps, it is God's will that I should not be a hermit but should devote my last years to the service of my fellow man. Perhaps, it is God's will that so many poor people flock to me in search of help?"

This conviction became more firmly rooted in his mind after a visit to the local cathedral during the Christmas season. Tomsk was on the most important route along which criminal and political exiles were transported to their more distant places of banishment, such as Kolyma, Magadan or Sakhalin. When the mineral resources of Siberia were discovered, the government realized that convicts could be useful in supplying the heavy labor needed in the iron mines of the eastern Ural slopes and in the gold mines of Kolyma. When in 1753 the Empress Elizabeth abolished capital punishment, murderers were condemned to exile and hard labor in Siberia for life. At the end of the eighteenth century, mutilation as a punishment had also been forbidden, and temporary banishment to Siberia was substituted for it.

While construction of prisons was expensive, banishment was of little cost to the government. For political reasons, as well as for crimes of violence, men were increasingly exiled into the endless, frozen wilderness. Such punishment was inflicted for even minor offenses such as fortunetelling, prizefighting, snuff taking, or even occasionally for begging in front of official buildings.

In the reign of Catherine II, when the demands for labor rose because of the increasing needs of the mines, the list of offenses punishable by exile tripled. Serfs were sent to Siberia for cutting down trees or for laziness, non-commissioned officers for insubordination, drunkenness or various other misdeeds. Jews were exiled for non-payment of taxes or for any plausible pretexts just to squeeze money from them as ransom, or bribes. The number of offenders who had fallen from political favor also increased greatly. "Siberia is the place where Russia hides her sins," thought Kuzmich.

Exiles were usually driven in large convoys, like herds of cattle, often begging their way because there was no adequate provision for feeding them. In the early nineteenth century this was remedied by the energetic and meticulously pedantic young Tsar Nicholas I. He ordered that exiled prisoners should be given identity cards to indicate their name, date of birth, term of exile, and their destination. Stationhouses were erected along the most important routes every twenty miles or so. The exiles were divided into three categories: hard labor convicts, penal colonists, and those "banished by administrative order." Those in the latter category were mostly political prisoners, more than half of whom had had no trial, but were sent to Siberia by order from the Minister of the Interior or of petty local official because of some politically subversive act or merely at the whim of a police or gendarme official.

Tomsk was one of the many relay points for the convoys of exiles. Kuzmich often saw an endless line of convicts, legs chained, trudging through the snow or mud and guarded by soldiers armed with guns and whips. Such spectacles made him cry and he resolved to be of as much help to them as he could. Kuzmich's moral authority was so great that when he asked the Tomsk chief of police to keep him informed of the dates that convict columns would pass through the town, he invariably did so. A short time before the arrival of a particular column, Kuzmich waited at the western end of the town, with an assortment of comforting items—jars of honey, smoking materials, bags of sugar and salt.

Many of the convicts were so ill that they could not continue their journey to exile and had to be confined to the local hospital. Kuzmich visited there and distributed little gifts, mostly food that had been offered to him as tokens of affection and gratitude for his charitable deeds. He was appalled by the indifference of the few doctors and nurses serving the hundreds of suffering patients. The most common diseases were scurvy, typhus, bronchitis, rheumatism and syphilis. Never before in his life had he seen faces so haggard and ghastly as those that lay on the greasy gray pillows in those hospital cells. The air was stifling, poisoned with the odor of perspiration and the stench of excrement. It was not surprising that the death rate ranged from 20 to 40 percent of each convoy.

All the acts of charity did not satisfy Kuzmich's growing desire to be useful to his fellow man. After morning prayers and breakfast, usually just a chunk of black bread and unsweetened tea, he would receive groups of pilgrims who came to see him almost daily with their problems. It was an exhausting job for a man well past his seventieth birthday. But he tried to cope with his demanding work as well as his failing strength permitted. There were days when he saw as many as fifty or sixty people, listening to their complaints and advising them on health, family and spiritual problems.

Years went by. Kuzmich's gray beard turned quite white and his hair became quite thin. He leaned heavily on a cane. Yet, his work increased steadily. One day as many as ninety petitioners surrounded him, begging for his help. When he tried to excuse himself, some of them cried, "For God's sake, Little Father, don't forsake us!" There were, in such throngs, many women who wandered from one hermit to another. Kuzmich knew this type of impatient, even compulsive pilgrim. Included were also older men, in greatly reduced circumstances and too fond of liquor, who tramped from monastery to monastery only to get something to eat or a warm place to spend a night or two. And there were peasant women seeking advice about their problems, mostly marital troubles or the marriage of a daughter, the purchase of a piece of land, remedy for a drinking or cruel husband, or a baby born out of wedlock. Kuzmich knew that he could do little for them but he invariably tried.

At the end of one of those extremely busy days, he collapsed and had to be carried to his cottage by two strong peasants who happened to be in the crowd attracted by the fame of the renowned "miracle worker." They put him to bed. The doctor summoned from the local hospital ordered him to rest for several days, eat richer food, and drink milk with honey. "You are exhausted. Take better care of yourself," warned the doctor.

"It's nothing, it's nothing," muttered Kuzmich, but he felt that this time he had seriously overextended himself.

★ ★ ★

At the end of January 1864 Kuzmich was very ill. He could not take any solid food and subsisted on only milk and water. Although his strength was failing rapidly, he kept a clear mind until his last hour. On February 1, he awoke in the night, raised himself on his bed, and said to Khromov's wife, who acted as his nurse, "My end is near. Please, call a priest." When Khromov himself, alarmed by his spouse, appeared in Kuzmich's cottage, he kneeled at his bedside. From time to time Kuzmich's lips moved as he prayed silently. Toward the evening Khromov noticed that his strength was waning. He was barely breathing, suffering great pain, but not a complaint escaped his lips. People hearing that the saintly old man's life was ebbing flocked to his cottage to pray. As Khromov was making the sign of the cross on the dying man's forehead, Kuzmich whispered, "I have an important document to entrust to your care. I am too weak to raise my head, but under my pillow there is a manuscript. It is my diary." Khromov dragged from under the straw pillow the thick file of paper. He saw on the title page the words "Diary of Fyodor Kuzmich." Under the title was a note in red: "Not to be opened until fifty years after my death."

"My last wish," whispered Kuzmich, "is that you swear to guard this diary faithfully and hand it, sealed, to His Majesty the Emperor. Show it to no one else."

Then his hand, that tried to make the sign of the cross over Khromov's head, collapsed. The Orthodox priest arrived to hear

Kuzmich's confession, he found him rigid and cold. His body was buried on the grounds of the Bogoroditsko-Alexeyevsk monastery in Tomsk on February 4, 1864. A simple cross marked his grave, bearing the inscription: "Here lies the body of Blessed Father Fyodor Kuzmich."

CHAPTER 18

Epilogue

Before Khromov could carry out Kuzmich's last wish, an official dispatched by the Governor General of western Siberia, Meshcherinov, confiscated all of the dead man's belongings, including his diary. The manuscript was sealed and sent to St. Petersburg, where it remained in the personal archives of the Romanovs until the Bolshevik Revolution of November 1917.

The Communist government, eager to discredit the Tsarist regime, published many selected documents highlighting various unflattering aspects of the old empire. The preliminary sorting out of a mass of written material was entrusted in 1918 to Felix Dzerzhinsky, head of the Extraordinary Commission to Combat Counterrevolution, better known under its Russian acronym of *Cheka*. The organization was described by its boss as "the eyes, ears and the mailed fist of the proletarian revolution." Busy tracking and exterminating its actual as well as suspected enemies, Dzerzhinsky delegated the task of selecting the most damaging accounts of Tsarist depravity to one of its secretaries, a dropout from the history department of Moscow University.

The secretary took seriously his task and, as he plunged deeper into the avalanche of documents, his fascination increased. But the job was so overwhelming that even working twelve hours a day was not sufficient. Consequently, his selection was perfunctory. When he came across the thick volume of barely legible pencil notes of Fyodor Kuzmich he found them intriguing enough to read passages. Knowing that Dzerzhinsky was fond of historical memoirs, the young man took the volume to his boss and reported, "Comrade Commissar, among the Tsarist documents, I have found an interesting piece of writing, filled with revelations. You know, of course, some of the fantastic legends and sensational rumors concerning Fyodor Kuzmich. . . ."

"I remember hearing all sorts of old wives' tales about him, but I refuse to believe them. Russian history is crowded with self-styled pretenders, adventurers and charlatans."

"But this Kuzmich was an intriguing charismatic personality, a faith healer, and, some people believed a miracle worker, Comrade Commissar."

"So, you, a progressive and educated man, a Bolshevik, are, at heart a superstitious peasant," snarled Dzerzhinsky. "Aren't you ashamed? We have had too many such faith healers and miracle workers, like Rasputin. We Communists have taken power in order to provide Russia with enough well-trained medical personnel to allow our people to dispense with shamans, charlatans, faith healers and witch doctors."

After a mere glance at the manuscript, Dzerzhinsky threw it into his wastepaper basket. The secretary returned to his task of searching for material requested by the editor of *The Red Journal,* a periodical established by the new regime to revile the old by publishing its secret treaties and political intrigues.

Three terrible years of civil war followed. As in all domestic struggles, there was incredible brutality and bestiality. Vindictive hatred made the maxim "two eyes for one eye, all teeth for one tooth" Dzerzhinsky's prevailing rule. He was convinced that it was better to shoot ten innocent men than to let one escape. At the end of the civil war his *Cheka* was renamed the State Political Administration and became known generally by its Russian abbreviation G.P.U. When the founder of the Bolshevik Party and the Soviet State, Vladimir Lenin, died in January 1924, and was replaced by

Joseph Stalin, Dzerzhinsky remained in office as his most trusted man, his right hand, or perhaps, his left hand. On a misty March morning, at the Lubianka, a former insurance company building, his telephone rang. He lifted the receiver and heard a familiar harsh voice speaking with a strong Georgian accent. "This is Stalin. Comrade Dzerzhinsky, I want to see you in my office at three o'clock this afternoon."

When Dzerzhinsky entered the study of the General Secretary of the Communist Party of the Soviet Union, he saw the powerful *Gensek* sitting at his massive oak desk. On the wall behind the desk hung a large picture of Lenin and in the far corner was his marble bust. Stalin's appearance was modest, even austere; he was dressed in a simple, light brown jacket, buttoned to the neck, and matching trousers tucked into high boots. Stalin's pockmarked face was set off by a bushy black mustache and a half-shy, half-sinister smile that revealed his teeth, yellowed from chainsmoking. Without responding to Dzerzhinsky's greeting, Stalin exploded, "Those incompetent idiots from the Commissariat of Foreign trade again report to me the difficulties they have in selling our jewels, diamonds, the Fabergé trinkets and old icons abroad. Our trade representative in Paris is especially inept. He has sold almost nothing. Shall we recall him and punish him for sabotaging our attempts to get hard currency abroad?"

"He may be inept, indeed, Comrade Stalin. But one must bear in mind that those bloody S.O.B.s, the white Russian emigrés, many in dire need of cash, are outbidding our agents and offering their valuables at ridiculously low prices."

"Can't we send abroad some items that those damn emigrés would not be able to match? What do you suggest?"

"As a matter of fact, for some time I have been toying with a new idea concerning this vital matter. May I share it with you, Comrade General Secretary?"

"By all means, do."

"Why don't we open the graves of the Romanov clan? Those bastards, like the ancient Egyptian pharaohs, were buried with many valuable objects on them. Some of their tombs, especially those of the Tsars and their wives, could be like small jewelry shops."

"A wonderful idea, Comrade Dzerzhinsky! A wonderful idea! Carry it out at once. We are in dire need of hard currency to buy the American machinery necessary to build a dam on the Dnieper."

Two weeks later Dzerzhinsky reappeared in Stalin's office at the Kremlin to report about his findings, "Comrade General Secretary, we have searched all the Romanov graves. We did find some very valuable items, especially on the women. Their diamond tiaras and magnificent necklaces will easily bring in many dollars and pounds sterling. As for the men, except for the rings, there were mostly military decorations, fit mainly for museums, but unlikely to bring in much hard currency. As to the grave of Alexander I, it was most disappointing. His casket was empty."

Index

abdication, Alexander's thoughts of, 57, 58, 59, 93, 103, 122, 334; arranges for succession of Nicholas, 335
acting, 42
Alexander I, after defeat of Napoleon, 261; appearance, 26, 40–41; at father's funeral, 120; begins reign, 115; birth, 26; breaks diplomatic relations with France, 166; Catherine's plans for, 26; casket opened, 304; childhood, 28–29, 54, 205–207; courtship, 34–35; decides to stop Napoleon, 167; depression after father's death, 120–21; "dies of cholera," 345; education, 26–31; funeral, 346–47; grave opened, 304; horse throws him, 182–83; languages, 31; marital life, 37, 46; marriage, 35–37, 77; military training, 29, 40, 41; opens negotiations with Britain, 169; rebels against grandmother, 41–42, 54; relationship with father, 39; religious education, 30–31; religious experience at Cathedral of Dormition, 246–47; restlessness, 316–17, 311; sense of responsibility, 139–40; social activities, 141–42; spurned by father, 55, 102; under Paul's regime, 72; youth, 32–33, 40, 42, 55; *see* Russian campaign
Alexander the Great, 21, 31–32
Alexis, 16, 90–97
Anne, Grand Duchess, 225–26
Arakcheyev, Alexander, 73–74, 104, 309–10, 313–16, 323–28; appointed inspector General of Artillery, 162; dismissal, 96
artillery function in battle, 70
Austerlitz, 165–84

Bagration, Princess Catherine, 282–83, 287–88
balls and gala affairs, 142–46, 283–85
Bariatinsky, Prince Theodore, 65
Beauharnais, Eugene, 251
behavior conflicts, 42
Bennigsen, General Levin, 75; commander of conspirators, 109
Beregina crossing, 259–60
Bezborodko, Alexander, 61, 70
Borodino, 251–54

Castrators, 312
Catherine, sister of Alexander, 204–11, 243–44; berates Alexander after Moscow lost, 257; correspondence with Alexander, 209–11; criticism after Tilsit, 210–11; dream of being Alexander's queen, 209; marriage proposal, 215–16, 223–24, 224–25; relationship with Alexander, 204–208, 209–212
Catherine, Grand Duchess (Princess Sophia of Anhalt-Zerbst), 17; birth of Paul, 18; body odor, 54–55; conspiracy against husband, 19; censorship, 57; court, 223; death, 60–61; decision to disinherit Paul, 58–61; empire under, 51–52; funeral, 66–67, 68–69; intellect, 17, 23–24; letters, 66–67; liberalism, 57; lovers, 22; marriage to Peter, 17–18; old age, 39; proclaimed self Empress, 21; and religion, 30; serfdom under, 24–25
Catherine Palace, 39

Caulaincourt, General Armand de, 212, 216, 226, 236, 238
censorship, 57
Chevalier Guard, 88, 105; banned from castle, 109
Chevalier, Mademoiselle, 83
conspiracy after Tilsit, 203–204
conspiracy against Paul, 99–104, 106–113; Alexander attempts to split, 125
Constantine, appearance, 26; birth, 26; Catherine's plans for, 26; education, 26–29; escapade without clothes, 140–41; Kostya, 140; military action, 92, 182; military training, 29, 40, 41
Continental Blockade, 202
court behaviour, under Paul, 71
cults, 312–313
Czartoryski clan, 52–53, 160–61, 165–84; *see* Secret Committee
Czartoryski, Adam, 52–53, 212, 275; and Elizabeth, 83–86; as confidant and advisor, 54–57; reacts to situation in 1806, 188–89; recalled, 127–28; *see* Secret Committee

Danilovich, Alexander, 10
Damas, Roger de, 203
deism, 30
disillusionment of Russian youth, 323–27; Alexander's attitude toward, 326
Divine Right, 71
Dolgoruky, Prince Peter, 159–61, 178
domestic issues after Tilsit, 212–215
Dormition, Cathedral of, 245–47

educational reforms under Alexander, 140
Elizabeth Alexeyevna, 34–37; and Adam Czartoryski, 54, 83–86, 282; and Gregory Ovechnikov, 148; coronation of Alexander, 137–38; critical of Alexander after Tilsit, 203; health, 77–78, 112, 339–42; marriage to Alexander, 36–37, 46, 77, 106, 148; reconciliation with Alexander, 335–42; relationship with Princess Golitzin, 82–85
Elizabeth, Empress (daughter of Peter I and Catherine I), 12, 16
Enghien, Duke of, execution, 165
Enlightenment in Russia, 24, 29, 30, 55
Erfurt, 215–22
Eugene of Würtemberg, Prince, 105–106

feast in honor of Alexander Nevsky, 302–303
Flagellants, 311–12
fortune telling, 47–50
Frederick the Great, 16, 70
Frederick II, 18, 51–52
Freemasonry, 75–76, 101, 102
French Revolution, 51, 57, 87, 165; and Alexander, 58

Gachina, 26–27, 40, 73, 184; escape to, 41, 42
Gagarin, Princess Anna, 105, 106, 111
Gatchina regiments, 40, 41, 42, 63
German campaign, 266–68
Girard, Mademoiselle Paulette, 80–81
Golitsyn, Prince Alexander, 42–43, 46, 50, 310–14, 323; relieved of duties, 331
Golitzin, Princess Varvara, 78–85
gonorrhea, 30
Green Lamp, 323
guards, as kingmakers, 16; refuse to pledge loyalty to Alexander, 121; under Catherine, 23
Gypsies, 43–51
headdress, 63–64
historical setting for birth of Alexander I, 9–16, 60–61
history during lifetime of Alexander, 51–52, 57–58, 88–105, 155–63, 165–84, 226–227, 228–31
Holy Alliance, 304–306

Isakey, Jean-Baptiste, 289–90
isolationist policy, 161

Joseph, Archduke of Habsburg, 208

Khromov, Gregory, 351–54, 358–66; and family Easter celebration, 362–68
Kobentzel, 168
Kochubey, 212–13
Kostya, nickname for Constantine, 40
Krüdener, Baroness Julie von, 288–89, 295–301, 303–304
Kutaisov, Ivan, 75, 97, 98; part in conspiracy, 104
Kutuzov, 249; death, 264; receives order of St. George, 261–62; regroups, 250–51
Kuzmich, Fyodor Pavlovich, 354–79; charity work, 374–77; diary, 378, 381–82; life as hermit, 368–70; illness and death, 378–79

Laharpe, Frederic Cesar, 29, 31–32, 93, 97, 246; dismissal, 51, 59; ideas, 32–33; influence on Alexander, 29; marriage, 51
League of Armed Neutrality, 93–94, 95
Louise, Queen, 157–58

Maria Feodorovna (Sophia Dorothea), 26, 27, 35; at Paul's funeral, 20; aversion of Paul, 103; birth of son Alexander, 26; critical after Tilsit, 203; reaction to death of Paul, 114; relationship with daughter Catherine, 205; refusal to be part of plot against Paul, 59; warns of dangers at Erfurt, 216–17
Mâria Theresa of Austria, 52
Marusha, 46, 51, 77
Memel, 157–58
Metternich, Count Clemens, 265, 273–74, 289, 292–93
Mikhailovsky Palace, 105, 111
military, Alexander courts the, 125; pageant at Vertus, 301–302; parades, 146–48, 195–96
military training, 29, 40, 56; Paul shames Alexander, 72–73; under Arakcheyev, 73
monarchy, 55
Morozov, Arkady, 354, 361
Moscow, contrast with St. Petersburg, 12; growth, 12–14; as winter quarters, 257–58; retreat from, 259
mourning for Paul and Catherine, 69
Munro the fortune teller, 48–50

Napoleon, 42, 60, 87–93, 155–63, 165–84; Alexander's fascination with, 199; after Tilsit, 211; at Tilsit, 185–99; and Paul, 95; destiny foretold, 50; Erfurt, 217–22; leaves Elba; prior to Austerlitz, 165–84; proclaimed Emperor, 166; return to France, 291–93; seeks marriage with sister of Alexander, 215–16; takes Lombard crown; *see* Russian campaign
nature, admirer of, 56–57
narcissism, 36, 42, 56
Naryshkin, Maria, 148–55; 204; children by, 153; first woman to spurn Alexander, 149; love affair with Alexander, 152–55
Nelidova, Catherine, 75, 98
neurasthenia, chronic, 336
newlyweds, 39
Nicholas, as Tsar, 346–47; chosen to succeed Alexander, 334–35
Novosiltsev, 169–70; 212

Old Believers, 311
Olmutz Council of War, 77
Orthodoxy, 14, 15, 30, 31, 246, 311, 332
Orlov Brothers, 18; mourning for Paul and Catherine, 69; Alexis, 18, 19; part in death of Peter III, 65;

Michael, 18; Gregory, 18, 22; letter about Peter III's death, 64–65
Ovechnikov, Gregory, 148

Pahlen, Count Peter von, 74–75, 99–100; Alexander warned of, 123; double intrigue, 109; exerts power after Paul's death, 121–22; exiled, 126; Paul suspects, 106–108
Panin, Count Nikita, 98, 123; exile, 105
Paul, Grand Duke 18, 35–36; accused, 112; appearance, 25; assumes power, 61, 63–64, 70–71, 87–105; death, 112–13; death foretold, 149; "Deaths Head," 25; early life, 25; father's death, 64–65; favoritism, 41; fear of plot, 105–108; funeral, 120; marriage, 26; middle years, 26–27; mother's plot to disinherit, 58–61; nightmares, 27–28, 59; plan to avenge father, 66–67; Russia reacts to death, 119–20; and serfs, 94; son of Saltykov, 18, 65; and upper classes, 119
Pavlovsk, residence of Catherine, 210–11
Paris, surrenders, 268; Alexander enters, 268–72
Partitions of Poland, 52; and Alexander, 56; and Paul, 58
Peter the Great, 9–10, 32; effect of death, 16; reforms, 14
Peter III, 16; abdication, 20; adulation of Frederick, 18–19; conspiracy against, 19; death, 20; foolishness, 17, 18, 19; funeral, 68–69; letter about his death, 64–65, marriage to Sophia, 17; search for body, 66–69; Tsarevich, 17, 18
Photious, Archimandrite, 314–16, 322–31; effect of visit, 333
Pitt, William, 170
Poniatowski, Prince Joseph, 251
population of Russia, 52
Potemkin, Grigory, 11, 55, 70
Preobrazhensky regiment, 16, 56, 73, 116
primogeniture, 16
Protassov, Madame, 22, 66–67
Pugachev, Yemelian, 24–25

Radishchev, Alexander, 14, 57, 130–31
Rastrelli, Bartolomeo, 12
Red Tavern, 43, 51
reforms, needed in 18th century, 14–15
regency plan, 102
religious experiences, Alexander's tolerant nature, 314–16; "most beautiful day of life," 302–303; reconciliation with Elizabeth, 335–39; seeking salvation, 318–23; with Baroness Julie von Krüdener, 297–99, 302–304
republican ideas, 33, 51, 55
Rostopchin, 245–46, 247
routine, daily of Alexander, 126
rumblings of revolution in 18th century Russia, 15–16
Russian destiny foretold, 50
Russian campaign, 237–243, 248–261; Alexander afterwards, 261; Alexander suffers depression, 256–57; approach to Moscow, 254; Borodino, 251–54; Moscow in ashes, 255
Russian empire, 51–52

Sasha, as nickname for Alexander, 54, 72
St. John, Order of, 88
St. Petersburg, contrast with Moscow, 12–14; during Napoleonic invasion, 248–50; founding, 10–11; proclaimed capital, 11
SS. Peter and Paul fortress, 52
SS. Peter and Paul cathedral, 68
Saltykov, General, 29

Saltykov, Sergei, 18; father of Paul, 18, 65
Samborsky, A. A., 31
Schenkenstrasse, 286–87
Secret Committee, 127–37, 139–40, 212
serfdom, 14–15; concern of Alexander, 31–32, 130–31, 139–40, 155, 174, 317–19; under Paul, 94
Seven Years War, 18
Siemionovsky regiment, 16, 19, 56; Alexander head of, 72, 116; part in conspiracy, 104
Simich, Tamara, 371–73
Slivov, Gregory, 355–57
Smolensk, 242–43
Smorgoni, 260
Sophia of Anhalt-Zebst, 17; marriage to Peter, 17; *see* Catherine, Grand Duchess
Speransky, Michael Michailovich, 213–15, 228–35; disgraced, 234–35
Staël, Madame de, 257
Stephens, Elizabeth, 214
Stroganov, Paul, 130–34, 212; *see* Secret Committee
Sturdza, Roxandre, 288–89
Succession, Act of, 59–60, 70, 334–335
Suvorov, Field Marshal Alexander, 52, 88–99; death, 92

Taganrog, 340; accident there, 342; stop at monastery, 340; trip to, 340–41, Tsar's death, 346–47
Tallyrand, 222–23
Tarassov, Dr., 342–45
Taurogen, convention of, 262–63; aftermath, 265–66
Tilsit, 185–99: cause of criticism of Alexander, 202–203; effect of on Russia, 201–202; historic setting, 192; meeting of Alexander and Napoleon, 193–94; parade, 193; treaties, 196–98
Tolly, Barclay de, 240, 243
Tsarskoe Selo, 27, 28, 39, 42, 54
Tula, 318
Tver, 225

uniforms, 41, 42, 56, 63–64, 88, 102, 106, 147, 180, 195–96, 203, 268, 284–85

Vienna, Alexander at, 281–88; Alexander enters, 275; Congress of, 275–281, 295; occupation, 227
Vilna, 261–62
Vladimir seminary, 320–21
Volkonsky, Peter, 103, 122, 204, 245; warns Alexander 123–24
Voltaire, letters to Catherine, 67; and Alexander, 97

Wagram, 227
Warsaw, Duchy of, 226
Waterloo, after, 299–301
Whitworth, Sir Charles, 76, 97–98; influence on Paul, 97–99; plot against Paul, 99–104
Wilhelmine of Sagan, 283
Wylie, James, 183

Zerebtsov, Olga, 100
Zhukovsky, Vasily, 206
Zinaida, daughter of Maria Naryshkin and Alexander, 153, 204
Zubov, Platon, 54, 60, 61, 67, 70, 74, 78, 98; part in conspiracy, 104, 110

Other titles of interest from Hippocrene:

COLLECTING RUSSIAN ART AND ANTIQUES

MARINA BOWATER

"The interest of all serious collectors extends beyond the pleasure of simply owning beautiful things, to an absorbing desire to acquire all possible knowledge of them—to resolve all the hows and whys regarding their origins."

Marina Bowater, herself of Russian origin, ran commercial galleries in London for 20 years. Entering Russian art when it was a little-known specialty, she has been an active and authoritative participant in the development of the field. With erudition and enthusiasm, she discusses the history, techniques and appreciation of collectable art forms from Imperial and contemporary Russia. Topics include icons and painting, the plastic arts, jewelry, folk crafts, and theatrical props.

224 pages, 7" x 9", 48 illustrations in black and white
0390 ISBN 0-87052-897-1
$25.00

NAPOLEON'S MILITARY MACHINE

PHILIP HAWTHORNTHWAITE

The renowned British military historian shows how the ragged armies of the French Revolutionary Wars were transformed overnight into the most efficient and professional in Europe. All aspects of Napoleon's military and naval forces are discussed, individual campaigns are analyzed, and the book is replete with period illustrations, maps, and formation diagrams.

200 pages, 8 ½" x 11", 40 color, 140 b/w illust., 38 diagrams, charts, maps
0241 ISBN 0-87052-549-2
$35.00